About the Author

I am a self-motivated guy with a passion for storytelling. A family man, I love my home and my native England. Writing is my creative passion, having my work read is my dream, having it enjoyed is the best achievement I could ever imagine. I write diversified stories that are always readily available in my mind and the ideas flow easily to manuscript. My family grounds me, I am thankful to inhabit such a platform of stability and I will hopefully continue to write for myself and others to enjoy.

This book is dedicated to
Kath & Ivor Dicks, dear friends, sadly passed,
native to Belleview & Painswick

Chris A. Evans

THE PAINSWICK CONSPIRACY

AUSTIN MACAULEY
PUBLISHERS LTD.

A CIP catalogue record for this title is available from the British Library.

ISBN 9781786125545 (Paperback)
ISBN 9781786125552 (Hardback)
ISBN 9781786125569 (E-Book)

www.austinmacauley.com

First Published (2016)
Austin Macauley Publishers Ltd.
25 Canada Square
Canary Wharf
London
E14 5LQ

The contents of this manuscript are fictional and have been written by the sole author Mr C A Evans.

Map data © 2016 Google

Acknowledgments

Debbie Evans – Illustration/Front cover
Submitted January 2016

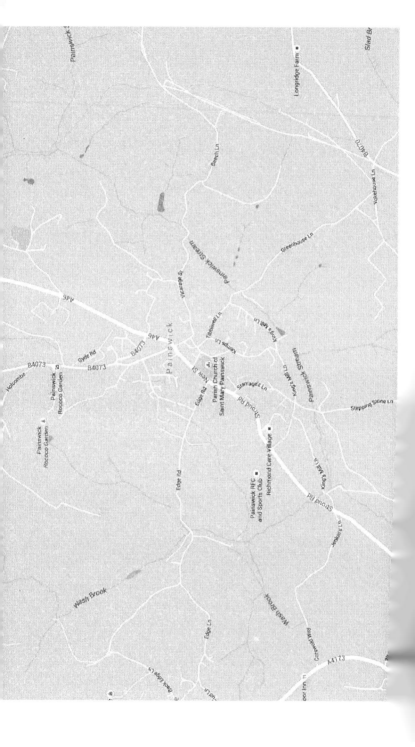

Food for Thought

What would you do if you woke up and found, after going for a walk in a quiet sleepy village, that your world as you knew it had irreversibly turned on its axis? How would you react if you were exposed to a single event which triggered circumstances so far removed from your normal life that it would be unimaginable to normal people? What if, in this modern technological age, you did not have any electronic signature and were being hunted by predators who wanted you dead? How would or could you cope?

What reserves and skills could an ordinary person invoke when they could not trust any other human being on the planet, and they had been stripped of any friends, family, home and vehicle, cards and were unable to be seen on any facial recognition cameras; where would they go? Just what would they do if their identity was the very thing that condemned them, and it was well advertised?

Just how far would a person go to stay alive and evade these pursuers? What desperate acts would they be prepared to implement just to stay alive?

The cable ties dug deep into his wrists, and he could feel the pain cascading through his entire body. Life could hang so precariously, and fortunes could change in one instant, but why? How could this happen and especially to him, an absolute nobody, a casual bystander. He was rendered almost motionless and felt so cramped and rigid; he realised that he had been dumped in the boot of a moving vehicle in the foetal position, like a piece of surplus meat. He swiftly ascertained that he must have been like this for quite a while, as he pushed his tongue out of his mouth and over his lip. They were bloated, and he felt the congealed blood that had coagulated whilst he was unconscious. This swelling extended around his nose and eyes, and his lip was split, tender and burnt when his tongue touched it. He was unable to see beyond the pitch darkness of his vehicular tomb, and it was extremely uncomfortable. He was scared, not normal scared, but scared like he had never been before. There was good reason for this fear; he was being disposed of.

He also knew the spectre of narcotics after having undergone surgery, and his body felt odd. He deduced that he had also been immobilised through chemical intervention of some sort. It felt like his skin was on fire, and his stomach was going around and around like a washing machine. He was acutely nauseous, anxious and his mouth was dry.

The car was moving normally. He guessed it was keeping to the speed limit so as to not to attract attention, and he listened to the droning of the wheel bearings and the tyres' rubber flowing over the miles of tarmac. He could detect faint and muffled voices within the car but with no clarity. The ambience was calm and serious with the occasional muffled laugh. The occupants sounded foreign, Eastern European, but what did he know? He was certainly no expert, but he deduced that he was in a large family saloon or a four by four judging by the space and feel of the upholstery.

He heard and felt the subtle change to the road's surface; it was quiet outside, so it was probably not a major transportation link now, more like a country or a B-road. This instantly raised alarm bells, as he was almost certainly on the last portion of the journey to his final last resting place. 'Why me?' he asked himself again over and over. 'I am not a super hero from the movies. I am not capable of martial arts, jumping off buildings and trains, or administering miracles armed only with a piece of cotton to stitch my wounds.'

He was just an average man, and his skill sets were honed on being able to navigate through a normal existence with a boring job with some social skills. His life was monotonous like practically everyone else's.

He had even failed at the marriage thing, so he was certainly not superman, far from it, and he was certainly not going to be a convincing James Bond. Was there a conspiracy of elements and events which could shape or create a situation?

Perhaps, it could even had been coincidence. John Parks did not believe in the possibility of the events that were happening, and until five days ago, he would have remained sceptical, but then a simple set of circumstances changed his existence. He became a victim of the very events that had been created around him, and unfortunately, there was absolutely nothing he could do, or so he thought…

Chapter 1

The Car

Breakfast had never been considered the most significant event of John Parks' morning, especially on a Saturday, so he opened the fridge, and as usual, he reluctantly removed a yoghurt and tore off the silver lid. The sun was shining through the windows, and it was warmer than anticipated. 'This would be a nice day,' he thought. He sat at the small gate leg kitchen table and ate the yoghurt, and unlike most people, he did not try to get every last bit out of the carton. He also tried to avoid getting most of it on his thick beard, which was too long and unkempt.

It was enough that the acidic offering had infiltrated his metabolism and not because he liked or wanted to eat at seven thirty in the morning; he just felt he had to.

Lots of coffee was his life support for the first few hours of daylight, so he made the first of many on his old yet proficient expresso machine. It was dirty, but he regarded the grime as adding to the coffee bean's flavour and authenticity. He discarded the yoghurt carton in the small bin in the kitchen, placed the spoon in the sink and then left the kitchen of the modest two bedroom cottage, his home since his marriage had formally broken down.

The cottage, Belleview, was on Vicarage Street in the beautiful village of Painswick, aptly dubbed the 'Queen of the Cotswolds'. It was an idyllic, quintessentially English setting and only became available to John through an inheritance; under normal circumstances, he never would have been able to afford such a lovely cottage. The famous St Marys church had ninety-nine yew trees in the churchyard. The one hundredth apparently never grew, and it was steeped in folklore and whispers that the devil forbade it. The grounds were meticulously maintained, and the church's spire sat central to the village. It was an impressive structure and an internationally acclaimed landmark.

His wife, Eileen, of fourteen and a half years and his two daughters, Jane aged twelve and Marie aged eight, had long since relocated to Australia with the new and improved husband. He was apparently everything John Parks was not.

Unfortunately for John, he was pretty much cut out of their lives, and in fact, he no longer even had their address. He had learned to cope with the parting by using a simple psychology: if they are happy, so be it; if they ever need me, I am easy to find. He also immersed himself in the belief that love could be achieved from a distance. If he held this thought close to his heart, his children would know where he was. He often repeated this to himself to ease the loneliness and his feeling of abandonment even though he completely disbelieved his own words and missed the girls tremendously. He knew he could attempt to contact them through their Aunt but he chose not to for now, he considered it too raw for everyone concerned at present.

The one lucky event to befall him post-divorce in his sad existence was his inheritance of the cottage from an eccentric uncle. The cottage had, therefore, remained outside of any settlement negotiations. His wife had made him sell their matrimonial home and was able to take most of the equity which left him living in a one room bedsit for eighteen months. He now had Belleview if nothing else, free from burden or greedy hands, and he was grateful of this fact.

He picked up his coffee, black and strong Lavazza, and the aroma pleased him immensely. He opened and went through the tiny, back double glazed door to the shared access, and went up the stone steps to the gardens turning right into Belleview garden. The sun was shining now, and the garden flowers were basking in the rays and dancing in the gentle breeze; it looked lovely.

'Brilliant,' he thought, 'absolutely brilliant.'

He climbed up the slight gradient in three stages, taking in the Aubrietia, snow in the garden, clematis and Jew's mallow and the assortment of rock plants he had finally been successful in cultivating. He then climbed the small sleeper steps to the patio and BBQ area and finally ascending the last sleeper steps onto a huge deck. This structure was built around a retaining wall fashioned from railway sleepers, and the steps were solid and gave presence to the gate exit. The upper floor decking was stained dark oak as were all the sleepers and fencing. The decking was elevated by two metres, giving radiant views and a beautiful ambience. He arrived at the top, and there it was completely peaceful. In fact, it was so tranquil and enchanting that he felt particularly restful without the usual factors that stressed his being.

Looking up he glimpsed the view, and this presented itself as one of patchwork fields separated by dry Cotswold stone walls that enveloped them and harnessed them to their owner. It was beautiful and the gentle breeze felt really good; he felt alive and content.

He sat with his coffee on a well-placed chair commanding the best position. It was one of four belonging to a garden table and chair set he had purchased especially for this reason, although three of them were never utilised. He was conscious he needed to hone his social skills.

He looked further across the valley to the beautiful hamlet of Sheepscombe. This also pleased him and gave him the satisfaction and knowledge that at least he had no mortgage any more. What a result at thirty-six years old! The elevated position gave him a clear view over the former weavers' cottages and adjoining cottage roof slates, some of which were nearly three hundred years old, acting as flat cap hats to the golden stone of the Cotswolds. The fields and countryside were especially green and fertile today, and the farms and houses were dotted up the hills. Window panes reflected the sun like strategically placed mirrors. Horses roamed in large fields, a few livestock frolicked and there was very little in the way of traffic, so it was mainly quiet.

Painswick had a rich historical underbelly of family feuds and land barons fighting which was now diluted and coveted with a thoroughbred of interwoven locals, and of course, now many 'not so local' locals who had infiltrated its ranks.

This was not uncommon in any small village anywhere in Britain, but Painswick was very close knit community and unusually proud of its heritage and beauty. Some distinguished families dated back centuries, as did the rich Cotswold stone buildings and structures that made this village so beautiful. This was undoubtedly why it retained the mantle the 'Queen of the Cotswolds'.

It also housed the wannabe rich, those people who had moved in who had the money but perhaps not the breeding to match and did not really fully gel but were able to buy into the postcode. These people could be perceived by the bred contingent as a slightly arrogant tier, as one cannot, of course, buy into history.

Then there was the week-enders, those who donned the hat 'rich' and maybe 'famous', those with coin but no intent to live here. They owned many properties in and around the village and surrounding countryside. They only visited when their busy and exotic schedule of mostly nothing allowed them, and they often moaned about parking, other visitors, tourism and apparently everything else.

Then there were the pretend owners of the coin, those who thought they were elite and rich but in fairness were not. They had enough money to give the impression they were local and had massive affiliations to the village, but it was obvious the majority did not.

Then there were the average 'everyday get on with it' people. They were rich and not so rich, but they were for the most part normal though. These were people like John, and he liked them all, as the real people were not pretentious or false and offered community spirit and always spoke to each other. He loved the jolly ladies who walked past daily and the working people going about their business. He loved that the village oozed pride and cleanliness. People cared for its appearance and lack of litter and human traits of abuse and laziness. He loved that artists walked the steep slopes to get to their tiny rented spaces in the Painswick Art studios, housed in the Painswick Centre. The architecture of the community and buildings were probably what attracted people from all over the world in droves. It was like a miniature *Inspector Morse* without crime, and a place that exuded eccentricity and all that is English.

'This is so lovely,' he thought. 'So peaceful. How lucky am I to be in a position to sit here.'

"Morning, John," said his neighbour, as he climbed his own garden gradients to a lower patio area.

He was in his fifties; he was a very old in his fifties and carried the skin and face of a man matured by weather and excessive lifestyle. He had worked for the diplomatic core in Lebanon and the Middle East, and John always thought of him as resembling the Major character from *Fawlty Towers*. He had a newspaper under his arm and carried a tray with a coffee jug, tea and some toast. He wore one of those chequered, old fashioned dressing gowns that looked like one that Scrooge would wear. It was red and copper in colour, and John could not help but think it was the most revolting garment, and it was only fit for the dog basket, if you wished to offend the dog.

"Good morning, old man," he blurted like an order because he deemed he was not answered swiftly enough.

"Morning Frank, how is it?" John responded cordially.

"OK, have you got much on today old man? You could shave that unsightly beard off, you know. Makes you look twenty years older and like you are going up a mountain."

"Nope, I will never shave it off. I won't do it for anyone. Anyway, I'm just doing the usual catch up on housework and other tedious things. Nothing much changes in my life."

Frank opened his newspaper and poured himself a coffee. This was his key to the conversation being over. His wife, an ex-Canadian now living under the flag of the United Kingdom, ambled up the garden in her dressing gown. 'She could be a bit more of a woman,' John thought, 'but she was slightly eccentric and liked being a bit off-the-wall and scruffy.' She also carried a few pounds where no woman should, and she looked haggard and worn by her lifestyle and searing desert heat. She was blessed with a shock of hair that reminded John of crystal tips, a white Diana Ross, or even Don King.

"Hey John, lovely morning isn't it?" she bellowed.

"Yes Barbara, it is lovely."

"You sure got the views up there, John. Frank, when are we going to get our elevated decking built like John?"

"John, when you going to stop hiding behind that damn beard?"

"Never," he said firmly. "I reiterate my comments made to your dear husband; it is never going to happen."

There was no reply, and she produced the latest romantic novel from her dressing gown and proceeded to read. 'Another would be conversation terminated in its infancy,' he thought.

John finished his coffee and collected his cup. He could hear a dog bark, and it was closely followed by the clip clop of two horses. This was a common occurrence through the street at this time, and it would be followed in a couple of hours by a gaggle of Hooray Henrys walking the Cotswold Way, shouting and adorned in the latest Barbour and expensive vortex footwear. Most walked about 800 metres or a couple of miles. Looking at some of them, John could not help but think that they probably felt like they had just completed the Camino de Santiago, all 800km of it.

He went into the kitchen, placed the redundant cup in the bowl and proceeded up the staircase to the bathroom. It was a modern cottage interior having been completely renovated, and the bathroom boasted a huge shower enclosure, Victorian bath suite and plenty of room. It had probably originally been an additional structure or a bedroom, since it was large, but it serviced the space of cleansing especially well. The conversion and décor were sublime.

John drew the curtain as both cottage bathrooms faced each other, and you could see in from the steps if descending. He turned the shower on and let it warm for twenty seconds. At the first sight of steam, he took off his t-shirt, jogging bottoms and got in. He washed his hair then his beard followed by his body. He then just stood under the cascading avalanche of water and could not help but think life was pretty empty at the moment. This was in complete contrast to his thoughts in the garden. He realised he lacked human content.

He switched the shower off, slid the door back, grabbed a towel and stood on the mat wiping himself vigorously. He dropped the towel on the towel rail and walked naked to his bedroom carrying his clothes. He passed the guest bedroom named the Bluebell room. The master bedroom, named Forget Me Not, was huge and located on the second floor and was accessed by a small winding staircase of no more than twelve steps. The impressive beams were displayed in all their glory, and the misshapen eaves lent itself to architecture that couldn't be replicated; he loved it.

He dressed casually in a pair of beige jeans, T-shirt and a sweatshirt, and he picked up his wallet, put it in his pocket and then his phone, which struggled to acquire any form of signal in the cottage or surrounding village. He decided to go for a walk. It had been a long time since he had just appreciated his surroundings, and there was nothing in his life that could not wait.

He locked the back door, put on his Vans trainers, walked through the lounge and exited the front door locking it behind him. He turned right and walked up the road to where Vicarage Street met Bisley Street. He saw Hamptons International estate agents on his right which was selling half the village to London's rich and people who could afford the prices that this beautiful setting commanded.

The Royal Oak pub sat proud to his left and was placed opposite the small village shop, and he walked past both and then turned left at Cardynham House. He breathed in the spectacular stone and views also taking in the beautiful sight of the churchyard and spire of St Marys. He walked down Tibbiwell Lane; he stood there outside the house that was adorned by a plaque for the Frederick Gyde Trust for the benefit of the people of Painswick, and he took in the sunlight bouncing off the steeple and houses. He set off down the steep gradient with the old Golden Heart Tea Room sign hanging where he imagined a pub originally was before it turned to the leaf and not the hop. The small bric-a-brac shop on his right was empty as was everything at this hour. It was very quiet everywhere.

He passed Kemps Lane with its impressive Cotswold 88 Hotel, magnificent in stature and commanding respect through vision and service, according to all. It was very grand, but he had heard rumours that it was closing down.

John continued to the bottom of the road where it joined Greenhouse Lane, and it also forked off toward Randal's Fields by the Painswick stream. He decided to go right, and he walked through some familiar buildings. It appeared that he was actually going into the farmhouses themselves, as the right of way literally went past the kitchen windows. It was a strange experience to those unaccustomed to right of way infractions into inhabited dwellings in rural communities.

He walked, following the stream in a parallel direction, at the end of the track and over a style. He then turned left and walked a few hundred metres to Hangman's Cottage. This was a derelict and eerie shell of a former hangman's house. Popular rumour had it that a couple of hundred years ago, he had performed a hanging without removing the mask of the unfortunate recipient of the then barbaric justice system. Once the man was pronounced dead, the hangman lowered the body. He then proceeded to, as he had many times previously, to remove the hood, only to reveal that the identity of the lad he had hung was none other than his very own son. Racked with guilt and remorse, he could not bear the burden of guilt and pain, and eventually he hanged himself in the cottage and was not found for months.

The house, some three hundred years old, still had the stone staircase, common in those times, chimney breast, outer walls, window openings, external doorways but no upper floor. There was no remaining part of the roof. The huge oak beams had fallen, like gods of architecture, to the floor within the building but remained on an angle. They were still defiant and not rotten through. There were some pieces of wood that acted like a bar across the far side corner, and kids were known to swing from them as a dare to the hangman.

There was an odd atmosphere, and this place was unusually quiet. There seemed to be no birds or any noise at all. The structure could offer some shelter, but it was ghostlike, and John felt uneasy, so he left the scene of the grizzly hanging and continued to walk up the narrow track. There was no road access here, just fields and tracks that did not respect the need of a vehicle unless it was a tractor and even then the ground was king.

He continued to walk until he met Stepping Stone Lane and thought he would just join Yoke House Lane and back onto Greenhouse Lane and once again Tibbiwell. He heard the birds reinvest in the landscape, and they sang and fluttered. He was immersing himself in the rural magnificence when the peace and tranquillity was shattered by a loud dull thump. It was followed by a crunching of metal, as if in slow motion, and he could hear wheels spinning following a high engine revving and then ticking over.

He was conscious that only one event mirrored this sound, so he hurried his pace and saw a gap through the hedge just before where the road forked. He peered over to see a car on its roof in a gully. The engine remained ticking over, the wheels were still turning in thin air begging the surface of the road, and he immediately smelt fuel. Instinctively, he ran through the gap, down the gentle incline into the gully and around to the to the driver's side.

He could see diesel coming from the tank, and he could also see the roof was badly caved in disfiguring the vehicle to the eye.

He put his hand in the door grip and inside the shattered door window and attempted to pull the door open, but it was stiff from the impact. It was also crushed which made it seal in its housing. He made three attempts to move it but without success. He managed to open the door after the fourth attempt.

He reached in and frantically hunted for the ignition start/stop button. He located it on the dashboard to the left hand lower side of the steering wheel, and he pressed it, stopping the power plant dead. With the engine immediately silenced, there was a strange and dubious ambience surrounding the event. He leant past the suspended driver, pushed the lever into the park position and the wheels ceased turning. There was a ghostly silence that gave John an uneasy feeling.

The driver was a middle aged man in what had been a very well cut grey suit. He had short grey hair, and he was quite distinguished looking, but the odd thing was that his eyes were staring at John, as if almost with pity and acceptance of the event.

"Hang in there. Don't worry, I will get you out of there," John told him reassuringly. "Don't move and I will try and perform a controlled release without damaging your neck. If you just drop, it may do some permanent damage."

The smell of fuel was strong, and John feared the car would ignite, so he tried to unbuckle the belt. It took some force, but he managed to achieve this by first placing his body and right shoulder against the man to ensure he did not just fall down on his neck or head.

John used all his strength to lower and pull the man from the wreckage without causing him further pain or injury. He knew it was of paramount importance to protect the neck and spine following any accident, let alone a collision of this magnitude. He had to move him swiftly and he quickly and deliberately dragged him some twenty feet from the car and behind a mound of earth. His thought process was that he believed that any imminent danger of explosion had passed, but he wanted to be sure.

"Get out of here. Get out of here fast!" muttered the man.

"It's okay. You may have sustained concussion, or a knock on the head may have disorientated you."

"Please go. Run for your life!"

"What are you talking about?" John replied smiling. "Don't worry. I will call for an ambulance."

"No ambulance!" shouted the man. "You must listen to me, and you must listen carefully. You are already dead, but you may as well know why, and give yourself about a five minute window of opportunity."

"Opportunity of what?" asked John.

"Life," replied the man coldly.

"What the hell are you on about? Don't worry; you have been in an accident," said John bewildered, absolutely certain now that the man had sustained concussion or worse.

"I did not have an accident due to the absence of concentration, my lack of driving skills or any road elements. I have been drugged with a chemical that shuts down all the body function and organs."

John struggled to digest the context of anyone being deliberately drugged. Date rape he had heard of, but off road accident death he was not buying.

"First it starts with paralysis," continued the man, "and an inability to move your muscles. This is what made me go off the road. After that, it gradually shuts down the heart's ability to pump with any regularity or power. The blood flow slows, and all function ceases. It will render me speechless in a few minutes, so listen to me, please.

"I don't know quite what to say, but is not really very believable. I am so sorry, but I am a real sceptic. I want to believe you, and I could humour you to make you feel better, but the truth is that you have simply been involved in an accident."

"No, you are so wrong, and this disbelief will place you firmly in the ground. I have been drugged man."

"How do you know all about this drug and that it has been administered to you?" asked John.

"Because my dear boy, I have used it myself, on others and on more than one occasion," replied the man nonchalantly.

"I am astonished! What a story," said John half laughing, but concerned for the man's welfare, he held his mobile in his hand. There was no signal as usual, nor would there be one anywhere near this.

"As we speak, time is running out for both of us," said the man, as he began wheezing and struggling for breath. "There is an internal tracker fitted to me which is my accountability to those I work for. It is active every second of every day, and although invasive on occasion, it is my lifeline to my operations team. It is monitored, and every event we contemplate and instigate is tracked from start to finish. It is also fed time elements. The journeys are planned and timed to ensure that we are not compromised, shall we say."

"I get it, so your own people will come and get you soon."

"No, not at all, the tracker will automatically generate and send a distress code, a signal that I am stationery. This in turn will activate a protocol, and a check will be conducted. If it concludes that I am not in traffic or at a toll, a team will be despatched to retrieve the key."

"What key?" asked John, now growing concerned that there may be some validity to this unbelievable yarn.

"This one," said the man holding out his hand. There was a silver device that looked like a flash drive but not a USB; it had a key type configuration where you would expect the device to dock.

"I don't want anything to do with it, thank you," said John. "The authorities can deal with this when they arrive. They will think I have stolen it otherwise."

"You don't get it do you? It is the very authorities that you reference that have orchestrated my demise, and believe me, they are going to kill you, too. No loose ends. It is not my operations team coming. It is the bird, and they have finally found me."

What bird? Human nature and anxiety were two of the strangest traits, and even in this horrible and unbelievable set of circumstances, John believed the man delirious and that everything would be OK.

'What the hell?' he thought.

John felt sick in the pit of his stomach. He was not connected to, or conversant with espionage protocol, and this was well beyond his imagination let alone his ability. He could never cope with such terror and conflict, and his emotions and powers of logic swung like a pendulum from second to second.

"Please listen to me and at least give yourself a fighting chance." The man coughed and wheezed badly now, and his breathing was becoming more shallow, and he was pale.

"Change your appearance. Drop your electronic footprint completely, no credit cards, no phone, no facial recognition cameras and stay off the radar. They already know who you are, where you live, all of your passport details and bank accounts. They know everything, and there is nothing left of you, so run and start again."

"Where would I run to, and anyway, how could anyone possibly know all this information so quickly?" asked John.

"You brought your phone. You simply brought your electronic signature, and this will be your downfall. They will have tracked your SIM in seconds which in turn gives your name, address and accounts. You, my friend, are sunk."

John felt the phone's presence in his trousers pocket. Why did he bring it when no one ever called him? There was absolutely no signal at times, so there was absolutely no need.

"Why John?" he shouted at himself inside.

"It will have been scanned and checked by now. The ownership and ancestry of your electronic life is up on a screen right now with surveillance personnel and ground teams on standby. Everything and anything you have ever done is up there for all to see."

Johns mind became a fragmented, frantic labyrinth of messages dominated by indecision and fear.

"What do I do with the key?" asked John frantically, partially buying into the unbelievable yarn spun before him.

"You must find, make contact and pass it to a man called Eric Jennings of the *Times*; he knows of its existence and will make sure the knowledge is shared and that the effects benefit all and not orchestrate war. This is the only way you can protect yourself and everyone else and keep everything visible; otherwise, you will disappear along with the key.

"And me?"

"You are lost. You are a dead man walking."

"Where can I find this guy? Are you listening?"

John glanced at the man. The corpse stared ahead with no apparent pain, but all signs of the living now sat in a hollow emptiness. John, like most people, was unaccustomed to being around the deceased and was distinctly uncomfortable, especially in light of the absurd content of the conversation that had just occurred. He heard a helicopter in the distance, and his heart sank. He attempted to swallow, but his mouth was too dry.

'This is not happening. This is not happening,' he repeated.

He looked at the man and searched his clothes to see if he had any identification on him, but he had nothing, not even a wallet. John considered returning to the vehicle to see if there was anything of validity inside, but he knew the position of the car and the leaking fuel made the environment unstable and potentially lethal, as might the helicopter cutting through the sky like a scythe in the distance.

John looked at the dead man, then at his mobile, then up toward the sky, where the rotors cut through the air effortlessly with their distinct sound getting closer and louder by the second.

'This just cannot be true. What a load of bullshit! Wait for them, John. Be logical and just wait.'

Chapter 2

Run Rabbit Run

"No," he said to himself, "it could not be, but who knew to alert the authorities? Why despatch a helicopter and not the routing emergency services? Why the key?"

He was suddenly acutely aware of the implications of what the man had said and if there was a shred of truth in his fable. He panicked, and his heart rate accelerated. He felt anxious and sick, and he felt a dryness in his throat that eclipsed the earlier shock. His stomach felt like it was rotating quickly, and it was churning. His chest was burning with a horrible tingling sensation.

He heard a noise from on the road behind him, and upon turning around, his eyes were met with the sight of a tractor trundling along. The weathered aging driver seemed extremely happy and without a care in the world. This was in stark contrast to the peril that John felt like a blanket had wrapped around him. The machine pulled a rickety old trailer which was loosely attached, and it bounced and creaked as it travelled. Instinctively, he looked at his mobile phone, and without questioning it, he waved at the farmer. The farmer tipped his hat, and as he passed, John threw the expensive phone into the trailer. It buried deep into the manure that was being hauled, and it had a pungent smell that offended him, but this would hopefully mask his immediate location and would continue moving in the opposite direction.

John ran; he ran like he had never ran before. He could hear the rotors getting nearer and nearer with every stride, and although he was pretty much out of shape, he kept running. He was drawn to familiarity. This would be a comfort and would be a productive route, easily accomplished without having to choose roads or pathways. The safety of the lane was obscuring him from above, and he sped toward Hangman's Cottage. There was an overhanging hedgerow and deep brush, so he could remain undetected from any helicopter for a while at least, but he was conscious that they would have equipment to track him down, so it would not be good to stay here long.

'This cannot be happening. It has to be a joke.' He kept repeating questions over and over again as this could not be John Parks' reality this sunny morning, no way; this was unbelievable.

The helicopter arrived noisily and now hovered over the crash site and looked menacing. It was not an emergency vehicle, and as such, it was obvious and conspicuous by its lack of signature or affiliation to the emergency services. There were no signs, in fact there was not anything to depict friendly help arriving. It actually portrayed the opposite image. The craft hung suspended in mid-air, and it hovered like a menacing huge insect ready to devour its prey.

He was unable to identify the occupants, but why should he recognise them? He was trying to recognise some form of uniform or medical equipment to allow him to dispel the stupid story and run for help, and this would be the normal course of actions following the discovery of a car accident.

He wondered how many the helicopter might carry, as it was a medium size machine. He decided to continue moving, and he walked swiftly to distance himself further from any potential threat. The helicopter lowered itself, and he was mesmerized and amazed by the next event. The rear doors opened and two ropes unravelled, thrown out of the craft by two men who now stood on the landing strut and then descended to the floor.

'Bloody hell, SAS ninjas,' he thought. 'No way.' His heart instantly sunk. They looked professional.

John was running as fast as he possibly could now. He was even more winded after the first burst, but fear and adrenalin had kicked in and became his energy and stamina. He arrived at the bottom of the track, turned right and ran past the houses and to the bottom of Tibbiwell. He then ran up the hill without looking back once, and he turned right, past the pub, flew past the Painswick centre and Hamptons International and down Vicarage Street and to the safety of his small cottage.

He knew that if the man had been telling the truth there would be some unwelcome guests visiting in minutes, and he had to make decisions based on logic and best practice to his code of life, which was having breakfast and taking a walk, not running from predators.

What the hell was he talking about? There had to be a reasonable explanation for all of this. He ran upstairs and lifted the bedroom carpet. There was a compartment under one of the floorboards in the left hand corner which was completely hidden. He lifted it and took out his passport and ten thousand pounds: his whole world, left to him by his eccentric uncle.

He then threw some changes of clothes into a backpack, which was by his chest of drawers, and took several hats, the biggest Helly Hanson coat that had lots of pockets and an overnight kit he had ready in his drawer but rarely used. He also grabbed a handful of loose change and put it in his pocket before running downstairs. He locked the front door, ran through the lounge, through the kitchen, through the back entrance of the cottage, locking the door on exit and up the steps taking two at a time. Luckily, the neighbours were not out there, as he did not want them to tell anyone what he might be wearing or which direction he might head. He heard a screech of tyres outside, and there were multiple vehicles. This was followed by the doors slamming and a big commotion and dogs barking.

"Christ, surely they can't be tracking animals," he muttered as he ran through the back gate. He turned right into the small alleyway and ran past the bowling green and entrance to White Horse Lane, the community hall and tennis courts and into the village park avoiding the open space of the football pitch. A different coloured helicopter now hovered right above his cottage making the scene even more dramatic as if not enough already. The whole area was like a scene from a *Bourne* film, only the star was an unwilling participant and a scared useless broken man with absolutely no skills for espionage or fighting.

John followed the hedgerow to the right, and a few metres in, he climbed under a gap in the steel fence and was behind thick foliage. He remained undetected, as the helicopter began to circle the park and roads within a small radius; it appeared to be performing a grid search.

He had heard the loud crashing of broken glass in his cottage when he was in the alley, and he was naturally terrified. He ran through the park and back through the fence just before the right hand corner met houses and residential property. He had to run fifty metres in the open, and he now waited until the helicopter had banked toward the cottage before he darted through the gate at the Lower Washwell Lane exit. He then ran down the road still hugging the right hand side of the lane where it offered more protection. He turned around the corner, and he was puffing. His heart and chest hurt, but he had no option but to keep moving, as he could hear the dogs in the park.

He ran around the corner. He heard the helicopter and hid behind a car in a garden hoping no residents saw him. The craft moved on, and he turned the corner and ran past Wernons. After passing several more houses, he turned the corner right and then sprinted to quickly re-join Vicarage Street and then he turned left and entered the slipway toward Beech Lane and Sheepscombe.

He ran with every stride and every breath burning his chest.

'Christ this is for real,' he thought. 'How can this be for real? Look at you, John, logic. Come on boy, apply logic. You need time to think. Dogs, what do dogs do?'

Track, they bloody track.

He turned the corner by the Mill House, and he heard the dogs getting closer and closer behind him, and they were far more vocal with the impression they were going to catch him. It was obviously that they had a decent scent and were not going anywhere but for his ankles and legs. Instinctively his need to survive and his logical thought process kicked in, and he threw caution to the wind and followed his basic knowledge of the area.

"Think John, think man," he uttered.

He leapt into the stream from the bridge. He stomped through the water awkwardly to keep his momentum, and he followed the weaving water trail past the Mill House and under the bridge there. He kept going, knowing not even the best tracking dog in the world could navigate scent through water.

He stopped momentarily, as the pain in his chest overwhelmed him. He placed his hands on his knees and bent forward. He wretched badly and the bile and yoghurt from earlier was expelled and woven into and all over his beard.

"Oh Christ," he muttered.

The regurgitated liquid smelt, and he felt even more sick, but he was conscious that the dogs and humans tracking him were noisy around his entry point into the stream.

'Think John, come on. What did the man say? Brilliant! Change your appearance: simple yet effective.'

He pulled at the backpack and pulled out the overnight bag. He had started walking through the twelve inches of water, as he opened the small shaving bag to reveal a small pair of scissors and a shaving kit that he had used once to trim his eyebrows. He placed the Phillips shaver at the top of the pack.

He placed the rest of the kit back in the pack, and while still walking, he started to hack off the long beard which had taken so long to grow, his pride and joy and his mask. He travelled past the big swimming pool conservatory to his right and almost back onto the road at the bottom of Tibbiwell Lane.

He had completed a circle in effect, and he could hear the dogs faltering in the distance by the Mill House. He stopped briefly, the once tangled mass that took patience and long years of growth was now all gone, but a mess of small clumped tufts remained. He replaced the scissors and opened the bag and retrieved the Phillips shaver he used for trimming.

"Please have charge, please have charge."

He placed the trimmer edge at the ready position and pressed the 'on' button, and it buzzed and vibrated. He pulled at the remaining tufts to leave an even surface of hair. He then turned the trimmer to shave, and he shaved vigorously, letting the three angled circular shaving heads to pull and cut the remaining hair from his face.

It hurt, as the hair was too long for a conventional shaver, but within two minutes, he was completely clean shaven and could feel the wind on his face for the first time since his wife had left him. He reached for and adorned a baseball cap that he pulled down at the front, and as he did, he heard the voices of a walking party. As they got close to him, he said good morning and they greeted him.

"Can I walk with you guys for a bit?" he asked.

"Of course, old man!" shouted a rather gregariously dressed would-be hiker, veins popping and hitting the floor with a stick he had found.

"Where are you guys from?" John asked.

"Oxford," answered a sweet girl. She was about thirty and had on a rather large sweatshirt, corduroy trousers, and a floppy hat covering a beautiful mane of auburn hair that shone in the sun.

John isolated her, as potentially she would offer the most convincing cover if they walked together. He walked quite close to her and in a fashion that would give the impression of familiarity and that they were together. He joked about the weather and the walk being arduous, and she smiled and was cordial.

"Where are you from?" she asked quietly.

"The Forest of Dean, Park End, in fact," he said confidently, knowing the area well.

"That's nice," she replied. "There are plenty of walks around there."

"Cannop is nice, by the ponds and stone works," he answered. "Speech House and the nature trail are worth exploring too but before the Hooray Henrys arrive on their bikes and with the screaming kids."

They both laughed and were unusually easy with each other having only met moments earlier.

"I am Jack by the way," he said, his sham growing by the second.

"Melissa, how do you do?"

"Pretty much OK," he answered knowing he was not.

They got to the top of Tibbiwell, and there was a huge commotion going on in the street. The road was blocked, there were cars backed up to the Main Road and the narrow streets were filled with agitated drivers. The police were trying to calm everything down and stop further vehicles joining the gridlock.

"What can be going on?" asked Melissa to one of her friends.

John felt his heart thump, as if to explode, and he burnt with anxiety. He felt dry in his mouth again and his body shook. He wanted to walk up to a policeman and explain the events of the morning, but there were men in the crowd that he did not feel fitted into the environment.

"Are you OK?" asked Melissa, showing great concern for her new friend and his welfare.

"I am fine. Just the walk I think," he replied carefully.

"There is a danger of a gas explosion or something, the Vicarage Street faithful have been emptied and evacuated," said one of the party laughing, seemingly all-knowing and very pleased with himself.

There were people everywhere, but John also detected there were groups of men in suits actually vetting the crowd, talking into invisible devices and going around everyone with more interest than would normally be associated with a routine gas leak. His first thoughts travelled to the fantastic and still unbelievable conspiracy theory, and it seemed that they could indeed have been well founded, or he was just becoming paranoid.

John moved to the left, and he was absolutely terrified and felt like a criminal for no reason whatsoever, an unfounded and totally unnecessary logic, but it existed and it was a dominant thought. He felt hunted and desperate. He was appalled and horrified by the situation he now found himself in. This was a feeling he had never encountered before. He was prey, human prey; just how could this be? He was also outnumbered, heavily out gunned and had no way of surviving, but he would, yes he bloody well would, even if he had to adapt somehow. But how?

This felt like a quixotic moment. He pulled himself together, and his heartbeat still rampant in his chest eased slightly. He took several deep breaths and slid past the unsuspecting group of walkers he had so readily harvested for his disguise, and he entered St Marys Street.

He headed for the churchyard by the stocks, and although he walked swiftly, he did not run or look awkward for fear of attracting unnecessary attention. He left the crowds behind him in his wake and did not look back. He walked through the famous yew trees and past the entrance to the beautiful spired St Marys Church. He went to the end that had number one yew tree, and this led onto New Street via the small exit by Lychgate Cottage. The actual Lychgate was attached to this, being an antiquated church entrance, it was a commanding sheltered structure that shrouded the exit and had beautiful external inscriptions. The interior sat on wood, claiming by inscription, that they were the original beams, recycled from the original belfry of the church.

There appeared to be traffic backing through the village everywhere, but the police chaperoned the jungle of engines and wheels and ensured service vehicles were kept moving.

Luckily, he saw the familiar sight of the Stroud bus trundling through the twenty mile limit without being hampered, so he positioned himself by its approach by the church wall. He flagged it down at the stop opposite the Falcon Hotel, and he got on without looking at anyone or attracting attention.

"Stroud please," he said passing over some change from his pocket, glad he had put it in now.

A ticket machine sprung to life, and he took the paper proof of purchase without achieving eye contact with the driver.

He walked to the third row, inconspicuous he thought, he rode the bus out of the village, past the retirement complex, past the rugby ground, and for a couple of miles. He kept his head down without looking or talking to anyone. He saw the old postal building and snooker club on his left and decided to disembark before the facial recognition cameras or CCTV could track him.

He walked down the aisle and got off prior to the town by the approach roundabout to the Tesco superstore, town and college. There would be no cameras here, and he needed to just relax and catch his breath for a few minutes and think. He decided to go up the Slad Road toward the Vatch, as he knew it would be virtually deserted and he could hide somewhere.

At the last minute he changed his mind and decided to go up Wick Street and the Old Painswick Road, as this would give him access to Painswick should he need to go back near the village. Even with danger everywhere, John was drawn back to where he would recognise more familiar, and welcoming, visual and emotional ties. He needed to reinforce and feel this and that this parallel haven that was Belleview, not only existed, but maybe he was having a bad dream, and none of this was real.

Even though he knew that Belleview must surely have personnel camped out and had the property bugged, he had to get answers from somewhere.

'How the hell can I contact Eric Jennings?' he thought. He needed a computer or at least a phone with internet, but how?

John pulled a stick from the side of the road and pulled off the twigs, so it resembled a walking or rambler's stick. He needed to blend in, and so he started to walk up the hill and into the quiet, the traffic dissipating behind him, as he distanced himself from the main road.

He could still hear several helicopters circling and searching the countryside. As he travelled, he maintained his position near the hedgerow and did not expose himself during the many sweeps of the flying eyes. He jumped over fences, walls and darted off road many times when the helicopters or any vehicles approached and passed, and he felt relief each time he regained his motion on the tarmac.

During the two kilometres or so that he had walked, he felt exposed and distinctly uncomfortable, and he kept questioning every element of the still unbelievable events and circumstance that were ruining his life. It was like a dream that was happening to someone else. He had not come to terms with any of it yet, and he had not processed it fully, but he needed information desperately, so he had to find Eric Jennings.

There were some rotors approaching. He felt them cutting through the air, so he immediately jumped over a shallow wall and landed in a field with a small wooded area to the edge, and he ran to it. He nestled into a shrub and relaxed for the first time in a couple of hours. He had to organise himself from here.

'What are you going to do, John? Come on man, there has to be a plan, or chaos will bring destruction. Come on man,' he thought to himself, 'this just cannot be happening. Why me?'

John was exhausted, and he was not only mentally drained but also physically shattered and sick in the pit of his stomach. He knew that he could never cope with such a situation. Even going shopping was a trial for John, so this was not only unchartered territory. It was obscene to him, and this was just not him by a long shot.

The present situation and ordeal he was placed in was bizarre, and he wanted out. He lay down, put his backpack under his neck and head, and he was amazed to find he drifted away from consciousness and fell completely asleep. He was startled by the thunderous roar of a helicopter, as it passed by at low altitude and seemed to be scouring every inch of the very woodland he was in.

He had a basic grasp of search patterns after watching the crime channel so much and understood the principles of a grid search through common sense. He just hoped there were no canine teams near to his present position as he was not familiar with this area on foot. Fearing the worst and erring on the side of caution, he decided to move anyway from the woods. He wandered through the trees and shrub, and to his joy, he came to a large clearing which housed a huge dwelling with a long drive off into the distance to a set of farm buildings, and he guessed the road was just beyond this.

John studied the house and decided there was nothing else for it but to investigate it closer. He decided that the best form of defence was attack and to hide in plain sight, so he walked to the back door and banged on it. He banged on it hard and several times, but it was obvious that the residence was not only empty but that there had been no one living here for some time. The mat was dry where there had been rain earlier on this week, so dirt or moisture would be expected, but it was completely dry.

There was no reply, and the house was motionless, and he could see an open window on the first floor and an access route using the drainpipe. He quickly contemplated his actions, after all, he was now about to break into a house, and this constituted a crime. John Parks was far from a burglar or a criminal of any sort. He felt slightly ashamed, and he was angry that he was being forced into the position of invading a hard working human's abode, but the obvious problem with this logic was that needs arise and he needed to stay alive.

He shimmied up the rickety drainpipe, crept over the roof edge and onto a ledge, climbed over a small apex roof and found the window which was easily opened. He entered and used both feet to land on the space near where the end of the bed stood. Without hesitation, he moved through the bedroom and listened carefully at the door to see if he had been mistaken, but the house was dormant, there was definitely no human presence.

He quickly moved back across the bedroom and to a set of doors. He opened them and looked into the wardrobe. There was a set of shelving and a long hanger with some clothes that looked like a middle aged woman's. He closed the wardrobe doors then moved through the doorway and into the next bedroom. He approached the sliding doors and opened them to reveal another larger wardrobe. This housed many sets of an older man's clothes, probably owned by a distinguished man, as it had a lot of Harris Tweed and Barbour.

There were also pairs of shoes and boots and an assortment of Wellingtons, all the wrong size. He did look at the bottom of the wardrobe at the back of the clothing and found a hidden laptop, an iPad and to his astonishment, an assortment of phones. He also found several sets of keys concealed behind a sliding panel, including what appeared to be vehicle keys, but he left them there for now, as he knew they were available. He took the other items and put them on the floor and married them to chargers which were in a box by the treasure. He chose the most modern looking phone, an iPhone 4 and the iPad. He took them to sockets and put them on charge and looked through the upper house and found four more bedrooms. He found a small set of binoculars and put them in his backpack and also a lock knife. It was well made and expensive, the blade measured twelve centimetres long and two wide, and this was a razor sharp deadly ally that could easily be concealed, so he placed it down his sock resting in his upper shoe.

He found little else in the way of productive bounty to help his present cause, but he decided to find something to eat, some fluid and to see if there were any vehicles on site. He went downstairs quietly and carefully replaced everything he touched before wiping everything with a towel he had found so as not to leave DNA or any fingerprints.

He found the kitchen, and there was little in the way of food. The occupant or occupants of the house were clearly on vacation, or it was a weekend retreat like so many in this region. It may have been that the house was just not inhabited, as it had the smell of being shut for some time. He hoped this was the case.

John found some bottled water, drank one straight down and put the other two bottles in his pockets.

He found only tinned food and elected to leave it as it was bulky and heavy and served little purpose if he had fluid for now. He did find a packet of shortbread biscuits, and thought this was enough, so he placed them in his pocket also after confirming they were in date, which they were but only just.

He moved into the lounge and opened all of the drawers and cupboards but found little apart from an old driving license with no photo id. Ideal he thought. The name on it was Carlton James Smythe. 'What an aristocratic name,' he thought. It would do, and he put it in his pocket. He also found another set of keys and wondered what they could fit. They were not house keys but did not look like car keys either.

He managed to see the faded words Peugeot on the rounded one and immediately remembered the mopeds that used to have this type of key a few years ago. He looked in the utility room and there were two helmets. If he was lucky, here was his transport and with his face concealed; it would be perfect. He could actually move freely for a while or until the bike was missed, if there was a bike at all.

He moved back upstairs and turned on the iPad. It immediately sprung into life, and luckily there was no entry code to get in or safety combination. Due to a landline server and being close to Stroud, a Wi-Fi signal was not an issue so he opened Safari and entered Eric Jennings of the *Times*. There were many pages of information about him but nothing substantial or that helped his present predicament. He held the phone he had selected to the picture of Eric Jennings, and he took a picture and recorded the details of his contact numbers. The best information he found was located via his Facebook page. He had a simple post, 'Off to the Cotswolds for the weekend'.

'Well I will be damned,' he thought. Just where are you Mr Jennings, and is it simply a case of coincidence or circumstance that places you by the dead guy and me?

John was baffled but motivated by this latest twist, and he was determined to find out where he was. The Cotswolds were huge, but if you put such a post on Facebook, there would be another for sure. The information could get a meet, and John could be exonerated of all evil and get on with life and back to normal. He also deduced that it was too big a coincidence that the guy in the car was heading for a rendezvous near Painswick. The reporter had to be at least somewhere nearby.

John went to the back door and turned the key, opened the door and made sure there were no eyes upon him or helicopters sweeping. It appeared quiet at least for a while. He walked over to a small outbuilding, not a garage or a shed, and it was one of the many old outbuildings that housed logs or a churn. He tried the door on the side, and it was locked, so he walked to the front and looked through a window, and there under a cover he could clearly see the outline of a moped of some description, as the stand and the bottom portion of both wheels were visible. He went back into the house and collected the Peugeot keys and other keys attached to the fob, and prior to returning to the structure, he ran upstairs, opened the man's wardrobe and took a large colourful sweater.

He was becoming slightly paranoid now and maybe with just cause. He believed the coat he had on was familiar to those seeking him, so he rolled up his coat, rammed it in his backpack and put on the awful sweater. This garment was not only too big, but it was also three shades of green and had some form of tree on it, a bit like a National Trust logo but more alpine.

He ran back down the stairs, returned to the garage and attempted to gain entry with the keys. The second key he inserted fitted, and he unlocked the padlock and opened the door. Just as he did this, there was a huge roar as a helicopter passed, as if it were only ten feet above where he had just walked. He swiftly closed the door behind him and immediately pulled the cover from the shiny, orange speed fighter moped.

I remember these he thought: noisy, loud, unsafe and went like stink.

He straddled the seat and shook the bike from side to side, as it looked as if it had been standing for a while, and there was a full tank of gas which slopped around. There was also the oil mixture tank showing full, so he decided there was nothing else for it, so he inserted the key and pressed the electronic ignition.

He was extremely pleased to see a fully operational battery and ignition, so he depressed the start button, and it spluttered a bit at first, but after two attempts and some panic setting in, he remembered to switch the fuel to the on position, re-engaged the ignition and the little engine erupted. It coughed a bit and then idled quickly, so he pulled the throttle a few times to loosen the mechanism and warm the engine and then the bike idled as well as a fifteen year old two stroke could.

He left it running and returned to the house and replaced all the things he had touched, including the iPad and chargers; he kept only the phone, another phone battery and a charger. He locked the back door, ran back upstairs taking a full face black visor helmet with him, went into the original bedroom of entry and climbed back out of the window pushing it to its original position. He then crossed the apex, leant out and shimmied back down the drainpipe and ran into the outbuilding just as another helicopter passed the house and roared off into the distance.

'Three in five minutes; they are grid searching,' he thought. 'There would be a human ground presence soon; he was sure of it.'

He went out to the front of the outbuilding and looked and listened; it was quiet for now. He went back in, and he found some old oil and a rag and rubbed the rag with oil. He then rubbed it in some dirt and cobwebs, before transferring the dirty oily mess to the rear number plate, just enough to obscure it and throw number plate recognition cameras into turmoil and remain undetected.

The downside to this was of course that the police or authorities may stop him to check, but he was small fish he thought. He straddled the idling moped, put the helmet on and gently eased the bike through the door. He put it on its side stand and shut the door, locked it and mounted the machine and headed down the driveway clinging to the woods and hedge.

He lifted the helmet to rest on his ears, so he could hear any helicopters, and it was only a few seconds and he heard the familiar engine noise and rotors cutting the air. John veered the small bike off the road and sat behind a tree, and the helicopter passed. He quickly re-joined the driveway and hammered the throttle. He went to some buildings, but they were empty, or appeared to be, and so he joined Wick Street and went down onto the Stroud Road by the roundabout where he had been dropped earlier by the bus.

He turned right and headed for Painswick. Luckily a large lorry occupied the road ahead, and he sat tucked behind it, completely inconspicuous, and he felt pleased with himself, but his stomach was churning, and he felt sick. He passed the snooker club, passed the garage forecourt with its assortment of shiny cars waiting for new homes, and he sped up the incline where things came to an abrupt halt just by the Gloucester turn off. Traffic was being redirected, so John rounded the lorry and eased the bike forward. There were police everywhere.

They were talking to each driver in turn and then letting them proceed but not to Painswick. John eased the bike back behind the lorry and out of sight. He turned it around in three moves and sped off back towards Stroud. He decided to go back up Wick Street and toward Hangman's Cottage and actually pass the crash site, then he thought better of this foolhardy, ridiculous and unnecessary risk and decided to go to Sheepscombe where he could see what was going on.

The little bike struggled up the hills, but it was a God send, and he made good ground quickly, although he didn't have a clue why he needed to rush, so he eased back.

'You are a dead man' kept ringing in his ears. 'You are a dead man, change your appearance, no electronic signature, Eric Jennings, you are a dead man, you are a dead man.'

"Like fuck I am!" he shouted into the visor.

He arrived on the approach, to the outskirts of Sheepscombe, and he realised he used to look at the houses here from his cottage's garden. Now using the small binoculars, he would reverse the activity and see what the hell was going on at his house. He stopped by a clump of trees, pulled right in, and concealed the small scooter completely. He peered around a tree. He withdrew the binoculars from his backpack, and removing his helmet, he offered the lenses to his eyes.

They were not the best binoculars on earth, but in the circumstances they would provide sufficient magnification to focus and see that there was a huge amount of activity at his house. There were a few utility vehicles in Vicarage Street, a token police presence and he noticed a few black SUVs and personnel resembling official types all up the street.

'Men in black,' he thought. 'Bastards.'

He could also see men with dogs and realised that Belleview was definitely going to be completely off limits, at least until things had played out for a while.

'Where was Eric Jennings? Who was Eric Jennings and what part did he play?' He was John's only chance of survival, and his ultimate salvation rested with this one person, so he had to find him. John retrieved the small phone from his pocket and tried to get a signal. He put data roaming on and opened Safari, and he then went to Eric Jennings' Facebook page, and to his utter amazement, it had a post not more than five minutes ago,

The 88 is lovely, magnificent views and Old England.

John knew immediately that this referred to the Cotswold 88 Hotel, since there was nothing else with the number 88 as significant in its name or description anywhere around this region. The hotel was tucked away just off Tibbiwell and was famous for having loud wallpaper and décor, inspired by mime artist, Leigh Bowery, and photographer, David Hiscock, whoever they were. He remembered the locals in the village calling it 'that arty-farty place' that needed revamping.

He googled the 88 Hotel and realised there was a huge flaw in the post, and this was even more worrying, as it was completely transparent and sloppy, but why?

The website confirmed that the Cotswold 88 Hotel had been purchased by Calcot Hotels and was undergoing an extensive refurbishment programme. This hotel could not possibly be extending its services to Eric Jennings in its normal everyday public operating capacity. It was to be renamed the Painswick Hotel, aptly so, and he had heard talk of a huge undisclosed sum for the business. The locals, who of course know everything and especially the Royal Oak faithful, were a huge source of grapevine truth and were known to elaborate, debate every event at length and knew every intimate detail. The purchase and subsequent proposals for the redevelopment of the beautiful old building had been one such source of great curiosity.

He knew he had to somehow get to Jennings, but how? The whole village was shut tight and buttoned up, and he wondered what the hell was going on around the hotel.

He picked up the binoculars and shifted his view from Belleview to the left where he could see the church spire. He dropped down from this, over the Court House and then he could make out the familiar distinguished outline of the 17th century hotel. It commanded the central position within Kemps Lane and could not be missed, but it was not a picture of a bustling hotel. In fact, it was the opposite, quiet with just two cars in the carpark.

The structure had a rounded almost castle-like extension on the right hand side appearing from the road that had been added after the original central building. It also had another annexe bedroom extension dated 1972 in the stone and this overlooked the lawn area and patio. He remembered this after going there once for afternoon tea on an offer and sitting in the garden thinking, 'This was not the Ritz but nor am I.'

He was in a quandary; he did not know whether to risk going there. Why would this guy, the very central pivotal piece of the puzzle, post a bizarre and almost stupid invitation to a local, to visit somewhere that was so obviously out of public operation and posed more questions than answers. He did not want to embark upon an inexpedient folly that would surely place him in an environment that seemed infected with entrapment.

John sat behind the tree and rubbed his eyes. His head hurt, and he had absolutely no idea what the hell to do next. It seemed that no matter what he did or which way he turned, he was going to be exposed and probably caught. Just then he noticed movement in Vicarage Street. The road appeared to reopen, and he noticed all the traffic being ushered to New Street and through the village. He also noticed that there were still men in the garden at Belleview and in the street outside the front.

There was nothing else to do, since he had to know just what was going on and how much involvement the locals and police had, so he put on his helmet and started the small bike. He was about to ride off when a thought occurred to him.

'What about the phone? Could it be tracked?'

This type of thought process would be paramount to his safety, electronic signatures and tracking. This phone was equal to the very device that had placed him in his current predicament. He did not know the capability of electronic tracking nor the extent of its reach or validation of ownership, even though not registered to him, he convinced himself that the surveillance teams and equipment could certainly detect all phones. He got off the bike, removed the phone from his pocket and placed it behind a stone near the tree where he had been hiding. He would remember this well enough and could see from a distance if it had been disturbed. As it was, the dormant device would merely represent another mobile device in Sheepscombe.

He mounted the idling machine and rode down the road toward the Mill House. He leant around the bend and watched the traffic disappear and some normality in speed and movement resume. He came up the slip road very slowly, as it was a 20mph zone anyway so this would work in his favour, and it would appear normal. He entered Vicarage Street and he anxiously passed the Artist Studio, the Quaker House and then approached White Horse Lane. As he drew up to it on his right, he could see a man guarding the door of Belleview, it had sticker tape 'do not enter' across the front.

The traffic moved slowly, but it kept moving, and he passed the Malt House before drawing level with his lovely cottage and caught a look in his peripheral vision. There were men inside which annoyed him, but there was nothing he could do. His breathing was heavy, and as he exhaled, he blew hard onto the visor. He felt hot and lifted the visor up to relieve the condensation.

He continued up the road and headed for the St Marys Church. He could park there and still remain anonymous with his helmet in place.

After sitting by the stocks for a few minutes, he decided to do a reconnaissance of the hotel, after all, he was inconspicuous. He thought about going down Hale Lane and parking by the Churn and going down the narrow walkway to Kemps, but it would attract attention as it was a vehicular cul-de-sac, even if a pedestrian exit, and locals were suspicious of any vehicles that did not belong there. Also, if he left it there, the bike would be noticed without doubt, but on foot he would be greeted by houses and gardens and these were probably occupied.

He pointed the bike back toward the Royal Oak as he knew he could not access Kemps Lane from Hale Lane. He turned right into Tibbiwell Lane and instead of accessing the hotel directly through Kemps Lane, he passed Kemps Lane turning and continued down to Kingsmill Lane and doubled back up through Knapp Lane and up toward the hotel.

'There is no point in being too easily spotted,' he thought. 'No matter what the disguise.'

He turned randomly into an empty driveway and hid the bike behind a garage; there were no cars in the drive, and the owners would probably be at work, so he hoped. He kept the helmet with him, and he worked his way to the big Cotswold dry stone wall in front of him. He loved the rich golden rock so much in this region. He ducked and followed it to the end of the driveway.

Chapter 3

The Change

He could see the hotel and its garden from his position. It was over the next garden wall, so he approached it carefully, climbed over the wall and slipped around the external circumference of the garden to a stone built potting shed that had a small door and a tiny window. He walked behind it quietly, as he could now hear voices and knew that the hotel was a front. It seemed as if it was being guarded, not occupied by guests.

"How much longer do you think we have to stake out this place? I am bored, tired and thirsty," said the first man.

"Stop moaning! You are always moaning. We do as we are told and that's all," replied a man with what John thought was an Eastern European accent.

"This guy ain't gonna show though. He can't be as thick as to come here can he, can he?"

"Be quiet. You talk too much and you never talk any sense, waste of language."

"I was just trying to make conversation. I hate this detail, so let's make it as easy as possible. That's all."

A crackling noise from a radio echoed, followed closely by, "Anything yet?" A very well-educated, very English voice asked.

"No," replied the Eastern European.

"Be vigilant. We have posted another note on Facebook to entice him over here, and he will take the bait for sure, and he will probably think it is his salvation. What an idiot," said the man on the walkie-talkie.

"If he comes, I will kill him," replied the Eastern European. "Make no worries. He will be dead."

"Not here though you fool. You have to dispose of the body elsewhere making sure he dies where the body is found, so it is not diagnosed as transported after death. Do you understand? It has to be set up like he could not live with the shame of being a traitor. Remember your assignment," said the man.

"OK, but I am still going to kill him," replied the Eastern European rubbing his hands with glee and anticipation.

John was physically repulsed and thought he would surely wretch. All this talk of death and disposal, and it was pertaining to him. He had to hold his neck to stop himself from being sick.

"I did not say you could not kill him; it is simply a case of how where and when. Anyway, we need to find him first."

"OK Eric, don't worry," replied the first man.

"Don't use my name you fool!" screamed the man down the device. "Are you crazy?"

"What a prick you are," said the Eastern European looking fiercely at the other guy.

He looked back in stone silence.

"I will communicate with you idiots later. Let me know if anything transpires," said the man and went.

"Yeah, I don't like him. He is right up his own ass, journalist, my ass, but what a front. He got really shirty just cos I used his first name. There's no one around here, its bloody dead, the whole village is dead, so just give me a city anytime."

"Will you shut up!" shouted the Eastern European. "Look around, do a sweep, anything but shut the fuck up."

So that was it, a complete front and a huge lure and trap. They had set the bait for the fool and look who was only a few yards away. John felt the sickness in his stomach intensify even further, and he was distressed beyond any normal comprehension, listening to talk about killing and disposal of him. It was beyond understanding.

'Christ, why me?' he pondered. 'What the hell am I going to do, or maybe I am just a dead man? Am I? Bollocks. I have a life, not much of one, but I have one, and I have kids.'

He rallied himself and sat for about ten minutes breathing heavily and trying to regain a normal rhythm. Just when despair and anxiety had subsided slightly, he heard a vehicle approaching and enter the grounds of the hotel. He saw a BMW X6 turn into the car park, and his eyes were greeted with the image of none other than Eric Jennings exiting the vehicle.

"Have you found him yet?" he bellowed at the men.

"No," they replied in unison.

"It's only been ten minutes," said the first man. "He will show up though."

"He is nowhere to be found, but he is a civilian, so he will make a stupid mistake. They all do," said the Eastern European over talking and over shadowing the first man.

"Well, be ready when he does. I don't want any loose ends, but try and be discreet, no newspaper stuff."

"We will get him. He is like a rabbit that is running into the headlights without knowing when to dodge the car," said the Eastern European, and he laughed sarcastically.

"Like hell I am," John whispered to himself.

John went to the door of the structure and found it was not locked. He went inside and there was a bench with drawers, some old curtains on the floor and some tools. He saw a small claw hammer and he put it through his belt, so it was hanging under the jumper.

'Little comfort against guns,' he thought.

He still had the small knife concealed in his shoe and he sat on a stool. He could see and hear everything and remain undetected. This was almost like hiding in plain sight, but he needed a strategy. He needed to think on his feet and attack rather than fall into acceptance of his fate at the hand of these men and the present set of circumstances.

"We can all be victims," he whispered to himself, 'but not me though. No bloody way."

It was now 2.35 pm and the afternoon sun shone down through the trees, the men continued to circle the hotel, and John remained hidden. Eric Jennings was inside the hotel, and all anyone could do was wait and see what developed unless one or more of them changed the game plan.

John got off the stool and sat on the floor on some old curtains. He closed his eyes, and he could see his girls running to him and telling him, "Daddy we love you. Why can't we stay with you?"

The separation had broken his heart, but now it gave him strength, and he was not going to just sit and take everything any more. He was really angry, but he drifted into a deep sleep.

John was jolted into consciousness by the sound of voices. He looked at his watch, 3.05pm, and he had actually been so mentally and physically drained he had fallen asleep again.

'Who the hell does this? Who the hell sleeps when they have people around them talking about killing them? Come on John. Get real.'

He was surprised but relieved he had napped, as he needed to be on his sharpest form to change his persona and have an acute reality check.

He looked out of the tiny filthy window and saw Eric Jennings, so he crept out of the shed and could peer into the garden through a small gap in the old stone wall. Eric Jennings was laughing and smoking a small cigar, and the two men were nodding in approval and humouring him. He seemed to be a man who always got what he wanted. John had long since thought that the world was run by people that went to that posh school together and the old handshake shaped the universe; nothing to do with morals or intelligence, just where Daddy sent you and who, of course, your daddy was.

"You absolute prick," he uttered under his breath. "You utter arrogant conceited unbelievable prick."

"Right chaps, don't cause chaos. I am going into Stroud to meet with someone special who cannot be linked or seen anywhere near here, so remember what I said, don't kill him here," said Jennings again laughing.

John saw a chisel on the bench, and he placed this in his backpack and exited the shed swiftly. He ran around the circumference of the garden, jumped over the stone wall and retrieved his bike. He started it and then he dropped down Knapp Lane, once again on Kingsmill and came to the bottom of Tibbiwell Lane. He was expecting to go up and through the village, but he was surprised to see the black X6 thunder down the hill, going too fast and with no consideration for anyone else.

'What a surprise,' he thought.

The X6 thundered past with Jennings at the wheel, smug and full of himself. John waited and then pulled out a few seconds after it had passed so as not to arouse any suspicion. He went onto Greenhouse Lane and sped up the hill, but as he went around the corner, the X6 was off the road and in the hedge. John approached with caution, pulled up alongside the car and looked in.

Eric Jennings was slumped over the steering wheel facing away from him. John put the bike on side stand and left it idling, the door would not open so he removed the hammer from his belt and hit the side window instantly sending shards of glass over the lifeless victim.

He recognised blood, loose flesh and bone on the back of his head, and lots of it, which was strange. He could see blood spatter all up on the back of the roof lining and backseat extending into the rear parcel area and back windscreen.

He then pulled Eric Jennings' head up and made it face him; it was instantly recognisable that not only could he detect that the man was not breathing, but he could also see that there was a small hole in his forehead. The back of his head was completely missing; he had been shot once through the head.

Instinctively, John ducked down just as a whistling sound passed by him, and he felt the helmet rock slightly. He stayed down, rubbed his finger over the helmet and he could detect a break and a furrow through the safety device. He knew he was being shot at, and he knew Eric Jennings was dead, but why?

This man had seemed pivotal in some major capacity.

'Maybe loose ends,' he thought, 'but still the question: why?'

He heard a car approaching. This was not good, and he decided this was his cue to risk all. He noticed Eric Jennings' phone and walkie-talkie were exposed on the seat, so he grabbed them quickly, and then he noticed something that tested his normal powers of process. Jutting out of the dead man's jacket breast holster, he could see the handle of a gun, a big gun.

'Oh for Christ's sake,' he thought, but unlike most films he had seen, no way was he leaving the gun like all the idiots he had watched. He opened the jacket, undid the safety catch on the holster and removed the shiny deliverer of death and four magazines that were attached to the holster. It was a heavy large gun, shiny silver with a black grip handle, and he felt instantly empowered. He put the gun and the ammunition in his backpack. 'No way was this falling out or getting lost, as this might be the only thing that saves me,' he thought.

He grabbed the scooter, and still crouching, he slid it off the side stand, and he straddled it flat and rode it around the corner at full throttle.

A car was in hot pursuit, a large black Jeep, and it looked menacing and had several occupants. He could feel its presence and could hear the tyres screaming, as it hugged the tiny lane at speed.

John sped off down Greenhouse Lane once again, even though hopelessly out powered by the big vehicle, he had the advantage of being on familiar territory. He could also manoeuvre more freely through small spaces and could navigate the winding lanes more efficiently and to go up pedestrian access routes.

He entered Tibbiwell Lane and up the hill with the Jeep closing in on him fast. Luckily, but easily predicted, there was traffic, and it was a nightmare with the added black suspicious vehicles trying, but without success, to park inconspicuously in the tiny narrow streets.

He slipped into St Marys Street by Cardynham House and the Jeep fell afoul of the queue by the paper shop and Royal Oak. John noticed some odd men outside Four Ways House, so he flew toward Vicarage Street, but this was too easy to fathom for those in pursuit.

Instead he threw a hard left at Hamptons International, passed the Painswick Centre on his right, up toward the charity shop and then he turned left by Olivas bar into Friday Street. He slowed right down and edged to a vantage point on the right hand side of the road. He edged around the corner creeping past the Roman Catholic Church of our Lady and Saint Theresa until he just caught the huge black Jeep aggressively trying to barge its way through.

This did not happen in Painswick. Locals were fierce about their rights of way, visitors and tourists speeding and on parking and any movement of traffic and the Jeep would have to wait.

"Believe me, you will wait," John chuckled to himself.

The Jeep finally moved and went passed the Royal Oak, and he saw it disappear down Vicarage Street as he rounded the circular entrance from Friday to St Marys Street. He watched as the men that had been outside Four Ways House started following it on foot, and they looked ridiculous, out of place and completely visible.

Unfortunately, John was only too aware that the scooter now represented a threat and instant recognition, so he decided to ditch it and quickly. He rode up St Marys Street, right up Victoria Street and turned left on New Street. He sped the hundred metres toward Stroud but then pulled a right into the entrance and back of the Falcon. He looked at the Shires. It was a beautiful building with a lovely round window, and it looked so peaceful. There was also a host of cottages near it named after yew trees, significant to the church, of course, but not very inventive he thought. He went to the left hand side of the car park, and he was conscious that he was also by the oldest bowling green in England. It had a lovely bowls house, and it was magnificently placed up in an elevated position and with peace and serenity.

'Not a place to die, though,' he thought as he continued with the tasks in hand.

He hid the bike as best as he could behind a large commercial green wheelie bin, and he lay it listing slightly but not enough to contaminate the fuel flow or let it leak away. He knew he had to preserve this little machine just in case he needed it at some point in the future. He then proceeded to cover it with some brush that had been cut from the trees and hedges and placed the keys in his pack. There was a broken wheelbarrow by the bin, so he leant it up against the hidden machine to lend even more authenticity to it being a mound of cuttings and rubbish.

He inspected the helmet closely, and sure enough he had been shot, and he was extremely lucky. The bullet appeared to have cut through the fibreglass external shell and entered into the polystyrene inner layer with ease, and it was only him dropping to the floor at that instance that had saved his life.

Luckily, it had not penetrated near enough to his skull to have hurt him, but he knew the bullet had nicked the helmet, as it had reverberated from the passage through. His heart beat so fast he thought it would explode. 'Me of all people getting shot at, what are the chances? Bloody high now I suppose.'

He could not help but think it was ironic that this morning he believed his life was boring, and up until a few hours ago, he was a monotonous nobody with no excitement.

'What I would give for that now?' he said to himself.

He took one of the bottles of water he had taken from the house out of his pocket and drank it straight down in one go. He threw the bottle into a green bin and tried to calm down and reorganise himself.

He took off the vile jumper. They had to have circulated a description. 'Santa on a moped,' he thought and started to giggle until it dawned on him how much trouble he was actually in.

He hid the bright garment in one of the bins, careful to cover it with some black wheelie bags that were in there. He replaced it with a Ralph Lauren black Harrington type jacket with a red pony from his pack, and he put on a black flat cap and sunglasses. He thanked Carlton James Smythe for the use of both the bike and the clothing and walked off down onto New Street, pulling out the walkie-talkie and phone. He waited until a gardening flatbed transit came parallel to him, and he tossed both into the back. 'Better they track them to the dump,' he thought. He had nearly forgot they all had GPS tracking capability. What was he thinking?

He crossed over the road, veered to the right and entered through the church entrance by Lychgate Cottage. He passed the trees and north entrance of the church which had a cannon ball imprint on it and then onto Victoria Street. He went by the town hall and where St Michaels restaurant had been, and he decided he would have to risk Hale Lane. There was nothing else for it, and they would surely be on high alert now for both the bike and John. Kemps Lane had cameras from the front entrance of the hotel and also the outer annexe and carpark.

John walked down the lane past the huge electronic gates of the Court House Manor on his right. Exaggerated accounts hinted that the four acre grounds were haunted by King Charles I following the siege of Gloucester in 1643.

'Good luck with that,' thought John. 'Another ruse to get idiots to book an overpriced bed and breakfast. What a complete load of bollocks, and anything for most haunted.'

He walked briskly, yet as normally as possible, not wishing to attract any attention at all. He had never been on the lamb, but due to his social awkwardness, he watched the crime channel all the time and knew the rules. He passed by the little cottages either side of the small lane, with their rambling trellis rose gardens and tiny courtyards. They oozed quintessential England and pushed the most idyllic scene forward to the eye.

He was confronted by a set of newish double gates on his left and just before the Churn. He peered over them to see if there was any visible signs of life. He noticed there were no vehicles present or any evidence of habitation. He looked at his watch, and since it was only 4.45pm, he decided to gamble and he scaled the gates and ran across the shingle drive to the edge of an outbuilding with a circular shaped roof and shell that belonged to the hotel. It reminded him of the tiny houses in Boscastle which were built in a round design, so the devil could not hide in the corners.

'They certainly did not hide here,' he thought. 'They are everywhere and I am *it*,' he uttered quietly.

He heard voices and decided the wall was too exposed at this particular place, as was he, so he moved towards the garden that belonged to the Churn. He climbed the wall and went toward the outhouse that looked like a small house. He could just see over the wall through a gap in the foliage to the lawn and drive of the Painswick.

What met his eyes was astonishing. There were two bodies stretched out on the floor, both with blood trickles coming from their heads and mouths. Whatever had occurred here had only just happened in the last few minutes. He instantly recognised the pair of men as the Eastern European and the English sounding guards that had been with Eric Jennings outside the hotel.

'Bloody hell,' he thought. 'Bloody hell, this can't be happening.'

This completely threw John, as before today, he had never seen dead people before. They were on the television not in real life, and now he had seen three corpses, no four corpses, today. This was somebody else's life, not his. He was ordinary, and the events of today were just too extraordinary for him to comprehend.

His stomach began to churn, and his anxiety once again peaked at a level he thought impossible. He had placed all his hopes on finding information from this very place, and the two lifeless corpses lay flat on the ground completely cutting off any chance of gaining knowledge. This had been his only direct hope of finding out who Eric Jennings really was, and now the Painswick Hotel probably represented a dead end in more ways than one.

He could not decipher in his mind how a prominent journalist was just snuffed out mercilessly. 'What of the media?' he thought.

What did that make his life worth, a nothing, a mere nobody. John was as good as dead, but at least he had a gun now, plus he knew everyone was after him, so he would trust no one.

He decided in his mind that he would not lie down and just take it easier said than done, but this notion gave him strength and hope. John realised that he had no idea of how to shoot the weapon or reload it, and it terrified him to aim such a thing at another human being. He was not accustomed to a world where human life was extinguished to order and to protect what, a key? Nothing was worth the price being paid here, not in his view.

He could comprehend a child killer being put down like an animal. If it were one of his children hurt, he always thought he would muster the courage to do something awful to the attacker and live with the consequences. 'That was a normal parental notion,' he thought reinforcing it in his mind, 'but to kill without any remorse for a key?' This was not in his mind set or capability,

'I could just never kill,' he said to himself several times. 'Not for this, not for any of this.'

If he was going to grasp any of the ever-changing circumstances he found presented to him, he knew he would have to gather information. He crouched by the wall and listened to what was being said.

"Get them in the van and out of here," an autocratic sounding man said to three others. He was obviously the conductor of this bizarre episode, the orchestrator of events. They all had on black military style trousers and a black jumper each with black leather elbow patches and black shoes.

'Bloody ninjas, men in black,' John thought once again today.

He watched as they picked up with ease and unceremoniously threw the lifeless corpses inside the VW Transporter parked on the driveway. It was as if they were tossing bags of supermarket shopping into the car, or garbage, not human beings probably extinct at their hands. One of the men then got into the driver's seat, another entered the passenger seat and they buckled their seatbelts and with the window down, started to bid the other two farewell.

"We will rendezvous at Wernons later," said the leader.

'I know Wernons,' thought John, 'but how could they be using that lovely old house? It was majestic and an integral part of the village history, and the locals always thought someone famous lived there.'

"Keep your eyes peeled for a scooter, you know, those moped type bike things that make loads of noise but have no power. He is on one and has a bright, ugly jumper on," said the leader.

"What do we do if we see him?"

"You know exactly what to do," said the leader.

John decided to hide and wait, as there was no point exposing himself now, and he needed to think about what he would do next, yet again.

"See you later." And with that, the engine started, and they drove out of the driveway and disappeared around the corner.

"I don't think he is going to show up here; do you?" asked the fourth man showing little faith in the present plan.

"We cannot take any chances," said the leader turning and facing the hotel entrance. "You need to hide out of sight and stay here for the night. I suggest you use one of the upper windows or balconies, as you will be able to see everything from there. You can also link to the cameras on the outside of the building, point the one over the door outward to see the driveway and road, and the other one is located by the extension completely hidden out of site. That one over there is inoperable, so forget it for now."

"Shall I set up an infrared beam, just in case?" asked the man.

"You can, but with the foxes and other local wildlife, it is your call. You may get a lot of false readings, but up to you, whatever it takes, old man," said the leader. "I will see you later. I am going to try and get to Wernons without attracting too much attention. The locals still think there is an issue with someone in the village, national security and all that waffle, so they will show patriotism and toe the line."

"Thick twats," said the man laughing.

"Keep your radio on," said the leader, and he walked off toward Tibbiwell Lane with a marching step rehearsed many times no doubt.

'Good luck with blending,' John thought. 'You look like Sergeant Bilko stomping all over the place.'

He watched the fourth man parade around the perimeter checking the camera by the extension and then he returned to the front of the hotel and redirected the camera to face the driveway and road. He was operating a small device, probably linking the cameras to a digital display screen somewhere or maybe his phone. He adjusted the front camera several times until he seemed satisfied that it was in perfect position for task. Once he had accomplished this sufficiently to convince himself that he had all angles covered, he entered the building and John could see him by the first floor window. It was adjacent to the castle-like turret that shielded the users of the balcony from danger.

John was content in the knowledge that he had in fact managed to ascertain their strategy and where the pitfalls might be around his next move. He decided to get into the next garden and locate himself in the potting shed he had been in earlier that day. He achieved this using all his powers of stealth. Fear was a powerful motivator, and he still felt anxious and exposed. He still fought the urge to vomit, as his anxiety was acute, and his body was burning with the thought of impending doom and the unknown.

"Come on, John," he said to himself. "Calm down, relax. You have a gun, a hammer and the will to live; come on man, survive."

He closed the door and instantly felt safer inside. It was familiar surroundings, and even though it was an absurd thought, it had become enlarged in his mind as a trusted hide out. He quietly made a makeshift bed out of the curtains on the floor, and he had a good look around. He found an old and very worn but heavy cricket bat. Its wear patterns boasted many years of good use in the field of play. Its appearance was ancient, but it had a good handle, woven well, and it had stood the test of time and was enough to deliver a blow.

He himself could not imagine putting leather to willow. He hated cricket and all the pomp and circumstance that went with, probably because like most sports, he was awful at it himself. He was in fact awful at almost everything, and he could not even talk a good game from the side lines because he either got too excited to watch or lost interest too quickly.

The bat offered some form of safety though, and it felt good in his hands, a little bit of comfort that he would gladly take on board at this point in the proceedings. He had little in the way of comfort at this junction in his life, and it was surprising that his best friends were now an ancient cricket bat and a gun he had no idea of how to fire, except to point and pull the trigger.

This sounded easy but the idea rested heavily on his mind. The taking of a human life would not be an easy task and would plague him forever should he have to achieve this. He lay down and thought about the day, the death and carnage surrounding him, the exposure to all that was evil, a different world, the world of others. This was not John's world. His was having coffee at Belleview, watching the horses frolic in the fields, being alone and not knowing how to fill the day. That was John's world, not international industrial espionage and routine massacres, and even as he thought this, it seemed even more ridiculous.

John lay down, drifted and was thinking of the girl he had met walking up Tibbiwell Lane. She had reacted differently to him, and she had responded to him more than he had ever anticipated, maybe losing the beard had made him more approachable, less Sasquatch and more human. 'Everyone had a beard nowadays,' he thought, 'but maybe mine just did not suit me, or maybe I am just not a suitable candidate for anything let alone romance, and maybe I am not a suitable candidate for life.' With that sobering thought clinging to his mind, he once again fell asleep.

John was awoken by the shed door creaking open very slowly, and he could see a beam of light, as if a torch was being held in someone's mouth or attached to a hat. He was aware he had been making noises in his half sleep, because, as he woke up, he snorted a familiar snort that often woke him up, and it was like a pig. He often thought of a local Old Spot pig when he woke up from this. Sometimes it frightened him and took him a few moments to collect his thoughts and bearings and to relocate to the conscious world.

His heart was beating so fast that he felt sick and was just about to reach for the gun when the door opened fully, and he could make out a small silhouette of a human before him. He noticed it had something in its hand, and it shone the torch by moving its head, as it was on some form of helmet or hat. The beam circled the shed and then as it descended on the makeshift bed, John, instinctively and without any warning, swung the bat. There was a dull thud as it connected with the side of the individual's head.

What happened next surprised John. He was so scared, and he had seen too many films where the ninja came back to life after being initially felled. The bad guy had always killed the victim because he was too nice, so John looked at him lying on the floor gurgling, and he hit him again, really hard and heard the bones in his face shatter as the bat dislodged the man's very means of recognition.

John looked at the man on the floor. His breathing was heavy and laboured and blood was coming out of a balaclava that indeed had the remains of a torch that had been strapped to his forehead. It was now firmly shattered and embedded in the man's skull. John lifted the balaclava slowly, unwilling to see the results of his actions, but he had to know. As the balaclava unfolded, he witnessed the true horror unfold inch by inch.

The jawline was odd for his face and obviously broken and completely pushed over the one side. The man's nose was shattered and resembled a lump of blood and gristle. John then noticed his eyes, he was of Asian descent, probably Chinese. He was no expert, but he looked Chinese. John felt in his pockets and found a wallet. He looked and it had an identification in it. This was composed of a picture with the name Chang Hock Sang, commercial advisor and an address of a company in London.

'Commercial advisor my ass,' thought John. 'If you are a commercial adviser then I am a Geisha girl.'

He felt in his other pocket and there was some information from Google about Painswick and the village. He also noticed that when he knelt closer something dug into his knee; it was a gun.

'I have never seen one or had one in my hands before today and now two,' he thought. 'John bloody Wayne.'

A radio suddenly crackled into life behind the groaning man. John saw it light up, and it was speaking in what he guessed was Chinese. He knelt down a bit further, collected the gun and radio, placed the small gun in his pack and then he removed the hammer from his belt and proceeded to hit the radio hard with it until it was rendered inoperable, and all life exited the machine.

John pulled the man backwards and placed him under the curtains and put some other items on him to conceal his existence. He exited the building slowly, and without hesitation, he went to the wall where he could see through a gap. He then saw the lights go on in the Painswick carpark, and he watched a dark shadowy figure run across the drive toward Tibbiwell Lane. The silhouette fell instantly, and there was no slow motion stopping and catching breath, clasping of any part of the body or dramatic exit. There was no prolonged stoppage in mid stride, or shaking or odd movement at all. He just instantly fell over and dropped on the spot as if he had been switched off somehow.

There was also a distinct and noticeable absence of any sound emitting from the body as it dropped. He had anticipated a gurgle, death croak or something, but it just fell lifeless to the floor, and there was a slight dull thud that would not be recognisable as synonymous with something as immense as the end of human life.

John was completely bemused by the event, but then he remembered the cameras, the infrared, and he noticed the front door of the Painswick Hotel open. He instantly recognised the man that had been left behind by the leader of the four. He emerged with a rifle still in his hand, and he was smiling. How could he smile after committing such an act? It was a large military type square rifle, and it had telescopic sights attached, and he carried it as if it were part of him. This was not a random shooter; he was an expert sniper to take a man out so cleanly in near dark conditions and with a moving target. Maybe he had the advantage of a night scope fixed, but even then, the shot had been exact and decisive.

He walked casually to the man on the floor, and he withdrew a handgun from a holster located under his arm. He then calmly and without emotion shot the man on the floor twice through the head. The body moved from the head up giving way to the impact of the bullets in turn. It was a pure execution, but the man on the floor was obviously dead before this barbaric act. This was pure overkill or was it just taking no chances.

The shots were muffled, obviously silenced by a suppressor, and John heard nothing but just witnessed the absolute finality of the act and the bullet with its high velocity and deadly accuracy was a silent assassin spinning through the evening air. He wondered if this would be the very means of his own demise. Would he just exit the planet with any knowledge of the act or why?

He saw lights enter the road and turn off Tibbiwell Lane, and he heard the engine of the vehicle as it approached. It came down the road, not fast, just as a normal vehicle would approach a murder. The shooter did not flinch, as he was obviously expecting it. A van swung into the driveway, and it was the VW Transporter that had transported the guards and the two dead bodies away earlier. The leader plus the driver exited and walked over to the lifeless corpse and the third man. The leader kicked the corpse.

"Good shot, old man. Was he moving when you got him?" asked the leader laughing.

"Yep, like a rabbit in the headlights," replied the man proudly, "but I had him in my crosshairs well before the lights went on. The infrared is brilliant, and I swear by it, but then you know I always have it set up wherever I am. It has cost a few dozy twats entry into the kingdom without them ever seeing or hearing it. Bang, and they are despatched."

"Is he the only one do you know?" asked the leader.

"Yes, I think so. I did not see or hear anyone else anyway," he looked at the leader and pointed to his eyes and then to the shed. He then put up one finger to obviously signal another single assailant and then he continued. "What shall we do now?"

"Go and have a look around just to be sure," said the leader to them both. "On second thought, I will go. You two can put the little wanker in the van ready to move out."

John crept away from the shed, and quietly but with speed and agility, he scaled the wall into the Churn just as the leader's torch beam hit the very area he had been standing in. He continued and shimmered around the circumference of the garden toward Hale Lane. He looked back and could see the beams of light, and he heard the shed door creaking and the leader entering it.

"Bloody hell! There is another stiff in here," he shouted to the others.

"How can that be?" said the driver.

"I have absolutely no idea, but he is dead as a doornail."

John entered Hale Lane and walked briskly but without running and went straight into the churchyard at Stocks Cottage. He walked past the church and to the exit at Lychgate Cottage, and he entered New Street with caution. He instantly returned back into the churchyard; he felt too exposed on the main road and had to find another way to get to the park and possibly Wernons.

He had already made his mind up that he disbelieved the leader's account of the condition of the Chinese man. 'This was a ruse,' he thought, 'a plot to amuse them and to destroy any moral of further assailants that may be hidden or listening. The man would have probably been rendered dead after the leader had entered, but there is no way he would leave him alive. Yes that was it, he had killed him.'

'Just what the bloody hell are you doing John?' he asked himself. 'You are discussing whether you are responsible for killing a Chinese ninja, a son, brother, maybe a father, or whether the UK ninja did it. This just cannot be happening; there is no way I killed him. I did hit him hard, and I did hit him twice. Bollocks it was him or me, and the leader killed him. I know he did. Yes, he did,' he repeated to himself.

John heard and saw the Stroud to Cheltenham bus trundling up New Street. Without too much planning, he ran and jumped the church wall by the benches, ran across the road to just before the Falcon and he beckoned the bus to stop, and it duly obliged. He pulled out some money, asked for a single to Brockworth, took his change and then sat down and looked down. There were only a handful of occupants, and he blended inconspicuously. As the bus waited at the lights by the Patchwork Mouse Arts cafe and chemist, he noticed it was very quiet everywhere. The bus rumbled on its way, past the entrance to Gloucester Street and Bisley Street, round past the lights and up the gentle incline. An old lady stepped into the middle of the aisle and rang the bell. She had two heavy bags with her and looked to be struggling a little.

The bus came to a halt just near Lower Washwell Lane. As she proceeded to disembark John took advantage of the opportunity and joined her. He helped her off and offered to carry her bags for her. He did and said enough to elude and dispel her fears. They subsided quickly, and she trusted him after he offered her reasonable conversation and threw in some familiar names of oldies he knew in the village.

It was just enough for her to relax and accept the help, as she needed it as the bags had become heavy. The old lady lived just opposite Woody Steeps, and he knew this would place him near enough to the park to be able to see into Wernons from a safe distance. He walked with her and she stumbled slightly, so John placed his arm through hers and joked that this was their first date, and that there should be no kissing or smooching.

As the old lady laughed, two ominous men in black clothing went past on foot. John did not make eye contact but his face was seventy-five percent hidden by his cap plus he was clean shaven; it seemed enough. For them, looking for a wild bearded man with an ugly jumper, they had been presented with an image of a clean cut individual in a Ralph Lauren coat, arm in arm with Super Gran and she was laughing and so content that they appeared to be satisfied that he was a local and not the fugitive they sought.

He felt his heart thumping like Apache drums and at speed, and he was dry in the throat again and just wanted to be somewhere safe. The old lady went to her door, thanked him many times and offered him tea. He warned her of the perils of letting young men near her virtue, and she giggled. He gave her a kiss on the cheek and walked off over the road and into the park.

He went to the bottom left hand side of the park by the fence and crouched down. He could see a lot of activity and what appeared to be guards all around and in the house. He went through a small gap in the fence where no doubt the kids had dens, and he got to a vantage point, but he could not hear anything.

He was aware of some crunching behind him, and he slid under a large bush and some fallen branches that had fallen afoul of some high winds in February. He could just make out some whispering, and he noticed two pairs of legs walking with stealth and looking into the undergrowth. For the first time, he undid his backpack and clutched the smaller gun from the Chinese man. He looked for a safety catch of some sort, but there was none, so it looked ready to inflict damage or even worse, death.

'They will kill you as much as blink,' he thought, 'so don't think too much, just shoot the bastards if it is you or them. Survival is key, so shoot them. If it is you or them, shoot them if it is.'

They turned and resumed their search in the other direction, obviously satisfied there was nothing of interest in this portion of the park.

John had held his breath and breathed reluctantly and conservatively. He relaxed slightly but quietly exhaled fully and inhaled with full capacity reached then repeated the process until his heart rate was somewhere near normality.

What the hell was going on? He climbed down a slightly awkward bank to a lower level of the upper garden he was now invading, but Wernons was locked tight. It showed little profit and probable death to try and get near it at present, and it was too risky where he was.

John was pleased that he had managed to survive through that day and realised he had to remain concealed at least for the night,

'So where do you go when you are on the lamb?' he pondered.

Now this was one area where John demonstrated an ability to apply his most logical thought processes. It was the one thing he was good at: analyse and react. He knew that there were a couple of new build houses nearing completion just up the road, and he immediately deduced the following logical facts.

They were being plastered and on second fix electrics; he knew this because he had witnessed the vans there and heard the workmen swearing at each other over who was making more mess.

He also knew that a new build had all sorts of warning signs about cameras and CCTV systems dotted over the mesh fences and gates, but in reality, there was rarely anything, and he knew there was nothing of the sort on these because he had witnessed some of the village children having a cigarette behind one of them.

He also knew that without power, he could resist temptation to use lights or appliances which would attract attention.

He also knew there would be plenty of dust sheets to which he could form some type of sleeping bag or cocoon to let him rest.

He slipped away from the vantage point and to the fence, and he was careful to remain in the foliage. He checked the perimeter slowly and could see the faint silhouettes of the two men disappear down the alley by the second bowling green and tennis courts, and pass by the community centre. This led directly to the back gate of Belleview, so he applied logic that they would check the property and then return this way shortly.

He scurried across the field and darted behind one of the huge old oak trees. He then peered over the gate and checked Lower Washwell Lane for any guards or anyone at all. It was empty in both directions, so he ran across the road, leapt up, lay his chest on the makeshift aluminium fence and dropped down the other side. It rattled slightly but not enough to set any alarm bells off. He ran to the back of the buildings and began to investigate the possibility of entry.

As he did so, he could hear the faint sound of a television in the property next to it. Although detached and with some distance, it was obvious that the old guy that lived there was hard of hearing and the television was blaring out the news. John climbed over a wall and crept up to the window that was ajar allowing the speech to be transmitted through the night air. He was amazed when a picture of Eric Jennings appeared with the information underneath claiming

Prominent journalist takes his own life after links to phone tapping scandal.

The newsreader proceeded to say what a good chap he had been, but of late he had been under investigation and was thought to be showing signs of depression.

"The only signs of depression was the bullet depressing into his skull," John muttered under his breath.

The next thing that happened rocked John's world. The station went to the local regional news, and John looked on in terror as his picture was paraded on the news with the writing:

Local Painswick man linked to death of a Chinese national.

The newsreader proceeded to tell the public that the police had issued a warning that not under any circumstances was anyone to approach this dangerous individual and also revealed that the assailant may be on a scooter and possibly armed. He had been linked to the death of a Chinese national, who was yet to be named until his family had been notified.

John looked in disbelief and tried to process the information. This could not be happening. The only good news was that they had used his passport photograph and he looked like a shabby member of ZZ Top or a mountain man. The newsreader informed everyone that this individual, John Parks, may have changed his appearance and had even potentially shaved his beard. John comforted himself in the knowledge and logic that there was no picture, computer generated or artist's impression, of him without a beard, so he knew that the average member of the public would soon forget this fact and look for the Grizzly Adams version, with beard and hair all over the place.

He moved back from the window and retreated over the wall and back to the new builds. As he did so, he heard muffled voices, and he watched as the shadows of the two men in black quietly and slowly walked down the lane shining torch beams into properties and hedges.

"What was that?" said one of the men standing at the front of the new build by the fence.

"Nothing," replied the other.

"I heard something; I tell you."

"Bollocks, it's nothing. Come on," said the second man gesturing to move forward.

Just then and with opportune timing, a squirrel ran passed them and up a tree.

"Did you see the size of that rat?" bleated the first man.

"It was a squirrel, you nonce," replied the second man and he started to move forward away from the fence and down the lane. The other man followed but kept looking around as if something of significance was being left behind.

John breathed normally again and was determined to get out of the open. He scoured the building with his eyes but could see no viable entry point. He then applied logic, it did not matter how great the doubled glazed door was or your conservatory, since the panels could be cut though like a knife through butter.

With this new planning lodged in his applied logic, he put his hand into his shoe and removed the small lock knife. The blade offered a means to achieving a transit square if he applied it correctly, as it was extremely sharp. He knelt down by the shiny back door and cut the panel by the beading, and after he had sawed it completely in a square, about 60 cm by 60 cm, he put the knife away. He then tapped the panel sharply but quietly with the side of his hand and pushed it through. He lay flat and pulled himself through the door and then placed the piece of door back in the gap and it sat nicely. It would be noticed by someone that looked closely, or the workmen or a professional, but as it was, in the dark and to casual bystanders, it would look no different to a normal untouched barrier.

He then proceeded to the upper floor and looked briefly at the outside world, full of danger and unpleasant acts. He came away from the window and went downstairs where sure enough, in the utility room he found a bundle of dust sheets and old blankets.

He elected to sleep out of sight and where he could escape from should anyone enter the building. He decided that the small bedroom at the rear of the upper floor would give the best defence and escape route. He could see that the window opened to become an escape window, so he could jump through onto the utility roof and be gone within seconds; guns blazing no doubt.

He lay there and the outside street light came into the front bedrooms through the hallway and gently illuminated the bedroom. He had carried the bedding with him, and he spread it out in a makeshift bed, and he lay down and covered himself. He used his backpack as both a pillow but also having the comfort of the gun near him. As he lay there he looked at the freshly painted ceiling with pendant wire hanging coiled up, he had some rather odd thoughts go through his head.

'What if you are downing in the sea or a river, and you fight and swim against tide and current for hours, at what point do you just give in and accept the circumstances, the circumstances of your death?'

'Never,' he reiterated fully in his mind. 'You never do.'

He felt very isolated and that he was marooned and swimming in a sea of loneliness.

He looked at his watch, and it was only 9.35pm, but he was shattered, absolutely shattered. With the fatigue yet armed with his new found confidence and wish to be a hero not a victim, John fell asleep without further thought for his predicament or what he was going to do. Everything would have to wait.

Chapter 4

Day 2

Daylight brought a fresh beginning. John had slept deeply, and with the house to himself, he must have snored without disturbance. He instinctively looked at his watch, and it told him it was 06.23am, and it was cold outside of his makeshift bed. The day looked bright enough through the window, and there was nothing to suggest bad weather or storms, but he knew there was a storm surrounding his existence at the moment.

He sat up and stretched. He stood up and gathered all the sheets and took them downstairs and replaced them as best he could in the position within the utility room that he had originally collected them from. He was hungry, so he reached into his backpack and retrieved the biscuits he had taken from the Smythe house. 'This now seemed months ago but was only yesterday, a few hours ago,' he thought.

He devoured several and took the remaining bottle of water and consumed it quickly. He was quite surprised how the events of yesterday had completely changed his habits regarding food. He could not even think about it and had felt sick all of yesterday, but good job he had ate the yoghurt at Belleview even though it had been regurgitated.

John checked his watch again. It was now 06.48am, and he needed a strategy. It was early in the morning, and he was going to look conspicuous leaving the property. He realised he would need to climb over the wall and leave via next door. Hopefully, the old man would be out of sight and unaware of his presence.

John collected his pack and slung it over his shoulder. He carefully inspected the Chinese gun and put it in his jacket pocket. The bigger gun he left in the pack. It was too big to carry given his present clothing, and no way could he conceal it or act as if it were not present. He looked at the bulge in his pocket and felt the weight in his pack, and he quickly understood that the magic ingredient to life was the firepower he had assembled. These elements narrowed the odds immensely, and no matter how bad a shot he proved to be, he had not only one but two very powerful and destructive tools at his disposal.

He also recognised that he might be at an advantage now. There was no way that his predators knew of his weaponry, and as such, they would be caught off balance should there ever be an opportunity for him to use them.

He felt somewhat better with his thoughts planting a little bit of confidence back into his shattered illusion of any sort of life existing for him. He went upstairs and looked out of the back window carefully, and nothing, no vehicles, no men in black, nothing but a couple of squirrels jumping about and looking extremely happy with their day. He envied them. He moved carefully to the front of the house and looked out, and he could see a man walking a dog in the park. He recognised him from the village and the black Labrador was familiar, so he dismissed him as being any threat, unless he recognised John and started screaming in the street.

John went downstairs and made sure everything was as it had been. If undetected, he could return again, maybe tonight as the weekend posed the possibility that nobody would check or come to work at the buildings until tomorrow. He also realised that it was now 24 hours that he had survived his ordeal, and it was a lazy day, Sunday. It had seemed like a year, and he felt exhausted but knew he had to do something, but what?

He examined the facts. Even though they were vulgar and repulsed him, he knew he needed direction. He needed a plan. Eric Jennings was dead, the guards were dead, the Chinese were dead, and his only lead appeared to be a band of covert operatives that seemed to have a pretty voracious appetite for his death. Even though he knew they had pretty serious intentions of killing him, he needed to get closer to these guys and try to establish a link with whoever was pulling their strings. There was no way that they were the brains of the organisation, although highly skilled in the trade of death, they were muscle, intelligent and high class, but still muscle.

He still felt queasy, and he needed to quell such feelings and try to remain calm. He took some deep breaths and went everywhere he had been with a cloth and destroyed any possibility of the authorities gaining his fingerprints. He ended up at the downstairs back window in the utility room. He opened it and carefully climbed out making sure he left neither shoe or fingerprints. He closed it to the frame, and although it was not locked, it appeared closed and would need close inspection to detect it was not sealed.

He checked all around as far as he could see from his position then he walked to the fence of the next building where the old guy had been listening to the television loudly. He climbed the wall and then made his way around the other side of his house and clung to the hedge.

A huge bark resounded and John fell into a phlegmatic trance for a second. His heart punched its outer wall with speed and sheer terror, and adrenalin drove the blood to be pumped at twice its normal requirement. He felt anguish and vulnerable, so he ran as fast as he could. He ran past the front entrance and straight across the road, jumped the railing and entered the park. He felt a perverse sense of betrayal by the dog, and worse, he felt pessimistic where some confidence had crept in. His plan was to penetrate a house with didactical stealth and disperse some of the shadowy undertones from the equation. Instead, he was running for his life, and had been cheated of his plan by a ferocious beast with no wish but to alarm the world to his presence. As he ran through the centre of the park, completely exposed and lit by the morning sky, he noticed movement to his left. It was not the local man from the village walking his dog. It was two men, both dressed in black, and they were running towards him.

John panicked, and he ran toward the alley directly toward Belleview past the tennis court and bowling green. He quickly turned down the small steps into White Horse Lane hoping they would continue down the straight alley passed Belleview and to by Hamptons International.

He ran down to the bottom of the road and joined Vicarage Street and turned left. He continued to run with categorical precision. This was not a game, and they were going to harm him. Without looking back at all, he ran into the Quakers Meeting House Alley and continued right to the bottom of the path. He then forked right and entered some brush and woodland.

John tried to breathe in tune with his bodily needs, not the anxiety driving his breath to be short and not productive to his lungs. He breathed in and out heavily to calm down the fear and the effects of running so fast after little occasions to do so in his life. He retrieved the smaller Chinese firearm from his trousers and looked to see if it had any form of identification. It was still quite heavy and big, and he had not realised how big Eric Jennings' gun actually was. The Chinese gun had a short screw-on suppressor on it and some Chinese characters and the engraving QSW-06 by the handle. 'Probably for export,' he thought. It had a magazine, but there was no apparent safety catch so probably ready to immediately inflict wounds.

John heard a dog barking and his worst fear was realised. He could see three men and a huge black dog running towards him, so he instantly got up and ran the other way. There was some shouting in Chinese, and he could see the man on the radio. John entered the bottom of Tibbiwell and ran toward the buildings that would take him and lead his party of marauders towards Hangman's Cottage. The dog was getting closer, and as John jumped the style and swung left, he glanced back to see the man release the blood thirsty hound. He could hear the panting and snarling approaching him at speed, and he could also feel the presence of the lead man gaining on him. John was out of breath and desperate. He was not as fit as he could be, and he stopped, turned, and without thinking applied logic.

The first bullet missed, but as the dog leapt at him the second bullet recoiled the whimpering then lifeless canine to the floor. John could not believe he had shot a dog, and he felt sick and was about to vomit when a man appeared around the corner into his path. He had a rifle, and as he lifted it to take aim, John, without any hesitation and still fresh with the knowledge that they had driven him to kill this animal, fired from the hip twice.

He would never know if it was good fortune or if he was a good shot, but the first bullet appeared to shred at waist height and the man's eyes bulged. He looked absolutely shocked that this 'rabbit in the headlights' could have been responsible for his demise. The second bullet had hit the man in the chest, and he recoiled and fell backwards, but even with this, he still felt the desire to kill and reached for the rifle that lay on the dirt track a few feet away.

John could not believe his next action. He walked to the man, pointed the gun at the man's head and gently squeezed the trigger.

"No way are you going to ever hurt anyone again," he said.

The bullet made a dull thud. The man's head turned on the side with the hole where the slug had entered, and he could see blood at the back where it had exited.

Immediately, John applied logic. There were at least two more adversaries, and he decided it was not his time to die. He could see the face of his children, thoughts flashed through his mind of their future wedding days, birthdays, and even if he could not be there, he was not going to be robbed of the dream of reconciliation by these cold, callous, heartless mercenaries.

He put the handgun back in his jacket pocket and picked up the rifle, looked through the sight and heard the crackle of the radio on the dead man. It was Chinese in his mind, Asian at least, and it obviously asked a similar question several times, but, of course, there was never going to be any form of response.

John picked up the radio and threw it about fifty feet into some brush on the corner of the track by a gate. He pulled the dead man into the entrance of Hangman's Cottage and hid it in the undergrowth.

Sure enough, one of the men appeared in his view. He was cautious and had a handheld device, in John's mind he was tracking the radio or some form of transmitter. He walked toward the brush where John had thrown the device, and he approached with his gun drawn and his arm extended. John lifted the rifle and placed the butt carefully into his shoulder to control any recoil. He noticed this too had a suppressor fitted, so he breathed in and out several times and tried not to contemplate the consequences of his actions, as he would surely vomit.

As the man got almost to the device, John took aim, looking down the barrel of destruction, and his hands were shaking, but he breathed deeper. The man's head was directly in the middle of his cross hairs, so John gently but firmly squeezed the trigger and watched. The man dropped instantly. The small *phut* of the bullet exiting the barrel and the dull thud seemed so simultaneous that the guy did not know anything of the event; he was merely meeting with his maker. John was conscious that he may need to shoot him again, as he was now paranoid about people doing him harm even if apparently carrying fatal wounds. This time though, he was confident that he had an ability that he never knew existed. He was a good shot.

'What a way to find out,' he thought.

He scoured the countryside for the third man. He decided that he was further behind as a backup, so John retreated further up the track. He could not risk hiding the second man's body, but it would have to be a patient game he played, or so he thought.

The third man exhibited obvious fear and impatience and was shouting to his colleagues. John homed in on the originating noise and lifted the rifle, steadying himself against the branch of a small tree. He could see the man hiding behind the style, shouting and frantically calling into his radio. John lifted the barrel to where the head of the man fell in the middle of the cross hairs. He breathed three times, in and out, and, in and out, and in and fired. The man dropped like a stone from a bridge, and he saw a portion of his head removed from the skull and flail outward into the morning sky. It was a miracle of technology that such a small piece of metal could be ejected so ferociously and accurately and cause such instant failure to live.

He felt sick and trembled. He also questioned was that all of them, and how long would it be until other would be killers were chasing him, and wanting to be the one that bragged of killing the bounty? He pondered everything apart from the fact that he had taken human life.

He had applied logic and fully appreciated the defence strategy was forced upon him. He was more concerned at taking the life of the dog, as it had no choice and knew no better. He decided he would not dwell on this too much, and he needed to survive at this point, and they were intent on stopping him achieving this.

He was undecided regarding his next steps, and unsure of what to do, not because of the horrendous fear that gripped him, but because he needed to find out if the lifeless corpses had any information pertaining to him on their person.

John withdrew the handgun once again and went toward the first body. The victim's face and head were a completely unrecognisable lump; it was hideous. 'This man would need to be identified by dental records or DNA recognition technology,' he thought. 'Your poor family.' There was nothing on his person of any significance apart from another gun, he placed it in his backpack.

'Quite the collector,' he thought.

He got up and approached the second man with caution, and with the gun extended and pointing at him, just in case. He could see even from a few metres away that the guy had half his head missing. He tried not to look or think about this too much, as he knew that his actions were actually responsible for the condition of his fellow humans, all be it expired ones.

John reached down and felt in the man's pockets, and there was a phone and some keys, but given the obvious tracking technology, he left both. He found a piece of paper, and it had Chinese writing on it. He had no idea what it might mean, but he knew if he could get access to Microsoft Translator, all could be revealed. He took the paper and put it in his pocket and then moved toward the third, and what he hoped was the final man, to be searched.

The man was shot clean through the head, and John was curiously proud of his ability to have survived a trained assailant and to have rendered him inoperable with one swift executing shot. He was never good at much, and now he had proved one thing: his quest for life outweighed the wages of an assassin as an incentive.

'They were merely out to kill him for profit, for some coin,' he thought to himself, 'but he was out to live for himself. He was only in it for survival, the most basic of primeval instincts, and there could be no more of a powerful ally than one that is driven by the need for love and life, and a new found ability to hit the target cleanly.'

The man gave up only some scribbled characters on paper. John put them in his pocket, found the man's rifle and slung it over his shoulder with the one he had collected. He moved quickly dragging the man into the brush opposite and throwing his radio into the same location as the other two. This would at least give him some covering time should other would-be assassins appear, as he knew they would.

He changed his mind regarding the keys at this point. He doubled back quickly and grabbed the keys from the dead man and put them in his pocket. The car may have a tracker fitted he thought, but the rest were normal Yale type lock entrance utensils, nothing more. He was contemplating his next course of action when he heard another dog barking. It had obviously been despatched with a backup squad, and he felt acutely nervous once again.

He heard the familiar noise of rotors overhead in the distance and knew a helicopter had been despatched to track and intercept him. If he was not careful he could become trapped in this triangle of death. He decided that he was not going to deviate from his quest to survive, no way.

He immediately removed the trousers off the last Chinese man he had placed in this direful state and he put his legs through, He then tied the bottoms to form a barrier from his own scent, and it would leave only the Chinese man's trousers touching terra firma. He knew this would slow him down considerably, but it was not about the immediate acts he achieved; it was the mid and long term strategy and patience that would fulfil his sense of logic and sustain his life on this planet.

He ran, not unlike a man attempting the three legged race, and he leapt off the public footpath, over a fence and dropped down the embankment into the Painswick stream. He hid behind a tree and discarded the trousers hiding them carefully, and he proceeded up the stream. The water shocked him. It was not only cold, but it made walking uncomfortable too. He came to the Mill Bridge and he hid under it, as he heard the dog barking, and the helicopter hovering in the distance.

'So, you are a thirty-something, white fugitive on the run and being pursued by God only knows men in black.

'You have two rifles, three handguns and a will to live. Apply logic, you wanker.

'Just what are you going to do now?

'Don't be a victim.

'Come on John. What the fuck are you going to do now?

'Don't be a victim. Don't be a bloody victim.'

With this debate concluded in his subconscious, John swung one of the rifles around and assumed the position to safeguard from recoil. He let the gun rest against the stone of the arched bridge, and remaining out of sight, he looked down the scope to find the bulging glass of the cockpit in his cross hairs.

'What are the odds?' he thought. 'Narrow them, and take plenty of shots.'

John waited, breathed and breathed again before his finger gently squeezed the trigger. He had the pilot firmly in his sight, but not a headshot. That was too optimistic and risky. He had the chest and lower stomach region lined up, and he released the boundaries of conscience from his mind. He was the bulwark for the common man, and this prompted him to release the missile, and he did so mercilessly. He quickly let off two more rounds and saw the helicopter screen cave in and the pilot slump over.

The helicopter revved dramatically and turned to face the other way but immediately dropped and plummeted to the ground. It was not quite like all the explosions John had seen on the films. The rotors tried to maintain their rotation, as they dug further and further into the ground and bent and buckled with the force finally stopping. The engine faltered and then the fuel line ruptured and black smoke started to emit from the cockpit and engine bay. The next thing was a loud bang, and the flame spun around the craft like an orange and yellow blanket flapping in the wind, and the machine was engulfed in fire.

'Oh my God,' thought John, 'this just could not be real.' He could not process what was happening before him.

He saw the dog run to the man and sit, while the man was watching in horror and amazement. John lifted the rifle, breathed deeply twice, engaged the trigger, squeezed gently to release the deadly projectile. Snap, nothing.

He instantly realised the chamber and magazine were empty. He discarded the rifle as worthless to him. Such comfort and carnage a short few minutes ago but only momentarily, it was now less than useless. He swung the other rifle around and into the same position. John lifted the rifle slightly, put the man's head and neck in the familiar cross hairs and breathed deeply twice. He engaged the trigger, squeezed gently to release the deadly projectile. Snap! The man fell like a stone, and the dog moved backwards as if it knew. John had however pulled badly at the last moment though. He knew that he had jerked, and therefore his aim was not true. He looked back through the sight at the helpless man floundering and trying to get balance.

He was on one knee and still looked menacing and needed to be despatched. John let the cross hairs compensate for the last shot, he went for the bulk of the upper body instead of the head. He squeezed the trigger, not once but twice, both in quick succession and he could see the man reel from the piercing thuds that were to be his final judges and executioner. He fell to the ground, and the dog whimpered and looked lost before it ran off into the distance.

John looked at the rifle and knew it would be a tool of recognition now, a hazard and a potential threat to him blending anywhere. He pulled at his backpack, pulled out a hoodie, took off his coat and discarded it. Massive plumes of smoke billowed from the crash site, and the whole neighbourhood seemed to be out on the track.

Although he had wet pants and wet socks, he walked through the stream towards the Wash Brook, and he followed it up. He moved quickly and then after some ten minutes or so, he approached the Stroud Road, crossed it and ran behind the Painswick Rugby and Sports Club. Here he decided to re-engage into the walking fraternity and to try and blend, as he was sure they had a description of him. He put on a pair of old shredded black Levi's jeans, some Vans trainers, and he tried to breathe deeply to get some normality back.

He discarded everything he thought unnecessary to him, and placed it at the bottom of a commercial green wheelie bin. He walked across the field and toward Washbrook Farm and Cottage where he joined the Cotswold Way and walked slowly toward Edge Road with Kingsmead and Hambutts Drive.

John churned over the events of the past few minutes. 'Just how much capacity does a human being harbour to change?' he asked himself. 'How could I go from a meek and mild boring twat to a merciless killer; this cannot be something I would ever envisage investigating in my wildest dreams. Can I ever come back from this? How could I take human life and not be affected?'

John could hear lots of sirens, and he was aware that the crash site would attract not only the police, probably terrorist branch, and medical staff, but the crash itself would fall under the scrutiny of the Civil Airworthiness Authority. He wondered what yarn would be spun, and how they would cover up five or six dead Chinese nationals?

A helicopter with at least three bullets through the cockpit screen and wreckage strewn from an obvious instant drop from the sky as opposed to some form of mechanical failure would be hard to hide or extinguish the real facts. Normally with a mechanical failure, you would assume the pilot would use all of his flight experience to try and accomplish some form of controlled crash landing.

Just then he felt the shift from his stomach to his throat and although he had no power of divination, he knew this felt awful. He had only consumed a few biscuits, but still the events of the morning generated the need to vomit, and he wretched. He wretched hard and it hurt. He expelled whatever had not been consumed by his metabolism and it was not much, but he felt better apart from the pain in his stomach wall.

He wiped his mouth and then, true to form, he heard the muffled rant of a party of idiots trekking down the path like lemurs to the cliff face. They were about a hundred metres from him, so he joined the path and walked slowly to let them pass, and he hoped he could tag along using them as cover.

They were, of course, some of the population of the now all too familiar rooting, tooting Hooray Henrys, stomping and walking with their makeshift sticks. They also adorned profoundly useless and over expensive rambling kit that they probably bought online. This for the most likely made them feel efficacious, and that was an easy explanation for why their clothes rarely fitted and were probably brighter in real life than where advertised, otherwise, why would one wear such vile, bright cagoules and such like?

The one good thing about walking in groups, and along the Cotswold Way and Painswick in general, was that it was not uncommon for people to just start a conversation with total strangers. Individuals could on mass, masquerade as whoever they wanted to be and pretend they knew what they were on about. What presented itself as amusing and quite extraordinary at times and even more surprising was their ability to believe that they actually were interesting in some way.

"Hello, where are you headed?" grunted some old Jock.

"Aberdeen," replied John sarcastically.

"You don't wanna go there, sonny," he said in a broad accent.

"No, I guess nobody does," John replied, "bit like the whole of Scotland."

The man looked offended and rambled on at pace muttering some obscenities no doubt.

"Good for you," came a small voice from behind him.

John reeled around. He was unsure of anything at this present time and every event, no matter how minute, represented a potential threat.

There before him, smiling at him, was what he envisaged as a sweet and effulgent girl. She was about thirty, with dark wavy shoulder length hair, almost Italian or Spanish in its presentation, and she had the nicest smile and bright teeth. She seemed to have an efflorescence in her persona, and she was pretty. She was very pretty. She also had a nice olive complexion and was wearing a pair of jeans, a chequered blouse, not loud, and a jumper tied around her waist. She also had a small rucksack hanging off her shoulder, and she had elected to walk without any form of stick.

"That old fart has bored all of us for ten miles, so I am glad you shut him up. I am Angela by the way."

"Hi, I am, Carlton," he said convincingly although the name reeled off, and he nearly said 'Parks'.

"Did you see the fire in the field back there?" she asked, pointing to the smoke that was now subsiding.

"Do you know what it was, Angela?" he asked her.

"It sounded like a light aircraft or a little helicopter, you know, the bubble shaped one with probably only two people on board. I do hope nobody was hurt," she said.

"I have no idea. I was over here taking a rest," he said nonchalantly.

"Have you walked far?" she asked.

"Not really, more casual and for pleasure than to achieve treckie badges, or the adoration of Hooray Henrys," he said smiling.

"I do hope that you have not confused me with those lot over there," she said firmly.

"With that smile there is no way you could ever be any form of Henry," he replied.

"You are a sweetie," she said smiling, and she skipped. She was looking very pleased with herself.

John felt a stampede of emotions well up inside him. Here he was presented with a lovely girl, who he would have thought completely out of his league mere hours ago. Yet here he was holding court, and she was attentive and happy. He had no future of any kind. Should he revel in this moment, or release her and keep her out of any impending danger. Association with 'John' was clearly dangerous and almost certainly represented incarceration at the least, death at worst.

She giggled, and as they walked toward the Edge Road, they realised they had drifted from the pack.

"So tell me dear Carlton, what do you do for a living?"

"I have a boring existence Angela. I work in an office, and I pretend to know what I am doing when I don't like so many others nowadays I guess, and you, what does a drop dead gorgeous girl do for coin?"

"What an odd way of putting it," she said giggling. "I work in PR, and I am good at it. I think."

"Good, I guess that works then. You are good at your job, and I have no idea about mine," he said confidently, being sure to joke without arrogance. "Here is the Edge Road, Angela, so which way are you travelling now?"

"To be honest, I have absolutely no idea. I am bored and I have really come to the end of my walking attention curve; it bores me now. How about you? Please say you are bored too."

"I am bored too. There is only so much walking a man can do."

"Shall we have brunch?" she asked flickering her big eyes at him.

"On one condition," he replied.

"And what would that be?" she asked.

"Let's just go left and walk to the Edgemoor Inn. I cannot stand the thought of bumping into those idiots in Painswick."

"OK, but how far is it?" she asked.

"Through the fields it is only twenty minutes, but thirty if I drag it out to be with you."

"An hour it is then," she replied giggling.

They walked back along the same path, through to Washbrook Farm and Washbrook Cottage, and they kept on the Cotswold Way path parallel to the small stream. The fields looked magnificent and were made even more pleasant, by virtue of her presence. John found her exhilarating and relaxing, and being together even as virtual strangers was effortless, and her company was not forced. They eased in and out of small talk and genuine companionship, and there was no awkward silence or hunting for appropriate topics to impress.

They joined Jenkins Lane and moved closer to the A4173 which John knew would be more utilised but would have more casual traffic. They got onto the A-road and turned right and presented before them was the lovely 19th century coaching inn. It boasted a nice outside sitting area and lovely uninterrupted views over the valley. Pitchcombe was close with its tiny community and the Cotswold stone buildings and dwellings under ancient tile reaching to the sunlight were in sight. It was an ambient and magnificent moment. It was also the first time that John had relaxed in what seemed a long time but was in fact only 28 hours.

"What sort of food do you fancy? Shall I go and get a menu and a drink?" she said playfully.

"I will go."

"No," she interrupted quickly, "my treat as you have saved me from death by boredom. The least I can do is feed you, and say I am eternally grateful." She continued to giggle, as she disappeared into the pub.

After a couple of minutes, John followed her in, asked the way to the toilet, and winked at her as he passed. He entered the toilet and relaxed, as he discarded what little fluid was ready to exit. He felt dehydrated and needed fluid. He returned to the bar as she was paying for a gin and tonic and a pint of Old Spot, local Dursley brewery real ale. It was lovely, and as she handed it to him, he put it to his mouth, and before he knew what was happening, he realised he had drank a large percentage of it.

"Wow, I have driven you to drink," she said as she burst out laughing.

"Not at all. I am so terribly sorry, but I was just thirsty."

"Another one of those young man?" asked the barman. She confirmed and he poured it.

"I have ordered us battered fish and chips; is that OK?"

"It most certainly is Angela, but you did not need to do this. Your smile is payment enough."

"I like you Carlton whatever your name is. You play your cards right, and I might give you my second name."

She was vivacious, full of life, and she reminded him of the fact that normality could be reached if he could rebuild a life and just get through this awful period. He also realised that there was no way he could reciprocate any information or divulge any key facts without deceit and lies. Whatever he told her would need to be rescinded later, and a positive outcome based upon his explanation would be difficult to achieve with conviction and forgiveness.

John decided that he would eat, go to the toilet and bail. He just did not want her to be involved or get caught up in whatever this was.

They sat outside and to the left hand side of the inn almost obscured, and they laughed and talked about things in general. There was no real need for specifics at this junction, and they were happy to be around each other. The food arrived. It was well presented and John was hungry. They both were, so in near silence, they proceeded to eat.

"I need some mayo," she said. "Do you want some?"

"Good shout, but I can get it," John replied.

"Just relax. I will get it." she said and went into the inn.

She returned giggling and clutching the bottle of mayo.

"You are a keeper," he said to her.

Angela leaned over to kiss him, but she then collapsed onto the table, and slumped over to reveal that half her face was missing. Her eye had disappeared from its socket and her cheek had exploded into a raw mass of torn and butchered flesh. John had blood spatter and chunks of her beauty all over him, and the shock sent shivers down his spine. He was instantly sick and vomited what little food and the beer he had ingested. A group of people, obviously friends out for meal, sat twenty feet away, and they saw what had happened without the knowledge of a gun being involved. They came over to see if Angela was OK.

"What happened?" said an older man.

John ducked under the table.

'Apply logic, John. Apply logic.'

"Get away from here! She has been shot!" he screamed to them.

Blind panic ensued and the crowd dispersed screaming and running into the inn.

'Where did the shot come from? The trajectory of the bullet had taken off her face, so it had to come from the right. Where is the killer hiding man? Think. Apply logic.'

John looked and saw an outbuilding across the road with a sun bleached rickety door; it must be the place. The people at the pub were all shouting and rang for an ambulance and the police. John opened his backpack and reached into it. His hand connected with Eric Jennings' gun, and he brought it into the sunlight, revealing that it had Beretta M9 written on its side by the handle. He looked at where the once angelic Angela had been giggling with him. He was now crying, and he thought this was a despicable act, and he stood witness to the matted mess where her beautiful face had pleased so many, that beautiful hair now so lifeless and so ugly crowning such a horrific view.

John could see a bus coming down the road, as it drew parallel to his table, he ran out and jogged with the bus until it had passed the building, and then he let it go as he darted across the road.

He saw some movement, and throwing caution to the wind, he abandoned logic and pulled back the top mechanism of the weapon thus loading the gun for action. This was an instinct and a blueprint that had been imprinted on his memory from a thousand action films. He lifted the gun and loosely lined the barrel to the door, and he started to dispense the evil contents of the magazine into the fragile decaying old doorway.

The shots screamed through the door at varying heights and angles, and there was thud after thud until the gun was relieved of its 15 round detachable box. The door, being so old, had succumbed to the velocity of the projectiles, and they had penetrated it with ease leaving a huge spiral of open spheres.

He put the Beretta into the belt of his jeans before reaching into his pack and pulling out the Chinese sidearm. He kicked the door in off its hinges to reveal the lifeless corpse of a Chinese man clutching a rifle. He was gurgling, and John looked into his eyes. He exuded pure fear, and as he was trying to say something and clasped his hands as if in prayer, begging for mercy, John placed his knee on his chest.

John casually looked around and with nobody else able to see or witness any of his onward acts, he became judge, jury and executioner.

"Why? She did not deserve any of this, and she did not see any danger or any death in her midst, but you can." John looked deep into the terrified eyes of the bleeding man.

"Look at me. I want you to know who is killing you and why. My name is John Parks, her name was Angela, and you stopped me from ever hearing her tell me her family name. This is the precise second you die."

He despatched a bullet into the man's forehead without flinching. It exploded out of the back of his head taking brain and segments of his skull. John was actually satisfied that Angela could at least meet him on the other side with the satisfaction. He had seen this coming, but she did not.

John reached into the dead man's pockets and found some keys, the usual standard issue radio and some cash. He took the keys and noticed there was a Ford Kuga key. He looked into and beyond the pub carpark and pressed the fob, and a brand new Kuga illuminated its indicators and made a clunk. John raced over to the car, knowing the Police would take about six to ten minutes to arrive from the time of the emergency call. He opened it and started it. He screeched off wheels spinning, and he raced down the road at full revs, every gear in the red zone. He veered left onto Wragg Castle Lane and came to the A46 Stroud Road.

He screeched to the right for a few metres and then turned abruptly left into Pincot Lane, tyres screeching and engine revving highly. He decided to tone it down as everyone would remember such a vehicle, especially driving so dangerously within the small lanes. He was currently achieving speeds that would normally result in a 100% chance of death by road accident, but he had to get out of sight fast.

He could hear sirens everywhere, and he knew that helicopters would be despatched, and any chance of redemption would be ruined if he was detected. There was also the issue of the tracker running through his mind, but he could not do anything about this now. He met the junction onto Wick Street and decided he would head for the Carlton Smythe residence, as it was his only chance. He reached across to the passenger seat where a cardigan and a bottle of water lay. He looked into the mirror and saw the blood spatter all over his face. That dear girl's existence shattered because of me, and now I am wearing her very face across my body. He wiped at it with the cardigan and kept rubbing. A large percentage disappeared. He opened the bottle with his teeth while still driving, and he emptied half of it onto the cardigan where he had not wiped himself. He then wiped as much of her away as he could using the damp absorbent material. It worked well, and he continued this process, as he proceeded for some way.

He decided at this point, to risk everything and he joined the main Stroud Road off the Old Painswick Road just before the college and Tesco roundabout. He then turned left and up Beeches Green and then he turned right at the roundabout into Merrywalks. He was almost certain that number plate recognition cameras would detect the presence of the vehicle at some point, so he turned left at the bus stops and pulled into the back of Halfords and parked up. He gave his neck, head and hands a thorough wiping down again, and he looked pretty normal for a man that had just experienced someone else's head being blown over his. He knew his DNA was everywhere in the car, but he still dusted down the car removing any prints. He exited the vehicle careful to push the door to with his arm. He knelt down out of any potential camera threat, reached into his pack and withdrew a polo shirt. He removed his jacket and t-shirt and discarded them into a drain. He put the polo shirt on, maybe it would not be recognised. He also threw the keys into the drain and put on a flat cap, and as he passed Halfords' window, he heard a young guy talking to his friend about wanting the bike in the window, but he could not afford it. He was clutching an average mountain bike, and the bike in the window was reduced at half price to four hundred pounds. John reached into his backpack, counted six hundred pounds and walked up to the man.

OK it is your lucky day young man. No catches, no gimmicks, but here is six big ones for the bike, your helmet and your jacket. You have thirty seconds to deliver your verdict. You may walk straight into Halfords after the transaction and purchase the bike of your dreams, or you can go and get drunk or order a hooker; it is purely your shout.

The man just looked at John in complete disbelief.

"10, 9, 8, 7, 6, 5,..." John started to look around for another candidate waving the wad of money in the guy's face.

"Yes, bloody hell yes; it is not funny money is it?"

"Don't be ridiculous man. Get in there and get the bike. Oh, and keep smiling and keep it as real as you can. No reference to me and my team; you never saw me, OK."

Now the guy immediately suspected he was part of a reality programme, and so his persona instantly changed. He snatched the money and started laughing and making stupid noises of sheer delight. He ripped the jacket off, gave it to John along with the helmet and bike and he bounded into the shop, wary of any hidden cameras or someone who was going to run and jump out into his face. He walked the walk but his friend just followed without emotion in a 'wish it were me syndrome', no doubt.

John put the helmet and jacket on, mounted the bike and rode off with his head down. His backpack was attached with a lighter load, but his uncle's hard earned cash was making someone happy anyway. He was not used to a bicycle and the Shimano gears left him treading thin air at first, but he learnt quickly how to engage them successfully, and he picked up speed. He peddled hard and the process was instantly pulling at his calf muscles. It was an awkward baptism into something he had done many years ago.

He went out of Merrywalks and then turned right toward Folly Lane, but he veered off left into some houses that formed a cul-de-sac and no through road to vehicles. He went to the furthest point, and there was a track, so the bike was amply suited for the terrain; it was just John that was not. It really hurt his legs, and he tried to find easier gears, but he realised he did not like bicycles at all. He joined the Old Painswick Road just before the Hawkwood College and he peddled harder as he entered Wick Street and felt some comfort, as he saw the familiar wood and house he had broken into yesterday. He steered the bike quickly into the wood, as he heard more sirens on the main road, and he saw a helicopter hovering about and another sweeping the roads overhead, but it was very low and slow.

John did not go near the main entrance, and he left the bike hidden against a tree. He also left the helmet and the jacket there. He ran around the circumference of the hedge before finding the shortest point from the fence to the outbuilding. He waited until the helicopter had passed, and then he darted like an Olympic athlete to the safety of the structure.

He could detect absolutely no change to the environment he had left yesterday. The window remained closed, but he could see it was not locked. There was nobody home. He waited until the helicopter rotors were a mere drone in the distance, and he ran to the house, shimmied up the drain pipe, over the apex and opened the window. He entered the window and closed it just as another helicopter banked loudly passed the dwelling.

"Bloody hell that was close," he uttered to himself.

John was determined to explore the house precisely from room to room and to see if any opportunities existed to make life safer and easier. He also needed to see if it held any key for him staying alive and indeed clearing his name at some point. He checked the rooms first to ensure there was no people anywhere near or in them. It was to his relief that the place was empty and appeared to have been this way for some time, more than he had originally suspected.

He found a lot of letters and documents in a bureau, and in sifting through some of the contents, it became apparent that Carlton James Smythe had died a year or so ago and that the estate had entered into probate a few months previously. The residence and all contents were to be kept off limits from the family members who were trying to get hold of them. There appeared to be two of them, a Miss Melamine Smythe and one Rupert Smythe.

'What a ridiculous pair of names,' thought John. 'Fancy calling your only son after a cartoon bear, a gay bear with a big red tartan suit on, and your daughter after a floor.

He opened a drawer and found a sample of strange keys. One was for a Range Rover, but he had not seen one anywhere. The keys were similar to the ones he had previously found hidden in the wardrobe upstairs.

"Where the hell are you?" he said out loud.

He also found more keys and looked around. He could see a wall cupboard that was opaque and well established but looked extremely well protected. John offered the keys to the large lock in turn, and it was the fourth key that entered, turned the mechanism and clicked. He was inspired. For once, something had seemed to have worked for him and delivered some luck. He opened the cabinet by pulling the heavy door towards him, slowly revealing a bank of rifles and shotguns.

"Come to Daddy," he said smiling.

It was a complete arsenal of quite old but very well cared for reapers of death. He could smell the oil and lubricants, and as he handled the first rifle, he realised that these guns were someone's pride and joy, and they would work without question. The person that owned these weapons was obviously a keen member of the shoot. There were also many boxes of ammunition left underneath the gun rests, and he removed a box of shotgun cartridges and thought long and hard as to how useful this particular gun could be. He pulled a beautiful shotgun with a cherry red butt from the rest, and he was surprised how heavy it was.

He walked down the hallway to the back door and checked outside to see if any helicopters were scanning the countryside. When he was satisfied that the coast was clear, he unbolted and then opened the back door which had the key in. He went to the outbuilding and found a chest of drawers and a cabinet at the back. He found a hack saw and some assortments of sandpaper and a wire wool mound. He noticed that under a blanket on top of the chest it had an old but adequate vice screwed to it.

Out of respect for old Mr Smythe, he wrapped the stock of the gun in the blanket and then he turned the vice slowly, gently and just enough until the gun was held and steady. He completely understood that Mr Smythe would exhibit repulsion and indignation at such an act, but he continued and marked out the double barrels. Once he was satisfied the gun could be carried and handled with ease, he then proceeded to saw through both barrels and the perilous instrument of death was fashioned to his satisfaction. He knew there could be no obstruction to the projectiles exiting the barrels, as this would constitute danger on all sorts of levels, so he set about reaming both barrels, and he polished them with the abrasive steel paper and wire wool. This took a surprisingly long time, but he was happy and content to be achieving something and not mulling over the events of the day.

He could not help but cast his mind back and started questioning himself and talking out loud. He had an image of her smiling face, her gentle way and the fact that she had found him easy to be with.

'How is it that I am in this predicament? I just happen to meet the most beautiful girl and then I am ultimately responsible for her being assassinated. See how ridiculous that sounds, 'me' 'John Parks' and 'assassinated' all in the same sentence. Bloody hell, I am not this person. How can circumstances orchestrate such a step change to my existence? I am a bloody office worker and a bad husband and father, not a bloody fugitive or killer or anything interesting. Even if the bullet was meant for me, I cannot believe she has gone. I cannot believe I did not walk away from her; I killed her.'

He stopped polishing the gun and a tear fell from his eye, trickled down his cheek and he wiped it away. It was the first time he had really let emotion take its rightful place in his mind since just after the incident. It was indisputable that he was fighting everything that was alien to him both physically and mentally, and he had not really had time to dissect the enormity of what he now endured.

His life had taken such a huge indecorous turn, the value of his insignificant acts, his normal day to day existence now harvested more pleasant memories, and what he believed an odious life now seemed golden. He now knew that this was obsolete and that he had to gather himself and move forward from the tyranny that hunted him. He needed to weather this turbulent time, and his misfortune must be placed somewhere in his subconscious, before it started to eat him away or influence his logic. After all, it was logic and application that had served him so well for the last few hours and given him sustained time on the planet.

With the barrel completely spheral, he had a sublime feeling of achievement, and with the shortened weapon by his side, he checked the outside ground and sky. When he felt it was clear, he removed the sidearm from his pocket, and he moved swiftly to the back door and entered the house.

'No use being caught unprepared,' he thought. "Keep the gun ready at all times, John, and apply logic," he said out loud.

His actions were becoming driven and spontaneous. Although a few short hours since his ordeal had begun, his mind set had changed considerably. Instead of finding things repugnant, he had developed a tutelage in his own mind.

He was determined to adapt to whatever circumstance was thrown at him and to quash the tide of death aimed at him. He would be his own saviour and repel the putrid attackers from his midst. He was starting to brim with confidence, and he realised quickly that this was a dangerous fool that sat on his shoulder.

He needed to be vigilant and logical, to take no unnecessary risks and to be cautious at all times. He would only need to lull himself into a false sense of security once, and he would join all the people he had witnessed depart earth in the last few hours.

John pulled out two more shotguns, and he repeated the process of shortening the barrels. He then lined all three weapons up on a table in the dining room, and he proceeded to unwrap fresh cartridges. Even for him, this was easy: break the barrel, fill the holes, put the barrels up and death ready to administer. He filled all three and then he went back to the cabinet. There sat a seven shot repeating shotgun, and he liked the idea of not having to change weapons or to reload every one or two exchanges. He did not shorten this one though, and he was unsure as to whether the barrel may get hot with multiple exits or whether it may affect the gun in any way. He had no idea, so he applied logic and caution and just left it as designed; it would work.

"You have three sawn offs, one full size with seven shots will be OK, as long as you can conceal it though," he was full on talking to himself.

Time had passed quickly, and he was quite hungry. He had been teased by the presentation of the food at the inn only to have the chance of consuming it taken away from him, as his new friend's face had exploded over him and the fish and chips.

He suddenly felt sick again, but he fought the urge to regurgitate what would only be nothing. He went to the kitchen, ran the cold water tap, looked in some cupboards, found a glass, filled it and drank it straight down. He then filled the glass and returned to the dining room. He glanced at his watch and it was just after 4pm.

A shocking thought entered his mind. It suddenly dawned on John that he had become somewhat proficient in despatching human life to the other side and that he was not as affected, as he imagined he would be. Was it that crucial and age old quest to survive, the basic instinct of man to overcome and conquer evil that drove mankind to do some of the things we do? Men and women had shown courage in the face of adversity for all of time and had managed to pull off amazing feats, overcoming overwhelming odds, just to save themselves or others.

"It is because I am just. I did not ask for any of this. I am just, just a prick," he said laughing to himself, "but I am alive, and I am no rabbit in the headlights nor will I be."

He remembered something his girls used to sing before they were taken away to the other side of the world.

I don't want to be a rabbit, they sang this over and over, so John sang, "I am not going to be a rabbit, my girls."

He remembered being teased by his father, he called him pusillanimous, not a normal word but the interpretation was cutting to a child. It meant cowardly and chicken-hearted, and he had never forgotten the taunts nor his dad smiling as he delivered the constant barrage of negativity. John knew this had in fact given him strength, and he wished his dad could see his last few hours. "Chicken my ass!" he shouted triumphantly.

John then rummaged in his trousers and found the piece of paper that he had recovered from the Chinese guy he had despatched earlier. He went upstairs remembering the laptop sitting in the cupboard. He found it and a charger, plugged it in and switched it on. It burst into life but painfully slowly. It was quite old and everything was out of date, but Windows sprung into life, and to his surprise, it was loaded with Google and Office. John looked up characters and could not find any reference to the meaning or validate the country of origin. He Googled characters in the People's Republic of China and came up negative, and then by chance, he stumbled across an offshoot of the page, and it was obvious that the writing was North Korean.

'Right, so I have North Korean ninjas posing as Chinese nationals armed with Chinese issue sidearms chasing me. Wow and bloody hell.'

He could not determine what it meant, but he at least had an idea of the enormity of the mountain he had to climb. He was unprotected by his own authorities and government and could trust nobody, so he was isolated and completely alone, but he was now prepared and ready to try and stay alive with a competitive edge. He was well armed.

He went into the kitchen and found some ancient but sealed coffee in the back of one of the cupboards. It was Carte Noire so he filled the kettle and plugged it in and hit the switch. It crackled and the element breathed life into the device, and it made the familiar noise at it raised the contents' temperature. He opened the jar, broke the seal by prodding it with his finger, then he opened a drawer and found a teaspoon. He put a heaped spoonful of the coffee in a mug he found, the coffee had a nice aroma emanating from it, and it was amplified when he poured the hot, but not boiling water, on the granules. He rummaged about but could find no food apart from what everyone has in the back of their cupboard and never gets eaten: sardines.

'It's funny,' he thought, 'how you just can't seem to resist two for one offers and yet hate the bloody things. They were never going to be consumed unless there was a stray cat somewhere.' He could not face them and left them where they lay, testament to good salesmanship and bad consumer spending.

John moved into the dining room once again and peered through the window. He was clutching and sipping the warm coffee, and it tasted really good, He had made it strong and black which was his preference, and he enjoyed a few moments of calm. He sat in a large wingback chair, and he felt the licence in his pocket that he had found when he first entered the house. Upon investigation, he realised that if he had produced it he would be 93 years old.

'No wonder old Smythe is not riding the moped,' he thought.

He then sifted through the documents again and found a letter from the land registry outlining the actual scale and extent of the property. He was instantly intrigued, and as he followed the plan, he immediately realised that the buildings toward the front of the drive on the left on exit, although separated by fences and gates did in fact belong to this property. He also noticed that scribbled on the back of the letter were the words, *don't forget the secret door in the den.*

Although worried about the chance of being spotted, especially from the air, John knew he needed to investigate the possibility that there was some useful meaning to this find, especially if the Range Rover was in there. He finished his coffee, found a large coat in the cupboard upstairs and put it over him loosely. He picked up the repeater shotgun and let it rest covered by the flowing coat, and he walked to the back door. He heard nothing. It was surprisingly quiet, and he walked on the fence line out of sight clutching the keys he had picked up. He got to the gate, climbed over it and proceeded to the large barn type structure with its large double door. It was an impressive building. He walked around the side to a door which he found locked. He presented the keys and the third one engaged and opened the door.

He slipped in closing it behind him, and there, sitting proud, was the glossy black Range Rover designed by Kahn with private plates SM11THE. At the back of it was a large tarpaulin covering something, probably an old tractor or machinery. John ignored it and pressed the car's key fob, and the indicator lights clicked and flashed. The clunk of the door release pleased him. He placed the seven shot shotgun on a bench by the door, checked he still had the Beretta and stepped over to the vehicle. He opened the door and entered the driver's side. He sat in, casually ensured the shift was in park and put the fob in the housing. He pressed the clutch in, pressed the start button and it fired first time with that lovely rumbling noise only a V8 could produce. John had a pious admiration and complete love of V8 engines and craved a Mustang or Camaro throbbing through the lanes, but this would do nicely.

"Good old Land Rover," he said to himself.

It was the most beautiful and tasteful version of this vehicle he had ever seen, and it had over four litres of power plant in its belly and it was a top of the range model. It had an extensive Kahn factory fit specification including sat nav, DVD player, drop down TV, perforated leather and dash; it was beautiful, and obvious this man was driven by chauffer. It boasted every conceivable extra including a body kit and fancy lights. He actually wished it was a little bit less conspicuous but decided to thank his lucky stars for providing such a good tool.

He let the engine idle, and out of curiosity, he walked to the tarpauling and pulled it back. It took some doing as it was the heavy-duty older type that used to be made, probably during the fifties. The action revealed quite a different vehicle, and there in all its glory stood an inconspicuous 25 year old Land Rover Defender with the keys left in the ignition. He jumped in, turned the key and it slowly rotated the starter motor, but nothing. He tried it again, and luckily it engaged, but then it coughed and spluttered and kicked into life throwing huge plumes of petrol fuelled smoke from the exhaust making it hard to breathe.

Even with the pollution, he let it run and it idled slowly then fast and then it found its pitch and the V8 completely overshadowed even the lovely tone of the Kahn's engine rumble.

'Well now, what a lovely inconspicuous farmer's tool,' he thought.

He walked to the lovely Kahn and leant inside and switched it off.

'You my beauty will have to wait.'

He left the Defender running for a few minutes, as the eight cylinders were now murmuring in tune, and it had found its pitch. The engine and lubricants were completely synchronising to achieving the purring sound with ease, and it exuded torque and power and the best off road capability in the world; he loved it.

John felt a sudden change in the air without knowing why. Intuition perhaps? Or was it logic that the calm was only a respite before the impending and almost certain storm. He instinctively leant into the Defender and switched the big V8 off, and he heard some voices in the distance and realised that both engine bays were warm and that the bonnets were a dead giveaway to the fact that the vehicles had been started.

Luckily, he applied logic. This analysis guided him to believe that anyone looking around the grounds or property would not feel the need to attempt to break into a garage structure just to satisfy their curiosity that nobody had attempted to start the vehicles. That would not make any sense at all. They would have already deduced that no vehicles had passed them in the last minutes, so there was no need for such a detailed search.

He returned the tarpaulin to its former resting place, forming a blanket for the Defender. He left the Kahn unlocked, as he knew it would beep loudly if locked, and he picked up the seven shot from the bench. He then exited the side door. He locked it and made sure there was no scuffmarks around the entrance. He literally retraced his steps to the back door, and he went through the opening quietly, locking it behind him as he entered. He then moved swiftly into the hallway, up the stairs and into the front bedroom. He carefully approached the large bay window. He adjusted the curtains so he could see out through a crack and remain undetected.

He waited there for what seemed an age but in reality was about twenty minutes. He decided that he was safe for now, and he regained enough confidence to go downstairs. He took the seven shot with him, and he decided he had to remain here for the night. It was early evening, he was hungry and tired, but he had relatively safe accommodation and water, so he went into the kitchen to make another coffee.

Once he had done this, he noticed a small doorway panel on the stairwell covered by coats. He saw a handle obscured by the rack, and he turned it and the panel clicked open. To his amazement, there was a light switch and some stairs. He turned on the light, as he could see no external light coming from any windows, so it must have been a dark room. It appeared to be safe, and he was sure that nobody would see the light come on and guess that it was inhabited. He carefully pulled the door. He had taken the Beretta out, and he walked down the creaking stairs and into a large space. Although a bit musky, it was habitable and obviously a den, as it had a couch with blankets and throws all over it, a television on a table and a couple of racks of wine, and hey presto, some beer with glasses.

John decided that if he could find an alternative exit from this room, he would utilise it as a safe room and sleeping quarters for the night. He thought it had one obvious advantage over any other room in the house. Any potential intruder entering would be susceptible to the den's alarm. The 'alarm' was really just the house's old age. Everything creaked, and you could not attempt to enter this space without letting any occupant know of your presence within the first few centimetres.

He scoured the walls and came across a row of panelled pieces with handles on each large side of them. He pulled on them all vigorously, and they opened slightly revealing shelves and ornamental racking. The panel he pulled did not fit in architecturally with the first ones. It had a more modern shelf lining, and most would not notice, but John had spent time in lots of old cottages and knew the wood was different and not aged appropriately.

He banged it, sure he was going to reveal a passage, but no matter how he tried, he realised the lining had merely been changed.

"So much for Sherlock Holmes," he muttered.

He walked back toward the staircase and that is when he noticed the change in colour of the stone under the staircase. It was very discreet, but it was like brad stone as opposed to natural Cotswold Stone. He knew that brad was formed and reconstituted to represent a mustard type colour, and he did not like it and always thought it represented the fake Cotswolds.

He ran his fingers over the wall, and sure enough, there was a gap about an inch wide. He pulled at it and the complete wall came out at a width of about 60cm; it was a doorway. At least he now knew what the words on the back of the letter describing the secret doorway in the den meant. He checked it and it only went a short distance, but there was a small iron ladder leading to a hidden grill with a hardwood inside cover. He undid a catch, pushed the grill, and he was astounded to find himself looking at the back door about five metres away.

He shut the grill, locked it and went back upstairs and checked to see if light come through the grill. It didn't. He went back inside, gathered up the weapons, his pack, replaced everything except the keys, the registry letter which he wanted to keep, and locked and shut all doors and windows. He then filled the kettle and put it on a tray with the cup, coffee, spoon, and he took them with him. He entered the den and pulled the panel shut after him, and then he placed a piece of wood he had found on the floor across the hooks inside which acted as a makeshift catch across the inside. He was acutely conscious that this would not result in the panel locking, but it would cause someone to tug hard on it to open it, and hopefully this action would serve as an early warning system to any attempted intrusion.

He then went downstairs and plugged the kettle into a socket by the couch and put some coffee into the cup and waited for it to boil. He poured the water, stirred the brown aromatic liquid, discarded the spoon and searched the room sipping his coffee. His stomach suddenly churned with anxiety. He realised that this would have to be the last cup of coffee he participated in until daylight. The smell of the coffee was a dead giveaway, to not only the residence being occupied, but also from where the aroma originated from.

There were many things pertaining to the private life of old Carlton James Smythe that John was aware of now. He had been in love, there were some pictures and letters by the television set, and he had also fought in the Korean conflict. What a commendable old guy! He was a decorated veteran, and he seemed to have lived a good life, being both socially and academically astute, both things John found hard to overcome or master. He realised that this guy had fought in a war, but he would bet that normal Joe here had actually taken more human life than he ever had; food for thought.

"Bloody hell," he said out loud. The sound of his voice seemed amplified, probably because he hoped he was alone, but also the large structure remained devoid of humans, at least living ones.

John wished he could build a portfolio of achievement and live a long and fulfilling life like the old guy. For now he would have to settle just for breathing, after all, he was living one minute to the next.

John pressed the on switch on the television, but nothing happened. He traced the lead from the back to a socket and switched it on. The television crackled and then in a few seconds later loudly burst into life. He quickly found the volume control and depressed the reduction side thus softening the deafening roar, obviously loud so the old man could hear. He switched the channel dial and selected ITV. He then impatiently waited as adverts were playing offering such delights as yoghurt, women's panty liners and life insurance.

"What a bloody concoction of shit," he uttered.

The news came on, and this was what John wanted to see. Local news and how the death of Angela had been reported, and of course the helicopter crash. How would they spin that bodies were strewn all over a quiet country village, especially one so affluent and well known as Painswick?

Sure enough the newsreader reported that a small helicopter, piloted by a businessman, had in fact clipped some overhead power cables following an engine failure and had made an emergency landing. John could not believe his eyes as a man claiming to be Robert Phelps had a microphone thrust under his mouth by the crash site.

"It is testament to my instructors and my own accumulated flight hours and continued vigilance that I managed to avoid a potential disaster. My co-pilot and very good friend, Jeremy Peters, also survived unscathed and got out OK. We both intend to celebrate tonight with a large claret of wine."

"In other news today, a Stroud woman was accused of claiming benefits..."

"What!" shouted John. "What about Angela? What about the bullets through the cockpit? What about the dead guys? Oh my God, this is totally unreal."

He realised the extent of 'their' power and how far 'they' could manipulate the media and contort everything to meet their needs. Human loss was great this day, in and around Painswick, Queen of the Cotswolds, not the ghetto or housing projects in Washington DC, bloody, quiet, idyllic, quintessential Painswick.

"How could no one notice!" he shouted realising this was not appropriate given where he was.

Besides being disgusted, John was even more frightened than he had been before. If this was possible, anything was. This notion was an amorphous collection of snippets of death, carnage, people, chases and what he believed to be someone else's life; this could not be him. It was also accelerated by fear and the unknown and due to the fact that he realised that the man he met in the car had been right. He now realised that their pursuit of him would remain relentless, and death was the only ending any logic could foresee. They would not be satisfied until he had only a toe tag on in the mortuary.

"Right, bollocks to that," he said to himself quietly. "Come on John. Logic man, apply logic."

He took one of the sawn off shot guns, checked that it was loaded correctly and placed it by the iron ladder. His escape route, freedom get out of jail card was ready. He checked that the Chinese sidearm was loaded and also decided to place it there, as there may be more than two assailants. He knew he had expended some ammunition, but it had some left and enough to at least help out. He walked back to the couch, sat, drank the rest of his coffee and produced the Beretta.

He depressed the catch on the left hand side of the handle, and the dispensed magazine fell out instantly.

"Well, at least I now know how to load and unload," he muttered.

John reached into the pack and took out one of the live magazines he had taken from Eric Jennings, and he pushed it into the shaft pressing it into place. He did not pull the mechanism back just yet, as it acted as a safety, and he had not worked out how to deactivate the death by shooting mode yet, including shooting himself.

He pulled the seven shot pump-action shotgun close to him and let it rest by the couch where he intended to sleep. He switched the television off and lay back. He could not rest. It was early and his mind was racing, so he placed the two sawn off shotguns carefully into his pack, ready to exit in haste if the situation presented itself. He had a feeling it might. He could see some machinery in the far corner, and he deduced that it was a small type of threshing machine, with spikes coming out at angles, probably used for irrigating the lawn surfaces allowing air and moisture to penetrate. It was a horrible apparatus, but John decided to place it by the bottom of the staircase after he had explored some options. He found some steel wire by the contraption, also an old heavy box, which had some tools in it, and some fixtures and screws in an old ice cream container. He found a Philips head screwdriver, selected two robust screws, and on finding some pliers, he applied the only form of logic that entered his head. What was transparently obvious and yet frightening was that all this came to him quite naturally.

He climbed to the second from top stair, knelt down and about six inches above the end of the stair tread, he screwed in one of the two screws. He then tied the steel wire to it, and with the pliers, he forced it into a cross thread and tightened the screw catching both wire and wood to an immovable housing. He repeated the same process on the other side but used the bannister for purchase, and he ensured the trip wire was both robust and taught.

He then grabbed a blanket from the couch and used it as a barrier to the sharp spikes and covered a portion and dragged the machinery to the bottom of the staircase, where it lay as an ominous tool, deadly to any adversary, analeptic to John.

With this ghastly safety measure in place, John removed the lightbulb from the only pendant fixture in the den, and he lay on the couch and clutched the seven shot which was cocked and ready to fire. He then changed his mind once again and removed one of the sawn off shotguns from his pack. He placed the seven shot upright by him and clutched the sawn off as he lay down, as it was smaller and easier to manoeuvre. He decided it was now time to rest, so he got up, switched the television off and retraced his step carefully to the couch, and brushed against the seven shot which comforted him. He finally lay down, and his mind was instantly drawn to the image of Angela once again and just how sweet she was. He also thought of the man's face, as John had despatched him. He had been consumed with fear and probably shock that the rabbit in the headlights had game and attitude. It served him right. His stomach welled and burnt as the anxiety washed over him, and he was convinced that he was ultimately responsible for her death and...

Just then, he was alerted to some muffled but audible words and noise emanating from outside, somewhere close to the back door of the house. Whoever the uninvited guests were, they were probably quite confident that the house was empty and that there was no real threat, especially from a novice and idiot running around masquerading as Jason Bourne.

I don't want to be a rabbit came into his mind again, but he was perilously close to being stumbled on and had to apply a steady patient hand; his decision was simply run or wait.

'Wait big guy,' he told himself.

He heard the gentle tap and the glass break upstairs as it fell into the hallway by the door.

'Not very discreet,' he thought. 'They must be pretty sure they can not only despatch me with ease but that there is no one here. More fool you guys.'

He heard the door open and the crunch of glass as a sole of the intruder's foot trampled it. He heard what he thought was two more crunches, so he was probably going to have to elude at least three people or despatch them. He heard them split up, and he could hear the upper staircase creak under the pressure of a human climbing it. He listened carefully, and his breathing was exact so as to not obscure his hearing, and his heart beat increased with the anxiety welling up in him. He heard them go into each room and he could see the flicker of their torch beams passing the minute cracks in the panel. He was breathing more heavily by the second, and it was the breath of a man in blind fear and panic, but he stayed exactly where he was and waited.

The panel was tugged at, as he had predicted and planned, then tugged at harder to slowly reveal the den to the intruder. It opened fully, gently creaking with every centimetre, and some light invaded the space from a torch beam and the light in the upstairs hallway. His heart rate was off the scale, and his throat acutely dry. He wanted to be sick, as Angela's face and smile flashed in front of him, and his children's faces raced by. He could remember and feel their sweet kisses on his cheeks, so now inspired, he remained still and tried to hold his breath.

He heard the foot tread on the upper landing of the staircase, and then as it moved forward, he heard it creak and then the heavy tumble of a man. It was an awkward, totally unexpected fall, and he tumbled the whole set of steps. As he reached the bottom, there was a deathly sound of spikes entering flesh and a gurgle like sound that John believed was a death rattle. He saw a beam of light from the top of the staircase, and it shone directly onto the crumpled heap lay at the bottom of the staircase. As it revealed the horror of the event, the beam fell on the trip wire and then there were several voices shouting and then he heard the familiar pull back of the sidearm engaging the chamber. John only needed to adjust the shotgun a few inches before he let both barrels go. It was ultimately very loud, as it echoed in the compact space, and it represented everything that was very final. He heard a scream followed by a dull heavy thud, a heavy thud that he believed had rendered the receiver of the chambers a complete twisted mess.

He rolled off the couch, dropped the sawn off and picked up the seven shot. He heard a hail of bullets raining over him, quiet and supressed, but many of them, and they were being released from a sidearm which was angled around the corner of the upper stair. The shooter remained completely obscured from sight by the landing partition. John realised that the seven shot could penetrate the partition but only if he could drop under the stairs and remain undetected.

He rolled across the floor and to a position directly underneath the staircase. It was obvious that the man had reloaded because the torchlight shone, and there was another hail of bullets, the projectiles buried themselves in couch, wall, and ricocheted around the den.

John leant backwards, and looking ahead and up, he gauged the best angle of entry, and he pumped the gun and released the trigger. He did this four times. It was so loud and echoed around the den so badly that he felt his eardrums cry for mercy as did the recipient of the shells.

The staircase shattered, and he could see through a large hole. The first man he had originally shot had been almost dismembered in the groin by the contents of two close barrels. The other man who had just been firing had little left of his head and upper body, neck and shoulders. It was a bloody sight of carnage and a complete mess, as he had anticipated.

John listened intently and waited. His breathing was exaggerated and he felt sick again with a dry throat. These were familiar feelings now and signs that he had taken even more human life. He could hear what he thought was gravel moving outside, and there was still someone left by the back door; he was sure of it. He moved from under the stairs, crept across the dark den to the iron ladder and gently scaled it. He gently unlocked the grill teasing it upward a centimetre and peeping through the small gap. His suspicions were immediately confirmed, as sure enough, there before him was an individual. The person was quite small in stature, dressed in black clothes which signified no affiliation to feminine or masculine, so he knew not whether it was a male or female. He removed the Beretta and pointed it at the shadowy figure that was against the wall, poised and sneaky, waiting for anyone to emerge. He saw the flicker of the moonlight twist off reflective metal, and he knew then that the assailant possessed a gun. It had turned dark, both in and outside his world, and this would help him, although the flash of the Beretta would give away his position temporarily to any further predators.

For the second time today, he abandoned logic and caution. He cocked the sidearm, threw open the grill and before the adversary could react, he discharged three bullets into the body mass. The dull thuds alerted him to the fact that he had hit the target. The air being exhaled and the whimpering also confirmed this, and as he exited the grill, he walked to the body that lay slumped and breathing heavily. He was contemplating executing this person, but he decided to see if he could gain any information from the condemned individual. He removed the balaclava to reveal a girl, blood oozing from her mouth.

"Why," he asked her. "Why me? Why would you do this?"

The girl just stared back with her hollow eyes.

He saw her arm come up and in a protective defensive move. Driven by instinct, he put his arm up as a shield to his body, as the blade glanced off him cutting him.

He leapt back and off her and shot once into her upper chest. He realised she was wearing a body vest and this is why she was alive. He also realised this is why he needed to shoot everyone in the head, so this type of thing could never happen.

She said something between the coughing and fighting for breath as one bullet had penetrated her neck. He tried to listen, as she was saying a man's name, repeating it over and over again.

Yuri, Yuri, Yuri.

Then silence and the open eyed death stare that he was becoming a little bit too familiar with. She slumped to the left side, and her body functioned no more; she ceased to inhabit the earth. John looked around, and it was quiet, so he tried to find any information, but there was little of anything on her like all the rest, but she had sounded Russian or Eastern European. He looked tentatively into the house, and there was no sound. He decided to go back through the grill, down the iron ladder and investigate the three bodies within the den with the Beretta loaded and ready.

As he entered the dark small confined space, he smelt death and lots of it. He moved forward carefully and slowly, through the musky Faust, heavily infiltrated by the smell of cartridges being expended and bullets wailing and hitting everywhere. John moved towards the man at the bottom of the staircase. He knelt down, but nothing could have prepared him for the abomination before him. The man had one of the spikes clean through his right eye, another through his neck and a couple more through his upper body. He was lifeless, and his shallow eyes looked forward in a death stare; he was impaled like a grotesque horrific caricature.

John could not have predicted the utter consternation and alarm his actions might have caused, but he wanted whoever came down those stairs to be gone, but the reality before him could not have been more repulsive. He shuddered with repugnance. It was all too vulgar, and the expression on the man's face was pure dread, utter horror and also complete surprise. He had not expected this at all.

John moved up the stairs a few treads to the enormous hole left by the shot craters. He looked at the man on the stairs with half his midriff blown away and his genitals and top legs completely missing. He then looked at the man just above and laying against him, and he was hard to recognise as a human being. His head had been completely dismembered and half his neck and shoulders had gone in chunks up the wall and all over the partition area.

Strangely, the scene reminded him of the film, *Saving Private Ryan* as he remembered the graphic scenes but then he also had a weird notion. John thought that the Smythe house price would now drop as a result of having such a barbaric massacre in it, but then no one would ever know would they? He could not understand how he had turned from a wimp who hated the thought, let alone the sight of blood, into someone who could search half a body for clues without vomiting or feeling any remorse at all.

It felt as if he had crossed a threshold and it worried him that he may not be equipped to deal with normal life again. He was angry at these individuals, but he had achieved vengeance for Angela's death. He had taken such an aggressive and forward stance of the violence aimed at him and twisted it into his own game, set and match.

'How is it that I am not feeling sick? I have normal anxiety but not like when I was around and in Hangman's Cottage or even the pub. How is it that my hands are not shaking? How is it that I feel that they just paid the ultimate price for the job they do, and the retribution exacted upon them was not only just but that it is a direct result of what their actions attract?'

He could find no clues as to their identity or anything else of interest, but he had confirmed one thing for sure, that none of them was of Asian origin. All of the three men were large in stature, and two had bits of blonde hair left, although the one he was looking at had no head remaining, and the little bit of matted hair left by his neck was completely red. John decided that there must be a backup crew and that they would know that they had met with distress if this lot had not informed base of their progress. John picked up his pack, the guns and reloaded the expended sawn off. He loaded the seven shot to maximum capacity and exited the den through the grill. He walked briskly to the hedge and trod stealthily, as he approached the structure housing the vehicles. He unlocked the door, went in and was about to open the Kahn door when he felt steel against the back of his neck.

Chapter 5

The Leader

John felt the barrel of the gun press into the nape of his neck and the sound of its keeper breathing gently with control. Next, his arm was unceremoniously yanked back behind him and up toward his shoulder blade, and he felt the presence of other black shadows in the room.

"Don't do anything stupid bonny lad, or you will just exit the planet if you do. It must be obvious to you that I could have killed you several times over already, but I choose not to, so relax. If you do as you are told and listen carefully, you might learn something of great value and importance that may just bring some clarity to your present predicament. Oh, and you will be able to continue breathing, but only if you do as you are told; if not, you are truly expendable."

John tried to breathe at a pace that matched his lungs' requirements, and he felt disappointed that even after all he had done that he had been outsmarted by the real elite.

"Who the hell are you?"

There was no answer.

"What are you going to do to me?"

There was no answer.

"Will you please tell me what the fuck is going on? I have just about had enough."

"Mr Parks," came a quiet voice from the darkness to his side, "you have been quite an amusing sideshow, exhilarating at times, pure stupidity at others but never failing to deliver amusement."

"I am glad you think so," John shouted, "but I am completely pissed off, so are you going to kill me?"

"If we had wanted you dead, we would have let the Koreans or Russians, or even Eric Jennings' crew expunge you ages ago, old man. No, you still do not get it. Do you?"

"Who the hell are you?" John shouted.

Out of the shadows, the leader emerged, the very guy John feared in his mind, and he knew that he not only sounded but was menacing for a reason.

"Who would you like me to be Mr Parks, friend or foe? Choose swiftly and wisely, my boy, as my next actions will be connected directly to the information you supply."

"Friend, of course. I could bloody well do with some."

"Really," said the leader, "so who do you think has been your guardian angel for the past two days, old man?"

All four of the men now emerged from the shadows, but the fifth still held the gun to his neck, and his arm was hurting.

"Can you let go of my arm please? I pose no threat," John asked.

"We know that Mr Parks that is until you get that sawn off or that Beretta in your hands. You like to shoot them don't you, and even if you could not hit a barn door from two feet. Priceless, old man, absolutely priceless, like a cowboy film watching you."

"I do not understand," said John, completely bewildered.

"OK, it's time to tell you some facts, and hopefully we can be on the same wavelength. First, come with us into our van, as we and you need food. We can talk on the way and at the pub."

"The pub," said John sharply.

"Yes, the pub," said the leader calmly.

John heard then saw the VW Transporter pull up outside, and he was led to it, placed in the passenger seat before cable ties were put on his wrists and connected to the overhead pull. The next tie was put on his right wrist and coupled to the seatbelt housing, while the leader sat in the crew cab seat directly behind him. Another three men got into the back, and the driver took off down the drive, turned right into Wick Street just as three white transit vans pulled into the drive. They all flashed their lights as they drove past.

"Don't worry, old man; they are the clean-up team, ghost busters," he said laughing loudly.

"I don't believe this," said John looking at him.

"Believe everything, old man," said the leader.

"So what is going on?" asked John earnestly.

"Well, to start with, the key that dear old Robert Thatcham gave you at the initial crash site was a fake. It has absolutely no meaning, and it holds no information. It is purely an encrypted piece of nothing, designed to waken interest in dormant operatives and those with traitorous blood in them."

The leader's phone started buzzing, and he answered it and started to talk in a sort of code. It was interesting, as it was not like any other language John had ever heard.

John noticed that they entered Stroud and turned right into Merrywalks and then onto the double roundabout, up to the rugby club and B&Q lights and over towards Nailsworth on the Bath Road. He noticed the South Woodchester turning, as they were all familiar places he had travelled many times.

"Anyway," resumed the leader, "the intelligence was deliberately leaked so that all the key players believed that the seabed project was finalised. This, in turn, would trigger a series of events and signify that the world would change significantly as a result. Of course with this, the financial balance of the world would undoubtedly spin off its axis in panic, and so the dangerous power players that lurked everywhere, needed to be flushed out. It was a simple, yet effective, strategy, but circumstances interfered in its execution."

"I don't get it though. Why me?" said John.

"You were just a complete tragedy of circumstance John," said the leader using his first name for the first time, maybe the formal approach was now lapsing. "You were the wrong guy, in the wrong place, at the wrong time, and as a result, you ultimately triggered a series of events that should have been significantly different. You did however accelerate the process, and I have to say, you got some of the difficult groundwork accomplished quickly and out of the way for us."

"But this Robert Thatcham, who was he and who did he represent?"

"Robert, bless him, was MI6, and he stumbled across a plot, or what he thought was a plot. We had deliberately leaked the intelligence, and he seized upon it like a terrier with a bone and would not let it go for anything or anyone. We tried to warn him, but we could not expose the ruse, and like a good operative, he continued to follow his instinct, but before we could get to him properly and take him out of circulation, he had been drugged and I believe you are more familiar than most with the rest of the story."

"Bloody hell," said John, completely aghast at the deceit and enormity of the situation.

"So Eric Jennings. Who was he in all this?" asked John, as he saw the old Rising Sun on his right, dilapidated and allowed to degrade, so it came under the right to demolish category for the builders. What a shame.

"Eric Jennings was a sleeper. His parents were Russian, and he was brought up hiding in plain sight. He was known to be involved in obtaining industrial or high commercial intelligence and selling it, but it suited the government to allow this to happen. You see he had no idea that his wife was a British operative who had been placed in his life twenty years ago and played this fabulous game of 'wifey'."

"He was as gay as a lord anyway," commented the driver. "Her protection detail used to go into their guest cottage for buddy sex with her. She hated Jennings, so good job he preferred young men, or she would have killed him."

"I can't take all this in. I just cannot comprehend any of this. How the hell could she live a life of complete deceit and lies and be on edge? I just do not know how you would do such a thing with your entire existence in this world."

"Crown and country, the Sovereign crown and love of all that is Blighty, old man," said the leader. "Plus don't forget, he was gay so she didn't have to have a sexual relationship with him. He was filthy rich, which by the way transfers on his death, so she is now a millionaire at thirty eight years old, not including the houses and social life. That will remain intact. Don't forget, to the universal masses and media, he killed himself and that is a bit of scandal but not too much, and it will be forgotten quickly. She is completely sorted forever without ever having to lift a finger."

"What about the guys at the Painswick Hotel? I saw them both lay out dead on the drive, and you guys taking them away," John said, as if they did not know.

"Freelance mercenaries, and not very good ones either. They were annoying as much as anything but easy to flush out and despatch," said the leader calmly and without any emotion at all.

"You act as if their lives meant nothing," John added.

"Do you think they would have inherited a conscience at the point of killing you, John? You surprise me, a man that seemed to shoot at anything without question, and you now ask me about my morals? Not good form, old chap, not good form at all."

John recognised the small quad section at Nailsworth. The tiny shops were now deserted and offered little in the way of traffic, by foot or wheel. The VW moved forward, went over the pedestrian crossing and turned abruptly left toward Avening. He watched as the garden centre appeared and disappeared with Tubby's restaurant attached. He had used this a couple of times when buying plants a while ago. He was astonished when they stopped the van and parked outside the famous Weighbridge Inn.

"Do you know where we are John?" asked the leader.

"Home of the famous two in one pie," John replied.

"Good man, I am starving and I have a need for steak and cauliflower cheese," said the leader. Everyone exited the vehicle, John had his ties cut and was unleashed under his own common sense, no use fighting these guys, they were in a whole different league.

They entered by the side exit, passed the toilets and snug door and went through the far bar entrance door. There were a few people in there, but John was ushered straight up to the loft. This was a lovely seating area that joined the garden through an access door on the upper level. It was a beautiful rustic inn. Lanterns, farm machinery, tools and ancient keys hung from the ceilings in the dark, smoke stained rooms, tarnished by years of huge open fires roaring in the winter, warming both travellers and locals alike. The pie was famous worldwide and worth every second of any journey to get there. John loved it and he ordered the traditional large steak and mushroom two in one. The others all ordered through a nominated man who disappeared down the stairs to the bar to get the food on its way.

"What about the Asian guy in the shed?" asked John.

"Christ, tell me that it was you that killed him, old man. You took his head off John, you completely smashed his skull and jaw to pieces, dead as a pigging doornail," answered the leader, and the other men started to laugh.

"It's not funny," retorted John abruptly.

"It bloody is for us," said the leader.

"I have ultimately killed loads of people, so how could you let that happen to me, and put a civilian in so much danger?" said John quietly, looking around the room and carefully examining the stairs for anyone who may be listening.

"Who have you killed John?" asked the leader, sipping on a pint of Old Spot that was brought by his man. He gave everyone else a pint, including John, and placed the tray on the big wooden table where they now all sat like old friends.

"I shot a bloody dog! Can you believe that? A bloody dog and then three men... and then a bloody helicopter," he blurted.

The men all started to laugh loudly. They were almost crying with laughter and just looked at each other as if they were attending a comedy show.

"It's not funny," said John sternly.

"You shot the dog," said the driver, "but since when does a bullet exit the wrong side of the head and body?" said the driver.

"What do you mean?" asked John.

"Not being funny, John, but you could not hit the ground with a stick," said the leader.

"If you jerked off like you jerk when you fire a rifle, you would have pulled your own winky off," said one of the men in fits of laughter.

"What do you mean?" he asked again.

"You are a disaster with a rifle John, no good at all. The worst thing for us was to try and shoot in a believable synchronised action with you, to make you think you had game," said another man, obviously the main shooter.

John thought back. He was sure he had them firmly in his sights and that he had despatched them with precision shooting. Then again, he was pleased to find out his kill threshold was less than his rampant spree would suggest, so he could live with this a little bit easier.

"What about the last lot at the Smythe residence?" he asked.

"We will give you three out of four there. The sawn off was a great idea, and we all thought you had grown some balls then, or thought you had game, brilliant though and you put them away no doubt," said the leader.

"And the fourth?" John inquired.

"The minute you came out of the grill and raised your weapon, she was taken out, as was the guy with the rifle by the garage, but you did not know about him though did you?" said the driver.

The stairs creaked and two staff brought up pies for all in two trips, also some bread and then they left swiftly. It was obvious that there were more men in the carpark, and the bottom of the stairs. He could see one guy outside the garden entrance door, which was ajar, and he was smoking and kept looking around.

"Who was the guy at the Edgemoor? The one that shot Angela?" asked John placing the first piece of steak in his mouth,

"Oh my God, that is so good," he said.

They all agreed, the shortcrust pastry lay as a roof for the steak, the heat and aroma emanating from the gravy meat and cauliflower was just enough to silence them all for a while.

"The guy at the Edgemoor was a mercenary, and we are still trying to get some details but probably Korean. You were lucky that we knew he was there. He took him out by the way," he said pointing to a muscular, hardened looking, quiet man at the end of the table who nodded and continued eating.

"You finished him off mind, and the kill was yours, but as you were firing all over the bloody building that guy down there put three into him from the outer roof to the back of the building. He was completely hidden, and you nearly shot him in the ass," said the leader, and they all started laughing once again and loudly.

"Angela should not have died. It is my fault," said John showing real remorse.

"I shot her," said another man opposite John, eating his pie and not moving his stare from John's eyes. He announced this as if he had put out the garbage, not taken an innocent girl's life.

"Why would you do that?" asked John loudly.

"Angela, real name Hellene Vinovich, Russian daughter of former agents in the Soviet regime, both deceased by our hands, I might add. She drugged your drink, John. You know, when you went to the toilet, powerful chemicals, too, the same ones that immobilised and killed Robert Thatcham. Luckily for you though, you drank it so fast, the pill at the bottom had no time to dissolve. Then you got a fresh one, and she looked so pissed off, as you walked out," said the leader looking straight into his eyes and laughing as did the others.

"Bloody hell, I don't believe it," John said.

"Believe it," said the leader.

"But she met me after I shot down the helicopter," he said.

"About that," said the man at the end of the table, "I had to fire three rounds into that mother to convince you that you hit the chopper. Your face was priceless, absolutely hilarious, fear meets pride of accomplishment. You were actually proud of yourself. Have you any idea how hard it is to bring down a chopper in real life? The pilot is really the only means of an instant drop from the sky. Then of course I had to rid the dog of its bloody handler! I thought you were going to shoot me the way your bullets were flying out over the countryside."

"Bollocks, I am bloody useless, but at least I am full. That was absolutely wonderful," he said looking at all of them finishing their food and relaxed. He was amazed how they were so calm in the face of their job title and work scope: eat, sleep, follow, execute, clean up, shop, execute and so on. What an existence!

Those choppers all have heat signature generated recognition equipment you know, and they have like heat sensors that can pick a man up at a few hundred metres away, no issue, further if directly above, so you cannot really hide.

"Get underwater, cold water," joked one of the men.

"Like *Predator*," said another laughing loudly.

"I need to go to the toilet. Is it ok down there?" John asked.

"Of course," said the leader. "You will be totally safe, trust me. It will probably be the first piss you have had without having to look over your shoulder in a while" He started laughing loudly. "Go with him," he said to the other man opposite.

The man followed John down the stairs, through the small seating area, into the bar and out of the door on the left, down the hallway and to the right. He looked as the man stopped by the door and smiled.

"I am not watching you syphon mate. You are safe in there, and there are men outside, so relax and have a piss."

John entered the toilet, he walked up to the urinal wall, undid his trousers and unleashed himself on the porcelain. It felt so good, and for the first time in ages, he felt safe. He realised he would be OK, especially with these guys. These men, they really were professional and well and truly knew how to ply their trade.

He also felt nourished and had information that cleared him of most of the sins he believed he had committed. Mostly, he was absolved of the evil that was the downfall of Angela or Hellene or whatever her name was. As the anxiety started to diminish, he heard footsteps outside, and he saw two men having a cigarette.

The taller darker man leant across and asked the other, "What the hell is going on then?"

"I think that Oliver said the twat knows absolutely nothing, so Jeremy will probably drug his pint, and we can dump him in one of the gravel pits in South Cerney."

"Where's that?"

"Up by Cirencester; it's not far," he replied.

John felt his stomach drop. His heart rate increased and he felt sick again. It was just about all he could do to stop himself vomiting there and then. He finished urinating in a fast pace, washed his hands and threw some water on his face. The dryer did not work, so he grabbed a paper towel and wiped his face as the door opened.

"You OK," asked the guy he had left outside.

"No worries," he said, walking back out, down the corridor, through the bar and seating area, up the stairs and sat by the leader. There was a fresh pint. 'The fluid of death,' he thought. He could feel nothing but betrayal and a strange sensation filled with humiliation, for believing them and being comforted by who he thought were his own government's allies. What an idiot.

'How the hell am I going to get out of this?' he thought.

Three other men had full fresh beers, so he applied logic, and he needed an opportunity to switch one without being detected, but how?

The men all continued to chew the cud, and then the leader went outside in the garden to talk in the code on the phone by the door. Just then, a girl started to come up the stairs. She had large breasts bobbing around but harnessed but with sufficient cleavage revealed by the low-cut shirt. It was just enough to distract the men for the *nanno* it took John to lean over and switch drinks with the driver opposite him.

With the leader out of the picture, no one else was taking any notice of John at all. He posed absolutely no threat to any of this band of elite mercenaries or government taskforce, or whatever they were now. He had an edge over them though, not in skills of expediting humans, but in that now they, of course, believed that he remained oblivious and unaware of his impending demise.

John pulled up his pint and taunted all of the men, especially those holding onto full pints, "Of mice and men!" he shouted.

"What?" said the driver opposite him.

"Are you a man or a mouse? Straight back chaps," he said upping his glass to his mouth.

They all laughed and raised their glasses. They were amused that the guy who was about to expire was actually hastening the process through trying to be friendly. John was pleased they felt so comfortable.

They all downed their respective drinks, and the leader returned.

"We need to go lads," he bellowed, and they all stood up like soldiers on parade.

It was the first time that John felt menace in the assembled strike force that surrounded him, and in the building. They were indeed a formidable crew. They even smelt of death. They were seasoned and hardened veterans who would not make many mistakes or succumb to easy manoeuvres, and they would need to be enticed into false security with cunning and playing to their modesty. After all, they firmly believed they were the best of the best, the worrying aspect was that they were.

He was still uncertain of how he could get out of this present predicament, but he decided to play the fool and maybe they would fall for it. He was still not convinced that he was such a shit shot with a gun, and he needed to retrieve his arsenal and for them to see him as the twat, not the reaper.

They were told to leave in groups. The driver and a further three men were to travel with John. The leader and six others would go in another vehicle, and the remaining six would travel in the third van when the rear exit was deemed safe. They would travel separately and in different directions and would meet later at the designated rendezvous at 22.30 hours. John overheard one guy whisper that they would meet at Wernons later that night after it was accomplished. This was extremely careless, but they now thought that they were dealing with an idiot civilian and little or no concern should be given to any capability he might have.

He instantly recognised that he was the 'after it was accomplished' part of the equation, but he was determined to avoid this.

He was led to the van but not put into the front, probably in case anyone saw him, but on the way there, he thought, never mind. He went through the side door, pushed the seat forward and climbed into the back row of seats. The driver got in and another man got in beside him. The other two got into the middle row of seats in front of John.

John smiled. they buckled their belts but John did not, he had noticed his pack on the floor and he knew it offered salvation and escape. He feigned feeling a little bit queasy. The operatives obviously deduced that the chemicals were starting to devour his senses, they looked at each other and he caught feint smiles appear on their faces.

The driver pulled out of the Weighbridge Inn carpark and turned right toward Avening but then left over the bridge toward Minchinhampton.

'Bastards,' he thought.

He lay down and pulled the pack to where he could access the sawn off and his Beretta. He knew he had loaded them, so all of the deadly contents of the pack would be ready to engage in his bloodthirsty activity. Once again, he was being asked to take human life just to survive. They in turn were determined to end his ability to bear witness to the events he had been part of.

John was mad; he was really mad. The driver breathed heavily and complained that he felt weird. John saw the sweat appear on his head, and he gently slid the sawn off out of the pack. He could not help but think that not only was it a bit more than just careless, leaving the pack in the back with him; it was downright sloppy.

The man on his right in front of him looked around and smiled.

"You OK cocker," he asked, without real concern for his welfare, obviously knowing he was dying. Well in his mind anyway, and he then faced the front of him.

"Christ I feel bad," said the driver, "really bad."

John placed the sawn off on his lap pointing forward. The van was travelling slowly due to the width of the road, terrain and steepness of the incline.

"What do you mean?" asked the man beside him. "Are you OK?

The man slumped a bit, and the man in front of John to the right moved forward. The driver blurted fluid from his mouth and coughed badly.

"Christ, he has been drugged," said the passenger beside him.

"That means," said the man to the front right of John. "Oh no, for fuck's sake!" he cried.

John released the contents of the chamber through the barrel. He caught the man full in the face and took off his head. He also hit the driver, crushing his skull with the close quarter pellets. The windscreen shattered outward, and John shifted across his seat to the right just as the man directly in front of him reached into his holster. John released the second barrel, and he made sure he took the front passenger and the man in front with the scatter of pellets. The front of the VW was just a red blood spattered mess. The roof, door cards, dashboard were covered in chunks of face and head, like bloody mincemeat, and the four men were pretty much rendered unrecognisable.

John felt nothing but outrage for the betrayal accomplished by people he had really trusted, and he began to question everything that they had said. He could believe nothing apart from the fact that he now knew that Wernons held the key.

John grabbed the backpack and watched as the van slowly moved into the bank. It made a thud, as it slowly came to a halt in the middle of the verge. John had to do the unthinkable. He needed to move the body in the driver seat to allow him access to enter and hide the van, but he could not face doing this; he needed another solution,

"Logic John! Apply logic!" he shouted to himself.

He got out of the back of the van taking the pack and sawn off with him and looked behind him.

'Perfect, absolutely perfect,' he thought as he investigated the low verge and steep bank. He went to the driver's side, opened the door, switched off the engine and lights, placed the gear lever in neutral and let the van roll back. He made sure the steering wheel reflected that a straight pattern of travel could be achieved, and he pushed on the door and guided the van until it was rolling sufficiently. He let it go, and it travelled back with enough traction and speed to mount the verge and go over the small embankment and through the green paddock before coming to rest in a large hedge. It was for the best part hidden, although he knew it would have a tracker fitted.

He was pleased that this alternative method of disposal. He had at least put the van and the remaining body parts of the occupants out of immediate sight. John ran from the scene to some houses in the distance. He would need to get away from this place within minutes if he were to survive the next stage of this titanic battle.

John noticed some sheds and outbuildings, and he went toward one, and a security light flashed into action sending its sharp ever revealing light across the shingle drive. A dog also barked, so John elected to go to the next house. Here he ran to the side and over a wall and looked into a small outbuilding. There appeared to be nothing, but as he turned the corner, a bicycle was leant against the wall. The reason that it was not locked here was that there was no need, or so the owner thought. This was in the wilds and the bike was also ancient, an awful example of self-propelling, two-wheeled transport.

John picked the bike up, went to the wall and threw the bike and the pack over. He leapt over and picked up the pack, but he suddenly remembered that he had expended the sawn off cartridges and needed to reload. He reached in the pack and brought out two cartridges, broke the barrel down and filled each barrel. He then relocked the barrel and replaced the sawn off in the pack before he mounted the bike.

Chapter 6

The Call

John peddled for all he was worth, back down the hill toward the Weighbridge Inn, but he did not stop. He went over the bridge, turned right and headed towards Nailsworth and Stroud. He went like the wind with the ancient rickety bike serving its purpose adequately, and he felt every muscle hurt again. He had to get over the crossroads in Nailsworth before the third van returned that way carrying the infamous leader. He would no doubt be aware of the fact that the position of the van was now stationary in the field. Protocol would dictate waiting a few minutes, in case it had met a tractor or lorry in the narrow lanes, but if it did not move, he would turn around and would come to see what was going on, as would the second vehicle.

John turned the corner by the garden centre, up the slight gradient and down the slope to the junction of the Bath Road. He did not even stop or look; he just kept peddling at speed and crossed the pedestrian crossing, shot into the crossroads and turned right, up the gradient, hid behind some shops, and stopped.

The phone rang and John was startled. He heard it and felt the vibration in his pack, and it continued to buzz begging an answer, but John was worried,

'Who the hell was it? Where the hell had it come from?'

He looked inside and saw a small mobile dancing in the pack, illuminating the inner sack and showing the assortment of weapons, plus a strange foil. He grabbed the phone, placed it to his ear and answered it tentatively.

"Who the hell is this?"

"Ah Mr Parks, who I am is of no concern at this particular moment, but if you do exactly as I say, I will keep you alive. If you falter or stray from my commands, you will surely expire. Your choice young man, so what is it to be: life or death?"

The man had an aristocratic English accent and exuded authority and class. He sounded like a man you could trust on a normal day, but this was not a normal day, far from it.

"Life," replied John.

"We do not have much time Mr Parks, so take the Bluetooth device in your pack and place it in your ear. Now, place the phone in a secure pocket or the pack."

John found it and complied, and it engaged the phone, so he placed the mobile in his faithful pack.

"They will come for you very soon. Ditch the bike, walk to your left and jump over the hedge. Go on."

John did exactly as he was told and was thrown into some bushes by his acrobatic leap. He saw a small stream, and he was about to ask when…

"Walk down the edge of the stream, and about a hundred metres there is a small bridge. Quickly now."

John could hear a helicopter in the distance, and he stopped to look up.

"Are you there yet?" asked the man impatiently.

"Almost," he said and he ran and found the bridge. It stood by a small wall and incline to the main road.

"I am at the bridge," he said panting.

"OK Mr Parks, in the pack is a foil suit and a plastic tube of about 40 centimetres in length; find them both."

"Got them," he said.

"Take your clothes off, put the foil boiler suit on, and when I tell you to, disengage the phone call and place the mobile and all other equipment in the pack and place it under the bridge. Don't worry, the phone is scrambled and cannot be traced."

John once again complied, and the night air chilled his naked body. He was really cold and started to shiver. He heard a vehicle, and when he looked up over the wall, he saw the familiar vehicle of death rumble past and head for the crash site.

"What now?" he asked shaking.

Get into the water directly under the bridge, and use the tube to breathe. Count to sixty slowly, repeat this fifteen times and do not surface before this exact time for any reason. When you do surface, retrieve the backpack and phone, you will have exactly two minutes to get dressed, run across the road and get into the doorway of the estate agents. A Travis Perkins flatbed with a crane will stop at the shop entrance. Get into the back of the lorry, and I will ring you again.

"Why fifteen minutes?"

"You don't have any time. It is their search protocol, and they will perform a grid search with heat signature surveillance. Get in the water now!"

The phone clicked off, and John put it in the pack, and positioned it under the bridge before slowly entering the freezing water.

As he lay down under the bridge, the darkness and loneliness added to the sheer horror of his predicament. He sat, water waving over him, and he put the tube in his mouth. He then submerged his lower body then gritted his teeth and lay back flat. The cold icy feel of the water stripping him of any warmth, found its way into every crevice and part of his body and he began to shake so much his head came out of the water. He quickly submerged it again and tried to control his breathing, conscious that he had to get the timing right, but the tube and the iced bath were proving a hard task to achieve.

'How long had it been so far? Christ, please don't make me fuck this up, please, bloody hell.'

Logic, he once again applied logic, one minute had gone, that is what he would say over and over. He started to count slowly, but then he realised he was wearing an Invicta divers watch.

"What a complete prick!" he shouted to himself.

He set the timer to 14 minutes and lay in the icy water. It felt like a tomb, and he felt isolated and exposed, and he could have easily given up at this point. He let his eyes come out of the water briefly. He looked up and out into the sky in the distance, and he could see the flashing light of the helicopter tail. This renewed his capacity to fight and survive, so he went back under. The water annoyed him, as it pushed the cold torrent against his neck and shoulders and then everywhere. He had a fight to control his breathing, and he had to take enough oxygen in to sustain his normal requirement but also to fight the onset of hypothermia. He tried to move his shoulders and neck, but it just made it worse, as it amplified the cold in segments that remained covered if he stayed motionless.

He glanced at the large dial several times and could not see much, so he decided to apply logic and started to count so that he would be close to the mark when he next looked. He was shaking uncontrollably and felt so uncomfortable and alone. He was a loner, but he had never felt quite so alone and exposed in his life.

He looked down to see the timer on the watch reflecting only twenty seconds off his allotted slot, within his tight schedule. He waited, counted to ten and decided he could not wait a single second longer. He leapt up out of the water, the torrent cascading off him, and he blew the tube out, breathed and panted hard. He took off the boiler suit, wiped what residual water he could off him with his t-shirt and put on his jumper, boxers, trousers and shoes. He checked the road both ways, ran across and darted quickly into the shop doorway as instructed.

He panicked, as he realised he had no pack. He ran and leapt the small wall and returned to the bridge just as the VW van pulled up at the crossroads and moved forward.

John ducked down and clutched the pack and invited one of the loaded sawn off shotguns into his hand, and for good measure, he also put the Beretta in his trousers' belt. Had this been a trick? No, surely not, but his heart was racing. Who could he possibly trust or believe? The VW slowly moved across the crossroads, through the tiny village and out of the other side towards Stroud.

John heard a larger vehicle approaching, and he saw the outline of the crane on the back with the familiar 'Travis Perkins' written on the side. Even though the current plan was flawed due to his position, as the lorry stopped momentarily, John raced over the wall, across the road and leapt into the back of the flatbed. There he found to his relief a blanket and a big coat. As he relaxed slightly, he realised just how cold he was, and he rubbed his legs and arms to try to stimulate circulation and warmth. He was shivering so much his teeth were chattering. He huddled at the cab end with the blanket around him and the pack and sawn off on his lap. He dug into the bag and put the earpiece back on, and as he did, the phone burst into life. He answered it still chattering.

"Ah Mr Parks, you live. Sorry about the timing," said the stranger. "I realised the van was on the move after the lorry had been given the green light. Very perceptive of you though, well done in evading the colonel, full marks to you.

"Who the hell is the colonel?" asked John still trying to regain warmth in his body and composure of speech.

"It matters not, but your welfare does, so you have to be clinical in your actions. I want you to be extremely careful, but you have to go back to Belleview," said the man.

"Who the hell are you?" he asked again.

"I am Bartholomew Theodor Knowles, Mr Parks, if that gives you any peace of mind. Now you can tell that no one could possibly make up such a preposterous name. It is real, but what if it echoes fable? It matters not, names are for tombstones anyway, and we are trying hard, both of us, to avoid that certainty."

"Who do you represent?" John asked.

"Why Mr Parks, all you need to know is that I represent life, for you, surely this is enough for now."

"I guess so, but please explain to me, why Belleview though? Surely the colonel's men will be crawling all over the place," said John.

"Hide in plain sight, and all that good advice. Where is the one place that they will least expect you to ever go? Belleview."

"But why risk it? It seems pointless," said John.

"I need you to disarm the one individual who now guards the house, and I need you to retrieve a small device he has. It looks almost identical in size and appearance to an iPad, but it is not. It is a decoder," said the man with an authoritarian voice.

"Surely you have trained men at your disposal, so how can you be sure I will accomplish this task?" asked John.

"Desperate times call for desperate measures, and you are desperate. I am not. I am not going to commit my people to going to a strange house and getting a decoder in front of the world and his dog. You know every centimetre of the house, garden and the layout, so who better to do my bidding than you?"

There was a brief pause.

"John, you need to evacuate the lorry, run into the park before turning and following the wall by the children's play items." The phone clicked off.

The lorry slowed down slightly, and it was obvious the driver had no intention of stopping. John grabbed his pack, sawn off and the blanket, and he climbed over the back of the bed. As it slowed to around 5mph, he leapt clear and the lorry revved, accelerated and the red lights started to get smaller.

John ran into the park, crept up to the hedge by the children's play area, passed the slide and rocking horse before running down to the tennis court.

The phone burst into life; he answered it.

"Best make your way to the steps opposite the bowling green, then around by the garage," said the man in a matter of fact voice. "I can inform you that the coast is all clear, so get over the Malt House fence and up onto the flat roof of your neighbour. She is out of town. You can access your cottage by the garage and across to your Velux window."

"How do you know that it is still open?" asked John.

"I do not know for sure Mr Parks, but I am assuming that no one has locked it as you left it closed and sealed. You never lock it."

"How do you know that?" asked John.

"You are a man, Mr Parks, and we don't lock things if they close sufficiently to work without any extra effort."

He ran down the steps, across the road and into the Malt House's driveway. He worked swiftly to scale up onto the flat roof and onto his neighbour's property. He jumped down the other side and scaled the incline to the fence that divided it from Belleview, and he went to the furthest right hand corner where he found his own bathroom roof and the adjoining garage. He climbed across the dividing wall and fence and onto the small walkway and leant forward to tease the Velux. He could see that the kitchen light was on, so someone was definitely in there.

John cocked the Beretta and had the shotgun in a position of instant access. He carefully opened the window, but he knew it had been recently lubricated and was going to be a silent process. He gently placed the blanket on the roof tiles to avoid the familiar crunching and creaking that always happened when under weight of foot. He stepped onto it, put both hands on the side of the opening and lowered himself down gently onto the side of the bath. He could hear that the television was on, not loudly, but any noise was in his favour, as it caused deflective sound patterns, and he would hopefully gain stealth and surprise.

With extra care, knowing his life depended on it, John then gently placed his right foot on the solid oak floor, then the left and let his full weight rest before closing the skylight. He elected to use and immediately selected the Beretta, the suppressor would avoid a full scale army of neighbours running around should the need arise to empty projectiles into the man, whoever he was. He knew if he expended the sawn off, total chaos would ensue. It was 10.46pm and the village was quiet and peaceful.

He ushered his body very slowly to the bathroom entrance, shrouded by the incredible distressed railway sleepers that had been so lovingly fashioned to give the perfect opening to a hand-built door. John always loved this feature and the fact that the bathroom was enormous. He looked at the beautiful Victorian suite and large walk-in shower that he had utilised only a couple of days ago when things were so different; he was sad and angry.

He crept through the doorway, onto the landing, careful not to knock into the table or vase holder. He moved forward with the Beretta extended in front of him, both hands gripping it firm. Every step seemed to take minutes when seconds was the reality. John looked up just as a man came around from the lounge and trod on the bottom of the stairway. He trod on the last step of his life.

"Oh shit," shouted the man, as he reached for his holster under his arm.

John, squeezed the trigger, conscious that this was one of the guys from the pub who had actually informed him that he was a crap shot. He released four bullets, and they all shattered his flesh above his armoured vest as they entered into him simultaneously, but the one that punctured the jugular vein in his neck was a repulsive and condemning sight. The man clutched the wound, but with every beat, the arterial spray spiralled two metres from his body and showered all over the staircase and up the yellow exposed stone.

The man gurgled, and since there was no ethereal intervention or splendid exit, within seconds his eyes were staring forward with that death stare yet again. The erratic yet powerful surge of blood now ceased. Life had abandoned this poor misguided soul with the most heinous of acts fulfilled, the taking of life once again accomplished with ease.

John moved down the staircase he loved so much, stepped over the lifeless corpse, and noticed on the table, there was indeed a tablet that resembled an iPad. He found a position by the front doorway, and he drew the curtains from the side to middle. He also moved toward the middle but he kept out of sight and drew the other, so he achieved privacy. He placed the device in his pack, checked that the

Beretta still had ammunition in it and stared at the corpse before an odd thought struck him.

'First there was Robert Thatcham, number one.

'Then there was Eric Jennings, number two.

'Then the Eastern European and the guard, number four.

'Then the guys in the field with the dog, three of them, number seven.

'Then the helicopter, man and dog, number ten.

'Then the Koreans, two of them number twelve.

'Then sweet or not so sweet Angela, number thirteen.

'Man who shot her, or not, number fourteen.

'Guys at the Smythe residence, four of them, number eighteen.'

"Now you sir, number nineteen," he said as he calmly reached into the dead man's holster and removed his gun.

"Well, well, well, a Beretta. What a surprise! And ammunition, thank you very much."

He placed the hardware in his pack and went back upstairs. He went to his bedroom up the small spiral staircase. He put on a fresh polo, hoodie, grabbed another Helly Hanson coat, pants, boxers, socks and some fresh trainers. He also threw a few bits of clothing into the pack to be sure of being able to change his appearance, they had all come in handy so far, and he threw several plastic bags in as well.

'You never know when,' he thought.

He went back down the small spiral staircase, closed the bathroom door to create dark space, and he pushed the

Velux open. He was super careful and grabbed a round shaving mirror from the sink and let it be his eyes outside. He offered it to the outside world by the exit by moving it around to see if there was danger in its refection. He could see nothing, so he climbed on the bath and then placed his hands on the side of the opening, and with one movement, heaved himself up and out of the cottage. He closed the Velux to the frame and moved to the side of the roof once again, taking the blanket with him and placing it in a fur tree. He was listening and careful, but the night air was a lone enterprise, and he could see and feel no immediate danger.

He realised he could get no signal here and thought how lucky that was as he had not placed the phone on silent mode, and he could have easily been given away by the tone of the ring. He also realised he had no further instructions, so he made his way along the same route he had used to get to the roof, but when confronted with White Horse Lane, he went to the furthest house by the turning circle and went to the back of the house. He went up the garden, over the wall and up to the large fence by the park.

He felt the phone vibrate. He had deliberately put it in the pocket of his trousers, and he dropped, cupped the bright illuminated screen and answered it.

"Mr Parks, your voice alerts me to the fact that you are obviously alive. Did you manage to retrieve my merchandise?" he asked.

"I did."

"Bravo, well done, and the man?"

"Dead as a door nail," replied John.

"Well it seems that everyone on this planet seems to have underestimated your capabilities, Mr Parks. I will not make that same mistake," said Knowles.

"By the way Bartholomew Knowles, answer me something please, if that is really your name of course. How did you manage to get the phone and the foil turkey basting kit into my backpack? How come the backpack was conveniently on the floor of the van?"

"Well Mr Parks, we simply used a double agent," he replied.

"Who?" asked John inquisitively.

"The man you just killed, John," he answered without any change in his tone.

"But why would you do that?" asked John, completely bemused.

"Collateral damage, and the fact that he was riding three horses in the race, dear man; damn bad form, leaking all sorts of information like a sieve," said Knowles.

"What now Mr Knowles? What is the next death defying stunt you would have the civilian undertake?"

"I think you need to rest, Mr Parks. We have a safe house you can use," he replied with an inviting tone. "Could you start by pressing the green button on the device?"

"No thank you. I intend to go off the grid tonight, and I will resurface tomorrow," said John much to the surprise of Knowles. "What's with the button too?"

"I don't think that is a very clever idea to say out and exposed old chap. We can protect you and you can rest," he said reassuringly. "The button merely activates the tracking device. It will activate itself in a few hours anyway, as it is on a timed pattern of protocol."

"No offence, Mr whatever your name is, but you can as easily kill me as protect me, so here is what is going to happen. I am going to place the phone and the device where I can access it tomorrow, and I am going to go somewhere to sleep and then at about eight thirty to nine am, I will come back for the phone," said John.

"I really don't think…"

John deactivated the call and placed the phone in the entrance to an old badger sett he knew existed by the fence. He then retraced his steps, placed the iPad looking device into a plastic bag. He placed it deep into another hole which was located ten metres to the right of the other one, and he buried it under soil and rocks and put foliage over the top. He made sure that he did not activate neither of the tracking systems, and he hoped that burying the phone and the tablet, he may eliminate any tracking before he recovered them tomorrow. He knew the signal would be hard to detect underground, but he did not want get caught because of it, so he walked away.

John retraced his steps and went back to the steps and down to the alley. He knew several of the locals were away because he had heard the idiots outside the village shop discussing their business for all to hear. They were screaming from the highest elevated pitch in their range about the best holiday on earth which was to be had shortly. They always tried to outshine each other, telling each other and bragging about their plans being better than the next, and so on.

He knew of one such pair of older idiots who had not only told everyone they were driving to Tuscany, but elected to share with the whole street and village that they would also be gone for over a whole month. He deliberately isolated this as the chosen palace of dreams, so he picked the most easily accessible route.

This particular cottage was called Steephill, an odd name, but as the name suggested, it was built on a steep hill and was easy to get to from the path. John jumped over a small wall from the path, onto a flat roof as the house was on tiers. He then walked onto the side of the house and tried the small green cottage window. It was always open, and even if the occupants were away, they always left it slightly ajar, as these cottages needed to be aired and could be musky if left completely closed.

He wrenched the fragile ancient window nearly off the frame and looked around. It was a noise he did not want to make, but it appeared that he had remained undetected, so he held the frame and pulled the old window out a few inches, and it broke the clasp inside and opened. John climbed in through the window and pulled it to the same position, slightly ajar and stood in the small bedroom.

He noticed the time was 11.46pm, and he realised he was practically exhausted and that it had been a very busy and taxing set of circumstances. He could trust no one, and he could not take any information at face value. He went into the landing and then into the master bedroom and looked out of the half-closed curtains. It was quiet, as this was the front of the house and it faced Sheepscombe. There was little in the way of light or travel path for anyone to be on which suited him perfectly.

For the first time in many hours, John relaxed. He went downstairs and entered the kitchen. He opened a cupboard and took out a glass, ran the cold water and filled it. He drank it, repeated the process and looked in the cupboards. He was not hungry now, but he would need to make sure he had supplies if he needed to return here or stay off the grid in the woods or anywhere else.

He went into the lounge and saw the photos carefully placed on the mantle shelf. They reflected images of happy people, and he briefly imagined a normal life once again, but knew that he had failed to make his wife happy, or the children, maybe. He still harboured the thought that just maybe there was still a chance somehow, somewhere for him to have a relationship and happiness. Given his present circumstances, he firmly believed that the notion of any normality returning to his life was highly unlikely.

He went into the small hallway and entered the tiny kitchen. He opened the cupboards and then a small door. Sure enough, it was the pantry stocked like the end of the world was nigh. There were cans of everything, but John knew it was about protein versus weight to carry. He did not want to carry bulky items that did not satisfy his needs or implements of eating or opening, so he elected to take just two tins of corned beef. The tins had the odd older type key opening device attached, and he was not sure if they even did this anymore, so he checked the best before date of consumption and it fell into the same year, that would do. He placed the two cans in his pack and did not eat anything. The pie and the events of the night still lay heavy on his stomach, and conscience and his appetite had all but vanished.

John was aware of movement in the road, so he crept back upstairs and looked out of the tiny window in the back of the house facing the road and the point of entry he had used. He could make out the silhouettes of four men walking in a controlled manner and checking everything and everywhere.

John was unaware if they were the instruments of death for the colonel or Bartholomew Knowles, and it mattered not, as he was absolutely safe and well hidden. He watched them disappear up the road toward Belleview, and the puppet master for the dead man in Belleview must surely know his fate by now, and because of this, they had probably instigated the search. John went downstairs, checked the windows and doors and placed a chair against the front and back doors to render any attempt to break in through these access points useless.

He went back upstairs and noticed it was past midnight, so he lay on a small bed in the back bedroom, placed the Beretta by his side, the sawn off on his chest, and to his surprise, he gently fell asleep.

Chapter 7

Day 3

John had left the curtains as he had found them, arranged to feign someone was in. At 6.15am, the light of the morning sun shone through the eight inch gap in the curtains and invaded the room, and it hit his eyes causing him to become aware of daylight. He rolled onto his right side and felt completely rested and comforted by the duck down duvet he had snuggled around him. He did not want to do anything but stay on this bed, wrapped in this duvet, for the whole day and days to come, so what was stopping him? Logic told him, he was alive, he was warm and he was hidden, but all of these things would be questioned and tested in the next two hours or so. He was aware that during his epic battle for life, he had not been to the toilet in days, and the two in one pie was making it known that he would have to reconcile this.

He went into the bathroom and pulled down pants and boxers and sat on the seat which he noticed was down. He was relieved that the process was swift and without effort, and as he wiped himself, he heard the rattle of the door handle downstairs.

"How the hell can you be caught with your pants down now?" he asked himself, gritting his teeth and pulling up his clothes.

He crept into the bedroom, reached for the safety of the Beretta and the sawn off, and put the pack over his shoulder. He then went to the window carefully and tried to see outside. The visibility was poor, but he could wait. He was not detected, and whoever it had been was merely checking, he thought.

The door handle started to rattle again, but he was indifferent to the idea of challenging whoever it was, or even placing him in a position of being seen, so he breathed heavily, held the firearms and waited. He waited for five minutes and timed it with his Invicta, and when he was sure the threat of his inquisitive would be perpetrator had elapsed sufficiently, he went downstairs and removed both chairs. If they want to come in, he would have to allow it, as it may be a neighbour checking the premises or a family member, a common event when someone went on holiday.

He placed everything back where he had originally found it, remade the bed and flushed the chain in the bathroom. He had not done this immediately on completing his ablutions, as it would have alerted any prospective attacker to his location and confirm human existence was present in the cottage.

John became very nervous and anxious once again, and the elusive feeling of security and the blanket of relaxed normality that he had found was now vanquished by the mere rattle of a door handle. He could not tell if it was innocent or ominous, but given his last encounters with humans, he chose to believe ominous.

He sat by the front window, put his hands in his head and thought about how cruel fate was right now.

"Who are you?" said a young woman standing by the doorway.

John reeled around to face the petit form in front of him.

"How the hell did you get in here?" he asked, staring into her eyes with menace.

"No illusion or trickery, I can assure you. I merely opened the door, you know, like most people do," she replied smiling.

"Who are you?"

"Hang on, you are the one that has broken into my Nan's house, but then I know who you are. You don't need an introduction, Mr John Parks. You have been advertised all over the local newspapers and the television. Tea, Mr Parks?" She filled the kettle and switched it on before producing a small carton of milk from her bag.

"Come join me in here, sit down?" she said, beckoning him to the tiny gate leg kitchen table. "It has to be time for tea."

John joined her, sat and just stared at her in amazement, she was a tiny woman, maybe thirty-five, no wedding ring, bobbed hair to her shoulder and smart even without significant make-up.

"How come you are not afraid of me?" he asked sheepishly.

"You did not do anything, John, and the whole village knows it," she said looking back at him from the sink. "There have been some pretty weird things going on for three days now, and everyone knows you are a hermit who is isolated at Belleview; people talk you know."

"Blimey, I just thought I was normal. I had no idea people thought I was a hermit," he said smiling.

"Wernons is positively crawling with people," she said as she poured the boiling water into two cups with tea bags she had prepared. "It is as if some dignitary is staying there, but in fairness, it is just a load of blokes. How strange is that?"

"How do you know all this?" he asked.

"My sister does some cleaning there, and she said that the first day, three days ago, it was almost as if some kind of special forces, or Thunderbirds had moved in. Tonnes of electronic equipment and military types everywhere including the perimeter night and day and then it all calmed down, as if they were trying to blend in. Some hope of that! That is when the rumour mill cried 'conspiracy theory' when you were framed. Chinese national, my ass. He was Korean."

"How could you possibly know this?" he asked again.

"My friend is a doctor and saw the body; the dead guy was supposed to be Chinese, but even though his head was almost all gone, he did in fact have a locket on him that must have become detached with all the impact and blood and guts, and, I am sorry, I am rambling and getting carried away," she said embarrassed for the number of words per second she was delivering to the world.

"No, please carry on. It is interesting to hear someone else's perspective, and I could certainly use an ally, if only briefly."

"We are an unlikely alliance, John, but anyway back to the blood and guts headless corpse. Sorry, I forgot you did that to him. Anyway again, my doctor friend found a locket where he had been laid out, and it was Korean, and the reason he knows this is that he went to some place in South Korea to do a month of do-goody work," she finally took a breath and stared at him.

John moved his eyes, as if to tease more information from her.

"He saw a picture in the locket, two people obviously in love smiling and happy, but he also saw behind the couple a large bellowing flag on a tower, and it was North Korean. How sloppy is that? An operative with love in his mind and leaving evidence of his ancestry and heritage for each and all to see."

"So what happened next?" John asked.

"He offered it to the authorities, and this guy in a black pair of military style pants and a jumper with elbow pads took it and said he was mistaken. Reeks of conspiracy, John, and that is how I know you are not a killer, well not of innocent women anyway. I hope I am right. I talk way too much, don't I? Sorry, sorry."

"There is no need for an apology, and you have just confirmed that Wernons is key to my future, but I am supposed to retrieve some things this morning, and well, you need to be as far away from me as possible. People around me seem to have a habit of falling foul to harm.

John looked around her, and she pushed his tea to him and sat. She sipped hers and smiled, and he sipped his.

"I know this is going to sound mental, but can you give me your tea?" he asked softly.

"Oh Christ, you think I may have poisoned you? Of course, here; sorry, I did not think. I am not completely tuned into radio *Austin Powers* and espionage," she smiled at him and passed him her tea. She grabbed John's and started to sip it in an exaggerated manner, as if to make a point and to harvest trust.

"Thank you, and I appreciate your understanding, so what is your name?"

"Cynthia, and don't laugh, Cynthia Lillybrook. I sound like a stream going into a pond don't I?"

"You sound great to me Cynthia, just great, and don't be so hard on yourself. I do want you to go, however, it is dangerous to be anywhere around me, and I cannot protect you or invite you to be a blip on my conscience. I just can't."

"Something else you cannot do, my man, is order me about. I shall do exactly as I please," she retorted with authority.

"Cynthia, trust me. The proximity surrounding me is poison and ill fated, so please I beg of you, return to your life and forget you ever saw me or had this conversation, please."

"Shall not. So what have you to do this morning that is dangerous anyway? I can be of assistance, and I can spy."

"I cannot tell you."

"Can't or won't?" she asked petulantly.

"Both," he replied instantly.

"I will follow you then."

"Cynthia, please."

"I know you don't trust me or anyone, and I do understand, but let me walk freely and be your eyes. I can even take a dog. Hey, I can stream images to you by phone. Come on John; what have you got to lose?"

"My life Cynthia and maybe yours; you do not understand. Look, people like you just don't exist, and I am convinced in my mind that you have been planted here, so sorry but that is the way it is."

"Who chose to break into this house John?"

"I did," he replied, almost with shame in his voice.

"Let me show you some things that will change your opinion," she said fiercely.

She went to a drawer in the lounge and pulled out an envelope and came back into the kitchen and sat down. She opened the envelope and emptied the contents onto the table. There were around fifty photographic prints of her and her Nana at varying ages in her cycle of life, doing things around the village.

"I was conceived, accomplished embryonic development and when ready, I was like many others before me ejected from a mother into this world. I was never planted," she had anger in her eyes.

"Calm down Cynthia. You must understand my first concern is for your welfare. My own protective instinct then kicks in for me and my resistance to believing anyone at the moment is kind of easy to see why, surely."

"I am on your side John, and I will prove it to you," she said, and she got up and opened the small kitchen door and went outside.

"Where are you going Cynthia?"

"I will go to walk around by Wernons and…"

"No Cynthia, please don't."

"The park then John. You tell me, and I can move undetected and at least see if there is any change."

"But why Cynthia? Tell me honestly, why?"

"Injustice. I hate it. I have my reasons, and I will hold them dear, so just trust me."

"OK, OK then," he said as he huffed. "The park it is, with your streaming whatever going, but the signal is at best intermittent and I have no device to receive. You mentioned a dog."

"Yes, Alfie, he is at mine, Cambridge Lawn, the flat built onto the side of Jim's house."

"OK, get the dog and just walk around the park," he said. "Remember, no heroics, don't look at anything, let the eyepiece point at different areas, and I will be able to see the rest for myself."

"OK, I will, but hang on. You do not have a phone do you?"

"I do, but it is currently underground," he replied.

"I am not going to ask you what that is all about," she said.

"It's not right you know. It does not feel right, and I cannot trust you Cynthia. I am so sorry, but nobody acts like you do in the wake of the current events and finding a criminal in your Nan's house. I just ..."

Cynthia moved to the drawer before he could finish. She was in the lounge and produced a file and a phone and returned, placing both on the table very quickly. She glared at him.

"When I have gone, read it and then you will trust me," she said with a look of betrayal and anger in her eyes. "Answer the phone too, and you may just learn something," she said before leaving hurriedly.

"Bloody hell!" he shouted.

He opened the file to see a smart upstanding youth dressed in full army uniform and smiling. He then read the headline, and he knew this could not have been manufactured given the time lines.

Family's Grief Turns to Accusations of a Cover up

John read the article, and the lad was Cynthia's brother, David. He had been serving with a patrol in Iraq and had gone missing. There was a lot of talk of friendly fire and a covert operation, but the family was never informed of the true facts. They were told he had died by claymore mine. There was no body to bury, and all of this weighed heavily on the family. Cynthia's mother had buckled under the mounting strain and committed suicide, and her father was dead, so she was now alone apart from her Nana and Grandpa.

There was a huge file dating back several years and the cuttings and reports and military fob off letters reeked of deceit. The information made John aware that this had been a crusade waged by Cynthia. No wonder she was the one person in the world that might actually truly believe him, but he still had a nagging feeling that would not pass.

The phone buzzed and vibrated and then finally the tone went off loudly and John jumped. His heart raced, but he answered quickly and then an app connected. He could clearly see the park.

"Here Alfie!" Cynthia shouted and the picture jumped, as she leaned over and picked up a tennis ball and threw it. She started to walk around the full circumference from the alley by the bowling green, and she went toward the kids play area first.

"There is a van parked at the top of the road by the corner, a VW Transporter thingy by the look," she whispered.

"Come on Alfie!" she shouted.

"Damn, you are good," he whispered.

"Thank you," she replied.

"Christ! You can hear me," he said surprised.

"Of course I can, but be quiet. I will sing if I need to or shout at the dog in a way that alerts you."

She said this without moving her lips at all in case she was being watched through binoculars, but she unfortunately sounded just like a drunken, bad ventriloquist.

John could not believe that ordinary people would sacrifice their safety and offer to help him, but the deep wounds that Cynthia exhibited showed a family in crisis and a girl who would do anything to subject the establishment to embarrassment or exposure.

"*Two little boys on two little toys*," sang Cynthia.

John could see two men by the swings, one was smoking, and they both moved quickly when alerted to Cynthia's close proximity. The dog barked and bounded toward them, and they immediately pretended to be performing exercises.

"Alfie, come back here, boy. Alfie, come back now! shouted Cynthia impatiently yet completely believable.

John caught the image of the two men jogging off, and he heard Cynthia start singing once more.

"I can see clearly now the pigs have gone," she sang giggled, as she delivered the line; she was actually enjoying herself.

"Take care Cynthia, and be super careful down by the gate and dog poo bins. There will be guys there I warn you," whispered John.

Cynthia passed the gate and sure enough, there were two guys, again smoking and looking completely out of character for the environment. They tried to act like they were walking toward the main road, but they just looked stupid after being caught off guard.

Cynthia continued walking down to the far bottom left of the park where she could just see over the wall of Wernons in the distance. The dog had disappeared through a hole in the fence in the park, and she could legitimately look over for him. Although a good distance from the house, she could clearly see lots of activity and men everywhere and vehicles assembled in the driveway.

"So, just what are you doing out this early young lady?" came a familiar voice from behind her.

"You bloody fool!" she shouted, completely outflanking him by being on the offensive. "Why are you creeping around and scaring people, you total idiot?"

"Sorry, I did not mean to alarm you," said the colonel calmly and taken completely off guard.

Just then, and as if on cue, the dog appeared panting and its tongue lay out of its mouth like a bacon medallion.

"You nearly gave me a heart attack, so who the hell are you anyway? I pretty much know everyone in this village, and I certainly don't know you," she bleated furiously, grabbing the dog and picking him up.

"My name is James Rawlings," he said and tried to share conversation, but she was marching off huffing. She started to shake, and she was not happy at all.

"Leave me alone you creepy, repulsive man. Scaring women and creeping about in the morning is not normal," bloody menace.

She turned to give him a further verbal battering, but it was as if he had completely vanished into thin air.

"He is not a magician, sweetheart; he has merely slid under the hole in the fence," whispered John. "He is a trained deadly force and not to be taken lightly. Believe me, I have seen him in action, and he is the one person I fear most. Cynthia, please listen to me carefully."

"I prefer it when you call me sweetheart, darling," she said giggling.

"Cynthia, please do not be flippant, not now. Act angry and bewildered, curse and walk on as if he has disturbed your karma but not enough for him to sacrifice you to the cause."

"Bloody men," she shouted and let Alfie down.

"Go on boy, have a good run because you will be cooped up for a couple of hours and wish you were back here, so enjoy," she said loudly, but she was incredibly audible yet believable.

"Man on a hot tin roof at nine o'clock. Can you see?"

John saw blurred images, and the phone started to crackle.

"Cynt…I… loo…are you th…"

"You are bre… up," she blurted, and she was gone.

The signal had degenerated over a few metres and then it had been lost completely. He was greatly concerned for her welfare but he decided to give her ten or so minutes. Sufficient time he thought for her to deposit the dog back home and come here. He was really worried, and he knew that he could not even attempt to ring her in case he compromised her position and placed her in danger, not normal situations in everyday life, mortal danger.

"Why did I agree to let you get involved, if anything happens," he said out loud.

"If anything happens to you? How sweet John! If anything happened to me, you would be haunted by the apparition of Cynthia Lillybrook, your sweetheart," she giggled. She put Alfie down on the ground and ran into John's arms and hugged him tightly and kissed his neck. She then leaned back, still in his arms, and looked at him with admiration.

"Although this is the best thing that has happened to me for many years, please explain to this idiotic old soul why you felt the need to hug me so beautifully?" asked John, smiling profusely.

"I told you that I believed you, John, and I did and I do. That complete *Men in Black* wanker in the field and all the other conspirators did nothing but confirm that my allegiance was not at all misplaced, that it was in fact on the path of the righteous and that I am completely in tune with what is just, truth and good." She hugged him again, gave him a peck on the cheek and proclaimed, "Tea."

"You are fabulous Cynthia, but he now knows you and will recognise you, so it is not safe for you here. Can you go somewhere?

"What, and leave you here to the wolves? Don't be absurd John. I am in this for the long haul. Someone has to pay and people need to know," she replied. "Anyway, I can help."

"How?" asked John.

"There is an anonymous site that you can drop any conspiracy theories to. It would mean typing everything, sending it by post to a PO Box and waiting, but it works. I embarrassed quite a few people with my theories regarding my brother's execution," she said.

"Execution?" said John startled.

"Yes, execution. I heard whispers and tales from the front, and he was executed by a rogue officer, not unlike the ones you and I are now dealing with."

"Christ, I have never been so confused or had such little faith in our secret service," he said.

"Welcome to my world, John."

"I do not want to welcome you to mine, Cynthia."

"Too late, I am in it."

"I have to retrieve the iPad thing," he said. "I have to somehow get into the park and get it. There is some leverage in it; I know there is."

"I could cause a distraction if you like," she said, eyes bright and full of enthusiasm.

An image flashed across his mind, it was unfortunately, an image of Cynthia lay with blood oozing from her eyes and mouth.

"No, you have to stay here Cynthia. No way are you going near him or the park," John insisted.

"I could walk the dog again."

"You have already done that, so think professional then think killer," he retorted.

"Sorry, just trying to help," she said softly.

"Sorry Cynthia, I just do not want you further involved, so let me think for a minute. I need logic."

It was now 8.06am, and he knew he was expected soon and that they were already prepared.

"I have an idea," said Cynthia, and she disappeared out of the door with Alfie in her arms. John had no time to question her or try to stop her.

About fifteen long minutes later, a van pulled up outside, a transit Connect with a lot more rust than it should have.

"Get in with all of your deadly force," she said.

John did not question her, and as time was running out, he grabbed his pack, shotgun and Beretta and climbed into the van.

"Get in the back, big boy," she commanded giggling.

"It's not funny," he said but he complied.

"Hide to the side," she said politely, "and put that dust sheet over you just in case."

She then drove the van toward the park but she turned off into White Horse Lane. She drove the Connect to the turning port at the end and reversed the van onto the drive of the furthest property.

"Wait here," she blurted softly.

John heard a rickety garage door open, and she jumped back in the vehicle and reversed into it. She then exited and closed the front garage door and opened the back door of the vehicle.

"Come on out. No one can see us from here," she said with renewed excitement.

"Where the hell are we? Who owns this house?" John asked.

"It is my Auntie's house, well, she is not my real Auntie, but she grew up by us and always… I am talking too much again aren't I? Sorry, I am really rambling on."

"You are lovely," said John and he leant over and gently kissed her on the mouth with just enough pressure to touch but not truly engage.

She grabbed him tightly and she kissed him full on, the sensation he felt was one of euphoria tinged with ecstasy, and he was in utopia. He pulled back instantly.

"Sorry Cynthia, but I shouldn't have let you do that. You are already in danger, and this makes you, not only a weakness and a bargaining chip for them, but a target too."

She moved towards him, but he repelled her gently.

"I won't have any harm come to you, especially because of me" he told her sternly. "I certainly won't be complicit and engage you in acts of stupidity. I like you far too much for that, and anyway, I want to get to know you under normal circumstances. There is that bloody word again," he said.

"What word?"

"The most frightening word in the English vocabulary, 'circumstance'. It conjures up all sorts thoughts of dastardly deeds and acts ranging from aggression to heinous merciless barbaric carnage. It is amazing how one circumstance can plummet you into a spiral of fear and death and dishonesty, followed by many other circumstances that fashion the outcome I guess."

"Mull these facts over, please, I met you and you broke into my Nana's house. That is a circumstance that brought us together, so don't forget, Johnny boy, circumstances can work in your favour too," she said gently and walked to the back door.

It was a single exit and it was completely covered by shrubs and a hedge. Over the years the hedge had grown over the shrub, and as they intertwined, they had formed a small arch about a metre high. The arch had been cut inside to form a small passage up the steep incline to near the park fence.

"We used to use this as our secret passage, David and I," she whispered, "when we were just little children."

"Stay here then please, and at least let me investigate if there are any baddies up there," he said smiling, but it was a fearful smile, tainted with nervous anxiety.

"Hang on," she kissed him, and when he released from the embrace, she was standing there with one of his sawn off shotguns in her hand.

"I used to go pheasant shooting every weekend, so don't underestimate my need for revenge or my accuracy with a twelve bore either."

"I think it is a five gauge," he said smiling. "This is just too farfetched you know, girl."

"Don't be facetious Johnny boy, a country girl that can fire a shotgun, duh," she said and beckoned him to follow her.

John quickly pulled her back, put his finger to his mouth to gesture her to exhibit silence.

"Don't you dare shoot me in the ass either," he said softly.

"Nice ass," she whispered, again giggling

He moved forward through the arch of foliage with his hands placed firmly yet silently in front of him, and he crept on all fours. His knee dug into a sharp stone, and it was all he could do to refrain from screaming out but that would have had devastating consequences. He came to the end of the arch, and it turned inwards, a clever ploy to stop anyone from the park knowing of its existence, and it protected the children in their wonderland as they played.

He looked all around, and he could neither hear nor see anything to give him any concern. He was only about twenty feet from the badger set where he had hidden the iPad device, and this was also located close to the phone.

"Do not move, Cynthia, and I mean do not move a muscle under any circumstances, no matter what prevails. Do you promise?"

"I do," she said looking at him with her big eyes.

John clutched the sawn off and left the safety of the arch and stopped as he walked to the metal fence perimeter of the park. It had a cold feel, and he was determined to, but…

"Good morning, Mr Parks. Fancy seeing you here," said the colonel, as he slid back the mechanism on his handgun, the one pointed directly at John's midriff.

He should have ensured it was ready to fire prior to the encounter, but this was an obvious display of egoistic machoism, and he revelled in his superiority regarding stealth.

John looked at the sawn off in his hand, and he now realised he had dropped the Beretta somewhere behind him.

"What were you thinking John? Wake the whole of Gloucestershire with a bloody sawn off in the early morning dew? What a frivolous notion," he said sarcastically.

"Are you going to kill me?" John asked almost resigned to the fact that this was more than likely the morning he would expire.

"Yes, but I need that device John. Thank you by the way for eliminating my double agent. You saved me having to dispose of a thoroughly nice chap, really just a double crossing traitor, but then, aren't we all?"

The colonel smiled, and he sickened John. People like him always got their way and seemed to be the old people on the park bench telling their life story and living to a ripe old age.

"Now John, if you wouldn't mind telli ugh, ugh, ugh," he could not finish his sentence.

The blood appeared on his upper shoulders and then his neck exploded, as the bullet exited. John looked into his eyes as he fell to his knees. He was clutching the wound then his eyes rolled. He had complete disbelief in his look, then he fell forward, twitched then nothing; he was dead.

Behind him, Cynthia had the stance of someone who knew how to respect recoil, aim steadily and to shoot true.

"He killed my brother. He killed David," she said with tears streaming down her face.

"Quickly Cynthia, get back in the arch! I need to collect the equipment."

"NO. Get it. I will keep guard," she said and waved him to go.

John ran to the set, squeezed through a gap under the fence and retrieved the device. He then ran, got the mobile and then returned to her. She was staring at the corpse on the ground. He grabbed Cynthia's arm, and they ran back under the arch and slid quickly down to its entrance and into the garage.

Cynthia was shaking and retching. She was visibly disturbed by what she had done and seemed emotionally broken, even a bit too much, so he needed to regain her attention and focus on the man she had despatched.

"Look at the arch, Cynthia. Look at where you and that dear little boy played. He took your brother and the future you could of enjoyed as siblings, he has been punished. Do you understand!" he shouted.

"Yes, I do. I just feel… I feel…"

"You feel hollow and anxious sweetheart, and you feel sick and dry in your throat and as if you will never recover, but believe me, you will," John said reassuringly.

John opened the door of the garage, jumped into the driver side and beckoned Cynthia to get in. He started the vehicle and drove out, exited the van, closed the garage door and got back in. He drove off just as the phone burst into life.

"Shall I answer it?" asked Cynthia.

"No, he can wait, and we need to get out of the vicinity. We will be tracked by the phone and device, but we can hide the device again. This is what is keeping me, well us, alive at the moment."

"We form an unlikely alliance; don't you think?"

"Yes, Cynthia, but how did you arrive at the point of no mercy with the colonel? How do you know that he was even remotely linked to the death of David?"

"That horrible man said his name was James Rawlings when I asked him this morning, and he gave you a different name; didn't he?" she asked through the tears.

"Yes, I believe he did," he replied humouring her and trying to steer the dilapidated vehicle through the lane up passed the Mill House.

"That was the name I was told was involved in David's execution. The man's name, the leader, was definitely called James Rawlings, and I am sure of it," she said with no element of doubt. She was absolutely convinced that her actions and judgement were right, and it was a righteous kill.

The phone rang again, so John stopped the vehicle.

"Wait," he said to the caller coldly.

They were in Sheepscombe, so he had veered into the side of the road by a few shrubs and trees. He put his hand over the mouthpiece.

"Get out and hide here. Hurry!"

She started to protest ,but John had pulled open the van door opener and ushered her out.

"Just wait here. I will be five minutes."

He then drove a hundred metres to the spot where he had stopped on the scooter to observe Belleview all those long days ago.

"Knowles, I presume," he answered putting the phone to speaker mode.

"Ah good morning, Mr Parks. I trust you slept well, but you have been a busy boy yet again."

"What do you want?" John asked impatiently, as he climbed into the back of the van and saw a very logical course of action laid out before him. He would keep this activity very quiet and see if the plan developed as he intended.

"Firstly, to congratulate you for the colonel's demise, priceless move, not even the best operative would expect a love struck co-conspirator to appear from the brush clutching a Beretta, then being able to shoot so adequately too. She is a keeper, John, but then you used that very term just the other day did you not, but that was not the happy ending that you were anticipating."

"You want the device Knowles?" asked John continuing to work industriously to ensure his plan would work.

"Indeed I do. Your perception is overwhelming."

"Then what? What happens Knowles? I get whacked. Everyone gets whacked, so is that the plan?"

"We have never met John, and you have absolutely no idea who I am, what I look like or where I am on the planet. I have no gain from your death, only from the device. I give you my word that I will not be responsible for 'whacking you' as you call it."

As the man was speaking, John had finished stage one of his plan, so he then put stage two into action. He got the device and wrapped it in a plastic bag that was in the back of the van. He found more bags and double and triple bagged it. He then got out of the car, went to the other side of the road where he made sure his actions were clearly visible to anyone able to watch. There was a silo tank through a gate. He walked over to it and he opened the top, he then let the device sink in. It smelt awful, but his actions would surely at least mask any tracking device.

"John, the tracking signal is due to come on soon, so where is the device? What have you done John? John, John…"

John left the phone by where the van was, and he finished stage three of his four stage plan and picked up Cynthia and drove off.

"What did you do that was so important I had to be in the hedge?" she asked obviously offended.

"They may have been following the tracker with cameras, binoculars, anything, so why expose you to any more harm than necessary? It would not have made sense, anyway, the device is sunk in the deep shit of the silo so they can piss off."

John and Cynthia parked the van up by a side gate in the lane by a field and ran through to the hedgerow and followed it up to the bottom of Tibbiwell. They quickly made their way to Nana's cottage, and as they arrived, they saw the helicopter hovering over the spot where they had discarded the device, and where John had carefully left the phone.

"Here," she said handing him some binoculars. She grabbed his hand and led him up the stairs.

"Thank you," he said.

"It's not called Steephill Cottage for nothing. Look out to the left. You can actually see the road where we were," she said smiling, and her eyes gestured him to get on with it.

John lifted the binoculars, focused the lenses to suit his vision, and sure enough, there were vans. Of course they were VW Transporter vans. John had been played once again, and it was blatantly apparent now, that the colonel and Bartholomew Knowles were in fact heavily linked in this fiasco.

"What is going on, John?" Cynthia asked inquisitively.

"You look, sweetheart. It is crawling with the Colonel's men, the same men from the Weighbridge Inn. It was all a ruse to flush out the device, no doubt of that, or they were in fact double-crossing each other for it, so there must be an extreme value to this thing. I cannot quite understand why this Knowles guy had his agent killed in Belleview then sent the colonel. It all seems weird and strange to me. There is no logic to these actions, and logic is what I process, not this crap.

Cynthia did look through and then dropped the binoculars. She looked tense and John rubbed her shoulders before she turned around to hug him.

"Just hold me please, John. I need to be cuddled."

"No problem, and forever seems good," he whispered.

They both went down to the kitchen. Cynthia proceeded to fill the kettle, no matter what had happened, it was still tea time. John reloaded the Beretta and placed it on the kitchen table.

"Cynthia, you need to put this in your bag, or hide it on you, but you need to have this," he said.

"What about you?" she immediately asked showing concern for what she imagined was unnecessary exposure.

John produced a fully loaded Beretta, exactly the same model, and he also pulled out some ammunition clips.

"This is the one I took off the dead guy at Belleview last night, but don't worry, I have a Chinese one too somewhere," he said.

"You talk about them like they are pens or pencils. Don't get too familiar or comfortable with them. Please don't forget that you need to head for armistice, disarmament and normality, remember that.

"I know. Three days ago, the very thought of a gun in my hand would have been completely ridiculous, let alone firing it," he said.

"If it's any consolation, Johnny boy, I did not have any intention of my week including the shooting death of a covert operative who had killed my brother. Look at my bloody hands, they are shaking uncontrollably," she shoved them out and they were trembling badly.

John clasped her hands in his and looked sympathetically into her eyes, and he noticed they were not shaking when held.

"I did not want you involved."

"I know, but what now?"

"Have you got somewhere to go where no one knows about? Somewhere that is completely off the grid."

"Yes, when I was winding up the newspapers and planting conspiracy theories, I had and still have a retreat. I also have some tricks, but I don't want to leave you."

"You will be the death of me, literally, if you stay. I will be more worried and conscious about you than I should be, and I will be careless. Please, I need you safe, so I can finish this, whatever it is."

"OK." She opened the door and disappeared shouting, "An hour, Johnny boy."

John had some terrible thoughts. 'Maybe she was involved, or maybe she had gone for help. Maybe she had.'

John ran to the van and unloaded what he needed and accomplished phase four of his plan. He was pleased that he had achieved so much in such little time, and this was undoubtedly a life saver.

"Hi, Johnny boy," she said as she bounded through the door.

She was now blonde by way of a realistic wig and had a pair of tight, revealing white trousers on and a t-shirt that heightened his appreciation of her being an attractive, feminine, sexy woman.

"Wow," he said.

"What do you think, Johnny boy?"

"You look fabulous girl, absolutely lovely, but strange, being blonde and all that."

"I used to do this regularly when I wanted quiet time away from the case and the limelight. We are going to take my Nana's car. It is parked in a garage down the road. I will tell the nosy neighbours that I am taking it to be serviced and that a guy from the garage will return it later.

They will not only believe it, but you can return without suspicion, and all will be hunky dory," she said satisfied with the plan.

"OK, and you, how do we get you safe?"

I will drive us to the wildest point that I know, and there I will catch a bus once you have driven off. You will not even know the direction I am taking, and I will change transport several times before arriving at my destination. She was writing as she talked to him and passed him a phone number.

"This way John, you cannot be compromised and nor can I. We will not know what each other is doing apart from you are going to return the car to the garage, go out the back door, follow the path and you will come to the front garden of Steephill.

"OK, but how will I know that you are safe?" he asked.

"Neither of us have that luxury John, and you know that, but we will meet after all of this has gone away. I promise you that. If you feel it is safe, or that you need to join me, or that you cannot see a way out, text this number. I will make sure we rendezvous and that we are reunited, somehow. I am only leaving because you are correct. I am a liability and will cloud your judgement, and I also need to secure a safe haven for you and I, either short or long term."

She smiled, but it was a nervous smile, and it was blatantly apparent that she did not really want to go anywhere.

"I will be reunited with you Cynthia. Count on it," he said.

"Come on. I will go and pack a small discreet bag and get the car. I will be up here in a few minutes, OK?"

"OK, Cynthia, but I don't like you being exposed like this," he said.

"And if I stay?" she said, leaving the cottage.

"Something does not feel right," he said to himself. "Something is just not right. Logic, John."

Fifteen minutes or so later, the car pulled up outside the house as she had said, and Cynthia bounded in the house.

"Come on, Johnny boy. Let's go. Get in the back and keep down."

"OK," he complied.

"I am driving to the common, Minchinhampton Common, OK?"

"OK," he said.

She set off and drove to the common. It was close by, through Stroud and on the Nailsworth road, and she veered off left, and after a couple of miles, she arrived and drove into the beautiful common with golfers all keen and ready to embarrass themselves, yet again.

She pulled the car into a side road and sat in a layby.

"Here we are, Johnny boy."

John climbed out of the backseat, and she got out, so he did too.

She hugged him, but something had changed. There was an urgency in her actions that defied logic, maybe she was scared now and things were beginning to sink in.

She hugged, kissed, and begged him to go quickly and not to even look back.

She gave him a locket she was wearing and promised that they would be reunited and that things would be OK.

John complied. He did not like it, but he complied. He went to the driver's side and got in, turned the key, placed the car in gear and drove off without looking in the mirror directly, but he watched her until he had to be out of sight.

When he returned to the garage, he passed right by it and parked by a cottage just down the road. The reason for this was that he spotted a well-known builder-come-decorator's van, parked in the driveway of a house in the lane.

The owner of the van was called Stan, and he was more than a bit of a womaniser, he was a philanderer of some note but also a likeable rogue to most locals. He was affectionately known to some due to his antics, and to many others he was just a good decorator, but for the most, he was known by many a husband in the village. They were not so affectionate.

There were exaggerated stories of his midnight retreats from first floor windows all over the village and surrounding countryside. It was also well-known gossip in the village that sexy Stan would not contemplate having any relationship with a woman who was married but who had a cottage with no upstairs escape strategy.

A popular Royal Oak outburst and slanderous affiliation to his antics from many locals was, "If the window did not open enough for Stan to jump out of, he did not try to jump into her front entrance."

"He is the Painswick prick," announced one drunken reveller at the New Year lock in. She was a councillor and popular rumour had it that sexy Stan had apparently had her fireplace stoked with something.

John picked up the locket and inspected it. The whole idea of it offended him for some reason, as it just did not feel right. He was conscious that he was becoming paranoid, but even when armed with this negative notion, he knelt down at the back of the van and tied it underneath on the rusty old exhaust clamp.

John also placed the completed phase four item into the car and drove to the top of the hill where there was a large field entrance and the land fell steeply to a gully. The gully was covered in brambles and thick dense undergrowth and then it was met by another field. He thought his plan was going to be derailed when he saw a farmer on a tractor, but the unsuspecting man turned in the opposite direction. The phase four complete item, which was heavy, was unloaded, and he used all of his strength to get it to the highest part and then he let it roll down the hill. It careered into the thick dense undergrowth with brambles and nettles covering it completely, the gully created a formidable barrier to anyone trying to reach it.

Chapter 8

Bartholomew Knowles

Bartholomew Knowles was at best, one of the most articulate yet ruthless and psychotic pathological killers in existence. This was a dangerous combination in itself, however, his mantle was further gilded by virtue that he had been diagnosed a sociopath from his early formative years. He had sustained the evil premise of barbaric bully, not normal bullying, torture, and he was linked to the suicide of a thirteen year old boy when he was himself only twelve, being cited as a contributing factor to the untimely death. He had been banished from three private schools for cruelty to fellow boarders and for killing animals in ways that made Genghis Kahn look like a reasonable guy.

Later in his early twenties, he had been excommunicated from the British army and any government position for crimes against humanity and was wanted for various crimes involving violence, fraud and commercial espionage. He was also highly intelligent. He was so far above average that he was diagnosed as bordering on the highest functioning plateau of the now renamed, autistic spectrum.

His gift for planning, executing actions and his absolute unwavering capacity to kill without flinching, made him an unparalleled and evil adversary for anyone, let alone the fledgling would-be hero, Mr John Parks.

He sat in the huge, leather, wingback chair in the study of Wernons. The chair was fashioned of red leather, worn but authentic to the character and décor of the lovely stately house and the grandeur of its ownership over the past and present years. It had button studs, lots of them, and before him was a solid oak writing desk with a green top inlay. He stared curiously at the screen in front of him. Nothing of significance was evident, just a grid map like Google maps, but he stared intensely at it.

"We underestimated this guy, Jenkins," he said quietly, yet when he spoke, everyone would listen and fear followed his every breath.

"He outflanked us because he had an accomplice," replied Jenkins.

"My dear boy, was that a pathetic attempt to shift blame given the damming evidence before us? Remember that all wars are not won or lost on what we know happened, it is that which is yet to happen that is significant, and surely this scenario sources our intelligence to gain our knowledge in advance. My team has let me down," he said.

"Sir, with due respect."

"There is absolutely no respect for failure, Jenkins!" he shouted, and he banged his fist on the table hard. His eyes glared, and the saliva left his mouth as he erupted.

Everyone in the room shook and Jenkins moved backwards and then regained his position.

The atmosphere completely changed in an instant, and Jenkins shuddered with fear. The three other men standing at the back of the room looked down to their feet.

"Yes, you do well to bow your heads in shame, you complete wankers. Have you seen this guy Parks' resume?" he said so quietly, as if he had not just achieved the levels of fear he had. "He is actually less than adequate, below normal, normal, normal! In fact he is not even normal. He was born a prick, and he has achieved all his living days lived like a prick, but he evades death like a fucking cat with ninety-nine lives," he said with his voice once again gaining deep loud decibels, and the men were rigid, trying not to be disrespectful yet not to gain direct eye contact with the ruthless killer before them.

"Even with all of the electronic tagging and surveillance at your disposal, the endless crews of highly trained operatives, endless budget, double agents and scams and trickery, helicopters, canine units, this prick not only kills the colonel and about twelve highly trained men, but he also gets someone to help him. And that's even after he is portrayed as a bloody wok slayer on the TV. What is he? A bloody magician?"

"Sir, I thought the colonel's team had killed most of the guys and kept John Parks alive," said Jenkins sheepishly.

"Well Mr Jenkins, this is where you have it all wrong. This is probably the most freaky element in all of this. I cannot even begin to get my head around this."

He paused and stared at the man in front of him, who tried his hardest not to stare back, then he relaxed, an unusual posture for this lethal individual.

"Tell me something. How does this mild mannered, complete life failure, Grizzly Adams looking, hillbilly hippy motherfucker, suddenly become Annie Oakley and hit absolutely everything that he aims at?"

"I don't understand, sir," said Jenkins quietly.

"You don't get it; do you man? Must be beyond the levels of what you can comprehend, Jenkins." He stood up and walked around the table, then moved back toward Jenkins who immediately cowered and moved backwards slightly and was visibly disturbed at the fact that he was confronted by Knowles. He did not cope very well, being so close to the threat of an imminent strike and pain, or worse.

"Everyone that this wanker claimed he shot, he bloody did. The colonel told me that if the prick got a rifle he was mental deadly. He called it something like sight receptive, and he said he did not have snipers recoil either, a rare gift."

"What is that, sir?" asked Jenkins, raising his eyebrows as he did.

"You know when you go the fairground sometimes or an arcade, well maybe you would not, Jenkins, as you are not human, but some people have a unique aptitude for shooting. These are rare individuals, but when one of them enters the army or services and demonstrates the uncanny ability to shoot a gnat's balls off at twelve hundred metres, he is cordially referred to as 'sight receptive'. This means that whatever is in his sight, is receptive to being dead, or at least shot exactly where he wanted to shoot him, or her, or the bloody dog. He even shot the bloody dog. What a complete bastard."

"And snipers recoil, sir?"

"This is where a guy can shoot shedloads of people but demonstrates no recoil himself," said Knowles, almost with admiration in his voice.

"Sorry, sir. I still don't understand."

"It means, Jenkins, that he has simply developed a numbness to killing, the taking of life, and he doesn't care like a civilian anymore. He has been pushed so far over the precipice of a normal everyday existence that he cannot remember the day it began when all the fear and anxiety made him feel sick, his stomach contorted, dry throat, the signs of fear and repugnant failure to live within normal Christian barriers. Now he doesn't."

He huffed and folded his arms.

"Do you realise that we have inadvertently produced a killer. We have pressed so much fear and so many adrenalin rushes into that boy that any normal human expectancy has diminished completely: old habits, expectations, love and life. He looks at everything in a completely different light now."

"Christ, he is a time bomb, sir," offered Jenkins.

"Worse. He is demonstrating logic and patience, and he is developing by the hour. Christ, is he resourceful for an everyday Joe! His own deep and hidden survival instincts and his high alpha male primeval desire to wipe out adversaries has surfaced dramatically. He is a dangerous man, in fact, he is bloody dangerous man, so do not underestimate him."

"How can we find him, sir, if there is no tracker and he has ditched the phone?" asked Jenkins.

"Bait, Jenkins. We now know there is no human bait, so we have to divert our efforts and change tactics. We will use his apparent love of crown and country, and we will encourage his patriotism to shine and be visible. We will lure him out with the prospect of telling someone he will trust, and then we will kill him after we get the device, of course. He must be kept alive, and I must have that decoder at any premium."

"Could we just let him go?" said Jenkins.

Knowles just stared at him, withdrew his sidearm and pressed it into the temple of Jenkins.

"People do not just get let go. He has the fucking decoder, you prick, so how do we get to extract the bloody plans if we cannot decode the entrance protocol?"

There was a muffled 'phut' as the bullet entered the open air, and the man standing in the middle of the three men at the back of the room fell to the ground like a rock. He was shot directly through the middle of his forehead.

"Would anyone else like to suggest something completely ludicrous? I have plenty more bullets."

"No, sir," echoed around the room.

"If any of you fail me again, you now know your fate. Now get rid of that asshole and clean up my office!" He marched out, and they all looked at each other and let out a loud breath of relief, apart from the corpse left on the floor with eyes staring ahead.

"Where the hell is my coffee?" he shouted as he entered the kitchen.

A man passed him a coffee, and Knowles sipped it slowly.

He marched off back to the office and watched as his men mobilised themselves under the threat of death if they were to fail. He was thinking that the world of industrial or commercial espionage was probably a more brutal theatre than any blood war. At least blood wars usually held a pride and commitment from the heart, not the wallet, but most had a noble motive no matter how twisted it appeared. Some even boasted having honesty of sorts and a sense of fair play, but war is never fair. Someone dies but still not to worry.

He loved the world of industrial and commerce, and the difference was easy to see. Everyone was driven by the coin, the most evil of enticement. Currency was as dangerous as religion, as it shaped the world in a way that only religion could many years ago when guidance was needed. Now it was a sustainable income and provided things for humans. The phone rang, so he left the huge bay window and sat in the throne.

"My dear chap, did you take care of the small issue that remained unresolved last night, old man," asked a voice that appeared to come from somebody who was accomplishing two tasks at once.

"No, but it is in hand. I can assure you that he will not breathe past this day."

There was a pause and deep breathing and some clicking as if a keyboard was being used during the conversation.

"Bravo, good man. You remain brimming with confidence, and this is what I like to hear, but let me remind you that this was the exact same answer that I received only yesterday," said the man.

"Listen to me carefully. I have never failed, and I am not going to start now," said Knowles sternly.

"Do you think he has affiliated himself with the Americans, Russians or the Chinese? What about the Koreans?"

"He has no affiliation. I can assure you, but he is using a Beretta, but not off an American. He may be an eco-warrior, as he is shooting up the world with sawn off shotguns," said Knowles.

"Bravo!" the man shouted.

"He is however like a pinball being pushed from pillar to post, and he has no idea who is who or what is what and he will trip up soon. I can assure you he will."

"I hear the colonel got iced by a novice, bravo! What a fitting end to a chequered career, but still, if he meets all those he despatched at the gates of hell, there will be a bloody big crowd."

"Won't we all have the same fate? We, none of us, are without acts of attrition that will surely catch us out one day," said Knowles.

"What is this chap like? How has he stayed alive so long?" asked the man.

"Good question. I believe he is incredibly lucky, but he is an assiduous foe. He applies logic, believes absolutely nothing of anything or anyone and seems to look at the worst case scenario in every situation; therefore, he compensates for it, very often with a hail of buckshot or bullets."

"Bravo!" the man shouted again.

"I am glad this amuses you," said Knowles.

"David and Goliath man, where is your sense of underdog association? He is your nemesis, but it is quite amusing, don't you think? He is a loquacious force without having to speak a word. Actually bloody good stuff if he wasn't causing me to be questioned from the board."

"Listen, this guy has a propensity for fair play and is a patriot. I can feel it. I am going to leak some information out there in the media then get him safe, back into Belleview and then dangle my trump card in front of him. I know he is a sucker for a female, the incident with the Russian at the Edgemoor proved that, so I shall employ virtually the same tactics, but I will place him in a 'him or her' situation. He will always be chivalrous and will comply because he won't be able to help himself."

"I thought you said he is ruthless," said the man.

"Yes, ruthless," replied Knowles, "but also completely lonely and has a feeling of terror and isolation, coupled with failure. Trust me, I have been in this game for a long time, and he will succumb to this plan. Just wait and see. Have we got the money arranged?"

"Ten million in all the currencies you requested, and all are, of course, completely untraceable notes. It is available and will be with you in the morning, but look after it. Men die for a lot less," said the man sternly.

"Excellent. I will have this sorted by tomorrow," said Knowles with utter and convincing confidence.

"OK, as usual I will trust your judgement, but the decoder is of paramount importance. Just where and how did he put the damn thing somewhere where we could not see?" said the man not really asking, more informing himself again.

"I will know this shortly, so don't worry. We can talk later, but I have to get things moving," said Knowles.

There was no goodbye, just the click of the receiver, and the conversation was over and the path clear.

Knowles checked his watch. It was 11.08am, and he felt tired and needed to rest.

"Good morning, Daddy," said a fragile female voice from just inside the doorway.

Knowles spun round and a smile appeared on his face.

"Good morning, Cynthia. Come in and close the door; did everything all go to plan?"

"Hook line and sinker. He is in love with me Daddy, after all, who could resist my charm though, no normal mortal?"

"Has he got the number?"

"He has. Don't worry, Daddy. He will call."

"Good, I have a press release and cover story hitting the twelve o'clock news, so hopefully he will see it and put down his guard," said Knowles.

"Are you sure he was one hundred per cent convinced that you are the brother of David Lillybrook? Did he buy it completely Cynthia? He is far more clever than we have given him credit for to date."

"Yes Daddy, and he is a nice guy really. Shame I will have to kill him, but thanks for letting me get rid of the colonel. He is, sorry 'was' always undressing me with his eyes and made me feel vile."

"He was a liability to be honest, a good and trusted operative in his time, but this is not the game of the old. Game of Bones is not going to sell. I have planned his demise for months, and he has nestled nicely into the façade. He made Parks feel comfortable and as if he were on the side of the righteous. What a prick really. I reeled Parks in when the colonel was looking for him, but who would have thought he would have guessed that Parks would have sussed the gravel pits plan and kill the guys in the van? Good stuff really."

"So what now? Lay low and do what?"

"You do absolutely nothing, and you have to stay completely out of sight. Don't even go by windows or in the garden. We will flush him out no problem, but he has an extra heartbeat for you, so we can use it to our advantage," said Knowles smiling.

"Did the team clean up the mess at Belleview? He may find it hard going back there, especially with all the blood up the stairs and on the wall," she said grimacing.

"It is spotless, as if nothing ever happened, in fact, it has been completely sanitised to eradicate any prints or even shoe prints or fibres or hairs, blah blah blah, the usual, Cynthia. How long do you think it will be before he calls you? After he sees the news perhaps?"

"Dear Daddy, he has a hard on for me and life, so he will call pretty much immediately I think. I told you that he is in love."

"OK, show me on the map where he placed the device."

"He placed it in the silo tank opposite those trees and that inlet there. It has some significance for him, and he

217

was sharing lots, but he is still reserved, and he is certainly abnormal for a civilian," she said.

"I know, it has thrown me a bit, his running around eluding everyone and capable of killing. That's the bit I cannot fathom, he has started to kill people at will, without showing the normal signs a civilian would. He is not being sick or feeling bad," he said scratching his chin.

"Perhaps he is turning into you, Daddy. Yes, he is a prodigy of you," she replied smiling.

"God forbid," he said smiling back.

"Worse if he started to change into me. Imagine if he wanted to be a girl? Perish the thought."

"Oh Cynthia, don't. Ugh."

"Oh by the way, where have the three stooges gone, Jenkins and the other idiots brigade?"

"Gone to kill Parks."

"But I thought you were going to?"

"Don't fret Cynthia. They never left Wernons and are dead already."

"WOW! I didn't see that coming," she said.

"We need to start to accomplish this task, be ruthless and get rid of waste and failure."

"I agree completely," she said, appeasing him.

"Anyone who fails will be terminated," he said coldly.

"Does that include me, Daddy?"

"Don't call me that for Christ sake. What if the men hear you? I need respect and no hint of favouritism. You have to respect the chain of command girl and sit with the knowledge that with the continuation of fear and self-doubt, they follow me without question. They are strong as a trunk but weak as branches."

"You did not answer my question, sir," she said.

"Just never test me," he said in an ice cold voice, devoid of any facial expression or emotion.

"I would never test you, sir," she replied formally.

"I want you to get some rest. We have a big day tomorrow, and I need to cap this one off before it blows up in all of our faces."

"Why did you use Parks to retrieve the decoder from Belleview? Why didn't you just let me go, so there was no chance of this situation occurring."

"He was free to roam, and any one of us that approached Belleview would have been killed. The agent inside was playing everyone and had tipped everyone off. This is essentially how I knew he needed to go but also that Parks was protected. He could accomplish this and walk. The rest of the players would simply let him breeze off into the sunset walk and lead them to me, but it is never going to happen now thanks to you."

Chapter 9

Faith

John lowered his binoculars. He felt cold and shivered. He was completely supine and overwhelmed with betrayal and anxiety at the image he had seen through the lenses. He had taken this innocent and apparently helpful girl into his confidence, nearly trusted her, and yet she hovered above him like the Sword of Damocles.

He had guessed there was some form of tyrannical undertone brewing and that evil was evident around him, and this was not just a gut feeling. Once again, this was deduced from overwhelming evidence, although not all of the pieces fitted the jigsaw. This was more due to the simple appliance of logic. Cynthia had simply made an error in her story.

She had claimed that the colonel had introduced himself as James Rawlings, the man in the file accused of the orchestrated execution of Private David Lillybrook, her brother and a martyr in her eyes. His absolution from disgrace and knowledge that someone was going to pay for his apparent unnecessary death, had, according to her story, been her sole reason to live and the driving force behind everything she ever did or was planning.

Just how was it then that she had got the name of David's killer wrong? It was an impossible mistake for a grief stricken, angry, resentful sibling, surely. When she was walking around the field, John had read every inch of the file and studied all of the data. The man named was in fact called 'John' Rawlings and not 'James' as stated. This was a simple, yet immature, mistake to make, especially for a trained operative. The same letter but a whole different name and an enormous miscarriage of justice for her brother. If she could not even collate the information that was so blatantly described, something had to be wrong, and he had known that she was fake at that very moment.

The date of David's killing and the hour date of his return home did not seem to collate properly either. He would have had to have been transported back the very same night as the perilous act or even before. Given the time delays and average flight time, this was an impossible timeframe to achieve even though she claimed there was no body, just fragments perhaps. The other worrying aspect was just why did he not get transported into Wotton Basset? It was a good story, but it did in her own words, leave room for credible, conspiracy theories.

John felt absolutely and utterly heartbroken but had to keep fully aware of his surroundings. He was obviously exposed, perched in the bushes above Wernons, yet again. This time he had more awareness of the dangers that surrounded him and the obvious stealth of the ground troops. He had placed twigs on all points leading to his present hideout with a view to them giving alarm to intruders. This would at least let a cracking sound be exuded, and the obvious imminent dangers would give him the chance to empty the shotguns and Beretta.

Once again, he trained the binoculars on the office window and saw Cynthia lean toward, place her arm on his shoulder, and give an older man a kiss and walk out of his vision and he anticipated, the room. It was not a sexual kiss, so he swiftly applied logic and in his mind he ascertained it was a member of her family, or an exceptionally close friend, as there was a comfort apparent in the embrace found only in a long or meaningful relationship. He then thought, what am I thinking? She is trained, she could turn that act on when she wanted and without trying, but he could see that she knew him well.

He could see the man now standing in the bay window. He had opened the window as a large cigar was being devoured and smoke billowed out of the man and the house. He was a very distinguished man, grey but well-groomed and thick hair, fit for his age, thick set, and he gave the impression from his stance that he was a trained and efficient man, and he stood proud and upright. This was no slouch. He was one of them and high up the food chain in whatever organisation it was.

John realised that he could go back to the house if he wanted, she had set him up, but it was for a good reason. He then watched as vehicles left the big gates of Wernons, turned acutely left into the Sheepscombe slip road, most having to double reverse to get around, then they went toward the Mill House. He trained his binoculars on the vehicles and watched them disappear under the foliage and trees and then reappear. He traced their journey to the very place he and Cynthia had gone to and where he had thrown what they thought was the decoder.

A team of men got out of the first vehicle, followed by a second team and then a third. They went across the road, entered the field and he guessed that they opened the silo drainage vent, allowing the putrid rancid spoils of the container to drain across the floor. It took about five minutes to empty completely and after they man handled it onto its side and then over, enough for the device to fall out, still wrapped in its container no doubt.

One man, walked into the mess and retrieved the bag containing the iPad, and they all looked pleased. They all returned to the vehicles, and the man cleaned his shoes off in the grass. They then all turned the vehicles toward Wernons.

John watched them, and these actions had eclipsed even his wildest dreams when they went off smiling with the machine. He would wait and watch as the events unfolded. He watched the vehicles retrace their way back to the huge gate of Wernons, and they all went in. The men disembarked and marched into the house; they were smiling and extremely happy. He watched, as they entered the room where the distinguished man still held court and was now smiling profusely.

He had difficulty seeing everything, but he saw the lead man hand the bag and device to the man. It took but two minutes for the atmosphere in the room to change completely.

"Just what the hell is this?" screamed Knowles to the man.

John could hear this as the window was open, and his voice travelled, in fact, half of Painswick must have heard his rage. He could not make out the others' voices clearly or sufficiently to follow their words, but it was easy to deduce the content and body language.

"This is the device, sir," he said looking at the others.

"NO IT FUCKING WELL IS NOT!" roared Knowles, moving right up into the man's face as he did.

"I don't understand," said the bewildered man.

He reeled back from the impact of the fist. His face imploded, and his nose broke instantly. He fell backwards on the floor; he had been knocked unconscious.

"Anyone else care to offer a stupid remark? Any comment anyone or hypothesis? Come on, you complete wankers! Where is that bloody device, damn it," he ranted even louder.

Cynthia ran into the room.

"Whatever is going on?" she said looking at the cowering men and seeing the one out cold on the floor, blood streaming from his nose.

Knowles picked up and smashed the iPad into the floor, then stamped on it several times.

"What are you doing?" she asked.

"KILLING A FUCKING iPad! What does it look like? A fucking useless iPad too, that just happened to belong to the wanker that was in Belleview that John Parks blew all up the wall. The bloody resourceful git only took the iPad and the decoder from the house and fooled you and everyone else. In fact, he has completely outmanoeuvred every one of us. He has completely fooled us all!" he repeated angrily shaking his head.

The men that were assembled in the room all looked down at the floor apart from Cynthia.

"How the hell has he disarmed the tracker though? I am completely baffled as to how he disarmed this technology and switched the product, bloody ingenious. I will have to kill him myself," he said menacingly, "You lot won't be able to."

"Maybe, but he has."

"Don't even think of offering me a lame idea. You were there my girl, DIDN'T YOU SEE WHAT WAS GOING ON AT ALL?" he screamed.

"I was not with him all the time," she shouted, "May I remind you that you had me running about like Mo Farah.

She hit the floor with a dull thud, following the backhand she received to the side of her face. "Daughter or not, don't you ever consider yourself my equal or that you are able to speak to me as anything but your superior and commanding officer. DO YOU HEAR ME!" he screamed.

She regained her composure, lifted her head, wiped the tears from her eyes and looked straight into his eyes with fear for her life. "I completely understand, please accept my apologies, sir."

"Get that press release out and get him into the open," he screamed, "I want him walking around believing he is out of danger, and this is the only way this wanker will fold. You, my girl, will seduce him and slit his fucking throat with me."

He charged around the table.

"GET OUT ALL OF YOU, BUT NOT YOU," he said staring at Cynthia.

He bellowed this command so loudly that John shuddered, and the men all scurried from the room quickly without looking back.

Knowles suddenly realised that the window was open and closed it quickly, checking who may be lurking under or around it. He casually glanced toward the trees but in a dismissive manner, and he quickly disappeared from the window and the room.

John was now unsure as to how to proceed, so he sat with the pack and guns and with the comfort that there would be an apparent respite before Armageddon descended upon him.

"The tracker you gave to Parks, the one in the locket, did he accept it?" barked Knowles.

"Yes, but he was completely paranoid at that point. Why?"

"Well, according to the locator, he has been driving or running around the village and neighbourhood in an erratic pattern. He continues stopping and starting, and it just seems odd behaviour for him at this time."

"What I think happened was that he was so spooked. He kept saying something was wrong and that he did not trust anyone," she said.

"But you are sure he trusted you?"

"I am sure, sir. He has the hots for me, and this I do know."

"We shall see, Cynthia. We shall indeed see."

"Have faith. He will be dealt with. Your plan is good, your troops are now back to full respect and commitment, and I have him reeling in as we speak."

Chapter 10

Bargaining Power

John put on the wig Cynthia had left at the house and that he had quickly hidden in his pack. He used a scarf to cover his face and moved toward the old lady's door, as he got there he went around the back. He knocked and took off the wig and scarf.

Hello sonny, fancy seeing you. Come on in for a cup of tea. Thank you so much for carrying my bags in the other day. If I had known you were a wanted man, I would have made you something to eat.

"But why?" John asked smiling.

"Because you didn't do it John. We all knew this and look, in the newspaper, you have been absolved of all sins, and it has been on the television. That Chinese man was involved in some form of turf war, Triad activity, and was killed in a gang related vengeance killing, not you sweet boy.

She beckoned John to sit at the kitchen table, and she sat opposite him. She was beaming, not only a visitor, but a famous one, too.

She poured a cup of tea from the china pot to the china cup, and she shook as she did so, but she was a canny old girl for eighty-six.

"I don't do mugs sonny, just China. Awfully crass of me, but I am old fashioned and proud of it," she said smiling.

"I think it is admirable of you to hold measure in your manners and habits, and even if new ones are thrust upon you all of the time, you keep doing it like you've always done. Just say no to tea bags."

"Quite and bravo," she said clapping her hands.

John sipped the tea. It was delightful.

"What do you think?" she asked.

"It always tastes ten times better when brewed by leaf and pot," he said. "Is it Miles tea?"

"How on earth do you know that? I am utterly impressed young man."

Her house phone rang.

"Excuse me, dear," she said leaning across the table and taking the phone in her fragile hand.

"Hello, Martha Anderson speaking."

John gestured toward the paper, and she gestured yes. He looked at the news article, and it said that Mr Parks needed to contact Stroud CID to clear up a few loose ends and then he could return to some form of normality.

"Hello Betty, yes, guess who I have sat at my kitchen table. Well, he was here," she said. "Goodness, he has disappeared."

John revisited a medley of circumstances, as he walked along the park in isolation but without quite as much fear. It felt odd to be out in the open and visible, and he felt that it had all happened a bit too quickly and a bit too conveniently.

He had decided that he had to return to Belleview, if this was a real lull, he needed to use the time productively. He realised that every call or any electronic signature he used would be tracked and traced and that he would not be able to fart or urinate anywhere without a sample being collected and taken.

He knew that he still represented a value, and he was being kept alive and groomed. He was sure of it, and he still had the deactivated decoder. This had managed to completely throw Cynthia and the strange man with the impressive voice on the telephone off the location of the decoder and onto him directly. Now he obviously knew the man at Wernons was the voice and close to Cynthia Lillybrook. He was gaining intelligence, and he was a step in front of them for once.

He walked through the alley to Belleview and found the gate was locked from the inside. With no energy left to scale the fence, he decided to walk back to the steps, down into White Horse Lane and then turned right up Vicarage Street and trudged the thirty or so metres to the entrance and sanctity of his beautiful cottage, Belleview. The door had been completely remodelled and it looked simply wonderful, a man stood there, obviously police.

"Yes, I am John Parks, but whoever wants to speak to me has to come here. I need a shower, shave and hopefully the other."

"I completely understand. I am Gerald Mallard, Stroud CID, but really," he looked around and whispered, "I am not going to start this relationship by being dishonest. I belong to a unit which is like special branch, housed in the Metropolitan quarters."

He showed John a badge and ID card.

"Look, the village shop is just up there, please get some milk and biscuits if you want tea, as I don't use it. I am not going anywhere, so you will have to trust me."

"It would be more than my job would be worth, Mr Parks."

"Christ, call me John. I need friendly conversation, not formality at the moment, so come on in."

He went through the door and looked at his lounge with all his familiar possessions. He did not tell Mallard that he had his hand on the Beretta and that he would shoot him as much as look at him.

He looked at the stair entrance and could not believe the professionalism of the clean-up team. There was absolutely no trace of the slaying, and he was pleased. It would be hard to live with this episode impressed upon his mind and being constantly reminded of it every time he went upstairs, or down, so maybe time would cloud the now vivid memory.

John walked into the kitchen, unlocked the back door and opened it right up to let the air in. The door of Southview which was adjacent immediately opened and his neighbour smiled.

"How are you John? We always knew you were a good guy, of course. Welcome back."

"OK Frank, thank you. I don't mean to be rude, but I have CID here. Do you have any spare milk I can have until I get to the shop, just enough for some tea for the guy?"

"Sure do." He went to his fridge, removed a litre container of milk and passed it to John.

"It's new and fresh, so keep it old man. We can have a chin wag later, and you can tell me and the sleuth upstairs all about it."

"OK Frank, I will do," he said accepting the milk and returned into the cottage.

"Best close the door," hinted Mallard.

John complied, filled the kettle, emptied it, rinsed it out again and then filled it for two cups even though he was not going to participate in tea. He placed the kettle on its base and flicked it on. He then placed coffee in his machine chamber and twisted it under the water exit. He then pressed the on dial and waited until the green light ignited, placed his small favourite French coffee cup under the dual exit and then turned the dial to activate the heavenly fluid.

The coffee flowed very slowly filling the cup in its own pace and with a white froth like it had cream or milk added. The aroma filled the room, and John knew that this was the most normal act that had happened in days, even though the presence of the stranger was invasive and was still disturbing him.

"John, I cannot make you trust me upon meeting you, and I know you have been through an ordeal. The full extent is cloudy, and I am not fully aware of everything, but I know most of your actions for the past days. I need to let you know that I am on your side and that I have some people that would very much like, an informal chat with you."

John's suspicions were immediately aroused and his defensive shield began to surface, as did the Beretta.

"I propose a meeting in plain sight, in St Marys church. It is safe. It is God's ground and house, and there will be tourists there. You know that John. What have you got to lose?"

"My head, literally, look even if I offend you I really don't care. I don't trust you or any living human being."

"OK, if you want to know who Cynthia Lillybrook is and what relationship she has to the man in Wernons, you will profit from the meeting. This is obviously your choice, John. You can also keep the Beretta on you, but I suggest we drop the arsenal of shotguns if we are going to enter into God's house."

John looked at Mallard, studied him, still with trepidation and conceit, but he realised that this was not an aggressive, arrogant man; he was different. He also had a burning curiosity as to the relationship between Cynthia and the man at Wernons.

'Logic John. Apply some logic.'

"Show me your wallet, Gerald. Would you please?"

"Of course, John. Why I have no idea, and I am not a rich man, but here you are," he said handing his wallet to John.

John opened it and the first thing it revealed on the one side was a bank of cards, nothing unusual. He inspected every one of them, and they all corresponded to his name as did his driving license.

He then opened a compartment to reveal a photograph of Gerald, standing proudly with his arm around a lady and a pair of children, one delightful boy and a pretty girl. There was a number written on the back, but it did not resemble a phone number.

"Anything to report, John?" Gerald asked.

"I will accompany you to the church, and I will keep my friend in my pocket. I will also hold you and the people in the picture responsible should any attempt be made to harm me."

"Not by me or my meeting contingent John. Now the other people are a different story, but you have something they want, so they will not harm you for now," he said.

"Agreed Gerald, so do you want tea?"

"No, let us walk to the church. It is light, there are plenty of tourists around and we can hopefully just walk there unmolested. Are you going to tell me why you suddenly see me as less of a threat?"

"Can I shower at least?" said John without answering his question, "I am humming a bit."

"Can you wait?"

John locked the back door, swilled his coffee down as it tasted really good. He followed Gerald out of the front door, into the afternoon sun and he locked the front door.

"Same lock at least," he said.

The men walked up the street without conversation. There were some tourists mulling around with cameras, some walker types and the day was dry and bright. They went past Hamptons International, passed the Royal Oak which seemed to have brisk trade, into St Marys Street and then onto the hallowed ground of the churchyard.

They both reached the side porch entrance door together and John gestured that Gerald should lead the way through the main church door, which he did. John loved the idea of the church, its history and majesty, the way it stood so proud and how it was once the hub of the community. The folklore fascinated him, the ninety-nine yew trees and the cannonball dent in the structure itself showing the scars of war. The church had been subject to many bell changes and historical deeds. The spire had been rebuilt due to lightning strike, and it was steeped in history. It had witnessed birth, death, marriage, heard desperate pleas and prayers of need and thanks. It was indeed a special place, and he felt calm and safe.

The tourist or visitors' book sat inside the main doorway and stood testament to the global gatherers that felt inclined to leave their paw print for all to read and witness their presence. Both men moved past the leaflet holders and donation boxes and onto the side of the church, facing the small area at the front laden with candles for those to remember and have quiet space. Behind this there was a large scale model of a galleon ship and the many decorative windows let shafts of coloured light gleam in from the sunshine.

John noticed a man and a woman, completely out of place, and Gerald looked at him.

"Tell them to sling their hook, Gerald. I don't need an episode of when tourists go bad. They look ludicrous in their creased corduroy and glasses on their heads."

Gerald gestured to the man and woman, and they walked off slowly, looking perplexed that a civilian had made them leave.

The main door opened and three suits walked in and toward them, while two huge military type guys waited by the door.

Two of the men sat behind them, and one in front, and the man turned to face them.

"Good afternoon, gentlemen," he said with a distinctive American accent, and he smiled.

"Am I supposed to say 'hi' and engage in small talk?" said John. "who the hell are you and what the hell are you doing here? What the hell do you want from me?"

"That's three 'Hell Marys'," he replied laughing. It certainly broke the ice, and John smiled too.

"OK, John, I am Mr Green, kind of CIA meets Bruce Willis, a nice guy but with a righteous purpose and will never stop until it is achieved. The guys behind you are Mr Black and Mr White, and you know Gerald, of course."

"Well I would like to be known as Mr Knob-end because that is just about how I am feeling now with your *Reservoir Dogs* shit.

"May I remind you that you are in the house of God?" said Mr Green.

"May I remind you that God sees all and that he has spoken to me to tell me you are full of the proverbial ass fodder," said John sarcastically.

"Feisty, Gerald. A true Brit, so no wonder he eluded capture and death so exquisitely. Please, let's start again, I am Martin Jacobs, US Government, and he put out his hand."

John did not shake it or move. He was clutching the Beretta and willing to start firing, even in this the house of God.

"Relax John, please."

"Relaxation is not on my agenda, Martin, and you might as well know that right now, I don't trust anyone, especially you guys."

"Cynthia Lillybrook, you not only trusted her, you liked her," he said.

"I liked the thought of an ally at that particular point in time. Remember that at that time I was doing my Arnold Schwarzenegger impression. I did, however, trust her about as much as I trust you, very little.

"Is that why you switched the decoder? I have to say, John, we were all mightily impressed with that decision. It has not only kept you alive, but it has caused, let's say, certain individuals, to take more risk of exposure and make some precarious moves."

"Who is Cynthia Lillybrook?" John asked impatiently. "And please enlighten me as to how all the pictures and information got into Steephill Cottage if she was a plant."

The door opened and a Canadian couple walked in and were ushered out with an excuse that some renovations were being discussed and that their window of opportunity to leave their mark would be in two hours. They walked off without questioning the perfectly plausible story.

"Cynthia Lillybrook is, in fact, one Cynthia Knowles," said Martin sternly, "the daughter of the infamous Bartholomew Knowles, industrial and commercial spy, assassin, a ruthless killer who would do anything to keep his position and grace of his peers. The amazing thing was that they followed you to the house, and they put a tube into your bedroom, used some form of sedation gas, and they had a jolly old time in there setting up the place with you having 'night-nights' upstairs like a baby. She was even in the house to familiarise herself. That part was really clever I must say. I liked this brash confidence, and the fact that she completely humiliated you and wound you in like a mackerel."

"And just who are his peers?" asked John.

"Well this is where the waters get a little bit murky. We know he has a top government official, probably a cabinet minister in London, who is pulling his strings, but we cannot identify him even though he has been active for years."

"We know they were talking earlier this morning," said Gerald.

"Is this the guy at Wernons, army type, grey hair about mid fifties perhaps?" asked John.

"That would be him," said Martin. "He has been playing everyone, but he is getting desperate as the game has changed."

"What do you mean?" asked John.

"The players are even more dangerous if that could ever be a reality. You had the Koreans, Russians, and the usual rogue elements involved a few days ago. Now they have been joined by the Israelis, Arabs, Chinese, and extremists. The British and the US are the thin blue line stopping them getting their hands on the technology."

"Just what bloody technology? The water thing?" asked John totally frustrated with the cloak and dagger surrounding the source of his plight and subsequent danger.

"The technology, as you call it, uses a pretty simple technique, thus it is priceless. It uses a system for converting common seawater on the seabed to drinking water. This can be done at any seabed location deep enough to exhibit the tidal undercurrents required to meet the physics of the process. The process of extracting the salt in this location and situation and providing drinking water in itself means that there is no need for water to be in short supply anywhere on the planet, hence stopping famine and crop disasters, as irrigation could be achieved if investment to pipelines is achieved."

"So world power changes and the third world could become equal given investment of money and intelligent training," said John.

"Yes, and the other upturn to this is that when they tested the process, they found that as the seabed was being disrupted, only in certain locations mind you, it emitted gases that could be harvested as fuel replacing the need to extract the usual fossil fuels. The big plus here is obvious: a virtually free by-product of an already world changing process is the fuel of the future."

"Wow, that is a breakthrough," said John.

"Sure is," said Gerald.

"What is significant is that the process not only provides water and the means to fuel its very process, the gas can be pumped to use in homes and cars all over the world," continued Martin. "This effectively eradicates the fight to control oil beds and gas farms and all those primary sites. It also means an end to the Arab stranglehold on oil, as gas and water would all become accessible and plentiful to all. The next millennium power and water problems all solved with a simple, yet effective process, that already exists, so as you see, some huge political leverage to those who control it."

"I can see why everyone wants the technology, so how is it going to be controlled?" John asked.

"We already have the process and the decoder. The United Nations and world powers will have access to the process, and everyone will benefit. There will be no one superpower John," Martin said reassuringly.

"We don't even need your decoder John. It is a fake anyway, planted by the Brits, cleverly I may add and put out as bait."

"So mine is a decoy to get Knowles out in the open."

"Not Knowles," said Gerald seriously, "the guy above him is the danger here, and we need to get him exposed soon."

"So just how did you stop the tracking device John? We are all pretty intrigued?" asked Martin.

"Simple logic really and good planning," he replied.

"And," beckoned Martin.

"The van I used was a working van," John said looking at Martin specifically, but Gerald was also very attentive.

"I noticed there was builders lead, you know, the sort used for flashing, thick grade too as Painswick is always needing some old roof or porch flashed. There were two full rolls of it in the back, and I thought at the time that they represented a lot of money as lead has spiralled upwards in cost and poor alternatives have been brought in."

"So you covered it in lead?" said Martin.

"More than that, I placed it in a plastic flat tool container, probably a chisel container when new, as it had screwdrivers in it, and I emptied them, put the decoder in, wrapped it around in lead several times, and when we returned to the cottage, and she went to change, I mixed some cement and put it in a big paint bucket. When I returned from dropping her off, I had a complete concrete jacket over it, and I simply rolled it to safety. Ingenious eh?"

"I am astonished," said Gerald, "Plan and execute all this when someone was trying to kill you. You are a more clever man than me and cool as a cucumber."

"If you were fighting to see the people in your picture Gerald, you would be amazed with just what you can conjure up," said John seriously. "I knew that the decoder represented value and that my life remained critical. If I was out of play, the decoder was lost."

"You surprised everyone," said Martin, "Well done."

"So how do I fit into all this? I guess it is because I have a decoder, or they think I do," he asked himself out loud. "Hmmmmm," said John glaring forward at the candles flickering away a few metres away from him.

"How would you like to play it, John? I do not want to place you in danger or advocate any form of involvement from a civilian, but I would be interested in any ideas you have," said Martin.

"Me too," said Gerald. "What do you suggest?"

"Kidnap Cynthia, and you can do it for me if you like," he said with absolute cold calm menace in his voice.

They all laughed including the guys behind him. John got up to leave.

"Hold on John. You have to understand that you are a civilian, and yet you talk like you are intent on bringing this whole situation to a conclusion yourself," said Martin.

"I am an integral cog in this unwilling farce," he replied, "I did not want any part of it, but it was thrust upon me, and here I am, right in the middle, without a paddle I might add. I don't like it; would you?"

"What would you do with her?" asked Gerald.

"Hold on a minute," said Martin.

"Look, I could use both the girl and the decoder as a bargaining chip. I could flush out the big guy, use a ransom as a ruse, you know like civilian becomes greedy and needs funds to disappear. It sounds plausible, and the lure of the decoder will be far too great for Bartholomew Knowles," said John.

"You know he would kill his own daughter as much as look at her, don't you John?" said Gerald.

"Yes and I pretty much wouldn't flinch if he did so either. That bitch played me. She made me feel human at a time when I was at my lowest and needed a friend most, then she was brutal in her betrayal. She is a prize cold callous bitch."

"Wow, remind me not to get you angry John!" said Martin, smiling but obviously shocked at the attitude of the once mild mannered man.

"John, can we take the liberty of relieving you of the Beretta?" asked Gerald, just around the village you understand.

A man behind John leaned over and handed him another Beretta, exactly the same.

"It has blanks in it," said Martin, "and it will scare anyone, but you cannot sacrifice anyone else, especially some innocent local."

"You can take the liberty of fucking off, all of you," John said standing up and first apologising to the master of the house for blasphemy and placing the Beretta filled with blanks in his left pocket.

"John please," said Gerald.

"I told you," he looked to the ceiling and chose different words than those that were to originally leave his mouth. "Get lost," and he walked toward the two gorillas that covered the exit.

John swiftly extracted the Beretta catching them all completely off guard. This was the live round version from his right pocket, and he pointed it at them both.

"Get out of my way, or I will surely drop you where you stand," he shouted to them, eyes fixed on them.

Martin gave the nod to comply and they moved well away from the doorway. John exited, placed the gun back in his pocket and went through the churchyard. He walked through the trees and when he was by the Royal Oak, he heard laughter. He did not go in but would. He had thought of something that would surely help him but later. He walked past Hamptons, down Vicarage Street and unlocked Belleview, entered it and locked it.

He went to his land line and dialled the number that was still in his pocket. The tone rang out and his heart beat faster.

"Hi, is that John?"

"Yes it is me, Thank God you are alright. I have a proposition for you."

Chapter 11

Foundations

John put down the phone. He knew it would be tapped, and he also knew it would set a series of events in motion and that he had to use all the circumstances that were to unfold to his advantage. He could now use his own vehicle. Yes, it would have a tracker fitted by one or more of the groups of people who had an unhealthy interest in him, and he knew he would be followed, but so be it.

John grabbed his car keys from a drawer in the kitchen and made sure he had his driver ID and his wallet, and he left the cottage and went straight to White Horse Lane. He pressed the fob and the Ford Focus lit up as if happy to see him. He entered, started it and drove up to the main road casually passing Wernons on the way. He got to the top of the road, turned right and went through the woods and down to Brockworth, across the roundabout and into more dense population. He headed toward Cheltenham, and he was there in about twenty minutes. It was late afternoon, and he needed to catch one specific shop. He looked at his pack on the passenger seat. He had emptied the shotguns at Belleview, but he had assembled some unlikely contents, and he would need them all. He parked by the general hospital and walked quickly through the park carrying his pack. He ended up running through, and he ducked into a doorway and took off the majority of his clothing. He changed into a bright jumper and jeans and continued to run with the pack hidden up his jumper. It was difficult to run with the Beretta digging into his belt, so he had to put it in the pack, although he felt uncomfortable once again and almost naked.

He discarded the old clothing in a bin and disappeared into the direction of the town. He entered it by the pedestrian walkway and headed toward Regents Arcade. He knew facial recognition software would probably pick him up, as they now knew he had no beard. He ran to the other side of the arcade, up the steps, into TK Max and he just grabbed lots of clothes in a blur, and for once gambled on the sized being somewhere near. He paid cash, exited and moved across the Bridge Café, through Cavendish House, down the stairs and walked up the road toward the Slug and Lettuce and past the Everyman Theatre. He dived into a party shop and grabbed some wigs and hats. He paid cash once again before walking out on the main street and entering an O2 shop.

He walked up to the counter and waited as an attendant walked over to join him.

"Can I help you, sir," he asked cordially.

"Yes, I would like ten mobile SIM pay as you go phones, loaded £20 credit each, activated for immediate use and please write the numbers of each one on the phone."

The man looked. He was puzzled, but it was a good sale, so he was eager to comply until he heard the word 'cash'.

John pulled out a wad of notes and informed him that there was sufficient funds available.

"This will take some time. They all have to be loaded and activated, so please wait.

"Stop talking and get motivated then," said John smiling, "I will give you fifty pounds, just for you, if you hurry."

It took the guy just thirty-four minutes to complete the request, and he was very happy with himself.

John paid him over eight hundred pounds cash and slipped him the additional fifty pounds. He then put on a wig, hat and a horrible loud hippy top. The shop attendant just looked but did not question him, and John exited the shop and turned right toward Boots and beyond.

He entered three different shops, changed along his route and also got on two buses for only a few metres. Each time he exited while wearing different tops, wigs and hats.

He arrived at the small shop he had been heading for and he entered it. He noticed there was a screwdriver by the counter which he immediately deposited in his pocket.

"I will have that one," he said pointing to a Chinese 125 CC scooter parked by the doorway.

"It has," said the salesman starting to explain the many functions of the 'twist and go'.

"Not interested," said John succinctly. "Just do the paperwork. I am in a hurry."

"Do you have ID? I need to register it," said the man now behind the counter.

"I do," he said passing it over.

They completed the transaction by way of cash including the 'L' plate and helmet. The money was retrieved from his pack, all twelve hundred pounds of it.

"You have to go on a course," said the seller.

"Of course I do," replied John, as he mounted, switched on the machine, placed his helmet on and rode off.

He immediately went to the university by Princes Elizabeth Way and there were a hundred scooters and motorbikes. He sized up an appropriate plate and unscrewed it by utilising the stolen screwdriver he had taken from the bike shop, and he exchanged it for the one on his scooter.

Now John needed to lay the foundations of his plan and to accomplish phase one. To enable this to move forward, he headed back to Painswick on the little bike, happy that number plate recognition software would not flag up the recently purchased scooter or that the rider had no insurance or tax. It had taken him forty minutes to get back to Painswick through the traffic, and the light had faded, but he was pleased to be inconspicuous once again.

John had worked out the architecture of his plan many times that day, both in his mind and by challenging every aspect over and over again. It had taken him an additional four hours in the darkness to set his tools in place to give the plan any chance to reach his objectives. Each part or phase of the plan was marked as an event and would need to be confirmed as each was achieved. It was as with all plans, fraught with danger and the capacity for failure, so he had built in many fail safe controls, and he was confident it would work. If it did not, it could cost him his life.

He returned to Belleview which was masked in darkness at 10.30pm. He entered and went into the kitchen. He also went to each room of the cottage and checked every inch. He knew every stone and piece of wood and mortar, but he was so tired. He knew it would be bugged, but he could not find any apparent devices for transmitting sound or images. He was no expert, but he knew damn well they were there.

John was too scared to take a shower, so he ran the bath. He looked at the Velux and made sure it was locked, switched off the light and placed one of the sawn off shotguns on the top of the bath. He disrobed and sank into the steaming hot water, and he lay there and wallowed in the creature comfort of cleanliness. He washed his hair with the tap shower attachment, but he did so with one eye on the door, the other on the Velux, one hand on the attachment and the other going between shampooing and the shotgun.

This he thought was bordering on the ridiculous, but he was so pleased to still be breathing and now clean; he felt great. He got out, pulled out the plug, towelled himself dry and then rinsed the bath to make sure it remained pristine and without the need for further work. He moved across the landing with the shotgun in hand and went upstairs to where his hanging rail was. He put on a pair of lounge pants and a T-shirt, and he looked at the tiny stairs leading to him. He decided to block them with a chest of drawers, but he went to toilet and cleaned his teeth first and thought he would be safe for at least a few hours.

He then lay on the bed after blocking the entrance, and he was certain that he had prepared adequately. His aim was simply to achieve a pleasant night's slumber plus the very real advantage of waking up in the morning alive. He had placed the sawn off by his side, the pack behind his head and the Beretta hidden under the covers. He was sure that short of having a howitzer on the cabinet, he could see the most evil of predator off, if only he could get some sleep.

Before he could really question the events of this day or analyse them any further, John closed his eyes, and no matter what transpired, he would not really hear it.

Cynthia entered the study where Bartholomew Knowles was sitting down smoking a cigar. She stood before the large desk with her hands clasped in front of her and waited for the attention she craved, for she was very pleased with herself. Knowles, on the other hand, was not too pleased to see her. He had always wanted sons and not a daughter, and she was needy and reliant upon him, and this was a weakness in her that he absolutely detested.

He raised his eyes to gaze upon her. He was flippant in his gesture for her to speak, as he simply held his hand out and pulled his fingers to his palms a couple of times.

"John Parks has just called, Sir; I knew he would, and he wants me to meet him as predicted. He must think he has been absolved of all sins, and he appears to be riding the crest of a wave. He will surely be off-guard now and easy to manage."

"Where does he want to meet?"

"I don't know. He just said I was to carry this phone and follow directions tomorrow because he knew I had a long way to travel. He actually thinks I am in Cumbria or in the wilds of Yorkshire. What a poor misguided little fool; he is quite a prick really."

"Don't underestimate this guy Cynthia. There is something about his methodology that intrigues me. 'Carry the phone' and 'new instructions'? He is actually turning into an operative or at least applying the very logic we ourselves would employ in the same circumstances."

"No Sir, I am not questioning your undoubted judge of character and awareness, but he is merely a love-struck prick who thinks he has gained a reprieve and has fallen into the trap of familiarity. He needs a friend, and he is desperate for some element of normality and comfort. Honestly, he will be like a puppy."

"I hope you are right, but where did he call you from?"

"That's the odd bit, the landline was traced to Belleview. He also sounded pleased to hear me, pleased with himself and he was not guarded until he mentioned the instructions, but I am sure he thinks he is protecting me not him."

"Let's have a think for a minute, Cynthia. If he is blatantly using Belleview as a base, he must feel safe and his guard will be down, and this much I agree with you. I imagine the phone line has been tapped, so we must assume the other players already know that you are being brought into the affray, and so there will be much movement in this arena over the next couple of hours. You are going to have to be extremely careful, even more than normal. The Israelis, Chinese and Koreans are formidable, but there are also the Russians, US and British involved."

"I can get him to meet me and then hurt him enough to tell me where the decoder is," she said coldly. "He will not expect it, and even if he suspects me somehow, he has no idea how brutal I can be, but he will surely find out very quickly."

"Good grief, Cynthia, if you were not my blood I would make sure you could never come after me! You are the most bloodthirsty and narcissistic person I know, apart from when I look in the mirror of course," he smiled, took a huge drag off the cigar and bellowed out a plume of smoke.

"Thank you, Sir. I think that is indeed a compliment I shall treasure for eternity."

"Let me know when he contacts you again. Get the tracking devices in place, and don't get isolated or caught by any of the other players. You know the rules, so no bargaining. I will abandon you, as you would me, our rules, OK," he said in a matter of fact fashion and gestured that she was dismissed.

"Of course, Sir. I know exactly how it works," she said confidently, as she exited the room, but deep down, she had absolutely no trust or love for this ruthless man that was her 'Father'.

She left the office, went to the operations room and looked at the four men she had assembled there.

"Right, we take the decoder; we take this novice out, and we finish this whole stupid episode without anyone fucking up. DO I MAKE MYSELF ABUNDANTLY CLEAR!" she shouted.

"Yes, ma'am," they said in unison.

"Right. Let me know what you have for me."

Chapter 12

Day Four

John woke up in his own bed, his own lounge pants on, his own smell on the bedding, and he felt great apart from the crushing weight of the urine on his bladder. He grabbed the shotgun and Beretta, put on his slippers and then he removed the chest of drawers from the entrance to the bedroom. He moved stealthily down the small spiral staircase, very slowly and deliberately.

He checked the whole cottage, and when he was satisfied that there were no intruders, he went to the bathroom and relieved himself. He then went downstairs and filled and activated his coffee machine.

'Could it have only been day four of this frantic myriad of events?' He had never been involved in such complex negativity and danger, and although exhausted recently, he felt somewhat rested this morning. He knew there would be eyes on him everywhere and more so ears. He was aware that absolutely everything he said and did, and the smallest movement from him would be listened to, watched, logged and contemplated by teams of electronic wizards.

He still found it strange that he did not feel remorse or any form of guilt for the demise of those he had despatched. This was profoundly odd and out of character, but he drew strength from the fact that humans can and do adapt to all kinds of diversity every day.

'OK then, to begin,' he thought confidently. He went to the bathroom and decided to shower prior to his coffee, as it took him two minutes. He was still cagy about re-enacting the scene from *Psycho* and being a victim, so he was fast, constantly watching the doorway, and the Velux, and he did not enjoy the experience. He dried himself very quickly, in fact he was still wet in places but did not consider this to be an issue. He walked onto the landing, and then the two metres to the bluebell bedroom on the same floor and dressed in a polo shirt and some jeans. He pulled some socks on and then he figured he was ready for anything.

He also placed the small lock knife in his sock. This had become a habit, and for some strange reason, he thought upon it as a lucky charm, a symbol of protection and a hidden plus that may help him someday. He did not even find the object uncomfortable when he walked around. He had grown not only used to it, but it actually gave him a small comfort that maybe someday, this would be significant.

He went out of the door but found himself going back into the smaller spare bedroom once again and to the built-in cupboard. He remembered where it was and pulled out an old rucksack. It was framed and sturdy and had an expanding capacity but was not too bulky when empty or half-full. He took it downstairs with him, along with his pack, and the shotguns. He placed the Beretta in his waistband and pulled the polo shirt down to conceal it. He then placed a bottle of tomato ketchup, a new cheese wire with grips he had purchased off eBay on a whim, some small 5cm by 5cm plastic click bags, and two rolls of cello tape in the pack and left it in the lounge. He went upstairs with another roll of tape, and he also had a pair of scissors. He proceeded to close every door, and he then cut a tiny strip of tape from the roll. He put it almost under the door but against the frame also to act as a seal.

He went back downstairs and picked up the rucksack, which he half-filled with clothes he had thrown by the washing machine days before, and he also put a coat in.

He then placed a big Sony CD player into the sack, and put some earphones in along with a specific pair of CDs. He smiled, as he did this as it would surely test any listening devices. He then exited the kitchen door, and as he did, he looked ahead, and he noticed the glass was different in the door, but he shrugged it off. He realised they must have broken through this the first day they saw him as a target and tried to get access to the garden when chasing him.

He went up the shared access steps and right into his beautiful garden. The cottage flowers glowed, and it was a picture of English cottage charm and tranquillity. He walked slowly, up the shingle to the first set of sleeper steps and climbed them, onto the second set and up onto the decking.

"Déjà vu," he muttered.

"Good morning, old man," was blurted like an order, as the old guy next door climbed his garden terrace to his breakfast table.

"Morning Frank, how is it?" John responded cordially; it was déjà vu for sure now.

"OK, have you got much on today, old man? Great to see that you finally shaved that unsightly beard off. You know it makes you look twenty years younger?"

"I cannot be having this conversation," John muttered under his breath and with his teeth gripping together he sat down.

"The beast just had to go; needed to make myself more attractive to the ladies, Frank," he said.

"Well I'll be damned, and how are you, young man?" asked Barbara, now joining her husband for breakfast but coming to the fence.

"Glad you sorted out that nasty business, John. Rough justice is never good, but we knew you were innocent. We told everyone what a nice guy you are. Didn't we Frank?"

"Not sure about that Barbara, but thank you anyway."

"We sure did, Babs, and there were lots of people to tell. Bloody place was swarming with suits and stuff, and your cottage was like a thoroughfare. I hope they left it nicely."

"They broke your back door pane when they first arrived but replaced it quite quickly," said Barbara. "We told them you could not do any bad things. You are so gentle and balanced. You could not hurt a fly. Could you John?"

"It's just humans. I only like to blow their heads off," he said sarcastically, guessing the conversation was being listened to.

"Oh you are funny," she said. "We have the decking being put in, John. It will give us a better view, so at last he has listened to me."

"You are so far up your ass, fatty," he muttered gritting his teeth and laughing inside.

"What was that John?"

"I am happy for you Barbara," he said.

Barbara sat and poured her tea, and Frank ate his toast. Some of the fragmented chaos seemed to disappear and interlinked back into the right places at least here. He was happy that this side of life had cemented itself once again and that it represented a normality that had existed, although he knew it would be short-lived, and of course, it could never exist like this totally, ever again.

John looked over to Sheepscombe and the gentle incline of the lush green fields with the farmhouses dotted around. The houses and the animals remained, but it was not the same. It had changed significantly in his mind and memory. They had spoiled this slice of Utopia for him, and the events and people who had invaded his life had ruined his very own castle.

Robert Thatcham, Eric Jennings, Bartholomew Knowles, Cynthia, the dead guys and, of course, the deceitful Angela had charred and maimed this once idyllic peaceful retreat and made it seem dark and macabre.

He realised that he could not ever sell Belleview. He loved it dearly but decided then and there that he would need to sever from her, just temporarily, just long enough to allow him to regroup and try to regain some of the softer memories and elements of the village he loved so much every day.

'Back to the job in hand though,' he thought. John walked casually out of the back garden and toward the park carrying the rucksack. When he arrived at green grass of the football pitch, he walked into the middle of it into the circle and centre spot, and he got on all fours, opened the rucksack and activated the phone. He turned the CD up to full volume, which was really loud, and it had Glitch Mob playing, which was heavy dubstep, mixed with dance. It was raucous and brilliant and what a distraction to anyone listening.

John put the earphones on, connected it to the phone and put his head inside the rucksack. No way could anyone hear him, but he could clearly hear the other receiver. Only those with knowledge of the number Cynthia had given him would know the content or context of the conversation.

"Hello. Hello, is that you John?"

"Hello, Cynthia."

"John, I have been so worried."

"Where are you?"

"I am on my way back. I can meet you, so tell me where."

"I have a series of instructions I need you to follow to the letter. You will find them completely bizarre, but you have to comply without question. Do you understand? Don't waver a millimetre from what you are asked to do, and no questions."

"No, I don't understand, John. You sound different, cold; are you under duress?" she asked.

"Not at all, I feel better than I have in days, and this is simply to protect you, that's all. I am completely in the clear now, but I am sure anyone that comes near me will have media attention or CID sniffing around them, and we want privacy."

"Oh thank you, John, but I am completely alright and nobody is interested in me."

"I would rather be cautious taking into consideration the events of late, and you really cannot be too careful."

"I think it is unnecessary, John."

"Humour me Cynthia, or we cannot meet."

"OK John, whatever you say."

"I am assuming you are travelling by rail network, so I need you to go to Stroud station. Is there a possibility that you can get there around noon time?"

"Yes, John, but what do I do then?"

"I will tell you when you arrive. Text your train time and ETA to this phone, but please do not call again."

"John deactivated the phone, turned the CD player off and then declared loudly, "Glitch Mob are brilliant, and it will be Sonny Boom Boom, my boy Skrillex, next so make sure your ears are ready for a bashing."

"Who the hell is Sonny Boom Boom for Christ sake?" said the surveillance guy with the earphones. "Look up Skrillex."

"Sonny John Moore, sir. Born January 15th 1988, better known by his stage name 'Skrillex'.

"What the hell is that!" screamed the man.

"Electronic singer, songwriter, DJ and dub step guru. He knows we are listening then, sir. It is obvious, and that's why we could not hear anything but Glitch Mob."

"And they are, as if I did not know," said the disgruntled man.

"American Electronic, three piece."

"Enough!" shouted the man. "He is onto everyone and clever. We cannot underestimate this man, but who the hell was he on the phone to, and who owns that number?"

"We are triangulating all activity in the region and directly in the area of Painswick Park, but it will take time. He used a pay as you go mobile that was purchased and only activated yesterday, and he called another device that, believe it or not, was scrambled. I mean professionally scrambled, and it appears to be even beyond our recognition capability."

"What do you mean?" hollered the man.

"It pings all over the Southern hemisphere, and it's not even our continents. It is bloody clever."

John picked himself and his rucksack up, and he walked to the bottom of the field to the left where he could clearly see Wernons. He looked through the binoculars, and sure enough, he could see Cynthia talking to Bartholomew Knowles. This was careless of them, even if she thought she was hidden from prying eyes. The issue was that they themselves had got caught in the trap of believing that they were clear and without worry. He knew he had a slender edge, but this may be all that he needed to get ahead of the game. It seemed that just for once, instead of constantly being the hunted, he would reverse the trend and that *he could hunt*.

"Everyone but me is relaxing," uttered John, as he moved away from the fence and went around the field and headed back to Belleview.

"We have pinpointed the call from the park, sir. He probably thought there is safety in being visible."

"Or just wanted a walk," said Cynthia.

"That could of course be the case, ma'am," he answered sheepishly.

"Go, leave us," said Knowles.

The man gladly disappeared.

"Well Cynthia, it is time for you to shine girl. Earn your keep, and make me proud for once."

Cynthia felt deeply hurt by the words of her father. He implied that he was never proud, and he was not, and she knew this. She had been born the wrong sex and then she was perceived as needy and reliant upon him. He had set her on a course in life from childhood where her only purpose was his gain, and she despised him. She was an attractive girl, and before she reached the age of fourteen, he had plied government officials with alcohol, sent in his little Lolita with barely any clothes on. Even if they were unwilling participants, they would be photographed and caught in the act, or just starting acts of gross indecency and enough to ruin them.

He had also abused Cynthia badly, worse when drunken rages fuelled his strange desire for sexual pleasure born of pain. Cynthia had become hardened and sociopathic over time and used men for whatever gain she wanted. She did not have the guidance or protection of a mother. Her mum had apparently disappeared when she was two, in less than convincing circumstances, and she had been guided by the ruthless and infamous Bartholomew Knowles.

She was also a highly respected assassin, due mainly to the fact that her victims never imagined a shy introverted little girl could deliver such a lethal cocktail of ways to die.

She decided to cast it off for now, as she had shrugged off many such digs and jibes along the years. She also dreamed of the day that she could actually despatch him to the other side. This was always on her mind, and he could answer to the real underworld for his barbaric cruelty and for making her life so uncomfortable.

"I will shine, Sir, and I certainly have no intention of failing you. He is an annoying tick, so just let me kill him. His boorish arrogance is really beginning to frustrate me now anyway."

"I am warning you Cynthia. Do not underestimate this man. He is not only resourceful, but he plies logic and he understands what everyone is doing, before they do it," said Knowles staring at her.

"We shall see, Sir."

"Yes, indeed we will," he replied.

Chapter 13

The Events

John felt the phone vibrate and the text tone go off. It buzzed away, and he smiled. He reached in his pack and pulled the phone out and read the text:

Train arrives at 11.52 XXX C

'OK, so you are going to pretend to be travelling. Everything is in place from my end, so here we go event one. Kiss kiss kiss, my ass.'

John made two phone calls to activate further events that he had orchestrated and secured both logistically and financially yesterday. He had achieved this with the old-fashioned, tried and tested, commercial transaction of half-payment already given up front, and, of course, full payment made today, when the events the three men were involved in were accomplished.

Cynthia got off the train that she had caught at Gloucester to give the impression that she had spent half the day travelling. She was looking around the small Stroud station for John and was surprised to see that there was a man with a card held up saying 'Parks/Lillybrook'.

"He has made contact," she said into her microphone without moving her lips or changing her facial expression, but it was an obvious event. Due to this simple act of stupidity, she had been exposed by the other man John had paid to watch and listen to just that event that he contemplated and anticipated well.

She smiled and made her way toward him.

"Cynthia Lillybrook, I presume," he said.

"I am," she replied.

"Follow me, please miss."

She followed him, she looked around nervously and was on edge. She then whispered, "I am leaving the station."

The man she was following gave the man on the station exit barrier a nod, as he went through. "Alright, Ted?"

"Absolutely," said the old guy smiling.

Now obviously, well-known taxi drivers had privilege in most situations like this, and he walked on through and turned to wait for her. She walked to the barrier, gave her ticket to the man collecting them and she followed the man to a taxi. He opened the back door to let her in and then he got to his driver door, entered, started the car and engaged gears and disappeared.

"Have we still got contact team one?"

"Confirmed on both audio and visual; keep her close."

"CMax, you follow as lead. We will take phase two."

"Affirmative AMG, in place and ready to go."

"Do we have street camera views at our disposal yet?"

"Affirmative, all systems, CCTV and traffic cameras are plugged and talking to us."

"Do not lose that taxi."

Bartholomew Knowles also anxiously waited with his team and was relieved to hear his daughter report that she had made contact.

"Have we tapped into CCTV and traffic cameras yet?"

"Yes, sir. We also have the helicopter available and heat signature, so there is no way he can get away undetected."

"Do we have snipers in place?" he bellowed.

"Four, sir, in strategic areas of the town and exit routes."

"Good. Now all I need is for Cynthia to come good this time, and I can get away from this whole shoddy affair."

"How many death squads are in play?"

"Four, sir."

"Any other players on the board?"

"US and British, sir."

The second man gave the ticket collector twenty pounds to reveal the ticket, so he did so quickly, Gloucester to Stroud one way. He rang a mobile pay as you go number and confirmed this fact.

"Where are you taking me?" asked Cynthia.

The man did not respond at all. He started the vehicle and drove out of the station taxi rank on Station Road and turned left and concentrated on the road.

"You like to rabbit on; don't you?" she said sarcastically.

Once again, the man did not respond at all. He glanced into his rear view mirror, briefly made eye contact with her and then concentrated on the road again.

"Stay with them; they are turning out of Station Road and left onto Russell Street, again Russell Street."

"Left onto Rowcroft."

"Travelling up Wallbridge turning left past Travis Perkins."

"Up Dr Newton's Way approaching roundabout, left onto London road. Onto Cornhill onto Parliament Street."

"He has stopped. I repeat. He has stopped."

"Get out here please Miss Lillybrook. Go through the alley and get into the next vehicle that has the door open."

"Where are we? We have been going around virtually in a circle. Are you sure you have the …"

"Just do it, and leave your bag here, please. It will be returned to you later," he said without emotion.

"I most certainly will not," she protested.

"To the letter, Miss Knowles," he said with his hand extended to accept the leather bag.

Reluctantly, she gave him the bag and exited the vehicle, and as she walked she whispered, "I am being made to walk through an alley; no idea where."

The driver drove off.

"He has taken my phone. I hope you are following me with the tracker," she huffed.

The man phoned a mobile number and told the receiver that the car had indeed been followed by a greyish blue VW Transporter van. In fact, he thought there were two of them and also a grey CMax. He also had an idea that a big black AMG Mercedes was a little bit too inquisitive but could not confirm. He would, however, inform number two who would do what he had been asked to confirm the players.

"Thank you," said John calmly.

She continued through the narrow alleyway and to a waiting car with the back door open.

"Get in," came a voice, again without emotion from a driver who was talking into a mobile phone.

"Oh bloody hell!" she blurted and sat. "This is ridiculous."

The man discontinued his phone call, put down the phone and drove off. He did not respond in any way at all to her comment and concentrated on the road.

"Is that the Ryeleaze Road? Are we on our way to the train station again?" she asked agitated and wanting to be in control.

The man turned right and entered Belle Vue Road and then Belle Vue Close.

"That is bloody ironic," she said.

Again, the man did not respond in any way and concentrated on the road. He turned quickly at the end of Belle Vue Close and turned back toward Belle Vue Road gathering pace.

"Tracker has package turned right. Ah we have visual, on Ryeleaze and right into Belle Vue Road. Hang on, that's a dead end! Bloody hell! Get out of there lads, or he will make you for sure."

The man made a call, as he drove out of Belle Vue Road.

"Everything we discussed is confirmed."

"All of them."

"Yes, absolutely."

"Initiate event three."

The man smiled, as he drove and passed the embarrassed occupants of the vans and cars and winked at each of them. It was so obvious that they had been seen, but they still tried to look as if they were looking for long lost family.

The man drove off and then he stopped the car in a factory entrance but did not go in. He answered the call.

"What do you mean he has made our surveillance team?" barked Knowles. "How the hell did he pull that off?"

"Went down a dead-end road, sir, and doubled back."

"Bloody hell! He is mocking us, but I admire his pure resilience. We thought we had a weak prick on our hands, but he is becoming not only resourceful, he is embarrassing everyone. Heads will roll chaps! Get me some results, and what the hell is Cynthia playing at?"

"What is going on?" she demanded. "Event what?"

"Take off your earrings, watch, locket, bangles, hairband, knickers and bra, Miss Knowles. Only your skirt and blouse must remain."

"What, I bloody well won't."

"Then get out of the car and commence your walk."

"Walk where?" she shouted angrily.

"Our business, and that of my client, is now concluded, so walk wherever you wish."

The man got out of his side of the car, walked around to her door, opened it and stood there like a chauffeur.

"Get out Miss Knowles. I have strict instructions, and you have strict instructions. If you cannot follow them to the letter, our business is concluded."

Cynthia was in a rage, but the threat of failure, and the thought of her father bearing down on her or worse, made her calculate that obedience at this point was in fact the only logic to apply.

She pulled off her earrings, bracelet, watch, rings, bra and then told him to look the other way. She removed her knickers, and he placed all the items in a bag.

The man opened the boot and extracted a sledgehammer before placing all the items on the concrete floor. He hammered them true and hard to the horror of the onlooker.

"You and John are just going too far!" she screamed.

"Who is John?" asked the man calmly, as he returned to the car with the contents of the bag smashed to smithereens. He threw them into a skip by the entrance.

"The vehicle is stationary. I repeat, the vehicle is stationary, so sit back and wait. I repeat, sit lads and be patient."

"What do you mean we have lost audio?" shouted Knowles. "You must be joking! How the fuck could he know that? He has rumbled Cynthia and that is a worry. Get more teams assembled and ready to go. He is too far ahead now with no tracking, and she is unarmed. Mind you, she will improvise. I am sure."

Cynthia's driver commenced upon the journey after confirming the third event had taken place.

He drove around the town and with an erratic pattern, using small side streets, narrow access points, one way streets and went exactly where a seasoned taxi driver could go, without anyone who followed remaining invisible. He picked up the phone again, and it dialled the pre-set number and was received.

"Still two vans, and the Mercedes. The CMax I believe has been overtaken by a Freelander. Colour silver/grey and I think there might be a bike in play. Looks like a Suzuki, big powerful one, too."

"Thank you, big party."

The taxi pulled up at a very narrow alleyway and stopped.

"Get out, follow the alley right through, get into…" he was interrupted fiercely.

"I know the drill," she said huffing and exited the vehicle.

She walked through the long winding alley and saw the main road fifty metres away in front of her, but before she could go any further, she was pulled into a rickety old gateway and told to be quiet.

"Follow me," said the man and the gate was closed.

She followed him down some steps and through a covered way and then through the side door into a van that was waiting.

"We have lost visual. I repeat, we have lost visual. She has gone into an alleyway off Upper Springfield Road, and I repeat, Upper Springfield Road, and on foot. Team one dismount and follow on foot."

"What do you mean disappeared? Don't be so bloody stupid man," Knowles snarled. "Get my car ready. This is preposterous."

"Is that wise, sir? Please wait just for a while."

Knowles sat down, his displeasure was blatantly apparent which usually would mean that people would die.

"Find me my fucking daughter, or you will answer to me! Do you hear? GET OUT! GET OUT!"

"She has not come out of the alley, and she is not on CCTV. The taxi has turned and gone, but it is unoccupied apart from the driver. What the hell is going on, chaps? Revisit the alleyway."

The driver threw Cynthia a bag of clothing and a helmet.

"Put them on. There is a towel to cover your virtue."

She looked into the bag, pulled out the knickers and pulled them on followed by chinos. She then put the towel around her top, removed her blouse and put on another blouse provided and a jacket.

"What now?" she asked.

"Place the clothes in the bag," said the man looking straight into her eyes in the mirror.

She did so.

He held his hand out and she gave them to him. He opened the window and threw them out and immediately doubled back and turned several times.

"In a few minutes, you are to get out, jump into the side of the road and behind the wooden structure. Remain out of sight, and do not attempt to move for five minutes, or until this phone rings."

He handed her a mobile phone and an earpiece.

"Do you understand? I will not stop the vehicle so you need to be ready; do you understand?" he repeated loudly.

"Yes," said Cynthia.

The vehicle slowed.

"Get out!" he shouted.

Cynthia jumped, rolled on the ground and darted behind the wooden structure.

"We have lost the package. I repeat. We have lost the package."

"Look at all the CCTV around the area. There must be something to link an exit strategy. Look at all surrounding streets and try all the gates and doorways leading from the alley itself."

"Get a team out of the van and into that alley. Find out where all the doorways lead to, and get me some footage. Somebody had better come up with something soon!" shouted Knowles.

"The other players will be swarming that area. We can track and follow them, sir."

"Are you questioning me? Do you dare to!"

"No, sir, of course not. Team one, get into the alley. I repeat, get into the alley and find out where the bloody hell they have gone! They could not just disappear; there has to be a logical explanation."

"What about remaining inconspicuous and not getting caught up with the other players?" came the reply.

"Do as you are told," screamed Knowles, "or you will surely face me for asking."

"Yes, sir, on our way."

The phone rang after exactly five minutes.

"Yes, this is Cynthia. Is that you John?"

"Hi Cynthia, look under the flagstone to the right hand side of the door. It is not heavy. You should be able to locate a set of two keys."

"I have the keys, John."

"The Yale will allow you to open the door in front of you, and you will find a scooter inside."

Cynthia opened the door and saw the small Peugeot scooter.

"I have located the scooter."

"OK, Cynthia, it was running an hour ago, so I know it works. Place the earpiece on and activate the Bluetooth, leave the phone on, put on your helmet and place the Peugeot key in the ignition. Press the start, and give it a little throttle. The fuel is already on.

Cynthia complied to the letter. She straddled the small scooter and started it. It spat and spluttered a little bit, but it soon found its pitch, as she gently turned the twist grip throttle on the handlebars.

"Ride out of the shed and turn left up towards the Uplands allotments. When you get to the end, you can manoeuvre the bike through the gate and up the track."

Cynthia managed to keep the bike stable and got to the allotments and then to the exit up the small track.

She rode the bike and was instructed to take the first off shoot to the left after a few metres which she did. She then continued up the track until she met a road.

"Ditch the phone in the trough on your left, and under it is another phone; do it now."

Cynthia threw the phone in the filthy water of the trough as instructed and heard another phone ringing. She got off the bike, leant it up against the trough, reached underneath and retrieved the phone. The Bluetooth instantly connected.

"Turn left Cynthia and keep going a couple of hundred metres. You will come to the Old Painswick Road."

She concentrated and then met the road.

"I am at the junction, John."

"Turn right and continue up Wick Street."

"Where am I going, John?" she asked.

There was no answer for a couple of minutes.

"Turn into Greenhouse Lane, but stop in the farmer's gate about a hundred metres into it. I want you to go through the gate with the bike, and it is unlocked, so be sure to close the gate after you and put it on its catch."

"I have done it, and I am inside the gate."

"OK, go to where the man did something to himself because he loved his son so much. First, lay the bike in the gulley by the hedge then ditch the phone in the trough by the entrance gate."

Cynthia was beginning to wish she had some back-up, as she trudged across the field toward Hangman's Cottage. Maybe her father was right about John. Just maybe he had been pushed so far that he himself had been turned into a killer. After all, what makes someone kill? What makes someone enjoy killing? She thought back to the first time she committed a gross act of violence. She had not killed the man in question, however, the act had led her on a path of sociopathic behaviour.

Her father had pimped her out to a government official, and she was told to lure him into a sexual position for the incriminating evidence to be gathered and recorded. They would also burst in and take a photograph, to add sheer horror to the event. On this particular occasion, when she was just fourteen, the crew took a little longer to enter through the door than had been anticipated, and the minister had become violent. He beat her badly and also attempted to bugger her. He ripped her virgin flesh so violently that she needed stitches and was unable to move for days.

The minister was a narcissistic bully and a disgusting blight on the human race. He only tolerated Cynthia due to not having a thirteen year old boy available. He was a sick individual. He showed no humanity and had no consideration for her. He was determined to satisfy himself in any means he felt he desired. She was, after all, paid meat for his entertainment.

Cynthia, however, had a failsafe plan that she had devised. She was young, but due to her father's paranoid lifestyle and her ability to read situations, she was ahead of her years, and she had to be. The man grew more and more aggressive and violent and hurt her more and more. He started to strangle her, but she reached for the razor blade that was concealed in her hairband. Without any hesitation and in rage, she withdrew it and slashed the guy in the face and kicked him as he reeled back in shock. Following this, she slashed at his genitals, nearly hacking them off, and created a scene likened to the best of any gory horror film.

By the time the crew burst in, the minister was bleeding out, and it took all of their resources to get him untraceable medical help and to push out a cover story as to why he was confined to bedrest at his home for weeks. It was, of course, the normal car accident story, and he was hailed a hero for surviving.

She had been lost in this memory as she walked, but when she realised she was at the track, she climbed over the small fence. She crossed the track, entered the derelict site and the building stood in front of her, moody and dark. It was uncompromising. It stood proud and had the feel of authority and age coupled with secrets and stories.

"Hello Cynthia," said John.

Cynthia reeled around shocked and startled at his capacity for stealth, and she was for an instant actually frightened.

"I am so glad to see you, John," she said.

After a pause of about two seconds, she ran to him and hugged him and kissed him on the cheek.

John could feel her taught breasts against him, and her arms giving warmth around his neck. She rubbed his back and let her hands wander over his waist, and then she stood back quickly. She pointed the Beretta at him and smiled.

"Foolish man. All that cloak and dagger, and you have your gun in your waistband. What were you thinking, John?"

"I was being ridiculous. I actually thought you might be human, but you are your father's girl alright."

"What do you mean, Johnny boy?"

"Bartholomew Knowles. Cynthia, please drop the pretence. I have been following both of you, and I am not stupid. That's why I offered you a proposition."

"My father warned me not to underestimate you Johnny boy, and he was right, too, apart from the part where you have a hard on for me. You see I have learnt that all men are testosterone driven and vain. I knew you would slip up and be caught off-guard."

She paused and was beaming. She was so pleased with herself. She revelled in her victorious condescending superiority over him, and she was, for once, the one her father would admire.

"Fair play though, getting rid of the teams the way you did. That was absolute genius! Who were the men by the way?"

"Taxi drivers. They were brothers who run a taxi firm, and it was all about money, pure and simple," replied John, who walked to a large piece of a beam and sat down.

Cynthia checked that his rucksack was in evidence, as she was convinced that this man would surely try to live after four such eventful and life changing days.

"Why are you so relaxed, John?"

"You are superior to me in every way, Cynthia, and I cannot compete with you. I am tired of running around and am completely worn out," he replied yawning.

"How do you know Bartholomew Knowles?" she asked, intrigued at his apparent knowledge of the organisation she guarded so fiercely.

"Ruthless killer, master of industrial espionage, trained international assassin, munitions dealer and so on. Takes tea in the office of Wernons. Doesn't everyone know him?"

Cynthia smiled. She was impressed and slightly concerned, as he may have more accomplices, and this would give credibility to the fact that he remained confident and was not showing the slightest bit of fear.

"How do you know I won't kill you right now, Johnny boy?"

"Don't play games, Cynthia. I still have the all-singing, lifesaving decoder, and if you kill me, my money is on that your father will kill you."

"How is it that you have become so clever and so calm, John?"

"Survival, the oldest of primal instincts. I did not ask to be involved in any of this, but it just kept dragging me in and spewing me out in different directions. I am sick of it Cynthia, so how do you live like this?"

"It is my life, and I have had no other options. I was born to it, manipulated and have plied my craft in the eyes of my father."

"Sit down Cynthia. Put the gun down and talk to me like a civilised normal girl. You can always lift it and shoot me if I move."

Cynthia just stood there, gun extended and stared. She was for the first time in her life confused, but in her mind, hesitation showed weakness which would never be tolerated in the Knowles regime, so she regained her composure immediately.

"Where is the decoder, John?"

"You really ask such a question while knowing it is the very reason blood remains in my veins and my heart beats; like I would tell you such a thing."

Cynthia looked up at the sky. A flicker of light kept catching her eye, and she could see a wire noose hanging from a bar over the expanse in the corner of the house where the back room used to be.

"That is a bit ironic isn't it? Has someone been having a spooky joke?" she said laughing.

"It is not a laughing matter," said John in a serious tone. "It is for you."

Cynthia laughed nervously and shrugged it off as an absurd gesture of defiance from a condemned man.

"So what now, Johnny boy?"

"Look Cynthia, I have something your father wants. In fact, I have two things your father wants, and you both have nothing except grief to bargain with. No matter how this proceeds. it bodes badly for both of us, and I don't think your future is rosy. Have you considered my proposal Cynthia? It makes sense."

"Preposterous, simply preposterous, John."

"What was the plan? Kill me, give the decoder to someone, Mr X, and then everyone lives happily ever after?"

"Something like that," she replied sarcastically.

"Open your eyes girl and get a life. There is still time."

"I am to get the decoder and kill you. That is my brief. There is then a transfer of the decoder plus ten million in untraced notes, and that is all I know. You will be dead, and I, well, I continue with my job."

"What's the matter, Cynthia?"

"It's just something my father said to the voice on the telephone," she said thinking deeply as she spoke. "I overheard them talking, and he said 'no one was to be left standing when the transaction is completed, not even kin.' I had no idea what it meant at the time, but now I am getting the feeling. No, couldn't be."

John stood up. He had a Beretta in his hand.

Cynthia pointed the gun and intended firing it several times.

John started laughing.

Cynthia was shaking. She had never hesitated before, but this man confused her. Her father detested her, did not care and was the darkest influence a child could have ever had bestowed on her. She had followed as a child would, obeyed into adulthood and here she was, about to kill the one person on the planet she had actually warmed to.

"Empty the magazine Cynthia. You have to think about your life: past, present and well, there is no future. I made you a proposition, and you elected to ignore it. You now have a gun, so just follow your heart."

Cynthia felt an emotion she had never felt before. She was willing to die here rather than shoot John Parks, but why? She could not place the emotion in a rational box in her head. She was cold, heartless and ruthless. Could she change, as John Parks had changed, but the other way?

John was looking at her, and he smiled. He pointed the Beretta at her head and started to laugh.

"It's not funny, John," Cynthia said with tears beginning to fall.

John continued laughing.

"You bastard," she screamed.

John fired until he emptied the magazine.

Cynthia closed her eyes on the first shot, but on the sixth, she looked up to see John firing towards her but nothing was happening. He walked up to her and took the Beretta from her hands.

She was totally confused. She had elected to meet her maker and let him live, and she knew she could not fathom why as she had never loved anyone or anything, so it could not possibly be love.

He fired one shot from the Beretta he took from her, and it broke a branch a few metres away.

"The one I let you take had live ammunition, while mine did not. For once and without question, please do as you are told, as I will not hesitate to despatch you."

"What are you going to do?" she said sheepishly.

"Take off the jacket, lie on the floor, place your hands behind your back and don't move, as I will surely put a well-deserved bullet through your head without any hesitation at all."

"You keep reminding me of this fact, John, but I may remind you that I was willing to die and let you live. Does that not mean anything to you? How have you become so ruthless and heartless?"

"You, Cynthia. You were the final straw. I wanted to trust you, and you let me down very badly.

Cynthia lay down and placed her hands behind her back. She felt his knee crush her waist, as he knelt down and held the barrel of the gun hard into her neck.

"Don't move, not a millimetre or I will despatch you to your maker, the dark one."

"I know!" she shouted in defiance.

John placed the cable tie on her left wrist first, then the right, then between the two and he doubled them all up.

"Get up, Cynthia."

"What are you going to do with me?"

John grabbed her arm and led her to the noose.

"Stand on the piece of wood on the beam there, young lady. You like to be acrobatic and to live on the edge, so stand right there for me, thank you. Now just bow your head."

John pulled the wire down a bit, pushed her head back and put the thin deadly razor wire around her neck. He then pulled it tighter, so it had contact with her skin and then he stood back.

"Perfect. You look less superior somehow, a bit embarrassed and shocked."

"Fuck you!" she screamed.

"Don't move Cynthia. Oh no, don't move sweetheart, or the wire will sever your neck like a knife through butter."

He wrapped cello tape carefully around her mouth and right around her head and told her to lift her right foot. He moved the piece of wood, then the left foot and repeated the process.

Cynthia was almost on tiptoe, and she could feel the steel wire taught against her throat. She tried to remain calm and composed, but this was a complete reversal of what she had anticipated today, and she could not help but hear the words of her father, "Do not underestimate this man Cynthia."

She tried to beg her release, but it was just a muffled sound, not words that could be deciphered through the bondage.

"Don't waste your words, Cynthia. Conserve your energy; you will need it. Now, what is the best contact number for Bartholomew Knowles?"

He pulled the tape down just enough to let her speak.

"You are kidding aren't you, John?"

"Why no. Number please, a mobile not a landline.

She reeled off a set of numbers, and he programmed them into his mobile phone.

"I do hope these are correct numbers. You see the sooner that I conclude my business with your father, I can then decide exactly what to do with you; I am leaving now, have a nice afternoon."

"Don't you dare leave me here like this John! I can help you. I know everything. John, I care for you, please, please, John."

John moved toward Cynthia with his small, yet razor sharp, lock knife that he had retrieved from his sock. He stared at her and looked front and back, then he strategically placed the phone on video mode and walked around her. He pulled the cello tape up over her mouth again and stared deep into her eyes.

She was terrified and tried to talk, but it was a muffled pitiful noise that emanated from her.

"There is always an alternative my darling Cynthia, but maybe not for you today, maybe this always was the day you die, you know, fate and the bigger universe."

Cynthia looked terrified. John paced around the ruins and he glanced back at her.

"I have, after careful consideration, come to a decision. I need to make you bleed out slowly, Cynthia. In fact, to satisfy my thirst for vengeance, I need you to bleed quite a lot. I know that if you slit the nose, this part of the anatomy bleeds like crazy, and I think the cheek does too but not quite as much as the nose."

His eyes were ice cold and fixed on hers, but she stared at him with pleading begging eyes. She realised this man not only had complete control over her life or her death, but he enjoyed the theatrics. 'What did we do to you, John? We chewed you up and spat you out,' she thought. 'Why couldn't I have met you under normal circumstances?'

"If I sever your nice nubile breast, I guess that would do or wrists. A head bleeds loads too. Thighs?" he said rubbing her upper leg. "You choose. What the breast, because you have no bra on? How considerate of you Cynthia, you do surprise me, but I will of course respect your wishes."

Cynthia was screaming but still held motionless by the wire that was becoming ever increasingly taught around her neck.

John undid her blouse by three buttons, revealing her ample cleavage and beautiful toned skin; her curves were perfect, taught and rounded. Her face portrayed a completely different picture. It was contorted in sheer horror, but she could not move. A tear fell from her eye, genuine feeling and remorse for a life filled with such unhappiness, disappointment and unholy acts. This, her final retribution, had surely arrived, and in the form of the new devil, John Parks. She had underestimated him, and for that, she would be cut up and left to die.

She looked down as he slipped the blouse over her shoulder, and her right breast and nipple was exposed followed by the left one. John found them a very pleasing sight from the bed of sacrifice. This was something human and nice, even if the circumstances reflected something quite bizarre and worrying.

He smiled, as he found them not only erotic, but it pleased him to have such control over a human being, especially one that had threatened his safety and existence. After all, this was the enemy, purely and simply the enemy, the daughter of Satan.

He cupped her right breast in his hand and soothed it gently, as it heaved with the anxious breath it needed. She was consumed with fear not without genuine reason.

He let the flattened knife blade rub hard against her areola, and he was smiling, enjoying her position of anti-ecstasy. He then turned the blade and placed the razor sharp edge against her proud nipple. She flinched. He then merely took one step back, switched the mobile camera off, pulled up her blouse, buttoned two fasteners and looked at her.

"Hell of a way to get a look at someone's tits, isn't it? Great pair by the way, really top notch."

Cynthia tried to regain her composure but she struggled. She was short of breath, her mouth was dry and she felt like being sick. Her eyes met his, and she was a different person, broken and defeated. The wire cut deep into her neck and was starting to draw blood on both sides; she was absolutely terrified and now completely confused.

John stood back and surveyed his quarry before taking out a fresh, unused mobile phone.

He walked up to her, still with the knife in his hand and cut some of the tape away from her mouth.

"Forgive me Father for my sins," he said looking up to the heavens, then he looked straight into Cynthia's eyes.

"Forgive me too, Cynthia sweetheart, but this is necessary evil," he said, as he held her head in his hand.

As he kissed her, she was twisted inside. She had and still did anticipate sweet death, and yet she was in ecstasy; it was another dimension to sexuality. She felt strangely elated. She felt her heart beating faster, and their tongues locked and investigated each other's mouths. He was so gentle, and she was surprised at just how gentle the kiss was.

She became completely engrossed and wanted to be naked and to writhe in his dominance, and she longed for his touch and to feel him all over her. Without warning, with the crashing totally unexpected act, instantly shattering the illusion that he may just love her, she felt the sharp steel followed by a burning sensation and a cutting pain. She opened her eyes immediately. The fantasy lay broken around her body, and she could not have been more destroyed in life or death.

John was just staring into her eyes without blinking and devoid of any real emotion. He held her and stopped her from tilting forward onto the wire. He stroked her face as she bled.

"I am so sorry Cynthia. I am truly sorry. Please forgive me, but it just had to be done. I think you know that ultimately, in your heart, it had to come to this.

Cynthia felt the blood flow. It was warm, and she was losing a lot from the fresh wound he had inflicted. She looked into his eyes but not with hatred or revulsion. She showed him a warmth that he had not seen previously, as if she had reserved her love for this very moment. It was as if Cynthia was actually re-joining the human race, and she smiled and her eyes were rejuvenated.

"Why, Johnny boy, why?"

He kissed her gently, "Because I could love you so easily, Cynthia."

He then briskly walked to a position of clear vision and could not hide his satisfaction. He then proceeded to place and break some bags and took a set of cleverly staged photographs portraying the grizzly sight before him.

John felt different. He had done a lot of things in the past few days that were alien to him, but this was the absolute biggest emotion that he had felt, and he could live with it.

Chapter 14

Unravelling

"We lost her, but we picked up a van in the street adjacent to the alley," said the team one lead surveillance operative. "There is no angle to see who got into or out of the van, if indeed anyone did, but the van, well it drove off and did some weird patterns, almost like it was trying to evade anyone attempting to follow it."

"Who does the van belong to?" asked another man.

"It belongs to Aswan Patem, an ordinary guy."

"Who does the taxi firm belong to?"

"Anwar Patem, sir."

"Ring any bells? Looks like we have a link gentlemen."

"Track them all down and bring them in, and tell them a girl was kidnapped. They will spill the beans if they think he has double crossed them."

John looked at the flat roof in the front of Wernons where the office was housed, and there in all his glory, sitting beneath the ornate ceiling, was the General of Death, Bartholomew Knowles.

"Yes, this is Bartholomew Knowles. Is that you Cynthia?"

"No, Bartholomew Knowles, this just happens to be your nemesis, John Parks. How are you on this bright and sunny late afternoon? Had a nice day? I do hope so."

"Congratulations, Mr Parks. I never underestimated you for one moment, and true to form, you have exceeded even my expectations. Well done, old chap, top skills."

"Thank you, Bartholomew, bit of a name if you don't mind me saying, never thought of changing it to a man's name?"

"If I did not know better, I would say that you are trying to antagonise me, Mr Parks."

"Stop waving your hands furiously to your team and trying to trace me, Bartholomew. I am watching you this very minute, so clear the room of those idiots. We are way beyond their involvement, and you know it. We are both in a different league."

Knowles bit. His narcissistic attitude and complete belief in his superiority over everyone made him vain, and sometimes his judgement could be manipulated to suit his ego, not necessarily his rational.

"What do you want, Parks?" he shouted moving to the window as if to declare his defiance.

"A rifle old chap. Now I wish I had the bloody rifle. *Click*," John said sarcastically.

Knowles moved away from the window swiftly and submerged himself in the darker shadows of the room.

"I don't trust you at all, John. Pardon me, if I don't just put a bullseye on my chest. I will stay concealed for now."

"What do you want besides the decoder Bartholomew?"

"Nothing, Parks."

"We all want something more, so come on, you can be honest. What do you want?"

"You dead, Parks, that would be an honest answer but that would be of no use to me apart from petty vengeance."

"What of your daughter?"

"Keep her. She is nothing to me, never has been, and I don't even think she is my blood, since she was born of a whore and a night of the standing prick, I am afraid, one of many pricks I believe. She's like a bloody tick on a dog."

"Wow, family values seem to have taken a downward spiral in the Knowles household today."

"You don't get it, Parks. They were never there. People are consumable items to be used and abused and discarded at will, and as you will not be here long from now, don't concern yourself too much. Everyone is looking for you. You have nowhere to go or hide; you are dead."

"You are not the first person to say that to me this week, and I have proved them wrong. You know what, Knowles, it is my intention to serve you with notice that you are in fact going to die within twenty four hours of this conversation."

"Grow up, Parks. You are outflanked, out gunned, and you are certainly out brained. You have no allies worth mentioning apart from Gerald and Martin, the ChuckleBerry idiotic twins."

"Well Bartholomew, I will give you ten million ways to recover your precious decoder, all wrapped in a pair of green holdalls, so take it or leave it, ten, nine, eight, seven, six, five, four, three, two…"

"OK, OK," Knowles barked loudly, "You can do as you wish with the girl, too. I don't ever want her near me, bloody parasite. She has failed me for the last time; I can tell you."

"You choose death for her, then," said John coldly.

One of Bartholomew's men walked into the office and handed him an image.

"This arrived on the secure mobile, sir."

"So you have already killed her, John. I am surprised that you dragged it out so long. Stupid bitch, Christ she was so damn annoying. Thanks, old man, for services rendered, and for free too," he said laughing.

Bartholomew Knowles looked at the picture of his daughter. She was hanging from the wire, neck bent to one side with blood coming from both front and sides, and she also had what appeared to be five or six blood soaked bullet holes in her abdomen, chest and stomach but the image was slightly grainy and unclear.

"A necessary evil, Mr Knowles," said John, now talking with an icily cold tone and a menacing atmosphere surrounding him.

"I really wish you had been working for me, Parks. I can relate to your efficiency and pride in achievement. You also demonstrate that most precious of products within our craft, logic. You have to analyse and react with logic not emotion."

"Thank you for the compliment. I have turned the corner so far from who and where I was last week. I don't even know myself anymore. I do know, however, that I intend to live a long and happy life and enjoy myself and the hell with everyone else."

"It is a shame you will never enjoy the money, John. There are those who are more scary, powerful and much more protected than I who will of course be coming for you. I will humour you, John. I will deliver the money for the decoder. Am I to be engaged in the same charade that Cynthia went through before her death?"

"Something like that Knowles but more elaborate."

"We questioned the taxi drivers in our own particular way, and they encouraged more force than necessary, but they were a good find for you and ultra-efficient for civilians. I guess they were paid handsomely. I hope so, as they now have some broken bits."

"It all boils down to coin, Bartholomew. It doesn't really matter how we try to fancy it up or make all this spy shit glamorous. It does not make all or even any of our acts courageous or incredibly meaningful; it is just about coin."

"Hmmmmm, looks like you have your own ideology firmly planted, John."

"It beats the public schoolboy mentality, trying to justify their actions. Coin is coin, in whatever race creed or language. The mighty coin speaks, and you know this is true whoever or wherever you are. I don't want to compete in the righteous stakes, since you are holding that mantle. I am happy to relax somewhere and watch the sunset with your money or the fat singer's money. It ain't over till it's over Knowles."

"What a strange reference, dear boy. 'Coin'? Never heard it quite put like that before."

"Bartholomew, please will you do me a favour and take the holdalls to the window. Go on. I am watching remember."

Knowles picked up the two large holdalls and went to the window as instructed.

"Open the window, and then please throw them both far enough out that they clear the main wall and land in the road.

"You must think me…"

"JUST DO IT!" screamed John.

Knowles opened the window, pulled the first holdall back and threw it over the wall, then the second. Then the phone went dead.

John scooped the suitcases up and put one over each of his shoulders before speeding off on the small machine.

Knowles ran to the front of the entrance and waited for the electronic gate to open. He then ran through it, but the road was deserted, and the holdalls had disappeared.

He ran into the building to the back room and demanded the surveillance footage. He watched, stunned, as the man, his nemesis and obviously John Parks, picked up the holdalls of money, gathered his bounty and just casually rode off. He appeared to be smiling, as he did so.

"YOU ARE DEAD PARKS! DO YOU HEAR ME? YOU ARE DEAD! You are dead," he repeated and he went into the office and sat down and put his hands in his head.

"We have found the taxi drivers, and we actually stumbled upon them being slaughtered by Bartholomew Knowles' gorillas," said one of the surveillance team.

"Are they alive?"

"Yes, luckily, a few broken ribs and such but OK. We have located the third driver too, and he evaded capture, bless him."

"What do they say?"

"They all mimic each other and tell the same story, the very same thing: simple set of instructions, to be followed to the letter or aborted at stages.

"Sounds professional."

"There were reported event achievements."

"What?"

"He had a set of events which had to be achieved and then reported, as each of the events were achieved."

"What civilian acts like this?"

"My guess is that it is one who is intent on staying alive and meeting the girl. The package was Bartholomew Knowles' daughter, Cynthia."

"I know, but did he succeed?"

"We believe so. He used multiple mobile sources, made her strip and lose all clothing and jewellery and had it smashed up. He either knew what he was doing. or he is a gifted individual, gifted with uncanny luck, which we know is not true."

"This Parks guy is beginning to worry me. He is no novice; he just cannot be, so where did she end up?

"At an allotment, Uplands Allotments."

"Is there any form of track anywhere near it?"

"Yes, it travels across the public footpath."

"Towards?"

"Old Painswick Road. Well, I'll be damned, the cunning bastard has only taken her and gone home again."

"Maybe not with the girl though. Where is she?"

"Hangman's Cottage perhaps?."

"Of course, it is by the original crash site, quick, get a team there in case."

"On its way, sir."

"I want you to report to me every two minutes. Do you hear? Every two minutes."

"Yes, sir."

John took the money and stashed it in the safest location he knew, and given the time restraints, it was also the closest and the quickest hiding place. He then casually parked the bike out of sight in a garage he sometimes used in White Horse Lane. It belonged to a guy in the road, and John had bought him a few pints on occasion. He stashed stuff in there, and it worked for both of them. They both had an unwritten trust, no questions and they also had mutual respect. John trusted this guy completely, he needed to.

John walked back to Belleview, unlocked and walked into the front door but only after putting the Beretta in his pocket with his hand on the handle and trigger. He was prepared for anything.

He went through the lounge and into the kitchen, and then opened the back door to let the dense stone structure ventilate. He then travelled to and went into each room. He checked the tape, "What a surprise," he thought and said out loud.

Each and every seal had been broken so he was instantly aware that intruders had accessed Belleview.

"I know you can hear me, and I know you have entered my property, so you can all FUCK RIGHT OFF," he shouted loudly.

"I do hope that doesn't extend to me," said Barbara smiling in her doorway and staring at John in a bewildered fashion.

"I am so sorry Barbara, but it is just that those 0800 salespeople make me so mad. Don't you get angry with them?"

"I tell 'em to fuck right off as well, John," she said laughing. "Him indoors, he tells them worse things in there, but I almost certainly can't repeat what he says, no way, not and remain ladylike."

"You just said 'fuck off' Babs," said a voice, and Frank appeared.

"Context, Frank, it was in context."

"Someone was in your house, John my boy. After you left, we saw them hovering around outside, so we watched, then we waited and went over to the Bentley Cottage entrance. We waited, and we saw someone walk past the bedroom window. It wasn't you, so we knocked loudly on the door shouting that we had dialled 999 for the emergency service police, and they scarpered through the back. They must have your keys. How could they have your keys, John? Bloody riddle."

"If you told them like that, they probably knew you were not to be messed with, 999 emergency service police," John said sarcastically but it just went straight over both of their heads

"When they changed the glass Frank," said Barbara, "they must have taken the key to have a duplicate made, cheeky buggers."

"That would explain the silent entrance, though. I will get it changed, but anyone can get in through a double glazed door," said John casually.

"I can't," said Frank, "not without the key, John. Anyway, let us know if you need anything. Strange goings on around here for sure, Babs."

"Sure are Frankie," she said as they both retreated to the comfort of their cottage and an evening of wine, no doubt.

John made a coffee, took it up the garden and sat next to the two men who occupied his seats on the decking.

"Hi John. Still alive then?"

"Hi Gerald, Martin. How are you both?"

"You are really leading an enchanted life, but you are also living so dangerously, John."

"Lead team? Where the hell are you?"

"We are ETA five minutes from offload, then five minutes from target point one, sir."

"Team two, where are you?"

"We are in place and circling from the Painswick stream end, sir. ETA a further five minutes."

"Team three, where are you?"

"We are already in position. Sniper one, two and three deployed and hostile to go, sir."

It was only one minute later that he repeated the same questions and received a slightly smaller translation in the timeframe of the answers given but the same version. He was anxious, the minister was also anxious and there was a whole lot more at stake than the others knew.

"Team one arriving, disembarking, team one on foot and spreading out, sir. Cover in place."

"Team two are in back up position and ready to go. I repeat we are ready to go, sir."

"Team three as were. Proceed team one."

"Go, let's get this over, and see what has transpired in this place. I bet it is not good, not good at all."

"Team one in position. All quiet, cannot get any heat signature, and it appears deserted."

"Go team one. Go to target."

"Copy, we are moving in."

"What is going on? Team one respond. What is current situation reflecting, team one?"

"Team one here, sir, and there is nobody here, but there is evidence of some harm befalling the young lady in question. There is no doubt in my mind that she is status expired."

"Gather evidence and trace for analysis. We need to find out exactly what she encountered here."

"Looks like John Parks murdered her, sir."

"That does not stack up. She was his bargaining chip, and he went to a lot of trouble executing the most elaborate planning just to get her off the grid and alone. So why would he just kill her? For what, where is the gain?"

"Revenge, sir, maybe a show of strength for Knowles. You know, 'look what I can do and to someone so close to you.'"

"Walk me through the scene."

"Grizzly, hangman's noose made from cheese wire, with blood all over it. Blood on the floor, and I mean quite a bit, and drag marks into the brush and track, and then they disappear. They or he might have had a quad or something to transport the body away.

"Not Parks, he could not have orchestrated the clean-up and still had gone home in the timeframe. We know he contacted Knowles too and went off with a package, probably sterling."

"There is a fully expended Beretta magazine here and blood everywhere. She is dead, sir."

"OK, we shall not cry over any loss of blood line associated with Bartholomew Knowles? Absolutely not! You guys get back here but leave surveillance in play."

About five or six minutes after the three teams pulled back, the familiar VW Transporters arrived and the occupants made their way to Hangman's Cottage. The lead operative scanned a handheld device, and it triggered a series of beeps when he directed it to the old original stone staircase. The man went over, found the device, smiled into it and stamped on it. He continued his sweep. "CLEAR!" he shouted.

"I believe she is dead, sir, based upon the evidence presented before me; how do you wish me to proceed?"

"Get Brian."

"Yes, Bartholomew."

"Don't use my name. Now walk me through the scene, but don't hold back. She was my daughter, but you know only too well my old comrade, I am first and foremost a soldier, and she is a casualty of this escapade and collateral damage."

"Looks like she was well and truly butchered. There's a lot of blood, and it appears she has been severed by hanging. Instrument of death: cheese wire."

"No sign of any struggle at all? No kick marks or movement within the theatre of the act? She had to be completely incapacitated, somehow subdued beyond any capability to resist. I do find this most strange for the individual involved."

"Spare the theatrics man. Fact and fact alone is my bounty, so tell me what you see. I will then act."

"Grizzly, hangman's noose made from cheese wire, blood all over it, blood on the floor, and I mean quite a bit, and drag marks off into the wilderness.

"He must have used the track as his route for disposing of the corpse. I cannot see that he would gain access to this point for any motorised vehicle, a motorcycle, perhaps, not sure, but to get a body out on it?

"He might have strapped her to something or probably straddled her over a bike or a quad, or even a tractor. That one may remain a mystery. Shall I come back?"

"Do, it seems of no further use to worry about her, at least I don't have to pay for a funeral, stupid mare. I think it is high time I had a very personal conversation with Mr John Parks. We ought to get acquainted."

"Did you hear that team leader?"

"Copy, got it all."

"It is not very direct. He just hated his daughter, and there is nothing really to go on in the conversation."

"Brian Cleed is there and that is significant. He is Bartholomew's accountant, scientist and medical guy, and he is a high ranking international industrial operative and wanted in several countries."

"Why don't we just pull them all in?"

"We want the big fish, lads. Exercise patience and always use a little fish to catch a big fish."

"He also has no living profile, surgically removed finger prints, no DNA on record, no name that can be traced and no history. He is a ghost, and even the girl he calls his daughter is not his bloodline.

"What shall I do, sir?"

"Redirect the drone to follow the vehicle and get it circling around Wernons. You never know, we might get some chatter. The men in his ranks are getting frustrated. A couple have left, we have them in black holes and we will learn more during the night."

"Affirmative."

"So John, are you really going to tell us what happened to the girl?" asked Martin knowing no answer would be forthcoming.

"You tell me."

"Come on John, this is getting more ridiculous by the minute. We all know what is going on, but we just need to get our heads around the facts, then we can move forward with the best solution," said Gerald.

"Best for whom?"

"For everyone, John," said Martin.

"You know who the big guy is don't you? You sit there smug and ready to hang me out to dry, and yet you need something from me. We would not be having this conversation if you did not boys."

"We have no intention of hanging anyone out to dry," said Gerald defensively.

"Yet you watched me."

"What do you mean?"

"You watched me. All of you watched me, and you played me, Gerald. I was running around like a frightened rabbit caught in the headlights, and you all watched and probably had a good laugh. The term you all used was 'probably', an expendable human no doubt."

"John, it was not like that."

"What was it like then, Gerald? Tell me because I am dying to know how a British subject is left dangling as bait in the midst of industrial espionage with the threat of world balance shifting, and against lethal gangs of assassins. I still can't believe I am saying those very words, and it involves running around Painswick, this sleepy leafy village trying to kill who, YOURS BLOODY TRULY, THAT'S WHO."

There was a pause and the men all just looked at each other in turn but said nothing. It was an awkward silence for the government officials, as they knew John was indeed correct in all that he said.

"That is exactly how it went down, and I still trust neither of you," he said, "nor anyone else for that matter. I actually think it is better the devil you know, that's my latest philosophy. At least I know where I am with

Knowles, everything is black and white, kill or be killed, life for coin. It's simple, but it works."

"John, please come on board and help us. We cannot help you unless you participate," said Martin.

"So what is it you want?" asked John staring at both of them.

"What did you do with the girl, John?" asked Gerald.

"What girl?" replied John.

"Have you made contact with Bartholomew Knowles? He received a call from a pay as you go phone that was triangulated to the park earlier today," said Gerald.

"Who is Bartholomew Knowles?"

"John, please. The girl, Knowles, the phones."

"And?" said John casually.

"A man matching your description," he said producing a photographic image from a file he had on his lap, "in fact you, right here in pure sight, caught on CCTV in Cheltenham, purchasing the very same phone and nine others from the bloody phone shop."

"He looks a bit like me, but it's not a very clear image though, in fact, it's pretty blurred, chaps. I don't imagine for one moment that this image would prove sufficient evidence in a court of law or would satisfy a jury beyond a shadow of a doubt, do you?"

"Come on, John. Work with us here," implored Martin.

"I lost that phone. It upset me, as I like a few of each things, like Berettas," he replied sarcastically.

"The same phones were also used to set up events around Stroud and Hangman's Cottage earlier today."

"Really? I wondered if anyone had found the box I dropped. Can I have them back, or have they all been used or sold on as I expect by now?"

"Don't be clever John. We triangulated them and they led us to the scene of what we think was the death of Cynthia Knowles."

"Really, who?"

"Cynthia. Don't be clever John. You know damn well who she is and that you are or were using her as a pawn against Bartholomew Knowles."

"What if I informed you, you of course being the tools of her Majesty's government, and you, the president's stooge, that I could not only identify and almost certainly expose the fat man? Could I disappear after?"

"It is an interesting theoretical notion, that given the full details, I could probably propose to the authorities and see what transpires. It would probably be favourable I imagine."

"Interested, aren't you, but don't play me though. It is a Home Office decision, and you Gerald are representing the Home Office here, so don't insult my intelligence and act like you are some lowlife, downtrodden government official. Please just drop the pretence and don't treat me like a child. I know you yield power and lots of it."

"What do you mean John? You have lost me."

"I played you, Gerald. I played along with our first encounter, but you really ought to have a chat with your Photoshop team."

"I don't understand, John."

"Give me your wallet," said John. "Come on."

Gerald retrieved his wallet from inside his trousers' pocket and passed it to John, Martin was watching intensely.

"The picture of you is with your baby in your arms, and the impression it gives is of a warm loving father. When was this was taken?"

"She is six now, John, so obviously six years ago."

"See the nice, shiny new red van in the distance? That one over there?" he pointed to it.

"Yes, what about it?"

"Look at the bloody registration, Gerald. It is not and cannot be a private registration, and you know why I know this little fact so well? It just happens to belong to one of Her Majesty's postal service vehicles, and the registration is this year. So was your daughter driven here by the DeLorean DMC-12 was she?"

"What the hell is the DeLorean DMC-12?" asked Martin, totally confused but knowing Gerald was well and truly caught out.

"The DeLorean DMC-12 was the car used to transport Marty McFly back to the future in the film *Back to the Future*," said Gerald smiling.

"Shit, good spot," said Martin.

"Let me ask you gentlemen the million dollar question, but really it is more applicable to Gerald."

"Fire away," said Martin.

"Do continue," said Gerald.

"Could you and would you allow me to get away with murder, for the greater good, crown and country and all that? Would the Home Office agree that all past circumstances shall we call them, get buried under an avalanche of shredded paper, and I become immune from any form of prosecution, and adorn the label of helpful innocent law-abiding citizen?"

"You said it yourself, John. You have done nothing wrong," answered Gerald without hesitation.

"Now I know where I stand then," said John breathing out heavily, "but I will never be free of everyone will I; not completely free?"

"I don't know," said Gerald.

"I do," said John.

There was a brief pause and all of the men just looked at each other not knowing what the next move would be, all apart from John.

"So what now?"

"That depends on you, John," said Martin.

"My rules gentlemen, in the name of crown and country, actually, as you know it is for my own absolution."

"We do, John."

"I need you to achieve some events that not only distract our adversaries but also stretch Bartholomew Knowles to the limit."

"OK, we are on board," said Martin nodding.

"Just one thing, John; do you have the money?"

"And just what money would that be, Gerald?"

"The money that was with Bartholomew Knowles."

"What money would that be? No idea what you are talking about."

"The money Bartholomew Knowles threw over the fence."

"Has it been reported stolen?"

"No."

"And you say it was thrown away?"

"Yes."

"Do I look like a rich man, Gerald?"

"You look like, and you are, an extremely intelligent and cunning man, John Parks, and this is in no doubt."

"Not me, Gerald old man. I am a failure at everything. You have looked into my life intimately, and I am good for nothing really."

"Hmmmmm, you are becoming quite the card, Mr Parks, quite the card indeed."

Bartholomew Knowles was livid. He was not concerned that his daughter had been slaughtered by a novice. He was incensed that a novice had relieved him of his money, and he would lose face with the man above.

"What do we know?" he bellowed at his assembled troops.

"We believe he has gone home and is in the garden of Belleview with the British and American contingent, sir."

"Arrogant bastard! I am going to kill him myself but first I need the decoder. I guess we wait for a while, then if nothing else fails, we will kidnap Mr Parks, and he will tell us everything, absolutely everything, then I will personally slit his throat."

"What shall we do, sir?"

"Monitor him and the others. I want to know where all the players are at all times. There are some visible and others are hiding in plain sight," he bellowed.

"Yes, sir."

"Get out all of you. I need to make a call."

"Yes, speak, he said answering the phone impatiently."

"It is me. I know there was a restriction on timing, but when is the package due for the party?"

"It's long overdue but no later than two days' time."

Click, the line went dead.

Chapter 15

Players

"We have intercepted cryptic but scrambled messages that have no fixed location. The signal is routed all around the globe and is sourced from a data network. It is impossible to trace," said the technician.

"Not good enough. There has to be a way to triangulate or follow with satellites; come on man, impress me somehow like the films, pull one out the bag for me."

"I am not Gabby off *CSI*, sir, and I know it sounds negative, but I know when someone is further advanced than our wildest dreams and cannot be tracked or breached for now. They are truly years ahead."

"Damned Chinese or Koreans I bet."

"More likely ours, the Israelis or even Americans, sir."

"I need to know how. I need something and to get ahead of this. Hang on, let me get this. Hello."

"Parks has the decoder hidden."

"And the girl?"

"Dead."

"Anybody to substantiate this?"

"No need, blood evidence is everywhere, and we cloned his phone. It is a grizzly sight, sir. This guy has turned to the dark side and is a full on sadistic killer. The pictures and video footage are particularly grotesque and horrific. He enjoys death. He simply enjoys it now."

"Well, she placed herself between good and bad, so she knew the risk she was taking. How does this prick evade everyone and turn into a bloody serial killer? He is now worse than a bloody assassin if he enjoys it, and it makes him sound just like someone familiar. It's a good job they are squaring up to each other, and hopefully we get to pick up the pieces."

"Sir, despatching an advisory is one thing, Quarter mass and the pit torture and sadistic perversion is another. Should we not pull him out of the theatre and try another angle?"

"Balderdash, move on man."

"Yes, sir, shall I stand down from him and see what he does?"

"Yes but keep an eye on him from the drone and ground operatives. He is beyond help now, so we will deal with him later, though, does he actually have the means to expose the bigger fish."

"We believe so, and the drone is set to follow Knowles, however, he plays classical music above the office, and the drone cannot pick up anything but... just a minute... Sir, what, ah OK, it appears he has been talking to one of the mobile phones from the ten identified as John Parks."

"So, he is planning an exchange then? It has to be, so triangulate that phone immediately."

"No need, sir. He is simply walking around the Painswick Park, and the only thing missing is a dog."

"He is either extremely stupid, arrogant or so confident that he is hiding in plain sight. Did you promise him anything, Gerald?"

"Yes, sir. I gave him my word that he could walk when everything was achieved and completed, sir."

"You did Gerald, but I most certainly did not."

"Whatever you say, sir."

"Too right, he will be fed to the wolves and rightly so. They are circling him anyway, and they will save us any embarrassment if he is found murdered in a ditch somewhere."

"Where is he now?"

"Wandering around the park like a man without a care in the world."

"Did he talk to Knowles?"

"I think he is talking to him now. He is quite comical, all this mayhem around and he walks about like a man looking for his dog. Hang on, he has ducked into the bushes beyond the park fence. He must have a clear view of Wernons from there, so I will ring you later."

The airwaves cracked, a different team started dialogue. "Did you deal with that other little issue?"

"Yes, they have been expunged."

"How many?"

"Four of them, sir."

"Any other news?"

"The merchandise was made in Korea, sir."

"Excellent, so what is he doing now."

"He had a meeting with the Brits and Americans, and then he appeared to go for a walk Sir."

"Where is the bloody tracker from the holdalls?" bellowed Knowles more agitated than usual and becoming deadlier by the second, even to those loyal and close to him, he was on meltdown.

"He has them both located up by the old church by the golf club, where the cemetery is. A team is on its way."

"There is a van leaving Wernons, sir. Looks like Knowles men are on the move."

"Use the drone; don't spook them."

"Yes, sir, drone deployed."

"Keep me on speaker."

The man blurted a series of information, "Van confirmed in sight. Vehicle travelling up to the main road. Vehicle turned right toward Brockworth and Cheltenham, out of Painswick. Vehicle turned left toward the cemetery, reversing and completing the turn, the road is almost inaccessible from this direction. Vehicle has turned the corner. Vehicle is parking by Gate House on verge.

Bartholomew Knowles growled and shouted, and everyone in his vicinity began to quake with fear.

The team got out and went over to the green pickup truck which had Painswick Council written on it. The caretaker and groundsman who operated the vehicle came out of the cottage in his official green jumper, and he smiled a courteous smile. He then went over to meet the men who had disembarked the van and were by his pickup

"Can I help you, gentlemen?" he asked cordially.

"Yes, I wonder if you could help me? A foolish and immature friend of ours thought it would be funny to throw our holdalls in your truck for us to have to chase. I guess you would refer to it as high prankster or maybe student stupidity. Whatever you choose to call it, I think you call it stupid," said one of the younger guys.

The caretaker looked into the back of his truck and sure enough, there were two holdalls lay there in the bed. He grabbed them and passed them to the young man.

"They appear to be empty," he said smiling. "They certainly are not mine though, that much I can tell you."

"Did you open them?" asked the younger guy.

"I didn't even know they were there," said the old guy.

"Thanks," said the younger man, and they all entered the van and evacuated the old guy's space.

He had no time to hide it, and he was genuinely surprised. Where the hell did Parks put it?

Knowles was neither amused or was he demonstrating any form of restraint or any patience whatsoever. He started kicking furniture, screaming and then ultimately he turned violent, and his temper erupted like a volcano of wrath. He punched and floored several of his men, as he marched about the building, he withdrew his gun when his phone burst into life.

"Knowles, and this had better be good."

"Do we have a problem, Bartholomew?"

"No, sir, everything is in hand."

"So you have the decoder or is its location known?"

"Almost, sir."

"Does the package still draw breath?"

"Momentarily, but I will remedy this in an hour or so. Sir, I can assure you his minutes are numbered."

"Not like you, Barty. You appear to be all emotional and irrational. Get a grip man! Is my cargo secure, the bargaining cargo that is? He seems to have you quaking a bit, old man."

"Yes, it is by my side, but don't worry, and no he does not. I told you that I will satisfy my need to kill with his blood."

"It is not I that worries too much, Barty. You have the ball firmly in your court, whether you choose to worry or not would be a decision based upon your own ability to recognise whether you are to fail or to achieve. The odds of this small riddle gesture toward your chances and whether you have worry or elation."

Click, he was gone.

The mysterious man dialled the phone number reserved for emergencies only, It rang and was immediately answered.

"The supplier has lost the money, I can feel it. He also does not have the decoder, and he is becoming a liability."

"Do we feed him to the others?"

"No, he might break and just feed us to the others. Death will be the only option to secure silence."

"He does not know who we are."

"He is not stupid though, and he will have fail safe plans around him."

"Hmmmmm, his daughter is dead though, that would take more than half of that away. She was so loyal and bloody dangerous."

"We can frame Parks by helping him to get rid of you know who and then frame his ass. This should be relatively easy, in fact, it should be a doddle with you around."

"Should I harvest crew members to assist? Should be easy enough if I taunt them with the footage of Cynthia's death. And twist it that he is an ex informant or something."

"No, this is now you and I, and no contact with anyone else. No more anything until this is sorted, so you must either orchestrate Parks' demise, or, well just eliminate him. Easy.

Click.

As the receiver went down on the other end, the dull thud of the first bullet caught him in the back of the head from relatively close range. His head changed shape with the following barrage of missiles burying themselves into his flesh and bone with merciless velocity. It was a final act, but the ferocity of the rounds tore up his face, as they exited through his shattered skull and severed brain. Little remained of his original features to allow visual recognition to be achieved.

The hail of bullets had rendered his carcass deceased and wrecked, and then as he fell dead on the floor, one eye remained. It was open and displayed the familiar death stare. Firmly in front of him, his assailant lifted his head to the side and slit his throat from one end to the other. This was a totally unnecessary act that was a statement to those that thought they were safe, anywhere.

The notes and folder in front of him were gathered up and placed in a rucksack, including the odd doodled drawing of a large dark bird with numbers. It appeared that Knowles was not the only person who had explored and instigated fail safe devices everywhere. The assailant also retrieved his wallet from his trousers, reached below the desk and retrieved the recording device placed there and directly linked to the scrambled phone and some keys.

The assailant then went over to the chest of drawers that stood against the far wall, moved them to one side revealing a large, impenetrable, fireproof steel door. The key opened the door to reveal a small safe contained inside the chamber with a combination lock and a key bar. The wallet was opened, the picture was removed and turned over, and the number was put into the combination lock. It clicked open, the other remaining unused key was placed into the lock, and the safe sprung open.

The contents contained within the safe could only be described as a Pandora's box. They were totally explosive and would bring down governments if given to the general public or shared with the opposition government. A foreign interest would kill for this without question.

The killer placed all of the contents into the rucksack, including a bag which contained what the assailant considered to be uncut diamonds. It was a large bag, the size of a bag of sweets, but it was manufactured in suede. The killer then placed the other similar, but slightly smaller bag, in the rucksack, and this was considered to contain cut and polished diamonds. They were worth many millions of pounds, and there could be no explanation for such a cache of precious stones to be hidden from general circulation, especially by the man who possessed them a little while ago.

The killer, as instructed, did not read the complete contents of the file, but just the notes that were in front of the man before the bullets destroyed him as a human being.

"John Parks is that you? This is getting bloody ridiculous. I have given you the package and complied with your wishes. Give me my package now; that's how it works."

"Tomorrow, Bartholomew. Everything is going to be completed, and everyone in the arena of shame will feel tickety-boo."

"I cannot wait until tomorrow Parks."

"Yes, you can."

Click.

"YOU ARROGANT LITTLE BASTARD!"

"What's going on chaps?"

"From what we can gather, Parks is actually winding Knowles up; he is taunting him."

"What do you mean?"

"We cannot get any audio from the drone, so we brought it home, but after one minute or less of conversation, Knowles was screaming and ranting, so the echo device placed opposite his house is picking up everything. He is getting sloppy, sir."

"No idea why he is doing this?"

"No, if you don't mind me asking, sir, is team leader one coming back into play tonight?"

"Why would Parks wind up Knowles?" said the man completely ignoring the other man's quest for information.

John walked into the Royal Oak and turned right into the bar. The large open fireplace pleased him, and the little jolly landlord was a sight for sore eyes. He walked the two metres to the rounded bar and was pleased to see a smiling familiar face.

"Hi John. Bloody hell, what do we call you? Killer-come-traitor-come-reprieved-convict-come… What are you now? Nice to see you, matey," he said smiling from ear to ear.

"I need a pint, Jim. Nice real ale, too. None of that gas lager shit either. Some local nectar."

"Of course," said Jim, pouring the pint of cask ale with perfection and pride.

"That one's on the Oak, old bean. I think you deserve it, but what the bloody hell happened anyway?"

"Leave him alone, Jim," said his wife Joan, coming in from the kitchen end. "He is probably sick and tired of questions."

"Joan, besides looking like a million dollars, how are you?"

"Good, and you?"

"Actually, I feel better than I have in ages," he said sitting on a stool closest to the window, so he could see most of the occupants of the pub.

"You are different."

"In what way?"

"Confident, almost cocky, assured and with direction, usually you sit like a mouse at the back of the room and never compliment or joke with anyone, but now, the new you. By the way, the shaved face is pleasing to the eye, You are a handsome guy, John."

"Thanks Joan, I never really felt very good about myself after the ball and chain ran off with the kids, but I think I just hid behind the big furry mouth rug to keep out of the mainstream bullshit, too. Bit of a beast too, wasn't it?" he said smiling.

"It was huge and ghastly, and you know we all called you 'John the Baptist' don't you, because you looked like a biblical man."

"What you saying, Joan, that he was a child ducker," said one of the locals who had gathered to listen to any potential gossip, with this comment, the whole pub erupted into spontaneous laughter, except for some tourists.

"What is he doing now?"

"He is having a pint, believe it or not."

"What's he saying?"

"Stuff about his beard and wife and kids running off. He is a strange guy that's for sure."

"Stay on him."

"Of course."

"Where is John Parks now?"

"You won't believe this, Commander."

"What? Try me?"

"He is holding court in the Royal Oak."

"You are joking. How the hell could he be having a pint now?"

"I swear he is, Commander."

"Do we have someone inside?"

"It appears that the whole place is crawling with every player; it is quite farcical."

"Bartholomew Knowles?"

"Oh he is pissed! He is so pissed you would not believe. We picked up another deserter today, and he had a broken nose where Knowles had head-butted him, as he walked past him in the hallway. No reason whatsoever, just dropped the nut on him."

"Did he talk?"

"Yep, singing like a nightingale, but he is unfortunately small potatoes. He did say that Knowles is on meltdown because he is not in the driving seat and has to complete his business by tonight."

"Parks is the business, I suppose?"

"Who is in the pub having a jolly old time unlike Bartholomew Knowles."

"Anyway, some Triad got ripped up by another member, and for some unexplainable reason, I was connected by PC Plod," said John to the madding crowd of locals who had gathered, determined not to miss such an opportunity of conspiracy theory openly discussed.

"Bastards," said one old regular.

"Idiots" was the cry of another, and it continued. The locals were riveted and hanging on his every word, as the inquisition dug into every nook and cranny of this incredible village story. Then John started to gather himself and was going to bid them farewell, and the assembled gathering were served notice that the conspiracy had been discussed more than enough for tonight.

"You can all have a good talk about me now. It's better if I am not here," said John as he got up from the stool.

"Good idea," said Jim, "and you know we will."

"Well, if you ever want to save the unholy, come and save me from him, John," Joan said, nodding toward Jim who was having another beer and smiling.

"I will give you ten pints if you do, John. You will fecking need them," said Jim, as he burst out laughing along with the occupants of the pub, apart from one who gave the special wife look. Jim immediately knew that he had crossed that old matrimonial line, and he quickly informed each and all that 'she was lovely' and it was a joke.

"The ironic, and yes comical, thing is ladies and gentlemen, do we really know who is in our midst?"

"What do you mean?" said a little old guy, lifting his head up and shifting on his seat, apparently pleased that there was more to this story than he had anticipated.

"I invite you to a five minute game," said John.

"I'm in," said the old guy.

"I'm in," said Jim.

"Me too," said Joan.

"And me."

So it continued through the twenty or so locals and staff.

"Look around you, village locals. We all know everyone, don't we? You all know each other, and you probably have done for the most part for many years. Of course you do, this is village life."

"What the hell is he doing now?"

"Playing a game, sir."

"What!"

"Playing a game, sir."

"What game?"

"Not sure, sir. Give me five minutes."

"Report back when you now something useful."

"Of course."

"What do you mean he is playing a game!" screamed Knowles, "I will show him a game when I decapitate him. I am going to dismember the bastard, so just wait and see if I don't."

"I will let you know where it leads, sir. Give me five minutes."

"Think about it chaps. You know your fathers, you probably know his mother, his father," John said pointing randomly, "sisters and brothers. You probably went to school together, played rugby and football, but who else occupies this bar that you don't know?"

The locals all looked at the other, more quiet and unobtrusive occupants, nestled into the other seats. The pub went silent, and John looked at every one of them creating an eerie atmosphere.

The Asian couple who were sitting at a table by the fireplace were intent on giving the impression that they had little command of the English language.

John smiled as he approached them. Jim and Joan were nervous, but the locals were impressed, and they absolutely loved it.

"Hello, sir, can you tell me if you are enjoying your meal?"

There was no reply. The couple bowed, nodded and smiled, but they did not reply.

"OK, contestants number one are portraying that they are of mid-Asian origin, here on holiday and yet they navigate the whole of the British Isles with very little command of the English language."

He paused and wound the audience in further, not that they needed it, for they indeed were hanging on his every syllable and letter of the spoken word.

"And yet my dear friends, these were seemingly innocent bystanders to our conversation. They knew exactly when to stop talking, stop eating and at the precise, in fact, the exact moment that I proclaimed there were those amongst us that may not be all they seem, they looked straight at me without hesitation. Now I ask you comrades, do these appear to be the actions of innocent tourists, or are there more transparent and sinister undertones? Oh and by the way, they have ordered traditional English country fayre, puppy dog pie. How the hell would they know what it was and how to pronounce it? I present the number one fake tourists, so a round of applause please."

The crowd obliged, the recipients of the loud applause melted with embarrassment.

John redirected his eyes upon the embarrassed couple and once more asked the question.

"Now would you care to comment on your food, or are you just going to pretend like others in here?"

John then diverted his attention and looked at the couple housed by the small window. They looked visibly worried as he approached.

"Good evening, can I ask you if you are a couple?"

"Yes, we are," the man said.

"For how long?" asked John

"Six years," answered the man.

John looked straight into the eyes of the girl, whose body language was imploding with every passing second.

"Could you be so kind as to answer a simple, yet common knowledge question, dear? What picture does your so-called husband carry in his wallet?"

"I don't know. Why would I look in his wallet?"

"Sorry sweetheart, you have just failed the test. Either you are having an affair, or you ain't married," said Joan from behind the bar.

"I beg your pardon," she said angrily.

"There ain't a woman on this earth that don't check her husband's wallet, sweetie. Every woman does it, in fact, we just can't help ourselves. Ask any woman."

"That's why I have two!" said Jim laughing.

"Are you beginning to see that my conspiracy theory is in fact real and active, even in this sleepy leafy little piece of the Cotswolds. Conspiracy, alive and present in Painswick, and who would have thought ladies and gentlemen, in our midst."

The locals stared at the two sets of people.

"I am not even going to mention the Israeli couple over there, probably Mossad or something linked, or the

CIA over there pretending to be gay. Only the Americans would attempt to sell a couple of guys and have a big rainbow over them."

There was a minimal pause, as John surveyed each and all, local and out of village.

"This is what I would like my local heroes to do. When I leave this remarkable and beautiful establishment full of Painswick patriotism, I would like you to make sure that none of these innocent individuals attempt to leave, follow me or make phone calls. Now we all know that they have absolutely no signal in the pub and would have to go out to accomplish this, but they have had no reason to do so, so if I leave and they do, it is a sign my friends."

John looked at everyone, the occupants and those outside listening, could have heard a pin drop.

"This will ensure that I maintain my privacy and safety and that they must be ordinary folk and I am wrong. If they do not comply, however, they are, well, they are not who they claim to be, and I am indeed in danger, so think long and hard all of you."

John went to walk out of the bar but stopped and then delivered a strange speech. He said something *really strange*.

"I like the Dark Knight. In fact, I love Batman, and I now know who he is, and I have also isolated Robin, although he is more like a raven. He is already known to me, and he will be exposed but only to Batman. It is strange. The Joker will be out of play tomorrow, and life must go back to normal, and Park Life must resume."

John then walked out of the bar and the locals' eyes pierced the strangers with patriotic unity and a friends' loyalty rarely witnessed. Three of them actually moved from their huddled favourite places in the pub, positioned themselves in front of the doorway to block any potential escapees and looked at the occupants. It caused an uneasy silence and the atmosphere was certainly not what it advertised on the sign outside, 'inviting, lovely local pub'.

"What the fuck was the Batman shit all about?" said Knowles to his men. I need to know about these references to the Dark Knight, Joker, and Robin. What the hell is he doing?"

"We are straight on it, sir, but he has chosen one of the biggest internet hits going, and it will have millions of postings. The literature on any one of these guys is almost impossible to link given the little that he said. It was cryptic, to say the least."

"He is either so clever that he is playing a game for everybody, or he is just plain thick, which we know to be incorrect. I think he is putting up a smokescreen to divert our attention and resources, and he is becoming so annoying, yet I have to admire him," said Knowles sitting back in his chair with his hands behind his head.

The second team of individuals that had been listening were equally baffled by his rant. "Where has he gone and what is going on about with all the Batman references? Is he pushing out shit for all to run around, or is he meeting someone?"

"He is beam riding somebody and sending out decoy flares. I have absolutely no doubt of this."

"What do you mean?"

He is deploying chaff to get everyone to miss the target and crash where no damage can be done. I told you that this guy is not stupid, and he has a healthy appetite for survival. He is doing everything in his power to expose every player and to bring everyone out. Who is Batman though? I mean his reference. I know who the masked marvel is."

There were some sixty or so operatives, collected from a mixture of organisations and government and the industrial world and the dark side of commerce, listening. Only one person within the human race truly understood, and he heard the one singular trigger, a word that isolated the transcript into a brand new higher plateau. This single word meant something far beyond what any of the other people listening could ever imagine. He smiled, and he felt somewhat uneasy that everything rested on such a novice, but then look how far he had come, but he was powerless to help as the circumstances unravelled, and he would only be able to seal the door closed upon completion.

The caustic crowd would eat John Parks alive if they knew the location of the decoder, so he was using all his cunning and bravery bringing all the elements of his planning to the surface. It was a clever move but ultimately the most dangerous to date.

The stranger also knew that he could never show himself to John and that the clandestine pedigree and architecture of his existence could never be revealed to the private or public world. He would try and help in any way that did not hold him responsible for anything and did not link him even indirectly. He had to be incredibly careful, as he had always been.

John walked back to Belleview with Beretta in hand; he checked both left and right approaches before unlocking the door and entering. He started to check the seals on the doorways upstairs. They had been broken again, so he knew that intruders had entered.

"Bloody hell!" he shouted.

He came down the staircase and into the kitchen, and he filled the old dirty coffee machine he loved so much with water, put coffee into the chamber and twisted it under the dispenser. He waited patiently as it turned from red to green to indicate it was the exact right temperature to deliver the water without scorching the beans. He was contemplating all of the next circumstances that should bring this ever changing saga to a close. Life had turned onto an illusion, and it was no longer his. It was manufactured by a series of negative events, and he was angry and aware of the need to sleep. He opened the back door, and it went dark.

Chapter 16

The Meet

The cable ties dug deep into his wrists, and he could feel the pain cascading through his entire body. Life could hang so precariously and fortunes could change in one instant, but why? How could this happen? Especially to him, an absolute nobody, a casual bystander. He was rendered almost motionless and felt cramped and rigid. He realised that he had been dumped in the boot of the moving vehicle in the foetal position, like a piece of surplus meat. He swiftly ascertained that he must have been like this for quite a while, as he pushed his tongue out of his mouth over his lip, which was bloated, and he felt the congealed blood that had coagulated whilst he was unconscious. This extended around his nose and eyes, and his lip was split, tender and burnt when his tongue touched it. He was unable to see beyond the pitch darkness of his vehicular tomb, and it was extremely uncomfortable. He was scared, not normal scared, but scared like he had never been scared like before, and with good reason; he was being disposed of.

He also knew the spectre of narcotics after undergoing surgery himself, and his body felt odd. He deduced that he had also been immobilised through chemical intervention of some sort. It felt like his skin was on fire and his stomach was going around and around like a washing machine. He was acutely nauseous, anxious and his mouth was dry.

The car was moving normally. He guessed it was keeping to the speed limit so as to not to attract attention, and he listened to the droning of the wheel bearings and the tyres rubber flowing through the miles of tarmac. He could detect the faint and muffled voices within the car but with no clarity. They just appeared calm and serious with the occasional muffled laugh, and they sounded foreign, Eastern European, but what did he know? He was certainly no expert, but he deducted that it was a large family saloon or a four by four judging by the space and feel of the upholstery.

He heard and felt the subtle change to the road surface. It was quiet outside, so it was probably not a major transportation link now, more like a country or B-road, and this instantly raised alarm bells, as he was almost certainly on the last portion of the journey to his final last resting place. 'Why me?' he asked himself again over and over. 'I am not like a guy from the movies. I am not capable of martial arts, jumping off buildings and trains or administering self-medical miracles armed with only a piece of cotton to stitch my wounds.' John Parks represented a normal average man, and as such, his skill sets were honed in on being able to navigate through a normal existence with a boring job, some social skills and family life; mostly monotony like everyone else.

'But remember how you have evolved," he said to himself. "Are you seriously going to accept this fate, trussed up like a turkey and bleeding, probably to be left in a gravel pit or worse.

John manoeuvred and arched himself, but the space was confined. He realised that time was probably ebbing away, and although feeling queasy, he was determined to fight. After all, he currently had ten million reasons to stay alive.

He reached deep into the depths of his reserves, and he almost dislocated his shoulder as he put his hand into his sock and pulled out the small, yet significant, life line, the lock knife. The men in the vehicle had obviously searched him and discarded his arsenal, but short of removing his shoes, there was no way for them to know he had a weapon concealed.

Luckily, he was able to unlock it easily and then cut the cable ties on his ankles. He then moved his arms around his feet and in front of him, and although it was excruciating, he felt positive and that he could change the circumstances he found himself in. He positioned the handle of the knife in his mouth and rubbed the tie on his right wrist over it. He had kept the blade razor sharp, and it cut though it with ease. He repeated the process with all the ties, and he gently and silently cut the rear boot cover revealing the occupants of the back seat.

John did not hesitate. He made a frenzied attack with lightning speed and ferocity with the element of surprise which completely threw the entire occupancy of the vehicle. He made hard slashing and thrusting movements with the blade, severing both neck and head flesh deeply. Both of the men recoiled, and blood spurted over the roof lining in great gushes. He had hit arteries, and the men clutched their wounds and were powerless.

He then grabbed hold of the man's head directly in front of him, and with all of his residual power, he pushed his head hard into the headrest of the driver. It connected with a big crack, and the car veered off the road. John leapt over the backseat and stabbed the passenger several times and then pulled the unconscious driver's head back and cut his throat deeply. He realised he still felt weird, but he had to get out of the scene before the authorities were alerted and worse.

He climbed over the man on his right, opened the door and evacuated the vehicle. He dragged the man out and noticed the death stare once again. He then dragged out the driver, and he had the same look, as did the passenger, but the offside back occupant had a horrible look with his face contorted and vile.

John searched them all. He collected four sidearms, lots of ammunition.

"And would you believe it?" he said with a smile, "Lo and behold, a rifle, my favourite toy with sights and lots of ammunition."

He hid the bodies as best he could, but the weakness he felt prevented him dragging them very far off the main highway. Luckily, he had been right in his assumption. It was a smaller road directly on the way to the gravel pits in South Cerney. Hopefully most traffic would be looking directly in front of the vehicle and would not be interested in the mound of human tragedy by the hedge.

John got into the vehicle. It was absolutely covered in blood, but a third class ride was always going to be better than a first class walk, and he had no strength or time for a big hike. He started the engine. It ran and he placed the shift to reverse, and the vehicle climbed out of the ditch with ease. If nothing else, the Jeep was built for task. He always liked the 'Just Enough Engineered Parts' scenario, meaning JEEP.

John was not sure if the vehicle would have a tracker, but he was determined to take no chances and to finish this clear objective: get out alive and bury the big guy.

He sped toward Stroud, turned up Wick Street and into the residence of his old friend, Mr Smythe. He parked the Jeep, ran into the driveway and toward the back door. He pulled out a gun as a cautionary act, but he knew this place was now no longer considered a place of interest by anyone.

He barged the door with all his might at the mid to top portion, and it gave way. He went in, and almost off balance, he collided with the hallway wall. He regained his composure, listened and then proceeded up the stairs and into the bedroom. He went straight to the wardrobe where he found the spare keys, and he pulled off his blood soaked polo shirt, put on a disgusting shirt and jumper, changed into a pair of corduroy pants that were hanging and two sizes too big before running downstairs, conscious of every movement and shadow everywhere, he left the house and went to the garage. The side door was locked, so without any hesitation, he pulled one of the silenced handguns, shot the lock to pieces and went in. He then opened, sat in and started the mighty Kahn, and the big V8 rumbled.

He just pulled the shift to drive, hit the pedal and the V8 engaged with a huge concentration of power and propelled the Kahn straight through the garage door. It

337

flew off its mountings, and he was clear as the door flew through the air and landed five metres away.

John engaged the lights and felt a lot safer in this vehicle. It was powerful and would go through anything, and it would also push a certain style VW van clear off the road if needed.

"So we think he was kidnapped then? Is he dead?"

"To be honest, we are not sure. We think he went into Belleview, and then the next thing we knew, nothing. The traffic cam by the road past the Patchwork Mouse, anything from there?"

"No, sir, nothing."

"So they were going to dispose of him, I suppose."

"Without the decoder, sir?"

"I think word got around that the decoder did not exist."

"Really, sir?"

"Really."

"What shall we do? Are we leaving surveillance on Wernons now or packing up shop?"

"Leave it there for a little while longer. There are a few loose ends, and this had not played out fully yet."

"So the bastard is dead? You are sure of this; you are absolutely positive?" Knowles said ignoring the man.

"Yes, sir. He was taken to the gravel pits as instructed."

"Where are the crew?"

"Not sure, sir."

"What do you mean you are not sure?"

"The tracker went dead, but they were right by South Cerney."

"So there is absolutely nil evidence of death yet. Go find some you moron. Despatch delta team now!"

"Yes, sir."

"We will leave tomorrow. Things are hot and sticky here, and it will only get worse." Said Knowles quietly.

"They took Parks to the gravel pits, sir."

"Is he dead?"

"Far from it, sir. There appears to have been a crash, and the impact must have deactivated the tracker in his kidnappers' vehicle."

"So where is his?"

"He flew off toward Stroud, and we believe he will ultimately be heading toward Painswick."

"What happened to his assailants?"

"That's the funny thing, sir. They appear to have all committed suicide by slitting their own throats and then hugging each other on the side of the road," he said smiling, the first time he had found the events too humorous not to laugh at.

"Well good for him! Bloody Bartholomew Knowles, a parasite and an evil mass. How he has kept breathing for so long eludes me."

"Do we have any idea where he is now?" said the Asian.

"No, sir, just that he is travelling somewhere in some vehicle, probably the crash car, the Jeep."

"Find him. Find him now!"

The Israelis were stone faced. They were unusually quiet and disappointed that they were, in fact, chasing the other players to catch up to where John parks may be.

"He is heading toward Painswick. I think he is going after Bartholomew Knowles. I would."

"What shall we do?"

"Follow, of course, and try to intercept him or find out where that device is; if it does, in fact, exist."

The man listened intently to all the comments. All the information was travelling through the airwaves, and he processed every sound and movement from a safe distance. He had to be so careful not to attract any unnecessary attention, and he melted into the background like a chameleon. He was in fact the most powerful player, and yet he was completely invisible and wished to stay that way indefinitely.

Martin sat there with the American operatives listening and following all of the events on the grid map that was moving with the oral traffic that now crowded the airwaves.

Everyone in the theatre of play were talking and beginning to lose some protocol too. Bartholomew Knowles had completely lost the ability for stealth and logical action, and he was so irate that he was shouting and getting sloppy. The other players were found so commonly in the same vicinity that they frequently turned away from each other to avoid eye contact; it was farcical.

"Sir, I don't believe it! Come quick."

"What the hell do you want?" growled Knowles.

"The device, sir, has been activated."

"What? Where?"

"Not far away."

"But how?"

"He must have hidden it somewhere, and somehow stopped the transmitter, but it has reactivated."

"It could be a trap!" barked Knowles.

"Parks is dead, so how could he set this event in motion?"

"Others are in play, but this is odd. Get the teams over there."

"How many, sir?"

"All of them, you fool."

341

"Won't that leave us exposed, sir?

"Are you frightened, my dear little boy? DO AS I SAY, AND DO IT NOW!" he screamed.

"Yes, sir."

The gates opened and Wernons emptied like the last inch of the bath. It was frantic and people jumped into the VW Transporters. Everyone was apprehensive.

"Sir, quick. The tracker has been reactivated somehow."

"I thought it did not exist?"

"Obviously it does, sir, and it looks like Bartholomew Knowles has sent an army to retrieve it."

"Best we do the same then. Send our boys in and secure that machine at all costs; do you hear?"

"Yes, sir."

The man sat watching and wondering what the next piece of the jigsaw would uncover when his private scrambled phone buzzed with a data message.

Gotham city is extremely busy tonight, 08.00 am tomorrow, you can rave on about it if you like.

The man smiled. He was highly impressed, and the cryptic clue left him feeling warm. He would have preferred to have concluded this awful business tonight, but tomorrow would come. He had been waiting six years, six long and hard years of cloak and dagger and anxious hard work, to expose this traitor, so he could wait another night. He would sleep well.

The airwaves erupted and just about every operative known and unknown started chattering openly. "Sir, the decoder is activated, and Bartholomew Knowles has sent just about all of his ground troops to seek and secure."

"Do the same as them. Quickly"

"There is a lot of activity at Wernons, and the traffic from the other players is that Bartholomew Knowles has sent an army to secure something, probably the decoder."

"Rally and despatch the troops. Come on, let's move! We cannot let the Asians or Brits get hold of the decoder."

"Commander, Painswick is alive with chatter and movement. The rogue has despatched operatives to secure the package."

"Go. Go quickly!"

"Holy shit," said the first team to arrive, "what the fuck is going on?"

Chapter 17

The Reckoning

Bartholomew Knowles paced up and down the hallways. He then went to the kitchen before the office where he lit a cigar. Suddenly, an audio recording began to play around the whole intercom system of Wernons. It was loud and seeped through every speaker in every room.

"Keep her. She is nothing to me, never has been. I don't even think she is my blood. She was born of a whore and a night of the standing prick, I am afraid, one of many pricks, I believe. She means absolutely nothing to me and never has done. She's like a bloody tick on a dog."

"Wow, family values seem to have taken a downward spiral in the Knowles house hold today."

"You don't get it, Parks. They were never there. People are consumable items to be used and abused and discarded at will, and as you will not be here long from now, don't concern yourself too much. Everyone is looking for you, and you have nowhere to go or hide; you are dead."

"OK, OK!" Knowles barked loudly. "You can do as you wish with the girl too. I don't ever want her near me, bloody parasite! She has failed me for the last time. I can tell you."

"You choose death for her then," said John coldly.

"So you have already killed her, John. I am surprised that you dragged it out so long, stupid bitch. Christ, she was so damn annoying, so thanks old man for services rendered, and free too," he said laughing.

"What the bloody hell?" he said turning around quickly, but it was too late to make any moves.

"Get on your knees, put your hands behind your head and interlock your fingers; you know the drill!"

"Christ, I don't understand; how?"

"I said get on your knees, put your hands behind your head and interlock your fingers."

"OK, but think about what you are doing. Come on, let's talk."

"I said get on your knees, put your hands behind your head and interlock your fingers!" shouted the assailant and shot him once in the upper right leg making him bend and buckle to his knees.

"Bloody hell! Come on. We can work something out."

He stayed down on his knees and placed his hands behind his head and interlocked his fingers. The blood was streaming from his leg, and the searing pain showed on his face.

The cuffs snapped close on his wrists closely followed by the tight cutting cable ties that were placed on swiftly after. He was not going to be able to escape out of them easily.

He felt his trouser legs material rise against his skin a few inches up to reveal his ankles and calves. He then felt the deep burning sensation, as the tendons were cut on both ankles rendering him unable to walk or run. He was completely immobilised.

The recording was on a loop. It just kept repeating itself, as his assassin stared into his eyes, revelling in the words.

"Keep her. She is nothing to me, never has been. I don't even think she is my blood. She was born of a whore and a night of the standing prick, I am afraid, one of many pricks, I believe. She means absolutely nothing to me and never has done. She's like a bloody tick on a dog."

"Wow, family values seem to have taken a downward spiral in the Knowles house hold today."

"You don't get it, Parks. They were never there. People are consumable items to be used and abused and discarded at will, and as you will not be here long from now, don't concern yourself too much. Everyone is looking for you, and you have nowhere to go or hide; you are dead."

"OK, OK!" Knowles barked loudly. *"You can do as you wish with the girl too. I don't ever want her near me, bloody parasite! She has failed me for the last time. I can tell you."*

"You choose death for her then," said John coldly.

"So you have already killed her, John. I am surprised that you dragged it out so long, stupid bitch. Christ, she

was so damn annoying, so thanks old man for services rendered, and free too," he said laughing.

"Come on, we can discuss this; it doesn't have to end this way."

"No, it doesn't, but it will."

"What about all the… I am everything to you. I made you, and I trained you from a pup."

"You see, you still cannot refrain from referring to me as a dog, can you? You total prick of a, well, you were never a man were you?"

"I have money and influence, and I can set you up somewhere and make sure you have everything you have ever wanted."

"All I ever wanted was a family, a degree of normality and, occasionally, just once in my life, maybe, some old fashioned parental love and affection from the one person I cared about."

"You can have all this, so give me a chance."

"Remember when you used to come into my room drunk and try to violate me? It used to take me hours to fall asleep after the abuse and violence."

"I don't remember."

"I WAS ONLY ELEVEN YEARS OLD, YOU FUCK!"

"I am sorry. I can put it right. Give me a chance."

"You must be joking, you animal."

"Oh go fuck yourself then, girl. I am not going to belittle myself trying to negotiate with a slut."

"What are you doing? Get off me, you bitch!" he screamed.

He could only look as his pants were pulled down to his knee, followed by his boxer shorts revealing his manhood.

The assailant grabbed it and looked straight into his eyes but spoke like you do to a cuddly dog or a child. "Did he not get excited when his little todger was pulled out? Who needs to grow a bit too?"

"Fuck off, you deranged slag. You were never good at anything, not even worth shagging."

"But you tried, didn't you? You ripped me, ruptured me and it was only that bastard Cleed that kept me from hospital many times. What a pair of bastards, and I will see him as well; don't worry for that!"

"Get over yourself. Christ, what are you doing?"

The member was lifted, pulled harshly and stretched. The sharp razor edge of the knife was put at the base.

"I am going to make sure that when they find you, they will laugh and say 'good tackle', *not*. You will in death be humiliated beyond your wildest dreams, and your memory will be humiliated. You will not even go down as the ruthless bastard and egoistic narcissist you want. You will go down as the prick with the prick lying next to him."

"Don't be stupid. You can't."

The blade severed the penis in one deep strong cut, and she held it to his horror-filled eyes.

"Prick by a prick. Remember me now? Remember coming into my room, pervert? How does it feel?"

"Christ, you are a demon."

"You are the demon, and you should have given me a choice or even adoption; anything but you."

The blood poured from him, not like the ketchup used by John to feign her death in the photograph, it smelt different and was warm, she pulled the scrotum tight, cut out his testicles and threw them at the wall.

He was going into unconsciousness and losing blood fast, but there was one thing left to be achieved, one last cleansing of the Knowles history.

The killer picked up his lifeless and limp member and rammed it into his throat, and he began to choke. She then lifted his head back exposing his Adams apple and the skin was taught and uncomfortable, blood from the dismembered penis dripping down his chin. It was a grizzly sight, but one that pleased the killer immensely. He made a futile attempt to regurgitate the member, to beg and then he attempted to swallow but could not. Their faces were literally inches away from each other, and their breath lay upon each other's cheeks, as she inhaled and exhaled heavily. His breathing becoming laboured and shallow from his nose.

Their eyes were as one, as the blade passed his neck gouging it open deeply. The blood spurted out of the arteries in a fountain of red, and high geysers hit the killer, but instead of moving, the killer bathed in the ultimate downfall and humiliation of Bartholomew Knowles. She rammed the member into his mouth further, and it exited the huge gaping hole that was his neck.

Cynthia stood up and basked in the glory of her revenge. It was pure evil carnage, but it was hers. She felt very good and exhilarated. There could be no remorse or any kind of sympathy for this was retribution for years of child abuse, rape, sodomy, murder, crimes against humanity, torture and for his betrayal. She felt cleansed. Her act of attrition was so vile and grizzly that it mirrored the life of the man she had so mercilessly executed, and in some sick way, it was a deserving and fitting set of circumstances for this human filth.

Cynthia opened a small safe behind a picture, emptied the contents into a familiar rucksack and walked from the office. She passed by the lifeless carcass of the surveillance operative and removed the disc from the intercom system. She entered into the bathroom, rinsed the majority of blood off into the sink and picked up two towels that were hanging on a rack. She towelled her hair as she walked through the back door and left the building. She walked past the circular shrub bed, down the embankment, climbed over the back wall and dropped down towards the Mill House. She then walked off still towelling the water and blood from her hair, head and body.

Cynthia smiled contently. She took the greatest possible gratification from the fact that the last thing that her father's, eyes were presented with on this planet, were in fact the eyes of his killer, his own daughter, if she ever was his daughter, which she very much doubted.

She had taken such pleasure in the image of what she had witnessed. She had watched him shift his mortal coil, watched in pure delight, as the blood drained from him. Bartholomew Knowles had slowly and desperately fought for air through his severed windpipe and bludgeoned ego, and the legacy of his own member being pushed down his throat would be echoed from many chambers for years to come, the ultimate humiliation. For the people who wanted revenge from the other side, they would have him now, to answer for all of his evils. The massing of the bright red gluey blood from his severed scrotum and manhood to his neck would now represent his uniform in death.

He had travelled through to another dimension. He was where no other would take him, hell.

The first van approached the site where the tracker led them. It whispered 'find me' through the letting of a pulsating beep every four seconds that glowed as a yellow dot on their grid co-ordinate electronic map.

"What do we do now?"

"Get hold of Knowles."

"Can't reach him."

"Well, we can hardly march anywhere near to the decoder with that lot going on."

"Can we shoot out the lights?"

"And then what? Everyone is here! Can you not see all the bloody vehicle lights moving around, and the shadows flickering with silhouettes of dangerous types? Get hold of Knowles."

"He is definitely not answering."

"Something is wrong then. He wanted progress reports every two minutes."

"What do we do?"

"Shall we just run?"

"Wait, we have two other teams in place. Tell them to hold fast."

"Team two, team three, hold fast. We are bemused as we cannot raise big leader, so let's just wait and be patient.

"Commander, I must report that the whole field is lit up by what appears to be a builder's halogen lamps, the big ones used in renovation when power is off. There are about eight of them all working off a generator, and it is like a fairground here. Bodies are moving all around and everyone is a bit on edge."

"The whole situation is discouraging anyone from actually moving at the moment."

"What is happening now with Knowles' men?"

"They seem disorganised and hesitant, not like them at all, so what do you think is going on?"

"I believe the head of the snake is missing."

"Really."

"Yes, if Knowles had been commanding, he would have sacrificed them all to retrieve the decoder. He is not a patient man at all."

"What do we do?"

"Wait a few minutes and see what happens."

"This is ludicrous! We can almost wave at each other and blow kisses we are so close. We are being played, sir."

"Get your logic working. Just wait. The first person who moves toward the device will open up the gunfight at the OK Corral."

"Well, I am not moving, and that's for sure, but where is Bartholomew Knowles? His teams are just stagnant and waiting. Why aren't they going in shooting?"

"They are waiting. Did anyone watch Wernons?"

"No, sir."

"Interesting. I would like to know something. How many operatives did Knowles have guarding Wernons when the tracker went off and all his men moon beamed to the chaff?"

"Ah, I see what you mean, sir. You really believe this was all a distraction to make Knowles vulnerable."

"It appears that everyone and his dog is at the signal site, and his men can't move, as they are waiting orders."

"Any orders, sir?"

"Yes, breach Wernons, send black team and do a full sweep after. I want everything that ever existed in there. Don't leave anything to chance either. These are desperate times managed by desperate men, so keep your lads safe as the priority."

"Thank you, sir, but what about Bartholomew Knowles, sir?

"Bring him in for some tea and offer him a slot on *Question Time* if he has the breath for it. I do, however, believe, well, let's just say that I have a feeling that something extremely clever that makes a mockery of everyone around us, and including us, just got achieved."

"Sir, it is pandemonium up at the signal. It is like the bit off *E.T.* when everyone has lights on and is scared of what is inside, the man said with an American accent."

"Save the theatrics man. Where is Knowles and his men?"

"All waiting."

"No way."

"Yes, sir. Everyone is just waiting."

"My, my, this is a calculated and premeditated movement of both low and high players in this industrial chess. To attract everyone to the decoder like moths to the light, literally, is a stroke of genius, but what does it gain for Parks? He has managed to expose all the players, and he has created a temporary stalemate that ridicules all best practice. No amount of training can give you the recipe for success, and just like he did in the pub, he is outwitting everyone through sheer genius, because he uses logic and keeps it so blatantly simple. Everyone looks for the more complex plan, pure genius."

"What shall we do, sir?"

"Well, that's the million dollar question. There had to be a motive followed by a plot and then a method of achieving some big act that would go by absolutely unnoticed. This is pure genius, a conspiracy within a conspiracy, pure fucking genius."

"I get that you are pleased, sir, but I am not sure I follow, sir."

"The diversion has to gratify the illusion of the decoder being the quarry, the main item on the agenda.

Let me calculate what else would be achieved and who would benefit most."

"Where did we say Knowles is?"

"Wernons, sir."

Martin smiled one of those smiles.

"I think I have it guys. He has gone after Bartholomew Knowles. Get some men over there right away."

"Martin, we are too late. We have just been informed that the SAS have gone into Wernons."

"Then I assume that the plebeian, scumbag Bartholomew Knowles will never see another second on this planet, nor deserve it. Have we located Gerald yet? He was supposed to shadow us and keep me informed."

"He has disappeared, sir."

"Hmmmmm, interesting."

The lights shone very brightly, the invasive halogen bulbs illuminated the whole field and surrounding area with tremendous and unwavering efficiency and created a blinding sight if approached from head on. The lights had been strategically placed, and there was no approach to the decoder that could not be seen.

The man sat back still listening to the riddle as it unravelled before him, but he already knew that Bartholomew Knowles had fallen afoul of his lifetime of unparalleled violence and brutality, and he would have been given no quarter and certainly shown no mercy at all.

The man watched and listened intensely as the pieces began to form, and they amalgamated and fell into place.

He had more than a vested interest, and he had developed a strange admiration for this unknown entity, this civilian.

He knew the latest distraction was cunning and well thought out and showed that there was a level of planning that all of the operatives currently in play could do well to learn from. It was a calculated, methodical and ruthless set of events, and he also knew that it would also gain John Parks something that he did not recognise. For the most part, he guessed and knew most of what transpired and indeed what had to transpire, but there was an element, something else that niggled at him, and he felt uneasy with not knowing.

He also knew that he had to obtain the information regarding the Raven at all cost and thought it genius that John Parks, the man with the beard, nicknamed 'John the Baptist' by the locals, the simple quiet unassuming man from the office with no training, no skills and no friends was spearheading the events before him. He was also extremely happy that John had demonstrated that he was indeed a true patriot and would serve crown and country before all else.

The lead armoured vehicle broke through the farmer's gate as if it were not there, and the green camouflage paint was clearly visible in the sharp cutting beams of light from the lamps. The additional two vehicles promptly followed and positioned one behind and one forward, flanking the lead vehicle. The vehicles made no attempt to evade anything, or anyone or to go faster than necessary or to bow to anything but task. It was a government making a statement of intent. The lead vehicle approached the signal, went past a few metres and reversed through the brambles directly over the signal. A large hatch door opened on the floor of the back area of the vehicle where the seats would have normally been. A strong hand reached down and tried to lift the decoder from the broken concrete, but there needed to be two people at least to achieve this. With some help from the driver, the lead outer casing that had been wrapped around the device several times was removed, the concrete pushed aside and the decoder was safely placed on the hatch as it was closed.

The night vision goggles and heat signature surveillance had every target accounted for, and eight foreign and unaccountable operatives were currently sat in crosshairs should anyone make an effort to interrupt the transition from collector to carrier. Another two ground teams confirmed they were in place, and another eight operatives joined the others on death row.

"Bravo one here. Package secure."

"Get out of there Bravo one. Return to sender."

"Bravo two, chaperone."

"Roger that, sir."

"Bravo three, I will loiter and remove some of the clientele from here. They look rowdy and out of place."

"Roger, Bravo three."

The decoder was removed and transported up the road where it was met with a hail of bullets from one side of the field.

"You are clear to play, Bravo four. I repeat. Clear to play."

The firing stopped immediately, and this was, of course, following the flurry of muzzle flashes from strategic points in the hedge line above the brightly lit fields.

The vehicle continued to the Brockworth and Cheltenham road, and it safely disappeared in convoy finally destined for its rightful home, GCHQ.

"Martin, just a courtesy call to inform you that we have managed to secure the package. British and US interests are intact."

"Thanks, but where the hell is Gerald? Does anyone know?"

"Affirmative, but that is a meet and discuss subject if you don't mind, probably a better subject for later on."

"I appreciate that, but who am I talking to by the way?"

"Andy Capp, a friendly British tourist, Martin. You know how these things rotate. I will contact you, but Cheltenham is probably a good place for a US official to have a nightcap right now."

"OK, I will make my way over there, thanks."

The third armoured vehicle circled while shining its own bank of spotlights on the heat signature bodies that the surveillance teams were pinpointing with ease.

The SAS team entered Wernons without opposition and immediately stumbled upon the lifeless bodies of the two guards whose necks were both deeply slit.

They also came upon what was probably a surveillance operative. He had headphones draped around his neck, and his hands were clean and not like the men in the field. The teams concluded a full sweep of the premises and secured all entry points. The scientific team would need to move in and would start to dismantle all the surveillance equipment, computers and search every single millimetre of the whole building and outbuildings.

The SAS black team leader stood over the trussed up dead carcass of the man he had offered to kill on many occasions. He despised everything about him as did his team, and where they had loyalty to crown and country and to each other, Knowles demonstrated no such traits and remained the most ignoble of humans.

The leader smiled and beckoned his men to come and see just how crestfallen the illusive Bartholomew Knowles really was.

"Someone only cut his fucking prick off, lads," he said laughing.

"Bloody hell! Leader, his balls are over there, and they look like they have been thrown against the wall."

"Aw, sick or what? Bloody brilliant, though! What a fucking statement, have it you pig."

He kicked him in the face, as his guys all lined up and participated. It was a ritual ceremony, as Knowles had been directly responsible for causing the death of one of their comrades several years ago, and they all took pleasure from seeing him so brutally dismembered.

The last armoured vehicle moved toward the broken entrance, and the gate lay on the floor testament to the force and nature of entry earlier.

"Sir, do we pull back, or are there any other targets to go?"

"How many on the far right?"

"Four and two, spaced out but in cross hairs, sir."

"Take them out! I repeat you have a green light to take them out."

The bodies dropped and the thud was enough to disperse the remaining personnel from the site. The cars sped off in different directions, and as one of the VW Transporter vans tried to escape, the armoured vehicle rammed it off the road.

The occupants were taken from the mangled wreckage and put in the back of a transit van that arrived within two minutes, and they disappeared into the night.

"Sir, Bartholomew Knowles has been well and truly slaughtered; it is like a scene from a horror film in here."

"What happened?"

"He had his dick and his balls cut off. Whoever did this, threw Knowles' fucking balls at the wall and shoved his own dick right into his mouth but it is coming out of his neck. Gross or what? Can you get hold of that, excuse the pun, but it is really bloodthirsty in here, and there's blood everywhere."

"Eloquently put, Leader one."

"There is no real way of making it sound anything but macabre, sir. Another thing too, sir, he also had a bullet in his upper leg and his throat was deeply cut, almost decapitated; I mean really severed. This was more than a killing for money; this was pure vengeance. I have never witnessed an assassination of such utter brutality and humiliation, and it is worse than any mafia hit. This was bloody personal."

"The killer is someone close with an axe to grind. It will be someone absolutely consumed with hatred, and we may never know who though, but still, job well done and all that."

"This was a trophy kill, sir, a quest of pure evil.

"Anything else? Any items of obvious gain?"

"No, technical is entering, so we will remain and keep secure."

"OK, let me know when you get back."

The phone buzzed into life startling Martin. He pulled it out of his pocket and clicked the answer mode.

"Hi, Martin."

"You are never going to guess what has happened?"

"What?"

"Bartholomew Knowles."

"Yes, what about him?"

"Dead."

"When?"

"Tonight."

"Don't tell me, when everyone was running around the floodlit hillside playing tinker tailor, I assume."

"Yep, but that ain't the best of it."

"Go on, treat me."

"Cock cut right off."

"Say what?"

"Knob hacked clean off."

"No way, *ouch*."

"Knob hacked off and rammed into his mouth, and his bollocks thrown straight against the wall and all while he was alive. Can you believe it?"

"Oh that makes me cringe and cross my legs! Who did it?"

"No one knows."

"Come on, someone knows. Someone always knows."

"Seriously, dark operation, no clues, no one left alive civilian or military. Knowles lay there in a pool of blood, and all of his men that were there are dead."

"How many?"

"Three at best we think, but the SAS are still in there, and it is buttoned up tighter than a duck's ass."

"I am on my way to GCHQ. I will find out."

"Thought I would let you know, knowing how much you loved this guy."

"Thanks. Imagine being remembered as the guy who had your dick cut off and rammed in your mouth?"

"Bit Al Capone," said number two.

"What a bummer," said number three.

"Not really," said number two, laughing loudly.

"No, thanks. Having a pussy rammed in my mouth, now that's another issue, but my own dick, no way."

"Here is a suggestion. Let's get off the airwaves and get back to protecting the free world, chaps."

"Very good, sir."

"Thank you, gentlemen."

Chapter 18

The Meetings

John pulled the Kahn into the trees by Sheepscombe and waited just out of sight. He also switched off the V8 to silence his position. The passenger door opened immediately, and a familiar woman entered the vehicle, still trying to towel blood from herself.

Cynthia leaned over and kissed John passionately on the lips and hugged him long and hard.

"Did you sort out your family problem, sweetheart?"

"Yes, John, but you would probably hate me, though, if you knew what I have done to him."

"I hope you cut the balls off the prick. He is not human."

"Funny you should mention it."

"Is it completely finished though? Are you alright?"

"I have no past John and no memories. I have only now, and we need to build the foundation of my life in our image, to bounce off a platform from when this episode is ended. I have to start, reinvent myself and forget that

Cynthia Knowles ever existed before the new era. I have to move forward and out of the shadows of that evil pig bastard lying on the cold floor in Wernons. I can never again kill another human being, except for Cleed, of course.

They both laughed, but they both recognised that this relationship was born from an uneasy alliance. Although they had respect and had fallen in love, they had to get used to each other on this dimension and also encourage trust. Loyalty was never going to be an issue since they were now fused together from the circumstances that had thrown them together and fashioned their path.

They kissed again and continued to kiss, and after several minutes, he wiped the tears from her eyes, leant back into his driver's position, started the Kahn and headed for Minchinhampton Common through the lanes.

"So, you have the decoder."

"Yes, Martin, we have the decoder."

"Is it actually authentic?"

"No, we had the original all of the time."

"Who entered this one into play? You?"

"Of course, we had to."

"Sneaky. Look what happened to Gerald? We got on pretty well, and he was getting on top of this whole John Parks thing when he literally fell off the planet and vanished."

"Gerald was found with an unfortunate 9mm realignment of his facial features. It was some surgery to his face! He was only recognised by print and teeth."

"Sorry, I had no idea. Was he in trouble or hit by the other teams?"

"No."

"Was he rogue?"

"We believe so." He had also doodled pictures of a bird on his desk, a crow or something similar, does this muster any images or thoughts?

"Jesus Christ, maybe a Raven."

"Yes or in my language, bloody hell."

"Does the Pentagon have clarity?"

"Yes."

"Is the White House OK with everything?"

"Yes."

"Good then I can go back to London and see where the other issues are leading."

"I think so."

"Do you know who it is?"

"I have no idea what you are talking about, Martin."

"That's OK. You play it all close, but he is going to move within the next twelve to twenty four hours."

"Is he? If I had any idea what you were talking about, I could comment, but unfortunately I don't, so I can't."

"I knew that is what you would say and do, so I am going to go. Thanks, once again."

"Goodbye, Martin."

The three vans had been accounted for. One was wrecked, and its occupants detained. The other had gone back to Wernons and tried to run for it, two dead two injured and detained. The other just ran for it and crashed, its occupants detained. All of Bartholomew Knowles' empire and operations were closed and would remain so until some other force or organisation picked up where he left off, but it was doubtful that anyone could do it with such brutality and cruelty and disregard for human life.

It was now late evening and all of the players were regrouping and thinking of how to move forward. The process of digesting the events of this day and the last few days was difficult. The intricate puzzle of deceit and disloyalty, death and destruction made it all seem futile, but it was necessary to ensure the project was a universal and shared miracle and not purely profit driven.

The man thought about the text. The Raven was such a large part of his life that it had consumed him. He lived life on a knife edge. He could never quite relax, always had one eye on the door and the other on the window when he slept and always had one hand on the trigger. The last five years had taken their toll, and he had become weary. He longed to sleep in and for a family that could just walk in the open without fear, and he wished the measures he installed were proven efficient. He knew that it had been the Raven, the very person who was supposed to protect the crown and country. But he had betrayed everyone, remained smug and conceited and who had caused another's life to be a tangled web of deceit and lies. He now had the very evidence to reveal the traitor and to push his seemingly obsessive pursuit aside. It was not a vendetta, but there had to be a wrong and a right, and the right just had to overcome the wrong too, or why were humans in conflict to protect them?

He sipped the fifteen-year-old single malt that he had poured, and it tasted smooth and the soft bite that entered his throat and stomach warmed him. The irony was that the very whisky he was drinking, had in fact been a present from the very individual, he was now planning to politically dismember tomorrow.

He intended to give this individual an option before the very public spectacle began. The individual was intoxicated with power, public office and showed a capacity for self-indulgence. The blatant irascibility he frequently demonstrated would prevent him from making a rational decision for at least an hour after he had the file revealed, so that would be the deadline. He would give him one hour to do the right thing or be publicly damned by the world.

He would not be able to quell his ego nor his insatiable appetite for success in the public eye. He demonstrated a particularly unhealthy need to be the influential cog to his mighty machine, and this character flaw would place him in a quandary. Could he face humiliation through the lens of the world? Perhaps not.

He had created a purlieus empire, one that he had defended vehemently. One even guarded by the death of others. The man flicked his mind back to when the power hungry candidate had asked him to participate in the defence of the realm. He had been a strong advocate for patriotism back all of those years ago, but greed corrupts men, and it corrupts the best of men if not kept in check. It appeared that throughout the ages and indeed now in the modern world, the higher the office, normally the greater the temptation, and the greater the abuse and the greater the greed. 'What a shame,' he thought.

These were, however, not in the main, righteous kills. They were for self-gain and to profit from the death of the innocent could not be construed as legitimate profit. The talisman would need to be paid at some point, and the point was here, and it was now.

Martin stood in front of his handler. He was invited to sit and handed a glass of bourbon.

"Thank you, sir."

"So, the Brits are playing it softly, softly and not telling you anything? Must be big then."

"It must be an ousting of cataclysmic proportion, sir, as they are really being cagey, and Gerald had his whole face shot off as if to obliterate him completely. Imagine having your face missing? I don't care that he is dead, especially if he was a traitor, but by whose hands? That is the piece of the jigsaw that I don't understand."

"Could the Brits have done it?"

"I don't think so, as they would have kept him for a while and let out some relocation garbage story, and not had his head shot to pieces. The way he said it too is interesting. He seemed almost disappointed, but also absolutely disgraced, that anyone from his team could have displayed such blatant disloyalty. What could you possibly gain from turning your back on friends and family and your country? Jesus Christ, a thought just crossed my mind. It is so simple, yet so true. *Trust him.*"

"What are you on about, Martin?"

Martin smiled and selected the word that he now realised had imprinted itself in his mind. "Coin, sir. It is always about and for coin, the currency of humans."

"I have never heard it quite put like that before, Martin."

"I have never heard a phrase more aptly put, sir. It could relate to most of what transpires globally."

Chapter 19

Day Five

John and Cynthia were wrapped up in the backseat, and John was shaking as he woke up. The sunlight invaded the car with iridescent shafts of light. Shapes were crafted through droplets on the windscreen giving birth to dancing orbs, if only momentarily. Even with the heavily tinted back windows, he could not deny morning was broken, and he had serious business this day. It was not the romantic rose petal filled bed of comfort he would have liked for their first night together, but given the abnormal and the highly unusual circumstances of their being together at this time, he was pleased that they had indeed actually survived the night.

John could not help but stare at Cynthia. She now exuded an innocence that had eluded her all of her life. One person, so broken and in despair due to the influence of just another human being, who had shown so easily that he was indeed devoid of any love, emotion and who had been brutal in his crafting of her childhood. He may have paid the ultimate sacrifice and in a way so grotesque that it made John shudder with revulsion, but he now wondered if Cynthia could ever integrate into any as semblance of a normal existence. Her torch had shone so brightly for the vulgar pursuit of her father's praise, and he had subjected her to probably irreversible memories and damaged her so far beyond what most psychotic killers could return from. Could love conquer this? Could John tame the beast within her? How and what would be the best way forward?

"I know you are looking at me," she whispered. "What are you thinking, John? Please be honest."

"I was simply deliberating as to the best way to bring you back from the brink of the devil's knee, my girl. How do I stop you sitting at his table and eat with the good guys instead?"

"Funny thing, John. I was thinking exactly the same thing about you. Are you now sat at the devil's table too?

"I have not considered the subject in that way, Cynthia, but I admit I am a completely different man, not through my own definition either. I have had triggers pushed and thought patterns embedded into my skull that represent nothing short of bedlam."

"So what do I have to do, Johnny boy, to pull you back from the brink of the devil's knee?"

"Do you honestly think we have any real chance or hope in hell of surviving into our old age?"

"Forget the planning. What about now? You are evading my question, and I think deliberately."

"I am afraid of the future, even of today and tomorrow, Cynthia. I was having breakfast at Belleview how long ago? I was watching bloody horses frolic, and within a few hours, I took a man's head off."

"They would have killed you, John."

"Do you want to know something absolutely crazy? During some of the quieter moments between shooting human beings and caving their skulls in with baseball bats, I actually had visions of my darling children in my head singing '*I don't wanna be a rabbit*'. How much bloody weirder could it get?"

"It just shows that you are human after all, John."

"Why did I make the transition from father, ex-husband, big softie John the Baptist to cold hearted killer with such ease?"

"Did you actually take pleasure from hurting anyone?"

"I was so scared and frightened at first that I was sick and had palpitations, but then as it went on…"

"Did you actually take pleasure from hurting anyone?" she repeated.

"Not in the exact definition of 'enjoyment'. I did consider what I believed to be the righteous kill to be sensible and permissible force, even with deadly force. The man in the shed, he was close up and personal, an invidious oaf, stomping around and shining a light on me. I was so frightened when I think back on it, but he was stupid. That's what gets me really, Cynthia. The SAS guys would have me absolutely in blind panic if they were after me for dark reasons, probably special ops Americans too, but your lot, I saw them as criminals, and I do the others too. They are easier to deal with because I know their motive is not just or patriotic at all; it's just coin."

"So, you still did not really answer the question though, John. Are you afraid to tell me?"

"I can sum it up pretty easily, but just not in my words, but I have something so absolutely fitting it could have been written for this very occasion.

Out of the night that covers me,
Black as the pit from pole to pole,
I thank whatever Gods may be,
For my unconquerable soul,

In the fell clutch of circumstance,
I have not winced or cried out loud,
Under the bludgeoning of chance,
My head is bloody but unbowed,

Beyond this place of wrath and tears,
Looms but the horror of the shade,
And yet the menace of the years,
Finds, and shall find me, unafraid,

It matters not how straight the gate,
How charged with punishments the scroll,
I am the master of my fate,
I am the captain of my soul.

"Oh my God, John. Where did you find that?"

"I didn't find it Cynthia. It is 'Invictus', a Victorian poem written by William Ernest Henley. He obviously had some bad shit going on at some time and pulled that gem from his mind. It's brilliant. Winston Churchill paraphrased the last two lines in a speech at the House of Commons in September 1941. Nelson Mandela used it when he was in prison and Barack Obama used it during the Nelson Mandela memorial service. It was also used by US POWs in North Vietnamese prisons, written in rat droppings on toilet paper. I believe it to be one of the most powerful scriptures of modern man and gives strength to a lot of people, but please don't take offence, but it is mostly a guy's thing; I think."

"None taken. It is lovely, dark yet lovely, so no more killing. We need a solemn oath from both of us, John. We need to be human again."

"When the business is concluded this fine morning and I am certain that there is no danger, I will gladly give you the vow. I will not violate it either unless I am ever presented with the threat of death or violence to you or to me, Cynthia."

"It's a start I guess."

"There was a pause for a few minutes. It was strange for both of them to just be in each other's arms, comfortable and feeling safe just for once."

"I stood up, Cynthia."

"What?"

"I admit that I was sat at the devils table, sweetheart. You asked me a question, and I want to be honest. I sat there with Lucifer, and I was not out of place. I have not left the table quite yet, but I have stood up ready to say farewell and go. This is where I am today, right now; is it enough Cynthia?"

"Yes, John and thank you for being so honest. I am not used to honesty or feeling this level of emotional warmth. You liked that Angela girl didn't you?"

"I liked the idea, Cynthia. She arrived at a point where I would have attached myself to anyone warm. It was still a horrible experience whatever her motive."

"This is one bit I don't get. How did she just happen to be there when you walked up the hill?"

"She didn't, and they probably had two or three girls waiting, so when she walked up, she was dawdling well behind and did not interact with the main part. When she broke off from them no one called back to her nor did not wait to see if she was safe. On reflection, it was obvious she was not in their group, but I was just naïve."

"But how? And why that part of Painswick?"

"Use logic, gal - the stream. I am chased by man and dog, and it is obvious I would travel through the stream since there are only two exits to cover. Bloody hell, I was foolish."

"You were human. Most people would be dead if they had endured your lot."

Cynthia cuddled him, and John was not sure if sex was an inappropriate suggestion, but when he looked at the time, even he could not break that record, and it would not bode well for the future if he did.

"We have to go. Are you all set? Whatever happens, you can walk from this, OK? You can get to where you want."

"Not without you, Johnny boy."

"Cynthia, please listen to me!"

"Not without you, Johnny boy. Now you have listened to me."

"Did you discuss an exit strategy, John?"

"Done."

"Will it work?"

"Does a bear shit in the woods?"

"OK, let's go then."

John exited the vehicle and urinated by a bush. He was still looking around for snipers or listening devices, and he even scoured the air for drones. He went back and got into the driving seat while Cynthia was in the passenger seat checking weapons.

"Well, Bonnie and Clyde it is then. You all set?"

"I am."

"Let's go."

The Kahn exited the hiding place, and the V8 roared as they made their way to a rendezvous point. They did not really speak, Cynthia held his hand and rubbed his arm and leant across and kissed him a few times. She was the happiest she had ever been in her life. John drew upon the elements of the poem that gave him such strength, and the love he felt from Cynthia eradicated all the negativity that had invaded his life of late, and to a lesser degree before.

"Is everything set do you think John? Are we going to be alright, please tell me we are?"

The explosion ripped through the Kahn and the vehicle was blown off the ground a metre with the enormous impact of the Centex detonating beneath. The fireball completely engulfed the interior, and the car landed on the ground and burnt like an inferno. The two bodies inside melted under the intense heat, and flesh became charred and mutilated in seconds rendering both unrecognisable. The picture was a sea of orange flames within the glowing blaze with crackling metal twisting and burning and disfiguring the shape of the Kahn.

Chapter 20

Exposed

The man sat there watching his timepiece and his heart rate increased, as he saw 08.00am. He knew that years of planning and hiding in the shadows would be rewarded in seconds, and he may be free of this terrible burden that he had carried for so long. He was ultimately responsible to one man to keep the interests of this country safe and without blemish internal or external. The threat from within was grave, and it would have to be dealt with without public scrutiny and without a witch hunt or investigation. He sat, exhaled and inhaled deeply trying to calm himself. The clock hit eight, and this man would have achieved walking the corridors of power and delivering the package and file as instructed and without attention being drawn.

The man was upright, an extremely smart and handsome older gentleman, and he walked with confidence but not arrogance. His suit was cut perfectly, his tie knotted to perfection and his shoes shone. The grey hair and deep blue eyes complemented his persona, and he had wrinkles but not deep. The only sign of his true pedigree was a small hidden tattoo bearing the familiar skull and slogan 'Death or Glory' on his arm. He no longer served in the theatre of war but was now completely domestic covert, and he blended adequately and without question. He stopped at the huge wooden door, knocked and stood back; it was almost 08.00am.

"Come," was bellowed.

The man entered and walked to the huge desk and chair. It swivelled around.

"Well, what is it man?" he uttered arrogantly, not even having the manners or common decency to look up.

The man placed the package on the table in front of him, turned and walked out and uttered 'arrogant prick' as he departed.

"What the bloody hell is this?" the man said impatiently.

Big Ben struck the first of eight resounding chimes.

The man remained sitting in his huge leather riveted chair and was delighted at his Westminster life around him... until he flipped open the page of the file. His heart sank, he felt sick and there was a burning sensation welling up inside him. He could hardly breathe. His throat was dry and he just stared at the information in front of him. It seemed like hours but was in fact a few minutes. There were two options, the pills inside the file, or the suppressed 9mm Beretta in the package; there was no third alternative. He looked at the pills and the gun, and he took the file to a shredder and it disappeared noisily into the rotating teeth.

He stared at and then he pulled the gun out of the package. He felt its weight, gripped the handle, pulled back the slide mechanism to load and arm and he put it to his temple. His hand was shaking and his stomach churned, but he just could not pull it. The sweat poured from his brow and he heard voices outside. He immediately ran to the door, locked it and sat back down and cried. He was not even man enough to pull the trigger.

He poured a large scotch, took out the two pills and placed them on his tongue. He then looked out of the window where he could see the London Eye in the distance. Big Ben's chimes had stopped, so he flicked the pills back into his throat and drank the whisky which washed them down into his stomach.

At 08.04, the familiar death stare emanated from his lifeless corpse as his head hit the table. It was done. The most dangerous, greedy and ruthless man, who was silently responsible for so much death and carnage in the pursuit of his own gain, had been brought to justice and made to pay the ultimate price. He was not quite as untouchable, as he had always believed after all.

The man got a call from the postman of the package.

"Recorded delivery signed for, sir."

"Well done, thank you. No trace."

"Goodbye, sir."

He did not even afford the man an answer, as this was the best of the best, and he would never ever be identified. His face, although caught a thousand times by facial recognition would be peeled away, as the latex outer layer of the wrinkled older man gave way to the younger handsome man. Grey hair would be replaced by the natural dark brown, and the blue contact lenses would be removed revealing big, dark brown eyes.

It would be a waiting game now, the discovery of the body of paramount importance. The gun was totally untraceable, having been assembled from a number of pieces from Bartholomew Knowles' own gun and that of his men's weapons. Any identification had been chemically etched off, so there was absolutely no chance of it being traced.

When the receiver of the package did not turn up for his 08.30am meeting, there was concern from the assembled group, as he was driving the agenda. Security determined he was present as he had signed in electronically and was seen going into his office. After knocking several times over a period of twenty minutes, the door was subjected to a controlled opening by security, and men in suits followed a protocol set up to protect everyone.

Upon opening the door, the men all stared in disbelief. The scene revealed an obvious suicide, but it was a shock and completely against what anyone would have believed. This man was destined for the great seat of government, and this was totally out of character, plus there was no note or evidence to suggest why he would take such a drastic measure. There seemed to be a discrepancy in the why, but the actions were clear.

The man sat there anxiously waiting for news, every second seemed to represent an hour, and he could not relax until he knew what had transpired fully. He never discriminated against a man's belief, but he did against a man's actions, and treachery and deceit would need retribution. He had disengaged from his knowing the individual and treated him as an enemy of the state. He wiped some beads of sweat from his forehead as the light illuminated on his phone and came alive. He answered it instantly.

"Yes."

"Sir, some bad news, I fear."

"What is that?"

"The Secretary of State for Energy appears to have taken his life this morning, and what's worse is that he executed this act at his very own desk in Westminster. Any ideas?"

"Was there a note found at the scene?"

"No, sir."

"Damn, we need to put a twist on this for the press. It cannot be seen as a weakness born of work overload or in any way family related. We will wait for a few hours, look at all footage of him and his office, and we will feign a terminal illness that he could not cope with, especially as he was running for the highest office in a few months."

"Good idea, sir."

"Thank you."

The man picked up the other phone, dialled 'one' and it went straight through.

"Yes."

"The Secretary of State for Energy appears to have taken his life this morning, Prime Minister."

"What a shocking and terrible tragedy. Was there a note?"

"No, but he had been Raven on about the election, and he was exhausted, so it could have been a lot of factors."

"Confirmed."

"We believe he suffered from a terminal illness, sir, and with the election coming up, he would have almost certainly of had to abort his participation. We speculate that it was all too much for him, sir, especially given how driven he was."

"Very well, I will make sure my people prepare a press release and condolences for his family. I appreciate your help in this matter; it will not go unnoticed."

"Thank you, sir."

The phone call was finished. It had only lasted briefly, but it was a cataclysmic step forward and relief for the man. He looked at his office, and he could not believe this day had come. He started to shred many documents and would personally incinerate the shred box. There could never be any link anywhere up or down the chain.

Martin was sitting at the American embassy. SKY news the BBC and ITV and every other news channel had breaking news.

"Shocking news from Westminster this morning after it was revealed that the Secretary of State for Energy has taken his own life earlier today in the lead up to the General Election. Mathias Croft was hotly tipped to become the next Conservative leader; it was muted."

"Well Martin, any comment?"

"Cleaning house, sir. I believe he was Raven."

"How can it be?"

"It fits but will never be proven, but my money is on this guy being the Raven."

"Anything else?"

"John Parks and a female have been found burnt to a crisp in a vehicle just outside Oxford."

"Hell and damn it, I thought he had nine lives, well ninety nine lives actually, but who was the girl?"

"This is where it gets freaky. We believe it was Cynthia Knowles, sir."

"How can it be Cynthia Knowles? Wasn't she butchered at that old derelict cottage a few days ago?"

"Yes, sir, Hangman's Cottage but there was never a body found, They have also confirmed ketchup present with the blood. It was all circumstantial at best, but maybe whoever killed Bartholomew Knowles caught up with these two."

"Why would those two be together, Martin? It is an unusual and precarious alliance. Would you trust either one?"

"Not likely but they both had one common denominator: they wanted Bartholomew Knowles dead and buried."

"What happened to the money and the other stuff reported to be involved."

"All gone, sir."

"What a story, Martin! You just could not make this shit up you know. Shame though, I kind of liked Parks. He had a bit of old English grit and determination."

"Me too, sir. We were always routing for him."

"Never mind, I will see the British later. See you, Martin."

"Goodbye, sir."

The man walked from the office with the contents of his shred box. He travelled to the basement and to a special room where he placed the contents into an incinerator and pressed the ignite button. The flames made small work of the small amount of paper and card, and when concluded, he opened the door, pulled the tray out and poked the ash until he was satisfied all trace evidence was completely destroyed.

He walked from the room, up the stairs, into the central outside space and he walked in the fresh air. He let the burden and the anguish of the past years float off his shoulders, and he smiled.

Chapter 21

Conclusion

"So what happened to the taxi drivers?"

"I Hid them twenty-five grand each from the holdall money and sent them the text of a lifetime as to where to collect it from. I am the new best friend to all three of them."

"Where did you hide the money when you threw the holdalls into the groundsman's truck in Painswick?"

"In the garage that belonged to Chris, you know, my mate from White Horse lane."

"Where did the lights come from in the field?"

"Is this thousand questions time just because you finally got what you wanted?"

"You promised me that you would disclose everything and then it would be done."

"OK, the lights belong to Chris as well. I asked him to set them up and set them off at a predetermined time. It was easy really. He hates the police or any authority figure, so when I told him I wanted to shag the law, he smiled and said, 'anything you want bro.' Good, eh?"

"That is so good of him and trusting. Did he know that there could have been danger?"

"Yep, I left fifty grand in his cement mixer in the garage and told him he could have the scooter. He was pissed within two minutes I think. I also left two grand over the bar at the Royal Oak, told them to be suspicious of everyone, and well, they probably had a great old knees up and talked about us with a drunken smile anyway."

"What about your family, your children?"

"They have been informed that I have been killed in an accident. I left one million pounds in an account for each of them which matures and will be accessible on their twenty-first birthday via their Auntie, she will handle it all as I can never reconcile now, I know this and dropped everything through the Grange solicitors door anonymously."

"Who was in the car John? Explain the burnt remains."

"Irony is something I will never cease to pull enjoyment from. It was Angela and Bartholomew Knowles, as he did not exist and nor did Angela, there would be no living person that would attempt to claim the bodies. Perfect, don't you think?"

Cynthia began laughing, "How did you pull this all off?"

"One man, the Raven's nemesis, a bloody good guy, who I never met, but he set it all up. It was your knowledge of his name, that piece of evidence, the Raven. Bartholomew should not have written it down on the file header. He had no idea it left the imprint on the blotter. How did you know it was significant?"

"He went quiet whenever he talked to this guy, emptied the room, the usual paranoid behaviour but after I found the name on the blotter, he cleared the room one night, and I cleared the surveillance team from the ops room and left the intercom on. I knew he was government and high up, and that's when I heard them talk about Gerald, and that's why I told you. I knew he was playing you, too." When I found the doodle in Gerald's study with the bird and number, I knew he was playing everyone, but I also knew that the guy at the other end of the number would help. He was his failsafe and luckily he turned out to be our salvation?"

"Good job we turned to each other and not to our predators."

"What was his name in the end, the main guy in Westminster?"

"Batman."

"Get on with you. I don't want to know really anyway. Bloody hell, John, I can't believe we are here and free from the chains of our former life. Can we get on with things now?"

"Do you feel safe?"

"Yes, I do."

"Well don't, not yet. One thing I have learnt, complacency is actually a killer, a magnet for bad deeds. Keep looking over your shoulder, keep out of the limelight, don't draw attention to yourself, don't make friends and don't socialise for a year at least."

"I don't need to John. I just want to bathe in our relationship and just get to know you without the stress and commotion we endured. I am fed up of people."

It was a beautiful morning. The sun was shining in through the bedroom window, and it was peaceful. Saint Raphael and France, in general, always made him very comfortable and relaxed. He loved this coastline and also being close to Cannes and Italy. The house was far more luxurious than he could have ever contemplated owning prior to his good fortune with the money from Bartholomew Knowles and Raven, plus they had diamonds. The house had a sea view from the master bedroom and a balcony. It was flawless in its provision of peace and tranquillity.

He held Cynthia in his arms and just stroked her head.

"You know what girl, it's going to take a lot of getting used to," he was laughing. "Cynthia, you don't even look like a 'Debbie'."

"You don't look like a 'Chris' either."

End